KT-554-283

The Water Theatre

ALMA BOOKS LTD
London House
243–253 Lower Mortlake Road
Richmond
Surrey TW9 2LL
United Kingdom
www.almabooks.com

The Water Theatre first published by Alma Books Limited in 2010
© Lindsay Clarke 2010
Reprinted September 2010

This mass-market edition first published by Alma Books Limited in 2011

Lindsay Clarke asserts his moral right to be identified as the author of this work in accordance with the Copyright, Designs and Patents Act 1988

This is a work of fiction. Names, characters, places and incidents either are the product of the author's imagination or are used fictitiously, and any resemblance to actual persons, living or dead, business establishments, events or locales is entirely coincidental.

Cover design: Rose Cooper
Cover images: Getty Images and Alamy

Printed in Great Britain by CPI Cox & Wyman

ISBN: 978-1-84688-130-5

All rights reserved. No part of this publication may be reproduced, stored in or introduced into a retrieval system, or transmitted, in any form or by any means (electronic, mechanical, photocopying, recording or otherwise), without the prior written permission of the publisher.

This book is sold subject to the condition that it shall not be resold, lent, hired out or otherwise circulated without the express prior consent of the publisher.

60000 0000 21464

THE WATER THEATRE

LINDSAY CLARKE

ALMA BOOKS

**Peterborough
City Council**

60000 0000 21464

Askews & Holts	May-2011
	£7.99

Remembering
V.M.C. 1914–72
C.C. 1916–2005

The author wishes to thank
The Royal Literary Fund
and
The Extension Trust
for their generous assistance
during the writing of this novel

CONTENTS

The Water Theatre

1
Fontanalba

A late-September afternoon, some time before the turn of the century, and all the hills of Umbria were under cloud that day.

I had flown to Italy at short notice on a mission for a friend and was driving a hire car southwards at speed along the shore of Lake Trasimene, when a violent release of lightning flapped out of the sky like a thrown sheet before crashing shut again in a close collapse of thunder. The squall gusted towards me across the lake, erasing the island first, and then the pleasure steamer making for the quay at Passignano. Moments later the reed beds nearer inshore had gone and the tiny Fiat shuddered under the impact of the rain.

I braked to a crawl. Lightning seared the clouds again, its glare prickling across my skin. With the windscreen awash, I could make out only the tail lights of the vehicle ahead, so at the first exit I swung off the *autostrada* to park by the flooded edge of a road overlooking the lake. Rain pummelled the car's thin roof. It sprang in florets from the drenched asphalt. Through a streaming side window I watched a horse prance nervously across its field.

When I checked the map, counting the kilometres past Perugia and Foligno, up a steeply winding road into the hills, I reckoned on at least another hour's drive to Fontanalba. My plan had been to get to Marina's house quickly, say what I'd come to say, and then hurry back to London before my life unravelled. The whole trip was supposed to take two days if I was lucky, three at the most. Either way it was going to be an emotionally expensive time. Meanwhile this storm showed no sign of abating. So I sat there in the heat, watching the lightning pitch and strike its lurid canopy across the lake.

I remembered how Marina had once told me that lightning bolts, like kisses, are mutual affairs. They strike only when the descending charge is met by a stream of energy rising upwards from an object on the ground – a tree perhaps, or a person, one who might be utterly unconscious of the way his metabolism has been flirting with the idea of an electrical embrace. Yet the flash, when it comes, always happens by assignation.

So I was thinking about thunderstorms. I was thinking how Marina had understood such acts of dalliance instinctively. She had been born in a tempest as a liner rounded the western bulge of Africa in the month before the Second World War began. Lightning heralded her arrival. It imprinted its tiny fern-like sign, the colour of coral, in the cleft of her infant chest. And as long as I had known her, she had always loved thunderstorms. So if this storm reached as far as Fontanalba, and the years had not sobered her beyond recognition, Marina would be out there, watching the thunder roll around the hills, inciting the universe; whereas I...

I knew that lightning strikes about ten million times each day. I knew that at any given moment more than two thousand thunderstorms are crackling across the planet. We can watch them from our satellites and calculate their number. We can estimate the voltage carried by each of the hundred, inch-thick lightning bolts that leap for many miles through the atmosphere every second. I knew that they singe the air, briefly, at temperatures hotter than the surface of the sun. But what I mostly knew was that in a thunderstorm the inside of a metal vehicle is a safe enough place to be. I'd once been told as much by a US Army medic as we rode out a storm of stupefying violence in a helicopter over Vietnam. That had been a long time ago, yet the memory retained the precise, epileptic clarity that warfare sometimes brings. Picked out of a firefight near the Perfume River only to be tossed about in a helicopter that felt ready to burst its bolts, I had been shaking with fear. But if the chopper got hit by lightning, the medic assured me with a grin, its metal shell would harmlessly soak up all the discharged energy like a Faraday Cage.

Now, I'd never heard of a Faraday Cage before, and I suspected that the medic might be lying to me as he had certainly lied to the black soldier with a throat wound over whose bloody field dressings he held a saline drip, but the theory met the moment's need, and I chose to believe it. Later I exalted it to a kind of principle, a law even – Crowther's Law – which had only a single clause: before entering a tricky situation check out the nearest Faraday Cage. In my work it was stupid to do otherwise. You calculated the risks and then took all precautions that didn't make the job impossible. It was how you survived. It was how you made the risks make sense. Though Marina, I guessed, would scorn such calculation.

As for her brother Adam, who was now living with her here in Italy and had once been my closest friend, I had no idea who he might be these days.

A week earlier I had returned from covering the civil war in Equatoria. The memories that came back with me were fixed in my head like the cutlass blade I'd seen in the skull of a bewildered tribesman who was walking away from his town along a dirt road. The death stench of that town was with me still – so many deaths, the rotting harvest of a labour of killing so immense it must finally have proved tedious. And when, two days after I'd got back to London, a call summoned me urgently to Yorkshire, to visit Hal Brigshaw, I was sure I knew what it was about. Hal must have been following the news from Equatoria, and would be anxious to hear more about the fate of his friends and allies, the men and women with whom he'd helped build that nation more than thirty years earlier.

Knowing that almost everywhere he looked these days Hal was confronted by the failure of his hopes and ambitions, I'd driven north in dread of telling what I had to tell. This wasn't the first time I'd made that journey filled with trepidation, but nothing had prepared me for what was waiting at High Sugden.

Hal sat blanketed in a wheelchair with his housekeeper, Marjorie Cockroft, fussing over the lopsided sag of his body. "Another stroke," she said, "only worse. It happened not long after you'd left last time. I did try to phone, but they said you'd gone abroad again. Anyway, he's mostly being very good." Dabbing a tissue at the corner of Hal's mouth, she spoke about him dotingly, as though he were deaf. "You're not to think we're not coping."

Hal sat desperate-eyed at the indignity of his condition. His right hand lay palm upward across his narrow thigh, while his head tilted to the left in a slack loll, so it looked as if he was straining to examine something filmy and delicate between the thumb and the forefinger of his defunct hand. Meanwhile, the air of what had once been the dining room of the grange hung motionless around him. At his back, by the mullioned window with its view across the Pennine slopes, a single bed stood on castors. It felt distressingly provisional.

I brushed a kiss across the old man's brow and tried to rally his spirits with a bluff joke, but I was appalled by the wreck of the once burly figure. Then still more so by the slovenly garble of Hal's speech.

Mrs Cockroft took it on herself to act as interpreter. "It's that war in Africa. We always watch the news together, though I'm not sure how much he understands these days."

Hal's eyes made it clear that he understood every intolerable word. Yet that wasn't why he'd summoned me. With scowling jerks of his good hand he dismissed the woman from the room. He wanted us to be left alone. The housekeeper sighed – she was only trying to be helpful. But her parting glance demanded that I appreciate the claims made on her patience.

Once she was gone, Hal tried to speak again. Marina's name emerged, buckled almost beyond recognition by the struggle of his tongue, and then Adam's followed. I should have caught on sooner to what he wanted, but Hal had spoken about neither of them for years. Only when I deciphered the word "Italy" did I grasp that he was asking me to go there and try to bring back his son and daughter.

I said: "It wouldn't work, Hal. They wouldn't come."

"For you," I heard him mumble. "They'll come for you."

"I'm the last person..." I began, but his damaged voice spoke over me.

"Been thinking... You've done it before... Got them to come home for me."

"More than thirty years ago," I protested. "And that was before..."

Again, even before that moment of hesitation, he raised the hand of his good arm and shook it as though to erase my protests.

"They'll come," he repeated stubbornly. "For you they'll come."

I did not share his confidence. And there were many reasons why I could have refused and perhaps should have done so. Circumstantial reasons, emotional reasons, reasons clamouring out of the present and even more strongly out of the disastrous past. Nor was there any need to scavenge for excuses. I had promised Gail, my American lover, that we would spend time alone together in the Cascades after the African assignment was complete. That time was now. The flight was already booked. I badly needed that respite. But in these desolate circumstances how to dash the last hopes of a man to whom I owed almost everything that mattered in my life? A man who had always put his trust in me, and who had once been far closer to me than my father had ever been? So I glanced away, casting about, wishing there were some other means to repay that debt of gratitude. But there was no way to say no to what Hal was asking.

And so it is, I was thinking now, as time and space shifted round me and lightning flared again above the lake, that, less in ignorance of our desires than out of fearful knowledge of how they might consume us, we send our streamers up into the storm. I sat in the hot car with thunder rolling round me. My thoughts drifted. I must have dozed. And thinking of thunderstorms, I fell into a dream.

I dreamt I was back in the old north on a day of bright June sunlight, certain from the idle air and the warm smells drifting from the terraced houses that it was Sunday morning, a little before noon, when all the mills and factories were still. There was no sound of traffic in the valley, no clank and rattle from the shunting yard, though distantly I could hear a peal of bells. Sunday then, and I was with my father and we were stepping out in the quiet morning to try the beer of a few pubs together. Over the next hour or two we would down three or four pints before making our boozy way back to where my mother would be waiting to lift the roast onto the table. And it was a good, warm feeling to be out with him like this, to feel the pleasure he took in showing off his son to his mates from the mill where he worked, for things had not always been so. Even in the dream, part of my mind stood aside, marvelling that things should be this easy between me and the father who, for too much of my early life, had been my most intimate enemy. But here, for once, we were at peace. I'd get in my rounds at The Royal Oak and The Golden Lion and enjoy the easy ritual of bar-room conversation. I'd listen and laugh, trade jokes and opinions about sport, about women, about the always unsatisfactory state of the world. Or that was how it should have been, for that was the feel of the dream at first, but then I saw that my father had fallen silent and was suddenly very weak. His limbs were so flaccid that he was unable to carry his own lax weight and I had to support him now, I had to get him home.

With one hand round his waist and the other holding his wrist at my shoulder, I was half carrying, half dragging him round the steep rim of the quarry on the hill above the town. We were making for the recreation ground on the brow. I could hear the swings squeaking in their iron chains. Not far now, but I was panting from the effort of it; and when, pausing for breath, I looked down at his face, I saw that the eyes were sightless and opaque, that he had been dead for some time, that his body was still as wasted and naked as I had seen it on the narrow death bed when I'd laid him out. I could feel the bed sores on his back. And the ringing I heard was the inane carillon of the ice-cream van which, on the hot day of my father's dying, had been the only passing bell.

When I woke in Italy to the thunder stroke, I was still carrying my father's dead body from pub to pub round the silent streets of the town, and there was no one near to help or carry him away.

Dusk was falling when I reached Fontanalba. The hillsides teemed with cloud. When I stopped at a crossroads to look for a sign, my headlights picked out a wayside shrine to the Madonna, dressed in her peeling blue robe. Some distance away, a street lamp glimmered through the mist. Having no idea where Marina's house might be, I turned the car in that direction and parked outside a tall stone house.

A small dog ran barking from a barn beside the house to yap at my shoes. Two small boys appeared. They stood on thin legs, their glossy hair cropped short over faces which stared aghast as I cobbled together a question in Italian; then they fled into the house. Somewhere above me clanged a single bell. Wooded mountains came and went among clouds the colour of burnt tallow.

I was about to turn away when a woman in a black frock came out of the house, wiping her hands on an apron. She called off the dog, then asked something – presumably what business I had frightening her children in the dusk. I tried again. She tipped an ear and lifted a thin, worried hand to her cheek. "*Ah, la signora inglese,*" she exclaimed at last. "*Marina! Sì, sì.*"

"*Sua casa?*" I pressed. "*Dove?*"

Her wrists twisted. Her tongue sped. As best I could I picked my way through the torrent of help and, when I thought I'd got things clear, she added more. Only later, as I braked in the narrow yard outside what I hoped was Marina's cottage, did I realize she'd been trying to warn me that no one was there.

By now the bell had stopped ringing. A wind had got up and was blowing holes in the mist. A single lamp revealed how perilous was the track along which I'd just rattled my car. It was so narrow that the wheels must have passed within an inch of where the edge sheered away in a six-foot drop to an olive grove. Looking up again, I met the dark, refusing silence of the house. The shutters were closed. I tried the handle on the double door, which barely moved. Under a bamboo awning built into a recess at the side of the house four chairs stood at a circular table. The dusk smelt of rain and draughty space.

There was no room to turn the car, and I was considering how best to back out of that dead end when the elder of the two boys appeared through the tatters of mist. He walked past me without a word, making for the low wall under the awning, where he tipped a plant pot and turned, pointing at me with a straight arm stiff as a duellist's. His small hand clutched an old pistol key.

A smell of dust and dried thyme. Then the frescoes emerging from white plaster in panels no larger than foolscap sheets. They showed turbaned merchants, sailors and cowled monks; a single-masted ship with two tiers of shining oars; an angel standing guard before a sepulchre; a woman praying in the desert, her nakedness covered by silver-white hair hanging like a shawl to her knees; a lion vigilant on a rock in blazing wilderness. It was as though the walls were trying to remember a dream and could recapture no more than these haunting fragments.

I took the paintings for medieval work at first, but a closer look showed them to be more recent, handled in an archaic style that somehow finessed pastiche and found simplicity. The Marina I'd known would have lacked patience with such obvious narrative intent. Yet if she hadn't painted these pictures, who had?

The boy smiled up at me and crossed the room towards the fireplace, where he pointed out a picture unrelated to the rest. A cheap, unframed reproduction, printed on board, it was a head-and-shoulders portrait of a jug-eared monk with hooded eyes and an unsatisfactory beard.

"San Francesco," he announced. I took in the golden nimbus around the tonsured head. The local saint, of course, St Francis of Assisi. Now the boy was pointing at his own chest. "Franco. Franco Gamboni."

I nodded, tapped my own chest. "Martin. Martin Crowther." Neither sound meant much to him, so I tried a variation – "Martino" – which elicited a nod. I opened a door onto a little kitchen. "Well, Franco Gamboni," I said, "I can't think there's a restaurant in this village of yours, so let's see if we can get some grub together."

Remembering forgotten instructions, the boy drew in his breath, gestured widely across the paved floor. "*Attenzione, ci sono scorpioni!*"

"*Ah, grazie, grazie.*"

"*Prego.*" He stood, smiling, with both hands clasped on top of his head, swaying from side to side. Then he turned and ran back up the track through the gloom.

Generations of olive growers must have scratched a living here before the house fell empty and Marina purchased it for next to nothing. She had intended to use it as a holiday cottage, but once life in England became intolerable to her, she had settled here in Fontanalba, living simply and cheaply, painting outdoors, content to be alone with her child. Then, much later, when he had nowhere else to turn, her brother Adam came to join her there.

The chimney corner of the frescoed living room had become a small study alcove. Beside it, an upright piano stood against one wall, its panels inlaid with fretwork patterns of foliage and masks. The trellised backs of two chairs were painted in peeling gold. A blue throw covered an old couch. On the desk in the alcove stood a paraffin lamp, a portable typewriter, a pencil case with a brass hasp and three books. *A New Pronouncing Dictionary of the English & Italian Languages* had been published in 1908 when, according to the table on page iii, a twenty-lira piece had been a gold coin worth fifteen shillings and ten pence farthing. Next to it leant a *Rough Guide to Italy*. It occurred to me that an entire civilization had vanished down the gap between those two volumes. Beside them lay the only other reading matter in the room – a skimpily bound book with the title *Umbrian Excursions* stamped on its spine.

The alcove would have been the obvious spot for a telephone if Marina had not refused to have one installed. Thinking of this, I took out my mobile phone and was about to dial Gail. But I was tired and fractious, the conversation would too easily go wrong, so I put the phone away again, knowing the call might now prove all the harder when I came to make it.

In the small kitchen at the back of the house I found the wine rack and enough bits and pieces for a scratch meal. I sat puzzling over those anachronistic frescoes as I ate. Surely monks and angels had no role in Marina's universe? If she had rejected everything else about her father, his atheism had gone unquestioned. Like oxygen or sex, it was a fact of life with which it made no sense to quarrel. So what were these paintings doing here along with an image of St Francis? They reminded me of the illustrations to the copy of Grimm's *Fairy Tales* that my mother had bought for me when I was small. In the stillness of the room I recalled the smell of that book and the way its pictures were like windows on a world utterly different from the grimy industrial landscape in which I grew up.

Then I remembered how I'd lain in bed with Marina once, chaste as a fabled knight, telling her one of those stories to still the rage of her grief. That state of almost innocence possessed me again in all its adolescent sensuality as, with a catch of the heart, I recalled the gift she'd given me later – a painting she'd made of a boy riding on a fox's back. These frescoes were more expertly done, but the same enchanted imagination was active here.

In the drawer of a bedside table upstairs I found an English translation of Virgil's *Aeneid*. Propped against a fat pillow, I opened the pages, and an old sky-blue envelope fell out onto the bed. To my astonishment, I saw that it was addressed to Adam in my own handwriting. Its postmark dated from the late '50s, at a time when we were both second-year undergraduates. During the bitter January of that year, Adam had suffered a brief episode of nervous breakdown. He'd been kept under supervision in a local mental hospital for a few days before being sent home to recuperate. I'd written this letter to him there, telling him how much he was missed by all his friends and trying to lift his spirits with a satirical account of our doings. Its tone was light but caring, even studiedly so in its preservation of a certain northern reticence. Adam had let me know how much it meant to him at the time, but I was both touched and amazed to discover that he had valued the letter enough to preserve it across all the years between.

My first thought after reading it through was that this mission to Italy might not be quite as hopeless as I'd feared. Then came a second, less optimistic thought. Hailing as it did from a time when things were still good between us, this letter might simply have been tucked between the pages of a book he'd been reading more than forty years ago and then forgotten. Thinking about it further, I could imagine no other reason why it would have escaped destruction.

I was about to switch out the lamp when a sweep of headlights brightened the bedroom window and a car approached across the valley, pulling to a halt somewhere close by. Unless the night had bounced the sound from elsewhere there must be another house, just below this one, on the side of the hill. A man and a woman got out of the car, laughing together. I caught a shushing sound, and then something muttered in a whispered exchange that ended in a brief contralto giggle. Perhaps they'd been surprised by the light in Marina's cottage? A key turned. There was more suppressed laughter before the door closed again and the lock clicked shut. Not long afterwards came the sounds of exuberant sex.

There are few more isolating experiences than that of lying alone in earshot of loudly rutting strangers. My mind illustrated the event, mingling fantasy and memory, and when at last all three of us were done, I lay in the silence thinking about the previous night in the Camden flat with Gail – how after the row over my decision to go to Italy we had struck an unsatisfactory truce and adjusted our plans to allow for time alone together. But that assignment in Africa had sickened my desire. Our lovemaking had been incomplete. It felt wistful as a fall of snow.

Later, her eyes grave among the mass of her dishevelled hair, Gail had asked me again not to go.

"I've made promises," I said.

"You made promises to me."

"I *will* keep them."

"They're broken already."

"But mendable. I'll make them good."

"It's the way you talk about them," she said after a time. "The people there, I mean. As if you were still in thrall to them somehow. Particularly Marina."

"It's more years than I can remember since I even saw her!"

"But you were in love with her once? She was the first, wasn't she?"

I said, "Marina left my life a long time ago. You have to understand: these are old loyalties. I'm doing it for Hal."

"No," she said, "I don't think so."

"If you had any idea how much I'm dreading this trip…"

"Then don't go."

"I have to, Gail. For Hal."

She shook her disbelieving head again. "No, Martin. Like always you're doing this for you."

And as if in ironic fulfilment of her declaration, here I was, alone in Marina's house under the Umbrian night, regretting that I'd come, knowing there were many reasons why I'd allowed myself no choice, and aching with memories of Hal Brigshaw's children who, together or apart, had long been capable of opening up a war zone in my heart.

I remembered the pain of my last encounter with Marina. I remembered the bleak hour in which Adam's friendship had turned to hostility. I thought about Hal stricken in his wheelchair and about the piled bodies of the dead in Equatoria. Again I shrank beneath the burden of my father's corpse, a limp, decaying load that I could not put down.

Knowing these things must keep me from sleep, I reached for the copy of Virgil. It fell open at the page where the letter had lain, and I saw at once that someone – Adam presumably; the book was his – had underscored three lines:

> *Your ghost, Father,*
> *Your sad ghost, often present in my mind,*
> *Has brought me to the threshold of this place.*

The night swung like lock gates around me, letting more darkness in.

I woke in a rose-madder room already steeped in warm mid-morning light. Pushing back the curtains, I saw a plump hill of olive groves topped by a cluster of houses, impasto pink and white, with terracotta roofing tiles. Sunlight flashed from a chimney cowl. In the hazier distance two thickly wooded hills saddled the horizon. Nothing moved. Even the swallows were silent on the wires, though somewhere a solitary cowbell clanked every now and then, jolting dry air that smelt of rosemary and thyme. Beyond the bamboo awning, a closer olive grove sloped steeply away down the hillside. The shadows of stone terraces tumbled in soft cataracts between the rows.

I was showering when I heard a sound beyond the clatter of water at my feet. When I called out to see if someone was there, a woman's voice lifted from the foot of the stairs. "I think maybe I have come at a bad time. Forgive me." I knew at once that it was not Marina. So whose was it then, this cloudy foreign voice that added, "I shall return again when you are dressed?"

I reached for a towel, calling, "Hang on, I'll be with you in just a minute. Don't go away." But the sitting room and kitchen were empty when I went down, though a newly filled bowl of fruit stood on the table in the dining area. Towelling my hair, I stepped outside and saw the woman sitting in the shade at the circular blue table. Sunglasses masked her eyes. A wide-brimmed straw hat with a silk ribbon hid most of her dark curls.

"Good morning," she said, "I had not meant to discompose you," and rose, offering a firm hand. Slim, in her late forties, she wore a shirt of lavender-grey silk hanging loose over ivory-coloured linen trousers. "I heard only this morning that you are arrived. If I knew last night..." Her ringed hands made a deprecating flourish. "There was no food in the house, I know. I have put milk and butter in the refrigerator and there is now bread in the box." With a hint of reproach she added, "We were not expecting you."

I took note of that familiar "we".

"There's no phone here," I explained. "I had to come at short notice and couldn't let Adam and Marina know. I thought I'd find at least one of them here."

"I see. You wished to jump a surprise on them!"

"Spring."

"Excuse me?"

"Spring, not jump."

"Ah yes. Forgive me... my English... I am Gabriella. And you?"

I told her my name, there was a brief beat of hesitation before she opened her mouth and said simply, "Ah!"

"They've spoken of me?"

"Of course." Her eyes, which had been briefly averted, returned now, bright with renewed affability.

"Do you know where Adam and Marina are?" I asked. "Is there any way to contact them?"

She gazed brightly up at me. "For the moment I don't think so."

"It's rather urgent. I don't have much time."

Somewhere higher up the hill a bell counted eleven in tinny chimes. We stood by the blue table in the fragrant day while she considered her response. A white sports car gleamed beside the shrine at the junction, where she had parked it. The morning basked in dry light.

She said, "I think you must wait for them."

This woman was no peasant, but the statement had a peasant's obstinacy. It assumed that waiting was the usual condition here. Things might once have happened; one day something might happen again; in the meantime, waiting was the thing.

But the prospect of kicking my heels in this uneventful place held no appeal. I said, "Perhaps the neighbours know where they are? I heard them last night. Down here." Crossing to the wall beyond the table, I looked over onto the salmon-coloured pantiles of a low-pitched roof. Another cottage was stacked on the side of the hill below Marina's, neater, in better repair.

"Ah," Gabriella smiled, "so Capitano Mezzanotte is back! But I doubt he can help us." I was about to suggest that it might at least be worth a try when I heard her chuckling softly at my back. "Of course that is not his true name," she said. "It is our joke, yes? He makes use of the place only occasionally. Adam

17

called him by that name because he comes by night and always leaves early."

"They," I corrected.

"Yes," she smiled.

"Captain Midnight. I see."

"He is a very private man."

"Public enough to keep me awake."

She nodded, her lips pursed, but smiling still. It occurred to me that she and Adam must be on intimate terms to share such a joke. Were they perhaps lovers? If so, this woman might be just as resolute to protect him from the past as he had been to sever all ties with it. She wouldn't want me "jumping" any surprises on him.

I said, "You really don't know when they'll be back?"

Frustration must have shown in my face, but with a wry tilt of her head she evaded my question. "Things don't always work out as we expect. You must not be dismayed." Abruptly she brought her ringed fingers together at her lips. "I have some small business to perform this morning. It will take me perhaps one hour or so. After then I will give you lunch at the Villa, yes? If you are agreeable, I will pick you up at, say, twelve thirty." The smile was warm.

Lacking options, I decided to be "agreeable", thanked her and asked whether it would be too far for me to walk.

She opened her hands and brought them together lightly at her chest as though catching a moth. "No, not far. But the road is steep," she said. "It will be a hot walk."

"I'm used to heat. I was in Africa a week ago."

The smile broadened, the narrow shoulders wriggled a little beneath the silk. "I am forgetting. You are famous for your *ardimento*. Very well, go round the hill and take the road to the left, past the *convento*. You will see. Cross a bridge and in perhaps three kilometres there comes a gate with birds. Mythological birds. *Grifoni*?"

"Griffins, yes."

"The drive will bring you. The door is open. Come through. I will expect you." Again she offered her hand and quickly slipped it free.

From the dappled light of the awning I watched the sports car accelerate away around that steep, heat-stunned theatre of olive groves.

I breakfasted on coffee and fruit with the *Rough Guide* open on the blue table. Fontanalba was of too little consequence to feature in its pages, so I picked up the slim volume called *Umbrian Excursions* and was about to open it when I decided I'd better call Gail. Only the machine answered me. I left a message telling her what had happened, gave a satirical account of the conversation with Gabriella and insisted that I had no intention of hanging about in Umbria for more than another night.

"You were right," I conceded, "I shouldn't have come. I'll make it up to you."

Then I sat, staring at the olive groves, marooned by the silence.

For want of anything better to do, I picked up the book again. The title was embossed on the cover, though neither the author's name nor the publisher's colophon appeared there. Only when I turned to the title page did I discover that it had been written and privately published by Laurence Stromberg.

That extravagant man had been my contemporary at Cambridge, though I'd seen nothing of him since we bumped into one another in the crush bar of a West End theatre at some point in the mid-'60s. "But you're looking so well," he'd crooned. "Quite the figure of the rugged hack, all tanned and rangy and doubtless badged with scars!" Then, with a wicked nudge he'd added: "Or has journalistic pribble-prabble merely deformed you into a cliché your trade?" But Larry's style had already begun to feel anachronistic, and his own career as a theatre director was faltering. The last I'd heard of him was a rumour that he'd been initiated into a secret order practising sex magic in South Kensington. It was the sort of gossip he might have started himself, which did not necessarily make it untrue. And the pages of his book revealed a familiar quirkiness now, for its various excursions were as much through the painted chambers of the author's mind as through the landscape of Umbria.

I skimmed through his account of the ancient augurs of Gubbio who'd read signs in the flight of birds, and then dipped into another on the oracular springs of Clitumnus. But I soon lost patience and put the book down. After a time I set out for Gabriella's villa.

Because Marina's cottage was perched halfway down the hill, some distance outside the medieval walls, I got my first real sight of the town when I looked up from the roadside shrine. Hunkered down behind its defences, Fontanalba was curled on its summit like a snail. Only a single bell tower and the crowns of two plane trees rose above the pinkish ramparts. The lane to the villa curved on round the hill, past the gate and a complex of buildings under a square tower topped by a Turk's cap dome.

The armorial carvings on the bastions of the town gate were hidden behind rough scaffolding, though I could see no sign of anyone at work. The dark archway opened onto a small piazza where the crown of the hill had been cobbled over. Houses sloped away along two narrow alleys, their roofs held down by top-heavy chimneys and flat stones. As far as I could see, there were no shops or bars, but midway down the wider alley an ornate niche had been built around the basin of a fountain. At the edge of the piazza, under the white glare of the Romanesque church, six plastic chairs waited for the shade.

Unaware of my arrival, a woman berated an old man from her vine-slung balcony. He brandished a bottle, stammered something back at her, and then slumped in the shade beside the fountain. Not wanting to get caught up in a neighbourhood wrangle that might have been going on for a decade or two, I backed away, out of the gate, wondering what else people could do in such beleaguered proximity but bicker in the heat.

I followed the lane past the *convento* down to where an ancient bridge spanned a river that tumbled among stones through a green glen. On the far side, a steep climb brought me to a wooded ridge, and from there I looked back down on Fontanalba. The air was heady and resinous, the noon light a somnolent blue shimmer punctuated by the shrilling of cicadas. I saw no one as I walked.

The griffin-guarded gates stood open. The last turn of the long, winding drive through trees revealed the palatial scale of the house. At the centre of a wide court with a parterre garden, water plashed from an elaborate fountain. Beyond it, a loggia shaded a number of doors at ground level. All of them were locked, so I climbed a sweep of stairs to the terrace above. From there, with its ochre stucco peeling in the sunlight, rose the main body of the villa.

I stood for a while beside a stone urn, taking in a view that reached beyond the statuary and pinewoods to the hazy plain far below. Turning back to the house, I saw that a door stood open in the portico beneath a second – and grander – upper loggia. I stepped through into the cool entrance hall.

The house was as silent as a painting of itself. Along the length of the hall's airy tunnel three chandeliers floated like tasselled marine creatures. Mellow light from a glazed door at the far end fell along walls painted with *trompe l'œil* prospects of trees and bowers and hills. I coughed to make my presence heard and, when nothing happened, walked along the hall to a central atrium, where a transverse corridor offered access to rooms on both sides. I was standing by a statue which had a missing hand, wondering whether to shock the place out of its trance by shouting, when a man wearing a white jacket appeared down the corridor. Startled to see me there, he advanced quickly across the tiles and listened, unconvinced, as I explained I was there at Gabriella's invitation. His chin was unshaven, his mouth tight, his blue eyes menacing. He growled something that might have accused me of breaking off the statue's hand and hiding it. His own hands, which were matted with black hair, gestured extravagantly. "No, no," he decided and, in the ensuing torrent of Italian words, two were uttered with emphatic force: "*La Contessa*".

When I failed to utter any intelligible response, he grimaced, indicated that I should wait a moment and turned away into the first room down the corridor. Leaving the door ajar so he could keep an eye on me, he picked up a phone from the desk and dialled a number. I could hear only his side of the conversation and understood little, so I looked at the bookcases. Many finely bound volumes were ranked there along with other books that looked dumpy and probably dated from the early days of printing.

With a twitch of his finger the man summoned me to the phone.

"Forgive me" – I recognized Gabriella's voice above the crackle – "I am delayed longer than I thought. But I have asked Orazio to take care of you."

I said, "I think he'd rather throw me out."

"Oh dear, he can be fierce, I know, but I have told him that the fault is mine. I will come soon. Please, make yourself at home. Enjoy the pool. There are towels and robes in the pool house."

I hesitated a moment before saying, "You didn't tell me you were a *contessa*."

"Ah! You do not care to have surprises springed on you?"

"Sprung."

Laughing, she said, "English has no pity."

On impulse I asked, "Is Adam there with you?"

"Adam? Why do you ask that?"

"I don't know. I get the feeling you're keeping something from me."

"And you feel you should have everything at once?"

"You think I deserve less? Besides, I told you, I don't have much time."

"Today is too hot to hurry," she decided. "Enjoy your swim."

I would have said more, but she was gone.

Orazio indicated that I should follow him out into a courtyard, where he opened a door concealed in the wall by a screen of boxwood. Immediately I heard the sound of water somewhere below. Descending a stone stairway, we came out into a secret garden. I caught the gleam of water issuing out of a lion's mouth to cascade down a channel cut into the steps of a small neoclassical temple which overlooked the pool. White parasols shaded two sun loungers in an arbour of bougainvillaea. A long marble table flanked by marble benches stood nearby.

Orazio beckoned me inside the temple, where a stone nymph poured water down into a basin shaped like a scallop shell. It wasn't hard to imagine someone bathing there, naked as foam-born Venus, but the steward was impatient to show me how a modern shower had been fitted into one side chamber, while a refrigerator, well stocked with drink, hummed in another. He poured me a beer. I thanked him for his trouble. Mollified, he brought olives and pistachios to the table outside, then he left me alone.

I swam several lengths, took a shower, dressed and lay down on the lounger. The beer was strong, the heat of the day soporific. A line of cypresses beyond the pool stood motionless. I might have been lying in a world where sunlight spellbound all things to stillness except water. Pouring from the lion's mouth, down the stairs into a shallow slipper bath and thence into the pool, it flowed out again unseen. It was as if this green and secret garden existed solely as a thoroughfare for water. Nature and art had consorted here to serve its purposes. The spirit of the place breathed in its sound, and now that sound was passing through me till I was left with only a diminishing sense of separate existence.

Gazing across the ornamental hedges at the mountains beyond, I thought – as so often on the chancy expedition of my life – *What the hell am I doing here?*

The pool panted in its net of lights. The sun stood still. I was recalling another arrival, in another place, as I fell backwards into sleep.

2
High Sugden

Grey goose and gander,
Waft your wings together,
Carry the good king's daughter
Over the one-strand river.

The push of cold wind at his cheeks had brought those lines to mind. It plucked them from somewhere deep in memory as he freewheeled swiftly down the banking swerve of the hill. Then, with the bike coasting on its own momentum up the lane out of Sugden Foot, the rhyme repeated itself in his head like flight instructions, until both slope and wind turned against him. Lifting himself from the saddle, he stood on the pedals to meet the gradient. His eyes were watering now. On either side of the lane silver tussocks of cotton grass glinted in winter light. He took the wind between his teeth, yet it buffeted about his ears so loudly he could hear nothing else and was unaware of the car climbing the hill behind him.

The car – a pale-blue Austin 7 – rounded a bend in the narrow lane as he tacked towards the next brow. Perhaps the driver had no time to see him. Certainly no attempt was made to brake or swerve, so it was merely a matter of luck that the side of the vehicle hustled past not quite close enough to touch but near enough to unbalance him. Panting in the stink of exhaust, he propped himself against the capstones of the roadside wall, looked up, and saw the car crest the rise and drop out of sight.

Alone on the side of the hill, Martin Crowther, eighteen years old, sweating inside his duffel coat, pushed back a lock of dark hair and shouted a pointless insult. But when he turned his head, the view down the valley was too elating to let him feel annoyed for long. On this last Saturday of the year the distant factories stood smokeless under dense cloud. Pale shafts of sunlight slanted down over the moor towards Crimmonden, while northwards there was already a pink glare to the sky though it was still only mid-morning. He saw that snow might fall before the day was out.

Martin let go of the cold handlebars and blew into his fist. Above him on the slope, a blackened slab jutted from a stack of outcrop rock. The light tipped and shifted again. He could hear the hum of the power lines, and everywhere around the gaunt horizon he sensed the depleted, psalm-like lamentation uttered by places where, for too long, industry and wilderness had been at war. Again and again he had tried to catch that note in poetry. He had brought some of his efforts with him in the folder in his saddlebag, and was looking forward to trying them out on Adam Brigshaw's educated ear, but that brisk, inexpressible alteration of the light robbed him of confidence. He ran some lines through his mind, thought he saw how they might be improved, then began to worry that they were no good. It might be wiser to keep them to himself.

Having been brought to a halt, he would have to walk his bike up to the next rise, so he swung his leg across the saddle and began to push. *Grey goose and gander*, he found himself muttering the old nursery rhyme again, *waft your wings together, carry the good king's daughter over the one-strand river.*

Over the centuries the slate roof of High Sugden Grange had buckled to a wave, so that the blackened Elizabethan house sheltered in the lea of its high stone barn with a head-down, introverted air. A lower range of outbuildings enclosed the yard where the Austin was parked beside a shooting brake. A skimpy figure wearing a red scarf reached into the back seat and took out two baskets before crossing to the porched door of the house.

Minutes later Martin's tyres whirred through the open gate into the yard. He propped his bike against a shed wall, removed his bicycle clips and put them in the pocket of his duffel coat. Under the noise of the wind he heard the clatter of beck water pouring into a stone trough, but so chill was the air that he thought it couldn't be long before even that sound was stilled to ice.

On the pediment over the porch, a mason had carved two free-floating cherubs in relief holding a shield on which a name – JNO. CRAGG – had been chiselled inside the angle of an open pair of compasses over the date 1596. Beneath it ran the inscription:

THIS PLACE
HATES LOVES PUNISHES OBSERVES HONOURS
WICKEDNESS PEACE CRIMES LAWS THE VIRTUOUS

The floor of the porch was flagged, and stone benches had been built into the recess at either side. A ribboned sprig of mistletoe hung above the door. As Martin stepped into the porch, the noise of the wind stopped, as though a switch had been thrown. Struck by the abrupt alteration, he took a single step back into the yard, and there was the wind instantly barracking at his ears. When he stepped forward into the porch, the switch was tripped again. It cut the world in two. It made things feel provisional and strange.

Martin lifted his hand to the knocker, and the studded oak door moved at his touch. He heard the sound of a woman's voice inside. "Don't be tiresome, darling," she was saying, "the day's quite complicated enough as it is."

"Then wouldn't it be simpler if I wasn't around?" The answering voice was also female, but younger, tetchier.

"Now you're just being captious," came the reproof.

"But I pulled my weight over Christmas, didn't I? I really don't see why I should waste half my weekend entertaining Adam's boring friends."

"There's only one of them."

Somewhere in the house a phone rang just once and was immediately answered. "Anyway it's not just him," the woman's voice went on after a moment. "You know Emmanuel's leaving tomorrow. I really think you have to be at dinner tonight. You can spend all day tomorrow with Graham."

"That's not the point. You know I…"

"There's a terrible draught in here. Did you leave the front door open?"

"I don't know, I had my hands full. I really think we should discuss this."

"Marina, I don't have time. The point is, Emmanuel's hardly seen you…"

"Well that's not my fault. I've been here kicking my heels, waiting for him and Daddy to show their faces."

"They do have more important things on their minds!"

"My point exactly."

Martin stood between the wind and the door, preventing the knocker's fall, admiring and fearing the suave way these voices performed their disagreement. What to do, in such company, with the thudding flats and twangs of his own rough vowels? Gentrify them? Speak as little as possible?

"Anyway," Marina pressed, "I can't think why you want me storming about the place in a bad mood before he goes."

"Oh do stop it, darling. What I want is for you to see if that door's shut. It's like the Russian front in here."

Martin let the knocker drop. It banged in his chest.

"Oh surely that's not him already! It's barely twelve. Go and see, will you?"

"Why can't Adam go? It's *his* friend."

"He's out on the tops with the dogs. He should have been back ages ago."

Martin heard footsteps on flagstones, and then the door was pulled open. Light from the yard fell across the girl's face, sharpening her frown. She said, "You must be Adam's friend."

His gaze dipped to the denim jeans rolled at ankle length over her loafers. "Well, you'd better come in," she offered, as though leaving him outside was a preferable, and perhaps feasible, option.

Martin stepped through into the hall and took in the sombre panelling, the tinted engravings and a newel post topped by a lugubrious owl at the foot of an oak staircase that rose to a banistered gallery. A smell of roasting meat warmed the air. He said, "I'm a bit early, I think."

"Yes. We're in the kitchen."

Would he have known this girl for Adam's sister in the street? Probably not. She lacked his sidelong air of reticence that might be either diffident or vain. The glance of her slate-blue eyes was franker. She was fairer of skin and hair, the latter drawn back into a ponytail at her neck, neither blonde nor mouse but glistening somewhere between. Martin found her frosty, snobbish, spoilt.

He followed her through into the kitchen, where a woman in her mid-forties closed the top oven of a cream Aga and smiled. She put a hand to the dark mass of her hair, in which millings of grey were threaded. Her eyes were a searching, rueful blue. "You must be Martin," she said, and before he could answer, "Oh for goodness' sake, Marina, do take his coat. We're in a bit of a muddle, I'm afraid. Adam should be back any minute. I've no idea where he's got to." She paused to take in the scale of additional difficulty presented by this young man. "You look pinched with cold. It must be horrid out there."

"It's not so bad," he mumbled as water drummed into the kettle that Mrs Brigshaw held to the spout of a fat brass tap.

"Not bad?" Marina echoed, incredulous. "It's going to bloody snow that's all. And we'll all be stuck out here for days and drive each other mad." She took his coat through to the hall. Almost eighteen years old, she was as tall as her mother, but lacked her comeliness and poise.

"As you can tell," said Mrs Brigshaw, "Marina's in a beastly mood. Earl Grey or Transport Caf? Or would you prefer something stronger?"

"Tea's fine. Whatever."

"So... did you have a good Christmas?"

"It was okay."

"Only okay? I should have expected a good-looking young man like you to have had a lively time. Do you have a girlfriend?"

Conscious of Marina listening at the doorjamb, he said, "No one serious."

"I should think not. There's plenty of time for 'serious' later. Right now you should be having fun. God knows, serious comes soon enough." Settling the kettle to boil on the hotplate, Grace Brigshaw wished that Adam would come back and take his friend out of the kitchen, where he was ill at ease and she had complicated things to do. None of this showed on her attentive face, but Martin sensed it as he sat in a stick-back chair, glad of the Aga's heat, wondering at this kitchen's airy space.

"You're from the grammar school in Calderbridge, aren't you?" Marina demanded. "I hear they don't rate women very highly there. On the evolutionary scale, I mean." She picked up a carrot and crunched it between her teeth, while her intent, grey-blue eyes traversed the kitchen, looking for some advantage with the matter that pressed more closely on her mind.

And this was unjust. He felt the heat of it. "Actually I have a rather high regard for Emily Brontë," he retorted, and thought he had established an ascendancy, until he saw the two women glance at each other. He heard his words as they must have heard them and flushed to his ears.

"She *was* quite exceptional," agreed Grace Brigshaw, and bit her lip. For a moment, sensing his misery, she wanted to pull him up from where he sat with his thick, flannelled thighs spread over large, cheaply shod feet, and hug him into relaxed laughter. But the boy would probably just stiffen like a hare on a poulterer's hook. So where to take things now? Oh dear, with

Marina already cross and tiresome, and the sky crowding with snow, this could quickly veer into a difficult day.

At that moment the front door banged open and two big dogs bounded into the kitchen with lolling tongues, their haunches shivering in an ecstasy of return. "Ah," said Mrs Brigshaw, "here's Adam at last," and Martin reached out with relief to the two dappled English setters that slobbered at his thighs.

"I didn't think you'd bother to come," Adam said, "not with snow threatening."

The absence of warmth in his voice left Martin wondering whether this friend he had met by chance was now regretting the invitation impulsively offered after they'd talked for an hour or so amid the steam and chatter of a coffee bar just before Christmas. They were of an age, both sixth-formers, though at different schools, working as temporary postmen during the Christmas rush, and both soon to go up to university. Conversation had revealed their shared enthusiasm for modern poetry, cinema and jazz. Each had been curious about the other's background, yet Adam's manner now suggested that what had seemed a discovery in the Pagoda Coffee Bar might prove an embarrassment among his family.

Martin said, "It didn't look too bad when I set out."

Grace Brigshaw glanced at where Martin kept his face dipped towards the warm, writhing smell of the dogs. "Well, at least Hengist and Horsa haven't forgotten how to welcome guests," she sighed, and glowered at her son, who said, "We'd better go up to my room."

Wondering what had possessed him to come here rather than joining Frank Jagger and the others at the Black Horse before bussing out to the rugby match at Crow Hall, Martin got to his feet. He stood awkwardly between the approaching mug and his departing host as Marina asked, "Don't you want this tea then?"

Leaving the room, Adam said, "Bring it if you want."

"Lunch will be at one," Adam's mother called after him. "Or thereabouts."

Holding the mug that had been thrust at him, Martin went out to where Adam waited on the stairs, frowning back at his visitor. "Marina's been a bitch all morning," he said. "It's because they won't let her spend the night with the tedious rugger-bugger she thinks she's in love with."

From somewhere along the gallery above, they heard the abortive clunk and gurgle of a lavatory chain pulled four times before the water flushed. As Martin reached the head of the stairs a door opened and he was astonished to see the tall but slightly built figure of a black man come out. He was dressed in heavy corduroy trousers and a thick roll-neck Guernsey over which he wore a knitted cardigan with leather arm patches. Even so the smile on his broad-browed, heart-shaped face amounted to little more than a gallant shiver as Adam said, "Emmanuel, this is Martin – the new friend I was telling you about."

Martin shifted the mug to his left hand and took the slender hand that was held out to him. The grip was strong. Adam turned to Martin. "This is Emmanuel Adjouna. You can talk at lunch. He's working with my father right now."

The African's smile widened. "You have fallen among good friends, Martin. In this place only the rooms are cold. Adam my dear, I think I would have died by now if not for these excellent trousers and sweaters you lent me." And he burst into a hoarse laugh. Martin found it impossible to say how old this man was. He wanted to laugh with him. Aware of the mug steaming in his hand, he said, "This tea might warm you up. I don't really want it."

"Thank you, but I have this." Grinning, the African took a flask from his back pocket. "From Russia, where they know how to banish cold. You like to try some vodka?"

At that moment a door further along the landing opened. A bluff voice called, "What's going on out here?" and a burly man with a strong, romanesque head and a broken nose stared out at the gathering on the gallery. "That for me?" he asked, and took the mug of tea. "Good, I'm gasping." He sipped at the mug, held it away from his pugilist's jaw, studied Martin for a moment, and said, "I'm Hal. This is my house. You're very welcome." Before the visitor could respond, the big man – he was taller than Adam, more vigorously built – turned to the African, muttering, "We'd better push on, old son, or we'll never have you in Government house." Then he went back into his study.

With a wry grimace Emmanuel Adjouna winked at the two young men and followed his friend. As the door closed behind him, the telephone in the study rang once and was again immediately answered.

Adam's was an attic room, up a further winding stair. Under the eaves by the dormer window, he bent to plug in a two-barred electric heater, pointed Martin towards a steamer chair that had seen better days and threw himself onto the plump eiderdown of the single bed. Above his head was pinned a Cubist poster from Le Musée d'Art Moderne. Martin took in the shelves stacked with books, the many Penguins in their orange livery with the white stripe; the leaning rank of records, many LPs among them; the slimline desk with its swivel chair; the air of inviolable privacy. He tried to clear his mind of envy.

"What are they doing?" he asked. "Your dad and his friend, I mean."

"Overthrowing the British Empire."

When Martin snorted and glanced away, Adam said, "You don't believe me?"

"Sure!" Martin got up and crossed to the dormer window, where he gazed out at the swollen sky over Sugden Clough.

"You haven't heard of my father?" Adam said.

"Should I have?" Martin turned and saw him balancing something on the thumbnail of his right hand. Light glinted briefly off an old silver coin as Adam flicked his thumb, sent the coin spinning into the air, and caught it in the same hand when it fell.

"He'd like to think so. H.A.L. Brigshaw? Author of *Inglorious Empire* and *The Practice of Freedom*?"

"Doesn't sound like the sort of stuff I read."

"But you read the papers, don't you? *The Express* thinks he should be thrown in the Tower pending execution at Traitor's Gate. Mind you, he'd be pissed off if it didn't."

"Politics isn't my thing."

Adam laughed, aghast. "Better not let Hal hear you say that – not unless you fancy being beaten into submission. We're all passionate about politics here, except Marina of course, though even she gets worked up about Africa. We lived there for years till Hal got the sack. Emmanuel's going back next week." Adam tossed the coin again. "Keep an eye on the news."

"Why, what's going to happen?"

"His people have already got the students organized, and the Trades Unions in Port Rokesby are with him. He's working with Hal on a strategy to get the miners on board, and once that happens the colony will be ungovernable." Again the coin span on the air between them.

"Which colony is that?" Martin asked, flustered by his own ignorance. But Adam seemed untroubled by it. "British Equatorial West Africa," he answered. "The Tories know they'll have to get out of course, and there's a puppet of their own they'd prefer to leave in charge, but Emmanuel's the only man who can keep the tribal factions together. He should be Prime Minister within the year, and then it'll be a clear run to independence." Adam shrugged airily at Martin, who stared at him as though listening to a signal from a distant star. "But then you're not interested in politics. I suppose you've got more important things on your mind." With studied casualness, he tossed the coin over and over again.

Martin frowned across at him, baffled by the shifting moods of this house. He felt he had stumbled into a culture of baseless discontent where, for all the authority and precision with which they were used, words had a slippery existence of their own. They seemed to correspond to nothing actually present in this privileged world – except perhaps for the anomalous African shivering in borrowed trousers.

"It's not that I'm not interested," he said. "Or that I don't care. It's just that I don't know much about it." He bit back the complaint that he had not shared the opportunities enjoyed by Hal Brigshaw's family. The coin sprang into the air again. With a swift movement Martin reached out, grabbed it, and turned back into the window alcove to examine his catch. Embossed with the garlanded head of a young man, the coin lay thin and mysterious in his palm.

"Give it back," Adam demanded.

"Hey, this is Roman, isn't it? Where d'you find it?"

"I was given it for Christmas. My mother had it from an uncle when she was a girl. I've always wanted it. Now it's mine. Give it here."

Martin was examining the coin by winter light. "I can make out an *R*, an *I* and an *A*…" He was reluctant to let this ancient thing go, could feel himself possessed by the desire to have it for himself.

"It's Hadrianic," Adam said. "There's a portrait of Antinous on the reverse. He was Hadrian's lover. Some legionary probably brought it here from Alexandria or Asia Minor." His voice stiffened: there was a peevish edge to it now. "It's quite rare and I'd like it back please."

"All right, all right, keep your hair on." Martin handed back the coin, but already Adam was ruing his failure to trust the possibilities of friendship: "I'm sorry." He tightened his fist round the coin. "I don't know what's got into me. It's being back home again – after school, I mean. Being stuck in this place."

Martin sat down across from his friend again. "You don't know how lucky you are. I'd give anything to live out here."

Adam slipped the coin back in his pocket. "It can get pretty boring."

Martin shook his head. "Not for me. I feel great when I'm out here, in the wilds." He glanced across at Adam, ready to withdraw at the first scoff, but encountered only an interested, affirming nod. "Which is weird really," he went on, "given that I've lived near the centre of town all my life."

"Not so weird."

"I suppose not, but…"

"What?"

"I don't know. Every time I come out onto the tops it feels a bit like coming home. As if the country where I belong is just over the horizon, and I know it's there, but I can only remember a few words of the language…"

"What kind of language would that be?"

The word "poetry" was at Martin's lips, but it would not pass. He saw it would render him too vulnerable to this new friend. So he merely snorted in demurral and looked away. In the meantime, Adam had felt it necessary to make amends. "Go on," he urged, "it's interesting."

"It mostly has to do with the wind," Martin offered uneasily, "and the way the sky reflects in water, and the sound of water, too. The feel of stone." He hesitated there, amazed that he had risked this much, then saw a way through. "I'd have thought you'd have sensed it. Living so close, I mean. You must have felt it trying to get through to us?"

Now it was Adam who frowned.

"You talk as though it were alive," he said. Aren't you being a touch anthropomorphic – muddling it all up with human stuff? What interests me most about these moors and crags is precisely the fact that they're inanimate. Not the foxes and the harebells, I know, but the rocks and becks, the things that aren't alive, that aren't messed up with life and living." Adam lay in the pallid shaft of light cast through the dormer window, staring, it seemed, into a close, countervailing darkness. "Sometimes I go out there and it feels utterly indifferent to everything – whether I'm there or not, whether I live or die even. It's just numb, unconscious of itself, as though it had been dragged into existence and was left lying there, sticking it out, enduring whatever comes because there's nothing else to be done." He glanced back Martin's way. "And you know what? I'm grateful for it. It clears my head. It reminds me that I'm human and, because of that, I'm not just trapped in the way things are. I'm free to act, to alter things, to make a difference."

Martin considered this, then said, "I know what you mean, but it's not the whole story." He was thinking about the days when he went out onto the moors or followed a beck down a crag, and it felt as though everything around him was breathless with a kind of expectation. "Perhaps it wants change as well?"

"What on earth does that mean?"

"I'm not sure. But it feels as if it might." Martin looked up to glance, cautiously askance, at Adam. "Change, I mean. As if at any given moment something new and marvellous is about to happen... if only someone said the right word."

Adam ran his fingers through his dark hair. He decided that Martin had taken Wordsworth too seriously, but there was something formidable in his earnestness, a feeling of weight and substance, and Adam was in no mood for that kind of argument. He got up off the bed and crossed the room to put a record on his portable gramophone. Carefully he placed the needle on the disk and, as music swung into the silence, he stood restlessly by the dormer window, fingertips tapping out the rhythm at his thigh. He had felt like playing something plangent and modern, but his father was working in earshot, so he'd settled instead for King Oliver blowing free and easy out of the Dreamland Café forty years earlier, with Jimmie Noone's clarinet syncopating at his side and Lottie Taylor at the piano.

Watching him, Martin thought about the ancient coin in his friend's pocket, the centuries impressed on it, the strangeness of time. He glanced away and saw the hollow place left by the weight of Adam's body on the bed. The music was filling him with longings so indefinable and obscure that he couldn't tell whether they were for something long since lost and gone or for a future that would always lie just beyond his reach.

Then Adam turned, frowning still. "Looks like you must have said the right word," he murmured. "It's started to snow."

But only a light smattering of flakes blew about the moorland sky, and none of it was sticking, so there was no sense of urgency in the air when Grace beat the gong that summoned the men down to lunch

Hal decided that he wanted a photograph of what was, for him, an important historical moment. As he instructed Martin in the use of his German camera, the big man's voice rang resolutely local in an accent pitched just east of the Pennine ridge. It contrasted so bluntly with the rest of the family's polished vowels that for a moment Martin wondered whether it was exaggerated for his own comfort. But this was not, he saw, a man likely to make adjustments to those around him.

Never having used anything more sophisticated than a Box Brownie before, Martin peered through the viewfinder of this snouted monster, fidgeting after the right focal length while Hal marshalled his family in front of the Christmas tree. Emmanuel Adjouna stood at the centre, a blue-striped tribal smock worn over two sweaters, with one arm at Hal's shoulder, the other round Grace's waist. Adam and Marina were at either side. The dogs lay panting at their feet. Conscious of Adam's discomfiture, and of Marina staring back at him with a haughty glare, Martin pressed the shutter switch. The bulb flashed – history arrested there, moment frozen for ever – then it was time for lunch at the round table in the spacious dining room at High Sugden.

Hal had been an amateur boxer once, and a swaggering contender's air still governed even his friendliest approaches. His hand lay big on Martin's shoulder now as he said, "Come and sit down, lad. You must be half starved after that bike ride." The others were already laughing at a joke Emmanuel had made, and Martin listened in fascination as they began recollecting anecdotes about past times in Africa.

From his readings in the *Empire Youth* annual, he knew something about that hot, forested world of Paramount Chiefs and painted mammy wagons and nomadic cattle drovers. But these people had lived in the colony, and it was more intimately *home* to them than England ever would be. Adam and Marina told him stories about Wilhelmina Song, who had been their nanny, and about the family's solemn steward, Joshua. Recalling close friends, Marina teased Adam about pretty Efwa Nkansa and spoke warmly of Ruth Asibu, who dreamt of becoming a lawyer. Emmanuel brought news of these and other people, whose exploits triggered long, amusing tales from Hal, until Grace put a stop to his flow with orders to carve second helpings off the roast.

Then she turned to the silent young man across from her. "So tell us something about yourself, Martin. Do you have any brothers and sisters?"

"No," he said, "there's only me."

"Singled out for a special destiny!" Adam darted a wry glance at Marina, "As I sometimes wish I'd been."

"So what does your dad do, lad?" asked Hal.

"He works at Bamforth Brothers."

"Does he now? I know Eric Bamforth. Not a bad sort, though some of his opinions are outrageous. Have you met him?"

"He came along to a works' cricket match once."

"Your dad's a cricketer, eh?" Hal beamed his approval. "Batsman or bowler?"

"Both really. He loves all sports."

"But you don't?"

Martin frowned at his plate, confused to find himself so transparent. "Not really my thing."

"Because he wishes it were?"

Unused to such close pursuit, Martin mumbled a dull confession that he'd never thought of it that way.

"At least you were supporting your dad," Hal said. "At the match I mean."

"I was scorer."

"I see," Hal pressed. "So what's your dad's job at the mill?"

"He's the boiler-firer."

"What's that?" Marina asked.

"The stoker," Adam answered her.

"Shovelling coal you mean?" She was looking only for clarity, intending no judgement or affront, but her frank gaze pushed Martin into deeper retreat.

"Then he is the powerhouse of the place," Emmanuel said. "Everything there depends on him. Isn't that so, Hal?"

"Absolutely right – except it won't be long before they're forced to electrify." Hal frowned his concern across at Martin. "I suppose your father knows that?"

"He hasn't said anything."

"Well, it's going to happen. And soon. It has to. While we can all still breathe."

"You mean they'll just sack him?" Marina put in.

"It depends," Hal said. "If he's a good cricketer, Eric Bamforth'll find some way to keep him on if he can."

"Let's hope so," said Grace, who was seated on Martin's right and sensed his discomfort. She tried to move things through onto safer ground. "So where do you live, Martin?"

"In town."

"Yes, I've gathered that," she smiled, "but whereabouts exactly?"

"Cripplegate."

"Really? I thought they were all commercial properties. I hadn't realized that anyone actually lived there." After a moment in which Martin failed to respond, she added: "It must be very convenient for the town centre."

Something in the young man's flushed silence had reached Emmanuel, who smiled across at Martin now. "I myself was born in what you would call a mud hut, my friend," he said, "and my father could not read or write at all."

Hal gave a little, chuckling laugh. "And now look at him – about to lead a whole new nation through to a time when none of them need say the same."

"God willing," the African murmured.

"It's in *your* hands now," Hal declared, then shifted his gaze back to Martin. "Believe it or not, lad, *my* old man shovelled some coal in his time as well. He worked as a fireman on the railways. *And* the old bugger voted Tory all his life!" Martin had sustained Hal's appraising gaze with some difficulty; now he saw it melt into an amiable grin as the man said: "So as for your own stoker dad – be angry with him if you like. Fight him tooth and nail if you have to. But never be ashamed of him. It only weakens your own spirit."

"Don't lecture the boy, Hal," said Grace.

"I was just letting the lad know there's no call to be embarrassed on our account. Quite the reverse, in fact. You understand that, don't you, Martin?"

"Yes, sir."

"Hal, lad. The name's Hal."

"Harold actually," put in Marina, "as in Anglo-Saxon. It means 'army rule', though he doesn't like to be reminded of it."

Briefly, father and daughter stuck their tongues out at one another in affectionate scorn, before Hal grinned at Martin again: "Hal to my friends, all right?" There was an eager, masculine warmth in Hal's gesture, a desire to be liked, to be approved, that took Martin by surprise. "My daughter likes to pretend I'm a tyrant," he said.

"Your daughter *knows* you're a tyrant," said Marina, "even if you have convinced everybody else you're a champion of liberty."

Martin swallowed and said, "Adam tells me that you and Emmanuel are planning to overthrow the British Empire."

After a quick glance between father and son, Hal grinned. "That moth-eaten old lion's already weak at the knees. What interests us is what comes after it."

"The difference between freedom *from* and freedom *for*," said Emmanuel.

"That's right. We're talking about people being free to make their own future through choice and action. We're talking about how the world gets changed."

Adam pushed his plate away and leant back on his chair. "If you're trying to get him excited about politics," he said dryly, "you've got an uphill struggle. Martin is a bit of a mystic."

"Is he now?" Hal cocked a wry eyebrow, more amused than surprised. "Not many of those in Calderbridge."

Amazed that his friend should expose him like this, Martin sat excruciated, until Adam prompted him with an inciting smile. "What was it you said about the clouds talking to you? Or was it that they're waiting for a word from you?"

"That's not what I meant."

"Then what?"

Martin glowered at the tablecloth. To hear his thoughts distorted this way left him mortified. He could hear the blood in his ears. He thought about the many times he had come out onto the tops alone, relishing the sharp stink of a fox's den in some abandoned quarry, listening for the curlew's cry above the cotton grass. Yearning for that kind of freedom now, he looked up with a hot glare in his eyes. "I was talking about the landscape round here and the way it makes me feel." They were looking at him, waiting for more, and he saw he could not leave it at that. "I mean, politics isn't the only important thing. Our life goes deeper than that, doesn't it? Politics always seems to be about what divides us. It sets us against one another. But at root we're all the same. That's how I see it, anyway – we're all part of the natural world, and it's part of us... maybe the most important, the sanest part."

"If only it was that easy," Adam said without any edge of sarcasm now, "but either it's too obvious to be worth saying or you really are a mystic, you know. Not so much a God-botherer by the sound of it, but a sort of nature mystic, right?"

Watching Martin suffer in his chair, Grace Brigshaw was moved by an intuition. "My guess is that Martin might be a poet," she said, beginning to collect the plates, "which is a noble and difficult thing to be."

"Indeed it is," Emmanuel smiled, reaching to help her, "and a true poet is even as much the enemy of oppression as some of us poor politicians are."

"*Do* you write?" Marina asked with new interest.

"I've done a few things," Martin admitted.

"Good for you," said Hal. "Grace is usually right about people. And there's nothing wrong with nature for a theme – so long as you hold on to what Emmanuel said. All the Romantic poets knew that. What was that thing Wordsworth wrote for Toussaint? 'Thou hast left behind powers that will work for thee...' He faltered there, frowning after memory. "'Powers that will work for thee...' How's it go?"

When he saw no one else about to help, Martin quietly picked up the verse:

> "'...air, earth and skies;
> There's not a breathing of the common wind
> That will forget thee; thou hast great allies;
> Thy friends are exultations, agonies,
> And love, and man's unconquerable mind.'"

Hal remembered the last two lines, and they declaimed them together, ending in a sudden alliance of laughter as Emmanuel and Grace applauded. Then, "Look," said Emmanuel, wide-eyed in wonder, pointing to the window as he got up to help clear the plates, "look at the snow."

While they had been eating and talking, a blizzard had set in. Swift gusts of snow were blowing and twisting beyond the window.

"It's been doing it for ages," stated Marina, pointedly.

"I'd better go," Martin offered, "while I still can."

"I can't possibly let you go cycling out there," Grace protested. "Not in this weather."

"Then you're stuck here for the night." Marina shrugged her narrow shoulders at Martin. "Like the rest of us."

Nobody had quite been prepared for this, least of all the young man who stood awkwardly by the table, gazing out at the thickening snowfall.

"I think you'd better ring your parents and tell them what's happening," said Mrs Brigshaw.

"We don't have a phone."

"Ah, I see. Well, is there someone who could get a message to them?"

"My dad might call in at The Golden Lion. I could leave word there. But, look," – Martin glanced at Adam – "I think I might just make it back before…"

"You'd better stay," Adam said decisively.

"Of course you must," Hal insisted.

"After all," said Marina, "he can always sleep in the haunted bedroom."

Grace sighed at her daughter in exasperation. "Oh don't be silly, darling!" Then she turned back to Martin: "But you must try to get a message through," she said. "We can't have your mother worrying."

"The phone's in here." Marina smiled at Martin with a kind of rueful sympathy as she opened the door onto a spacious sitting room.

Only rarely had Martin used a telephone before, and he was amazed to have the privacy of a whole room for the purpose. He saw more crowded bookshelves – so many books in this house, there had been stacks of them along the landing and elsewhere. Now here were hundreds more, along with piles of pamphlets, newspapers and magazines. An African mask studded with cowrie shells glowered down at him with steady malevolence from over the stone arch of the fireplace. Its eye sockets were slotted like a goat's.

A pile of three new books lay near the telephone. On top was a translation of a work by Leon Trotsky, *Literature and Revolution*. Opening it at random, Martin read how Communist Man would improve on nature's work, removing mountains and redirecting the course of rivers until he had rebuilt the earth. Man would become "immeasurably stronger, subtler", he claimed. The average human type would rise to the heights of an Aristotle, a Goethe or a Marx, and "above this ridge new peaks will rise".

In that moment Martin felt, by contrast, subterranean. He was worrying that he had come unprepared for an overnight stay – no pyjamas, no toothbrush, nothing but what he stood up in. But then he had been prepared for nothing here. In this ancient place anything might happen. There might well be ghosts – for the house did feel haunted, but as much by the future as the past, and the shades of both agitated him. And to talk with these people left him straddling a gulf between what was said and what was thought. Nor did he see how their hospitality could ever be repaid. When he tried to imagine taking Adam into his own home, his imagination shuddered and baulked.

Martin thumbed through the pages of the local directory, thinking that it was all very well for Hal to pontificate about not being ashamed – he did so from the accomplished heights of a civilized life in this Elizabethan grange; he had a good-looking upper-class wife; he sent his children to expensive schools. If he had ever known the humiliations of circumstance, they were far behind him.

Martin found the number and dialled it. He waited through many rings, imagining the crowded Saturday lunchtime bar of the Golden Lion, and Ted Ledbetter, the lame publican, swearing as the phone called him away from the pumps. He dreaded that his father would be in the pub, that he would have to speak to him. He stared out of a narrow window where there was now nothing to be seen but driving snow. When at last the phone was answered, he stumbled into speech.

As he came back into the dining room they turned to look at him. "My dad wasn't there," he said. "He'll probably drop in later. Someone will tell him."

"That's all right then," Hal said, and tapped Emmanuel on his shoulder. "We'd better think what this snow does to *our* plans." The two men got up, but Hal stopped at the door and turned to look at Martin again. "About you and your father – things are difficult between you, right?" When Martin nodded uncertainly, Hal went on: "Well, for what it's worth, I bloodied my nose against my own dad time and again before I worked out something that proved vital for me." He paused for a moment, perhaps for effect, perhaps deliberating, then drew in his breath. "The thing is, if a man wants to widen his horizons and make something new for life, he'll do well to make sure he has at least two fathers – the one he's born with, and the one he chooses for himself."

For a moment Martin seemed to be standing at the centre of a huge silence in the room. It was as if he and the big man with the knocked-askew nose were alone together. But it was Adam who spoke: "Are you volunteering?"

Hal studied his son a moment, sounding out that louche, elusive smile for jealousy and rancour. "Don't think it doesn't apply to you too," he said quietly, and winked at Martin. "In fact," Hal added, "I might just be daring you both to start making your own big choices."

"What about me?" Marina said as she began gathering the plates. "Or don't girls count?"

"You, my darling, don't need daring," Hal said. "You've never done anything else. I don't suppose you ever will." And he planted a kiss on her head. For the moment at least she seemed acquiescent in the philosophical silence of snow that was settling across the house.

"One day," said Emmanuel, "I think Marina will have something to teach us all about freedom."

"God help us when that day comes," her father laughed, shaking his head. "As for you, Emmanuel my friend, I'm afraid that history will have to wait a while longer. We'd better make some calls."

"It's been a century since Sir Elgin Rokesby deprived us of our liberty," Emmanuel smiled. "I dare say we can endure a few more hours of servitude."

"In the meantime," Grace frowned out into the gusting white whirl, "it looks like we're all in jail."

Once Hal was gone, Adam seemed to relax back into friendship with his guest. When they returned to the attic, he became more talkative, less barbed with sarcasm. Their conversation moved onto the safe ground of their common interests – music, films, books – and this led to the question of whether or not writers should be politically engaged, and whether their writing could ever amount to more than bourgeois self-indulgence if they were not. Which brought them back to Hal and the question at the back of Martin's mind.

"So is your father a communist?" he asked.

Adam raised his brows at him. "Why do you ask?"

"Some of the books I noticed downstairs. And didn't Emmanuel say something about having been to Russia?"

"He's been to many places. Washington is as interested in him as Moscow."

"That doesn't answer my question."

"Now you sound like that grubby little demagogue Joe McCarthy: *Answer the question, answer the question. Is Hal, or has he ever been, a member of the Communist Party?* Would it bother you very much if he were? I mean, if you don't care about politics, what's it matter either way?"

"It's just that I'd like to know what I'm dealing with here."

"In case Hal might try to brainwash you? What kind of people do you think Hal and Emmanuel are? If you want to know about their politics, you should ask them. But ask seriously. They're serious men. The issues they care about are serious. Probably the most serious issues in the world right now"

Until this moment the wider context of Hal's endeavours had seemed too far removed from this house perched on the Pennine edge for serious consideration, and too distant from Martin's own preoccupations to excite more than puzzled interest. But now, even as the snow shut them in, he sensed horizons sweeping open round him.

"I can see that," he said. "It's why I want to know more."

"All right, then forget your prejudices, forget the propagandist labels. Hal's thinking owes a lot to Marx, but he's not in the Party, not any more. He's his own man, a thinker in his own right, a political theorist. Emmanuel has the chance to put his theories into practice. It really is about changing things... and not just in Equatoria. In fact, independence for Equatoria is only the start. They're working on a development plan that will transform the country in ten years and set an example for the whole continent. Africa has vast resources – which is why it's been carved up and plundered by the imperial powers to no one's advantage but their own. Imagine what it could be like as a continental union – a federation of independent countries, each running its own affairs, resisting exploitation by international capital on the one hand and the crude oppression of state control on the other. In fact, absolutely refusing to take sides in the paranoid madness of the Cold War. Its influence would be unstoppable. It would be like accelerating history."

Here was a dream on a scale unfamiliar to Martin's thinking. Caught up in Adam's enthusiasm for Hal's plans, he was told how the long collaboration with Emmanuel had given Hal a rare chance to realize a philosopher's dream that was at least as old as Aristotle: to shape world events through the proper education of a man of action. To most people Equatoria might be no more than a minor page out of a stamp album, a sweltering stretch of rainforest and savannah, populated by half-naked savages. But it had an ancient tribal culture of its own – in the sixteenth century the Portuguese had been sufficiently impressed by its wealth to send ambassadors to the court of the Olun of Bamutu, the region's most powerful king. And the country was rich in minerals – diamonds, copper, zinc, and possibly uranium. If properly administered on behalf of the people by the new radical intelligentsia, the country could quickly be transformed. A hydroelectric dam in the Kra River Gorge would power new industries. The profits would finance a national programme of education for all. Ancient tribal rivalries would be dissolved by a growing sense of a national commonwealth. As a place to make a stand for the future, Equatoria had much to commend it.

With growing wonder Martin realized that the telephone in Hal's study really did reach, operator by operator, and often with difficulty, from this remote Yorkshire house to secret rooms in Africa, where brave men were conspiring to end a century of imperial oppression. And once you were put through, the whole mysterious continent might have lain steaming just the other side of the Pennines. His heart beat high in his chest when he considered how he had cycled out to High Sugden and stumbled on these new horizons. He was a privileged insider, close to the start of what might be world-shaking events.

Yet his images of Africa were coloured by Hollywood and Rider Haggard and the comic books of his childhood. Emmanuel was the first actual African he had met. In no way did that engaging man resemble the cinema's leopard-skinned warriors and witch-doctors, but surely no one could call him typical? And what about that mask over the sitting-room fireplace? Its barbarous grimace had left him wondering whether Africa might not still be more preoccupied with superstition and magic than with politics.

Yet Martin was too hungry for a larger sense of life to dismiss everything Adam said as fantasy. And too canny to swallow it whole. So he drew in his breath and marshalled the first arguments he could find against his friend's overwhelming ardour. Then he applied himself to learning, fast.

3
Sibilla

I came awake to the sight of a woman in a black swimming costume at the edge of the pool. She was drying her tanned thighs with a white towel. A fuzzy aureole of sunlight glittered off her limbs. From the mouth of the lion, water poured loudly into the slipper bath. The sun had shifted. When I sat up, she turned to look at me.

"Ah, you are awake at last," said Gabriella.

"Have I been asleep long?"

"You were dreaming when I arrived." She removed the swimming cap and shook her hair free. "I hope it was a good dream."

"I don't remember anything about it."

"Then you must try to catch it by the tail, quickly, before it vanishes."

Massaging the back of my neck with one hand, I said, "If it's anything like the last one, I'd rather let it go."

She studied me a moment as she dried her upper arm, eyes narrowed, lips lightly pursed in disapproval. She draped the towel over her shoulders, closing its edges with one hand across her breasts. "Even troubling dreams mean well by us. We should hear what they have to say."

"Oh dear," I said, "are you some kind of therapist?"

"That would please you less than my being a contessa?" She laughed at my embarrassment. "Did not some clever person say that all professions are a conspiracy against society?" she said. "I agree with him."

"Perhaps you can afford to." The doze, the beer, my frustration at the unanticipated delay, my reluctance to be in Umbria at all

– this dislocating mix had made me needlessly rude. She knew it, and I regretted it.

"In any case," she replied, "is it not good to take an interest in the mysterious facts of our condition? I enjoy working with dreams as I enjoy good conversation or swimming. As I enjoy eating also. Look, Orazio has laid out lunch for us. There is salad, cheese, *prosciutto* and bread. If you like, he will make us omelettes with *tartufi neri*. It will taste of Umbria, I promise. The truffles were gathered this morning."

"I trust the dew is still on them?"

After a moment, she smiled in response. "Excuse me while I find a robe." If she was conscious of my gaze as she walked away, it did not trouble her.

The robe was silk, its design Japanese. Under the shade of a mulberry tree, we ate at the marble table in the heat of the afternoon. The Contessa was talkative about everything except Adam and Marina, but I was enjoying her company and in no hurry to ruffle our conversation with pressing questions. Once we had agreed how delicious were the black *frittate* that Orazio had cooked for us, she informed me that truffles were the fruit of lightning. We talked about the previous day's storm, which had been the first of the season, but I said nothing further about my dream. I congratulated her on the beauty of her home and, more wryly, on its grandeur.

"Yes," Gabriella agreed, "it is perhaps extravagant." A gesture of her hand dismissed the thought. "Now we shall be serious. You will tell me all about your work. It interests me very much."

Over the years I had evolved various strategies to deal with such approaches, and could slip into whichever mode seemed likeliest to impress or deter, silence or seduce the questioner. But what I'd seen in Equatoria had left me finally sickened by all of them. I made evasive noises. She pressed me to say more. The Italian light dissolved around me, I frowned down into the dark of memory. The stench of the death pits hit my nose again, and I was speaking about people driven to a frenzy by forces beyond their understanding and control, about the grief-crazed women and silent children; tormented and tormentors alike unprotected by ease and privilege, by the glib, talking-head culture that distances us from raw suffering and depletes us of an immediate sense of what is real on the earth. Mentally I ran through footage that would never be screened, the literally obscene out-takes which cannot be erased from the observer's mind, yet slink out of history unshown. I told her about them as plainly as I could. *If you want to know what I do*, I was saying, *this is the bleak news I have to bring you on this bright afternoon.* It left me feeling ashen inside, as though a once ardent heat of moral passion had burnt itself out some time before, almost without my noticing.

She was not looking at me directly when she said at last, "I believe there are more than fifty wars happening right now. Can you tell me why it is men love war so much?"

"I've seen more of it than most people," I answered, surprised to find her so well informed, "and I can think of nothing loveable about it."

"Then I wonder why you return to it so often?"

I remembered the despair with which Gail had put the same question only a few weeks earlier. Even then I had not believed my answer. I had no better one now, for the truth was that on each return I'd found it harder to cleanse my thoughts, to be simply present anywhere, least of all inside the care of touch. Out of her rage and hurt, Gail had branded me a war-zone addict, accused me of infatuation with the evil in the world, of eye-fucking its horrors with such lust that nothing could ever hope to match the intensity of its hold on me. Under Gabriella's patient scrutiny now, watching the dazzle from the water drift along a line of cypresses, I saw that I might already have passed beyond such virile craziness into a still more frightening condition.

When I did not speak for some time, she said, "The question disturbs you?"

53

"Not really. I've lived with it far too long for that."

"Of course," she nodded. "And when a man is carrying the troubles of all the world, the taking care of his own soul does not seem so important?"

"I wouldn't say that either."

"Then what would you say?"

"That there must be better things to talk about on a hot afternoon."

Gabriella shook her head in mild exasperation. "You are such bewildering creatures."

"Do you mean foreign correspondents in general," I smiled, "or men in particular?"

"Men," she answered. "Men! Yes, men. Men!"

"Spoken with true feeling. So tell me about the Count. I've been wondering where he can be?"

She considered me a moment, aware of the deflection. Very well, she too could be frugal with confession. "My husband lives much of the time in Geneva. He performs work for the United Nations there."

"A good man then." Invited to pursue the intimacies of her life no further, I sought a light way out of the corner in which I had left myself. "And does he also believe in oracles?"

"Of course. He too is an Umbrian."

"That makes a difference?"

"Sometimes I think that in Umbria even those who believe in nothing else believe in signs and portents." She turned her gaze to where the mountains floated in the haze. "It is our custom. Ever since we learnt to read the fortunes of men in the flight of birds. Perhaps long before that time."

"I've always thought bird-watching harmless enough."

"Now I think you are making mockery of me! However, if you keep your eyes wide, there is meaning to be found everywhere – not only in the birds, but in the murmur of trees, in the pictures made in fire or water. Even a voice heard in a crowd may say something that can change us. As with the radio, there are many places to listen. It all depends how you are tuned – yes?"

"Or which kind of universe you think you live in?"

"Exactly so. I know how it is not respectable now to believe in such a spirited conference of things. But the ancients were wiser. They had great respect for our Umbrian soothsayers." She glanced away, pointing down the slope of the garden beyond a dusky clump of ilex trees. "For example, there was a powerful oracle at the springs of Clitumnus down there on the plain beneath us. And not far away," she lifted her gaze to the horizon, "in those mountains, is the cave of the *Sibilla cumana*. From Virgil? You understand?"

"The Cumaean Sibyl? I thought she lived near Naples."

"Yes. But they say that when Christianity came there, she moved north, to Umbria, to the Monti Sibillini. Regrettably, *la grotta della Sibilla* was closed with stones, a long time ago, by men who did not understand the true nature of her *negromanzia*."

"Black magic?"

"Of course that is what they thought. That is why they exploded the entrance to her cave with dynamite. But it was not like that. There are many stories."

"Tell me some."

"So that you may scorn them?"

"Because I like stories."

Gabriella studied me. "In that case, I will tell you about Guerino il Meschino. You make me think about him a little. *Meschino* means... how shall I put it into English? A poor fellow, a man who has something perhaps a little disgraceful about him?"

"A tramp?" I suggested.

Dubiously she shook her head, fluttering the fingers of one hand.

"A rogue then? A rascal?" Her shrug was unconvinced. "How about a wretch?"

"Yes, a wretch. A wretch will do very well."

"And he reminds you of me? Perhaps I don't like this story after all."

"But he too has *ardimento*. And a cunning mind. A mind for opportunities. I think you will like him. Anyway he comes to Norcia in search of his lost father…"

I flashed involuntarily on the image of my own father as I'd seen him in the dream. Thunder rolled inside me. *Truffles are the fruit of lightning*, I thought in swift recoil. And then: *the world is full of signs and portents*.

"…and in a pass through the mountains he meets his Excellency the Devil, who says to Guerino that if he wants to know who is his true father then he must consult the *fata* who lives in a cave nearby." Gabriella gave me an interrogative frown. "You understand this word *fata*?"

"Fate? Fortune-teller?"

"No, perhaps not fate." She frowned again, then found the word she wanted. "Fairy – yes, fairy. The Devil says, 'There is a fairy who lives in a cave in these mountains. Her name is Sibilla. Enter her cave and you will come to a country where the trees give fruit and flowers at the same time, where there is no pain or sorrow, where no one grows old and everything gives pleasure to the senses.' So Guerino, of course, asks the Devil to tell him the way to this cave of marvels. 'But you must take care,' the Devil warns him, 'because the cave is guarded by a terrible serpent called Macco, who was once a man but has been enchanted by Sibilla and is now become a snake.'"

Gabriella paused there to sip her San Pellegrino, then put on her sunglasses and moved to the edge of the pool, where she sat in the light, dangling her legs in the water.

I said, "I'm wondering which side the Devil is on in this story."

"I am telling you the story as it was told to me when I was a child," she reproved me. "I too had questions. I was told not to interrupt. So – Guerino has no fear. When he comes to the cave, he walks the serpent under his feet and goes into the underworld looking for the *fata*. And it is just as the Devil has promised – not dark, but a bright garden of figs and apricots and pomegranates. There are orange groves and lemon groves filled with singing birds, and the air is still fresh with flowers of spring. As for Sibilla herself – she is a woman of great beauty who welcomes Guerino with sweet words. Yes, she says to him, she will reveal who is his father, but first he must taste all the pleasures of her *paradise*, where the banquet lasts for ever and the music does not grow tedious, and no one gets sick or feels bad from drinking too much, and time itself stands still so that no one grows old. And then, when they have become lovers, she and he, she will tell him everything he wants to know."

Gabriella turned her head to glance at me briefly through the dark glasses that concealed her eyes. "But Guerino is not a fool. Even as he tastes the pleasures of her cave, his clever mind asks questions. He learns from her servants that she is the famous *Sibilla cumana* who had prophesied the birth of a Saviour from a Virgin. But she had believed that she herself was the chosen one, that God would enter as flesh inside her virgin womb, and she was so filled with grief when Santa Maria was chosen in her place that she has come to this garden beneath the earth, where she will live till the end of time. Now Guerino is excited very much by her soft voice and eyes that speak of bedtime, by her white skin as she lies down beside him. But he resists the desire to make love with her, and the story says that he is glad he did so, for a day comes when he peeps his eyes through the drapes of Sibilla's boudoir and sees that, beneath their skirts, the legs of her servants are... *squamose*? Scaly, yes, like those of reptiles. So he thinks that Sibilla too must be a serpent, and when she next comes to make love with him, he rejects her. She pours her fury and venom on him, but he runs away, back into the upper world. Once there he finds that a whole year has passed. Because he is a good Christian he goes to Rome to give thanks for his salvation, and the Holy Father absolves him for the time he has spent in Sibilla's company." Gabriella glanced my way and took off her sunglasses. "So what do you think of my story?"

"I expected Sibilla to get a better press." Smiling at her puzzled frown, I added, "I thought your story would speak well of her."

"You think it does not?"

"Well, I can't say I've ever been keen on scaly legs!"

Gabriella gave a little laugh. "There, did I not say you were like Guerino? You see only from his point of view."

"But that's how you told it."

"That was how you chose to hear it."

"Didn't I hear you say the Devil was behind it all?"

"He too has his work to do. And did he not speak the truth?"

"That Sibilla had turned some poor soul into a snake?"

"Have you not heard of the wisdom of the serpent?"

"Now you're trying to have it both ways," I protested. "And either way Sibilla doesn't come through for him. Guerino didn't find out who his father was."

"But was he prepared to pay her price?"

Looking away, I said, "I suppose you can read it any way you like."

"Ah! Now you are thinking that it is just a story."

"But if it's any consolation, I prefer it to the stories I report out in the real world."

"And of course such stories are more real than mine?"

"Bullets are real," I said. "Cutlass blades are real. Nobody would want to argue with their reality."

Gabriella sighed, got up and came back to the table, suddenly businesslike. "Tell me," – a hint of challenge sharpened her tone – "what do you want with Adam and Marina?"

I said, "I'm not sure that's any of your concern."

She tapped the table briskly with one finger. "They are my friends. I love them and care for them. I know they feel they have good reason not to trust you."

"So you have been talking to them? Now, I mean, since I came?"

"Marina knows you are here, yes."

"Where is she?"

"Not far away."

"Is she here, in the house?"

"You may be a good journalist, Mr Crowther, but you are also a guest in my home. I do not care to be interrogated by my guests."

I said, "I've come a long way to see them. I also have a life of my own to live and I'd like to get back to it. So forgive me if I seem impatient. What about Adam – have you spoken to him?"

"No. He is not... available."

"What does that mean?"

"Precisely what I said."

"And Marina won't see me?"

When she did not answer, I got up, stared back at the villa with its many shuttered windows. "Look, I knew she wouldn't be exactly thrilled that I'd come, but... It was all so long ago..." I turned and saw Gabriella, upright in her chair, observing me, with both hands resting at the stem of her glass on the marble tabletop. "She must know I wouldn't have come near her if it wasn't important."

"Important to whom?" Gabriella answered quietly.

"More important to her than to me, if that's what you're thinking."

"But have you not thought that Marina might have other important matters to attend to at this time? Matters that are none of *your* concern."

This did not surprise me. Once I'd learnt that Gabriella had discussed my arrival with Marina, I expected reticence, hostility even. So realizing that my frustration stemmed as much from gloomy predictions fulfilled as from the actual obstruction, I changed register. "I wanted to speak to Marina because there are all kinds of sensitivities in what I have to say. I wanted to be sure she got the message clearly. I even hoped she might take it more seriously precisely because I'd chosen to bring the message myself." I caught the dubious tilt to her gaze. "But perhaps I was wrong. Perhaps it's better if it comes from someone else."

Gabriella nodded thoughtfully. "It seems you must decide whether to trust me." Then, with a soft winsome twist to her lips, she added, "You have seen, I think, that my legs are free from scales!"

It was impossible to resist the smile.

Imagine it then, I thought, the uncovered underworld realm, inverse of all dark expectations, sunlight radiant where only igneous gloom should be, the globes of oranges, sharp lemon waxiness, ripe figs, unseasonable flowering and plenty. No sorrow, no war, no famine, illness, death. No reports to file, no tyranny of deadlines, no news at all, just permanent sensuality and peace.

"Fortunately," I said, "it's not *my* father who's in question here."

"Then… Marina's father?" Her face clouded at once with the realization.

"Yes. Adam and Marina's father."

"Ah! Hal has asked you to come?"

"He very much wants to see them again. Both of them."

"I think that may be difficult." She turned away from my gaze, frowning, uncomfortable. "I think it's impossible. I think he has given you the trouble of a wasted journey." I studied her expression, puzzling again over her relationship to Adam and Marina, sensing a close collusion that passed beyond mere friendship. Her voice pushed on hesitantly into the space I'd left. "Marina… her feelings in this matter…" Gravely she shook her head.

"I know," I said, "but things can change, can't they? Everything *has* changed for Hal. He's very frail. I don't think he can have much longer to live."

"And now, after all that has happened, he wants to see his children again?"

"Is that so terrible?"

"No. It would be moving – and pathetic even – were it not for the terrible things that drove them apart."

"A very long time ago."

"Yes, but… some wounds do not heal."

"Especially if we decide to keep them open," I said.

"Sometimes such things cannot be decided."

"No," I shook my head, "we have to live by our choices."

"So you want me to tell Marina that her father wishes a reconciliation?"

"That's not quite how I'd put it. I think I'd say he's looking for forgiveness." Again I read only doubt in her face. "But then perhaps I do need to say it to her myself after all. I made Hal a promise that I mean to keep, and it's not that I don't trust you, but… I'm wondering why you feel you have to protect Marina from me?"

Averting her eyes, as if making further space for calculation, she gave a brisk, decisive sigh. "It is not Marina I have been trying to protect." For an instant I thought she meant Adam, but then I saw my mistake. "Please," she said and raised a hand to prevent me speaking. "This is embarrassing to me. The truth is that Marina entertains a great scorn for you." She opened her hand, disclaiming responsibility for a judgement against which no appeal was likely to be heard. "However, if you insist to see her, I will try to speak with her once more."

"It would save time if you took me to her."

"Perhaps, but something else might be lost."

I saw there would be no budging her. A few moments later she excused herself and went into the pool house to change back into her clothes. I sat, staring into the water, thinking about what she'd said, unsurprised by it.

When she reappeared, offering to drive me back to the cottage, I said, "If Marina is here, in the house, I think she should come out."

"Do you think she is hiding from you?" Gabriella snorted. "Then you know her less well than you think. Marina does not hide. Not from anything. You may search the house, if you wish." When I made no move, she said, "I think you do not trust very much, Mr Crowther. But now you must trust me or go home."

She turned, led the way back up the damp stone stairs, and said nothing as we drove back at speed. I tried to end the silence by saying quietly, "I know Marina better than you think. She meant a great deal to me once." But Gabriella chose not to reply as she drove on across the humpbacked bridge, back towards the town.

Having dropped me off at the junction by the wayside shrine, she told me to wait at the cottage. She would be in touch again as soon as she had word. When I gave her my mobile number, she took the card with pursed lips, her mind elsewhere.

"What is it?" I asked.

"I am thinking that maybe this is no longer just for Hal."

"Few things are simple," I said. "Especially where Marina is concerned."

"Or you too, I think." Her hand moved to the gearshift. About to pull away, she paused, tapped the steering wheel with her fingertips. "And then there is Adam also." The dark lenses stared again, I saw my reflection there. "Explain this for me," she demanded. "Adam said something strange about you once. He said that you and he are living each the other's life. What did he mean by that?"

But that was a question I couldn't answer without emptying out my heart, and I wasn't ready for that. I might never be ready for that. So I shrugged and shook my head.

Gabriella studied me, undeceived but not insistent. Then she released the handbrake and drove swiftly away, leaving me to walk down the track to the cottage, so preoccupied with old, rekindled memories of loss and betrayal that I might have been wormholed by her question directly back through time.

4
Troglodyte

That night at High Sugden the electricity and telephone cables went down, leaving them with only candles and oil lamps for lighting. On Sunday morning the sun rose late over the white silence of snow. With the television set and radio out of action, no news came in from the outside world. For a time they were even shut inside the house by a drift that leant its soft barricade against the door, and the lane down to Sugden Foot proved impassable. Yet, far from imprisonment, that exile from the world spelt release for Martin Crowther. And the key to his release was conversation – exchanges rambling far into the night with a depth of intellectual passion so far beyond his previous experience that he was left staggering about for arguments.

On the Sunday morning he and Adam dug a path out of the house where snow had drifted into brilliant dunes across the yard. The digging ended in a brief snowball fight with Marina while the dogs bounded around them, barking. Then, after lunch, the three of them went sledging in the frozen afternoon.

Later, as a bloodshot gloom gathered over Calderbridge, Hal, Grace and Emmanuel strode out to watch them. Careering feet first and upright, Marina whooped and screamed as she slid out of control and poured herself smoothly into a drift. The sledge skewed on down without her, but she was quick to her feet, brushing snow from her coat, disdainful of Adam's jeers. By the time Martin had retrieved the sledge and drawn it to the top, Hal had decided that he and Emmanuel would ride it together. The African crouched at the prow, wide-eyed with laughter, gripping the sides as Hal pushed off from the rear, leapt aboard behind him, and the two friends skidded away in a swerving dash that tipped them both, giggling like drunks, into the snow.

"Bugger it," Hal shouted back up the hill, "one of the runners has come adrift."

"In Hal's schemes," Grace muttered to the wind, "there's usually a screw loose somewhere." Beside her, Martin stared in amazement at the two men, his breath condensing to laughter on the winter air.

Walking back home across the hill, Emmanuel clutched his coat collar at his cheeks as he told Martin that one day he must come to Equatoria and learn how life should truly be lived. He spoke of the fragrant rainforest heat that dampened the air of Fontonfarom, the town on the upper reaches of the River Kra where he had lived as a child. He told Martin how he had been born on a Monday sometime in the second decade of the century, the youngest of six children fathered by a peasant farmer who had served for many years on the council of elders. Their people, the Mdemba, were the smallest of the tribes whose traditional lands had been colonized as British Equatorial West Africa. "It was our good fortune also," Emmanuel smiled, "to live far from Government House in Port Rokesby. So now you are thinking, 'How does this black man come to be shivering here in the snow?' I will tell you."

Not long after his arrival among the Mdemba, a Methodist preacher called Goronwy Rhys had recognized the precocious intelligence of the eight-year-old Keshie Ofarim Adjouna. The boy already sat at the feet of the Paramount Chief on ceremonial occasions, his face painted white to signify his office as ritual soul carrier. Baptized now as Emmanuel, he was also the devout young Christian who sang soprano in the Mission Chapel choir. Over the years, the Welshman had supervised his protégé's progress through elementary, middle and secondary education, and on Emmanuel's return from military service in the Second World War he had arranged for him to go to the newly established Teacher Training College at Port Rokesby. It was there that this eloquent and ambitious young man had first encountered the charismatic energy of H.A.L. Brigshaw. "And the rest," he grinned, "will soon be history."

Just then, as they approached the house, they heard a ringing in the dusk.

"They must have fixed the phone line," Marina shouted, and ran on ahead.

She was standing in the hall with a resentful face as the others came in. "It's for you," she said to Martin, and went up to her room.

"You might have put the kettle on," Grace called after her, but there was no reply.

When he went through into the downstairs study, Martin was astonished to hear his mother's voice down the line. "This is the third time I've tried," she said, slotting more coins into the box. He knew how much effort it must have cost her to risk this call to people she had never met. Was something wrong?

"The line's been down," he said. "We were out sledging on the tops."

"You're having a nice time then?"

"Yes, it's great."

"Your dad got your message at the pub, so we knew you were all right. But you've not got a stitch with you. To put on clean, I mean."

"It's all right. Adam's lent me some stuff."

"Oh, I see. Well, so long as you're being no trouble."

He glowered at his reflection in the dark window glass. The silence of the line stretched between them. He withdrew inside the walls of that ancient house, inside the thick dusk of the high hillside moor that was already stiff with cold. What could he say that would make sense to her about the life of this extraordinary family?

She said, "We'll see you when we see you, then."

"Tomorrow probably."

"Right."

"Or the next day. It depends when they clear the lane. It's isolated up here."

"I should think so. Wouldn't care for it myself."

"No, I don't suppose you would."

"Well, you won't forget to say thank you to Mrs Brigshaw for me. For putting you up and looking after you, I mean."

"Course not."

"All right then. Take care of yourself." Before her money had expired, she put down the phone. Martin replaced the receiver and stood in the book-lined study filled at once with relief and remorse. His hands, he realized, were throbbing from the snow. Almost immediately the phone tinkled as a receiver was lifted somewhere else in the house and another call made.

Grace and the men were in the kitchen by the Aga, waiting for the kettle to boil, so it must have been Marina on the telephone, impatiently making contact with her own world. Not until half an hour later, when her father picked up the receiver in his study and told her to clear the line, did she stop talking. Martin was coming down the stairs from the lavatory as Marina walked head down into the hall. When she looked up at him, her eyes were raw with tears.

"Is something wrong?" he asked.

"Everything. Just every bloody thing, that's all!"

"Anything I can do?"

She glared up as though bewildered by this concern, then she shook her head and brushed past him, making for her room. Called down to dinner an hour later, she refused to come. Hal was all for fetching her to the table, but with a wan, apologetic smile at Emmanuel, Grace advised her husband to let their daughter be.

"She seemed very upset," Martin put in.

"Trouble with the rugger-bugger, I expect," said Adam.

"Which one is that?" asked Hal.

"The Holroyd boy," Grace supplied. "Graham."

Adam said, "He probably got seduced by some other tart last night while Marina's back was turned."

Grace winced at her son. "Must you use that awful word?"

"But I think her heart will be aching," said Emmanuel.

"She'll get over it," Hal decided.

"Of course," Adam added, buttering a thick slice of bread, "once she's milked it for all the drama she can!"

After the meal Grace said that she wanted an early night and left the men talking together before the open fire in the sitting room. On her way to take a bath, she knocked at Marina's door and was told to go away. Rather than provoke a fit of rage that her daughter might later regret, Grace sighed and made her way to the bathroom, where she soaked for a long time by candlelight with a gin-and-tonic beside her. Downstairs the men talked on.

The independence of India. The defeat of the French at Dien-Bien-Phu. The ignominious debacle of the Suez Crisis. The triumph of the People's Army in China. The callous exportation of conflict from the prosperous northern hemisphere to the rainforest farms and flooded rice paddies of the south, and a growing understanding of how an inexorable cabal of political, military and economic interests was disfiguring the lives of millions who lacked any notion of geopolitics. Until this snowbound weekend at High Sugden, Martin Crowther had been only dimly conscious of such issues and events, or blind to their significance. Now, as Hal and Emmanuel explained their relevance to the coming struggle in Africa, they became matters of urgent interest to him. At the same time he saw surprising connections made. He had never realized, for instance, that the muck-and-brass, industrial enterprise of the hard-worked landscape around them had first been financed by profits from the trade in slaves between Africa and the Americas. Nor that the population of Equatoria provided one among many captive African markets for cheap cloth made just across the moor in Manchester. Nor that the colony had first tasted freedom when its young men were conscripted to fight in England's war against Hitler. It was, said Emmanuel, a taste that could not now be taken from their mouths.

That evening Martin also learnt how Hal and Emmanuel had been expelled from the colony several years earlier when the government tried to break up their Popular Liberation Party and install a lawyer called Ambrose Fouda as a more biddable political leader. Hal's response was to write *The Practice of Freedom*, which quickly won him a reputation as a champion of revolutionary thought across the colonized world. Meanwhile, Emmanuel was working with the small band of exiled politicians living a half-starved life in the cheap lodging houses and grubby coffee bars of London and Paris. He and Hal watched from an impotent distance as their allies in the colony were sacked, beaten up or imprisoned. But Fouda's United Democratic Convention failed to win popular support, and in recent times the tide had turned in favour of the PLP.

With increasing excitement, Martin listened to these two zealous men urging him to see how his own energy could, and should, be put in service to the worldwide reach for liberation which was now the noblest struggle of mankind.

"Do you realize the scale of resources they're squandering on the arms race?" Hal demanded in response to Martin's ill-considered remark about the peacekeeping value of nuclear weaponry. "A fraction of it would banish hunger and preventable diseases from the face of the planet for ever. Children who are dying of starvation this very moment, or living out stunted lives in a wretched daily struggle with want and sickness, could be healed and housed and educated. Our governments choose not to do that. They prefer to keep the Soviet Union surrounded by an obscene arsenal of weapons powerful enough to destroy every trace of life across the planet. I wonder how long you would continue to endorse their priorities, my bright young fool, if you knew that most of the news on which your views are based is so much propaganda?" Hal left a pointed moment, then pressed on. "For God's sake, Martin – or better still – in the name of common humanity, the world needs intelligent young men like yourself to get out there, have the courage to see for themselves, and tell the truth about what's happening. Things *can* be changed. They've got to change. And it's not just a matter of principle. Our decent survival as a species depends on it."

Feeling at once admonished and adjured, Martin spoke to Adam about that moment later, when they were alone.

"Of course he'll bully you if you come out with stupid remarks," came Adam's wry response, "but it's only because he doesn't like to see a reasonably good mind abused. Hal likes you. He wouldn't bother otherwise." Smiling, he added, "We all like you. At least, I *think* Marina likes you – though she's capable of changing her mind at a moment's notice and you may never work out why."

A few minutes later, as Adam was showing Martin to his room, Marina popped her head round the door and said, "You've warned him about Jonas, haven't you?" Her mood, lighter, capricious, must have shifted during her time alone.

"I thought you'd already done that at lunch," her brother answered.

"Oh yes, I forgot. Anyway he should be all right." She glanced wryly at Martin. "There haven't been any sightings for a while. Not since the nasty shock he gave our uncle George a couple of years ago."

Adam said, "I'm sure Martin's made of sterner stuff."

"And it's all a sad story really," Marina sighed. "Jonas Cragg built this place, back in the olden days you see. You must have read the inscription carved over the front door. You can tell from that he was a crazy mixed-up sort of Puritan. But he died a hideous leper's death in this room, cursing the name of God for all his suffering." Then she added with studied nonchalance, "If you stay awake, you might just see him walking in his shining shirt."

"I look forward to it," Martin grinned in answer. "I'm good with ghosts. I'm sure that old Jonas and I will get on just fine."

Marina shook her head. "Better men than you have come out of there crying for their mummies!" And, making wailing noises, she went off to her room.

But as he lay alone later in the panelled chamber, Martin wasn't thinking about ghosts. He was pondering Hal's remark about a man's need for more than one father, and found himself thinking about the one he'd been born with. If you asked Jack Crowther about politics, the only answer you were likely to get was an obstinate insistence that it didn't matter who you voted for, they were all the same, all out for Number One. Yes, there had been a time, during the war, when he'd sailed the world as a merchant seaman and must have sensed the pressures building in many of the places of which Hal had spoken. But set beside Hal Brigshaw's visionary imagination, his world felt as cramped and dark these days as the boiler house where he laboured. For him, Africa and the Orient were fading memories of coolies and traders, of skinny children demanding baksheesh, of waterfront bars and dusky whores. Bits and pieces from his travels were still kept at home – an ebony figurine that had caught his eye in Mombasa, a pair of carved elephants from Rangoon, the crocodile-skin handbag he'd bought for his wife in a Cairo bazaar. But only the sea, in which he had drifted close to death for a time when his ship was torpedoed, remained vast and restless in his mind. Otherwise his perspectives reached little further than ambition for his cricket team, the odds on the next race, or wondering whether Calderbridge Rovers would ever climb out of the Third Division of the football league.

This was Martin's birthright father, a man who had come back from the war as a stranger to terrify his infancy, and whose quick rage could still shake and silence him. Yet gradually the man's power over his son had diminished as his bewildered pride in the boy's accomplishments had grown. No longer afraid of him, Martin tended to think of his father now with a rancorous kind of grief. Yet he suspected that, as long as they kept off politics, his father and Hal might get on well enough together. They shared both a bluff air of conviviality and that canny north-country manliness that prided itself on being nobody's fool. Both men seemed built on a bigger scale than either Adam or himself – as though, in their different ways, they were relics of a mighty culture that had spent itself in warfare and would never know such days again unless new springs of energy could be found. But Hal Brigshaw recognized this as Jack Crowther did not, and in that vision lay the evolutionary difference between them. Martin's father was stranded in the unsatisfactory past. Adam's was designing the future.

Torn between newly excited ambitions and the familial ties he resented, Martin lay awake, ruing his predicament until it occurred to him how much more bewildering must have been the life of the African who slept along the landing with the destiny of a whole nation in his dreams. He remembered Emmanuel talking about a huge crocodile he had seen dragged alive out of the Kra's brown water when he was a child, and how his mother had hidden him away one night lest he be carried off to accompany a newly dead king into the spirit world. Wondering at the distances the African had travelled, and whether his own life might one day be catapulted into strange orbits by Hal Brigshaw, Martin eventually fell asleep.

In the dream that came he was approaching his father, who sat, robed in ermine, on a royal throne. When Martin stood at his feet, this kingly figure reached out, roaring, with his mouth gaping open, to seize his son and cram him head first down his throat. Uncertain whether he had actually shouted out loud, Martin woke and lay trembling. Except for a slant of moonlight through the curtained casement, the panelled room was all thick darkness round him. Wide-awake now, he lay in the rigid silence of the house. The luminous hands on his wristwatch leant at ten past two. He was afraid, though it made no sense to be afraid. Shut inside a dark world, he knew what time it was and nothing else. Then he heard the sound of someone walking on the old boards of the landing beyond his door. Gripped in silence, he turned his head and made out a faint radiance there. The footsteps passed, stopped, turned again. With absolute certainty he sensed someone standing at his door. Martin was reaching for the bedside lamp when he remembered that the power lines were dead. Because the silence was intolerable now, he said, "Who's there?"

The latch jolted and the door opened. Marina stood there with a dim battery torch in one hand, holding her blue woollen dressing gown closed at her throat with the other. "I thought you were awake," she whispered. "I was going to make a cup of tea. Do you want one?"

"I don't know. I don't think so."

"You shouted something." She swung the torch towards his face. "You look terrible in this light."

"For a minute there," – he smiled weakly – "I thought you were Jonas Cragg."

"I feel about as cheerful."

At that bleary hour he had spoken without thought, and was amazed she'd let slip a chance for mockery. Then a phrase from Shakespeare, that had recently meant much to him too, flashed across his mind: *the pangs of disprized love*. He said, "You should have talked to someone."

"Do *you*, when you're miserable?"

"No, I suppose not."

She stood at the threshold, assessing his uncalculated honesty. The night was cold at her cheeks and ankles. "All that stuff about Jonas – Adam and I made it up to scare each other when we were kids."

"I guessed. I bet you haven't got an Uncle George either."

"But it could be true," she said. "All kinds of spirits haunt these moors. I know you think so too, because Adam told me."

She crossed to the casement, drew one curtain slightly and shone her torch out across the snow. "*The little lamp burns straight*," she whispered in a hollower voice, "*its rays shoot strong and far. I trim it well to be the wanderer's guiding star.*" But only when the rhyme came did he recognize the poem she was reciting.

"You love her too," he said.

"Of course. How could one not? Emily was a rebel and a visionary. I bet her dad found her even more impossible than mine does me." Marina had not turned from the window, nor did she now as she quietly declaimed:

> "*Frown, my haughty sire! Chide, my angry dame!*
> *Set your slaves to spy; threaten me with shame!*
> *But neither sire nor dame, nor prying serf shall know*
> *What angel nightly trails that frozen waste of snow.*"

though as the stanza reached its climax, she held the torch under her chin and confronted him with features that would have formed a still more spectral mask had not the battery begun to fail.

"This is hopeless," she said, scowling at the frail beam, "I won't be able to see what I'm doing." She turned towards the door, then hesitated and looked back again. "I'll talk to *you* if you like."

"You'll catch your death standing there."

"That bed's fairly big." Before he could respond she was crossing the room, saying, "Edge over a bit." He hesitated, conscious of his body, of hers, of her parents asleep along the landing. "Do you want me to freeze?" she said.

With his breath tight in his throat, he withdrew as far as he could to the far side of the bed as Marina climbed in.

After a time, he said the first awkwardly consoling thing that came. "He can't be the only man who fancies you."

"But I thought I was in love with him." She lay with her knees drawn up, tenting the blankets, her fist holding the dressing gown closed at her throat. "I probably was." He could smell the clean warmth of her body; otherwise she was no more than a vague blur in the darkness. Then, as she swallowed, he sensed the shudder of her tears.

"I know," he offered quietly. "It hurts."

Marina turned her face towards him, surprised by the quality of his sympathy again as she had been a few hours earlier on the stairs. "Yes," she whispered, regaining control of her breath. Then Martin lay there, listening to her express a tumult of thwarted feelings for another man.

Much of what she had to say was of no interest to him. There was, in any case, little space left for response. So he became preoccupied with the sound of her voice in the darkness, and with the untouchable closeness of her warm figure. He felt like a specimen sealed in a jar, motionless, in cloudy suspension.

"You're a strange one," she said at last.

"How do you mean?"

"Listening to all this, saying nothing one way or the other, as if your views don't count. Or as if you're too high and mighty to share them with me."

"It's not that," he said.

"Then what?"

"I don't know the man," he glowered at last. "It doesn't really matter to me."

"So why not tell me to shut up and go back to bed?"

"Is that what you want to do?"

"I don't know. I don't know what I want. It doesn't help to talk about him. It just makes me angry when I think of him falling for that scheming little cow." Impatiently she began to flick the torch on and off as though signalling across space. By the light of a longer flash he saw, where her dressing gown had fallen open, a coral-coloured birthmark near the top of her breast. Making no effort to conceal it, she said, "I won't be able to sleep. I don't know what I want."

He felt the heat and fury of her grief, and that in some obscure and unjust way he was now being held in part responsible for it. But she made no move to leave his bed. Unsure himself whether it was intended as a taunt or a sop to her childishness, he said, "Shall I tell you a story?"

"What kind of story?"

"I don't know. An old story."

After a pause, she said, "Go on."

"Switch the torch off first and put it down."

When she'd done so, he thought for a moment or two, then he told her the story of 'The Golden Bird' out of Grimm's *Fairy Tales*. He had always loved the ambiguous relationship between the youngest son and the magic fox who was his guide, and the way the animal's seemingly callous advice steered the soft-hearted youth away from temptations that would have wrecked his quest to gain the Golden Princess. Marina listened in rapt silence as he spoke, uttering a small moan of dissent only when, as a reward for its faithful service, the fox finally asked his friend to cut off its head. Moments later, Martin smiled at her sigh of pleasure when the fox was transformed by the bloody act into a prince.

"Ruth Asibu would like that story," she said. "She's my friend. My best friend. She lives in Equatoria."

"I remember," he said. "The cook's daughter who wants to be a lawyer."

"She will be one day. There'll be no stopping her."

"Like you," he replied. "I can't see anyone stopping you either. Not for long." But Marina didn't answer, and they lay together in silence for so long that he wondered if she had fallen asleep and, if so, whether he should wake her, because he would never be able to sleep himself with her lying there.

In the darkness, she said at last, "You were looking at my birthmark, weren't you? Earlier I mean, when I was playing about with the torch."

"Not really," he said, embarrassed.

76

"You were. I saw you. It doesn't bother me. They say it came just after I was born. We were on a ship out of Africa, coming home. There was a storm, lots of violent lightning. They say the mark appeared during one of the flashes, as if the lightning had stamped it there."

"Extraordinary!"

She made a small affirmative noise, unsurprised, having already heard that response many times. Then she said, "Tell me about you."

"What do you want to know?"

"Where you live, for instance. Why are you so cagey about that?" She felt him turn his head away. "And about your parents. Your mother sounded really nice when I spoke to her on the phone." Still he did not speak. Marina shifted to confront him, propping her elbow on the pillow, and cupping her cheek in her hand. "I don't know why you have to be so secretive about everything. Come on, it's dark," she said. "I can hardly see your face. Tell me."

Still he did not respond. She reached a hand to touch the skin of his cheek. "I trusted *you*," she said.

After a time he began to talk.

Martin Crowther had not always been ashamed of his home, for at first sight Cripplegate Chambers was an impressive Edwardian office block on a prime commercial site overlooking the busy centre of town. Slate-roofed, the grime-blackened sandstone of its staid façade exuded an air of respectable probity. The name of the building was announced on a glass light above the porched front door. Beside each of its pilasters a number of brass plaques advertised the various businesses it housed: CHAMBERLAIN & HALLOWES, Solicitors & Commissioners for Oaths; THEODORE NASH, Dental Surgeon; GREVILLE EAGLAND ARIBA, Architect; CLAUDE HORSFALL, Estate Agent; NETTLESHIP, LUKINS & MIDGELY, Chartered Accountants.

Each morning, at all seasons of the year, Martin's mother, Bella Crowther, could be seen polishing those plaques. By that time, in the cold months, she would already have laid and lit the fires in each of the offices. All of the chambers would have been hoovered or mopped the previous evening, the ashtrays cleaned, the wastebaskets emptied, the desks dusted. But though her family lived in the building, their name went unmentioned on the door.

They had come there when Martin was nine years old. At that life-altering moment, his strongest emotion had been wonder at the worlds revealed inside the building. A spiralling staircase with a mahogany handrail ascended through all three storeys from the chequerboard tiles of the hall. The child had never previously seen stairs on that scale, and their curving flight struck him as an airy miracle of suspension. Following his mother on her rounds at the end of the working day, he quickly discovered that each office had a distinctive smell, and that each had its particular mysteries to disclose.

The outer rooms of the solicitors' chambers were a cubicled warren of roll-topped desks and safes, typewriters, telephones and tall tin filing cabinets, but the inner sanctum had a clubbish air, redolent of cigar smoke and old leather. Between the ornately tiled fireplace and the window stood an imposing desk from which Clarence Hallowes proffered his expensive advice to clients seated across from him on a buttoned brown Chesterfield. Against panelled walls, glazed bookcases housed the blue ranks of *Halisbury's Statutes*.

By contrast, an astringent, antiseptic smell sharpened the air of the dental surgery, where metal drills hovered above its chair of torments, attended by a battery of lamps and an eerie carmine spittoon. Best of all, the architect's office was a bright studio smelling of cigarette ash and Indian ink. Among its sloped drawing boards, high stools and plan chests, Martin found a trove of graphite pencils and stiff tracing paper, of protractors and shining compasses in suave leather cases, of T-squares and elegant French curves.

Outside, in the yard at the rear of The Chambers, stood an old coach house and stable block which was now a plumber's workshop, crammed with cisterns and lavatory bowls, boilers, pipework, sinks and taps. Soon after he arrived, Martin discovered that by climbing the outside steps that led to the old hayloft, sliding down the slate roof of the building below, and clambering round the corner of the building beyond, he could look down into the yard behind the Majestic Cinema. The door of the projection room often stood open onto the fire escape, so he could hear the blurred boom of the soundtrack above the whirring reels. Sometimes he could smell the hot, electric glare in there.

"It sounds amazing" Marina said in the darkness. "What a great place to grow up in!"

But she spoke only from boredom with her own privileged home, he thought. Nor had he yet disclosed any of the circumstances that had come to blight his life. Having begun, however, there was no stopping now, so he told her how, at the back of the vestibule, a door gave onto a gloomy staircase that led down into the cellars. This was where the Crowthers had their kitchen-living room. Its scant daylight came from two frosted-glass sash windows that reached only to pavement level on the street outside. All that could be seen through the foggy panes were the shadows of passing feet. If the windows were opened, dirt and petrol fumes blew in.

His mother had done what she could to make the place attractive with wallpaper and linoleum, but there was no disguising the bloated lead pipework under the sink, and no defeating the musty odour of damp that seeped in from the other basement rooms beyond. One of them was a larder with arched stonework, where spiders, silverfish and cockroaches thrived; another the coal hole that was filled by the lorry load from a chute in the yard. Neither had windows. In an otherwise bare room with whitewashed stone walls and a flagged floor stood a copper for boiling clothes and an old stained bathtub.

The lavatory lay beyond, outside, its door at the foot of some railed stone steps which climbed up to the yard. In winter it was a cold place to have a shit.

None of this had bothered Martin at first. It was how things were, the received order of things, his life. Then he had passed the examination that took him to the grammar school, and it wasn't long before he realized how different were his own circumstances from those of classmates who lived out in the new housing estates or among the tree-lined avenues of Heathcote Green. Once he had become aware of the difference, only one or two trusted friends were ever invited back to his cellar dwelling in Cripplegate. Even to them it was hard to explain that he had no room of his own, for when the Crowthers moved into the Chambers, they were given only a single bedroom to share on the top floor. Not until the lad was twelve, and increasingly taciturn, could his mother persuade Clarence Hallowes, the feudal ruler of the Chambers, to have a small attic cleared of half a century's junk so that parents and son might pass their nights apart.

Once he had his own room, Martin would spend hours alone up there, reading, listening to his Bakelite radio, or staring at the busy street below like one of God's spies. For hours at a time he watched people going about their lives utterly unaware of how closely they were observed: the shoppers and strollers, the queues forming for the Palace of Varieties across the way, pedestrians hurrying homeward in the rain, the lovers meeting at bus stops, their kisses sometimes, and their public quarrels. It was only when he started to take an interest in girls himself that things began to darken for him.

By the time he was fifteen, he was attracting the attention of high-school girls, all of whom came from respectable middle-class homes and had little notion of how anyone else might live. Mostly he met them in the coffee bars after school, or walked with them in the parks, but sooner or later their parents would expect to meet him. Having invited him out to her semi-detached home in Manor Drive two or three times, one of his girlfriends insisted that it was time he took her to meet his parents, and at last he ran out of excuses. She had looked around in some amazement as they entered the vestibule of Cripplegate Chambers. At the head of the cellar stairs, she hesitated when he led the way down. He looked back and reached for her hand but, presumably imagining that he was taking her down into a dark place with illicit designs, she turned on her heel, ran out of the building and would not come back. After that he kept quiet about where he lived.

This, he admitted in some wonder to Marina now, was the first time he had talked about it since. He lay, rigid, waiting for her to speak.

"So you live in a cellar," she said eventually. "So what? Do you think it makes you some kind of troglodyte?"

Lying in the darkness, hot and furious, he felt himself grow into the fit of the word. A troglodyte, yes. Low-visaged, clumsy-footed, grim and sullen, a beast stumbling up out of the bowels of the earth, half-formed by contrast with her dancing-princess hauteur. "Why not?" he snapped. "What do you think?"

"I think you might be a bit of a snob."

"I should have known better than to tell you."

"It must be such a luxury," she said after a long moment, "to be able to feel sorry for yourself like this all the time."

He rounded on her then. "You should talk! Who's been lying on her own all night trying to make everybody else feel guilty? You've no idea how lucky you are – living in a place like this, with parents who can give you everything you like. *You* want to try being holed up underground like a bloody badger!"

For a moment he felt vindicated, one of the wretched of the earth raising his voice at last, casting his shadow over the ignorant airy world of the privileged. He was high on the anger that throbbed inside him.

"Mind you," she went on undeterred, "I *can* see one big disadvantage with living where you live. If you spend half your life squinting up at people from under their feet, and the other half gazing down on them like some superior being, then it must be hard ever to look them straight in the eye. You should be careful of that. If you don't put it right, it could cost you friends. Friends who want to care about you for who you are, not because of where you live or what your father does, or how many exams you've passed." He was about to shut her up with a blistering retort when he was silenced himself by her afterthought: "People like me I mean."

It left the darkness strumming between them. He wanted the night to hang still for a moment. Needing some firm hold on the shimmering thing this confusing creature was making of his world, he felt a barely governable urge to turn over, pin her down by her wrists, and demand that she say the last thing again, slowly, without irony or ambiguity. But that would only prove he was the lumpen brute she'd accused him of believing himself to be.

So he did nothing, said nothing.

"Actually," she said after a pause, "it's a pity you're not a bit more of a troglodyte than you are." And then, to his amazement she raised herself on one elbow and leant through the gloom to kiss him, a little awkwardly, on the brow. For an instant the soft warmth of her breast pressed against him, but before he could respond she was out of the bed, making for the door, where she stopped, turned on bare heels and said, "Thanks for letting me let off steam."

"Wait."

"I'll see you tomorrow," she smiled, then she whispered, before vanishing, "For everybody's peace of mind we'll pretend this never happened. Okay?"

5
Proxy

When Martin came down to the smell of bacon late the next morning, he found everyone except Marina up before him. Only the two setters greeted him with unmixed pleasure, beseeching attention at his knees. Grace Brigshaw seemed less patient of the young man's presence in the kitchen than at any time since his arrival, and when he carried his plate through into the breakfast room Martin found Hal and Emmanuel worrying over the African's delayed return to London while Adam applied himself to buttering his toast with gloomy concentration.

A few silent minutes later, Grace brought in a second pot of coffee, sighing, "Do you think Marina intends to lie in bed all day?"

"If she's going to sulk, it's probably the best place for her," Hal grumbled. "I can't be doing with her emotional tantrums right now." He stared across the table at his son. "Why don't you make an effort to cheer her up?"

"Actually," Adam answered, gazing out at the drifted snow, "I don't have much time for her right now. If she throws herself away on idiots like Graham Holroyd, then she deserves all the grief she gets."

"Well, that's not very helpful of you," Grace declared. "The trouble is, she won't take any notice of a word I say, and the two of you haven't the faintest notion of how she feels."

"In my country," Emmanuel said, winking at Martin, whose heart had jumped at the first mention of Marina's name, "they say that women should be kept laden, pregnant and six yards behind. I wonder if everyone isn't much happier that way."

"I'm quite sure the men are," Grace replied with an air of exasperation. "However I wonder if it's ever crossed either of your minds that it's not only African men who are in need of liberation?"

"Now hang on a minute," Hal put in tetchily, "you know damn well we've gone to a lot of trouble to get as many of the market women involved in the movement as we can."

"If you think that's what I'm talking about," said Grace, "I give up." And she returned to the kitchen.

Martin stared at his plate, uncomfortably aware that he knew more than anyone else about Marina's condition, though he had no idea how her mood might have shifted since their night encounter. But when she came into the room a few minutes later, wearing a roll-neck sweater and jeans, Marina exclaimed with cheerful nonchalance at the smell of fresh coffee.

"I'm glad you're in a good mood," her father scowled, "having managed to upset everybody else."

"I'm sorry about that," Marina said, with no trace of sorrow in her voice, "but it was a bit of a blow at the time – you must see that?"

"Well, you seem to have got over it remarkably quickly," said Hal. "I wish my problems could be solved half as fast!"

"I think you must have passed a better night than I did," Emmanuel smiled at Marina. "I was disturbed by so many noises that I thought the ghost you were talking about must have come in from the spirit world."

In the instant before he averted his own gaze, Martin saw Marina's eyes avoid the tilt of the African's smile. He thought: *Emmanuel heard us; he must have said something to Hal.*

Cool and unruffled, Marina said, "Old Jonas, you mean? Perhaps he did. I seem to remember hearing one or two odd things in the night myself."

Martin could not look at her. Instead he glanced across at Adam, who was frowning at his sister. Then Marina turned her smile on Martin. "You look a bit washed out. It wasn't you wandering about in the night, was it?"

"Me? No. It wasn't me."

"I've been on the phone to Jim Lumb down at Sugden Foot," Hal said. "He reckons that if it stays like this, his tractor should make it up here tomorrow morning. So we'll just have to keep our fingers crossed." He looked at Marina. "I think your mother could do with a hand today. Mrs Tordoff won't be coming in till after the New Year." Then at Adam: "And we need more wood brought in." He turned to Emmanuel, shaking his head: "I should have had more sense than to bring you up here."

"Not at all," the African grinned. "Being confined like this is good practice for when I shall be locked up inside Makombe Castle."

"You expect them to put you in prison?" Martin said, taken aback, but glad to keep attention elsewhere.

"I intend that they should." The African widened his eyes in a smile. "Actually, Governor Dawnay would prefer not to arrest me, but I shall make it impossible for him not to do so. Then everyone from Fontonfarom to Port Rokesby will be on the streets demanding my freedom."

"So a week or so from now," Hal said to Martin, "you can think of this cool customer sweating inside a hot cell."

"While I shall be remembering this preposterous snow," the African added, "and all of you shivering in Yorkshire, and it will make me very content to be where I am!"

Meanwhile Marina was picking at a scrap of cold toast, alert to every nuance of feeling in the room, discomfited by none of it and so poised in her detachment that Martin was left wondering whether his memory of their time spent in bed together was merely a figment of some midnight fantasy. So he was glad to get out of the house and fetch logs from the woodshed. The air there smelt of frost and sawdust. Its chill smarted at his cheeks as he and Adam worked together in silence, taking turns to swing the axe and carry the filled basket through into the house until a stack of split logs stood high at either side of the open hearth.

They came back into the kitchen in time to see Marina lift a tea towel from a bowl of risen dough. Closing her eyes, she leant over and pressed her lips to its soft dome. When she looked up, she saw Martin staring at her.

"Do you want to kiss it?" she invited.

He snorted, blushed, looked away, aware of Grace and Marina grinning at him.

"Here," said Adam, "let me." He kissed the dough, tipped it out of the mixing bowl onto the tabletop and began to knead. As Martin watched the smooth rolling motion of his shoulders and fists, Grace bent to open the oven door. The air swirled with the smell of baking bread. She prised the loaves from their tins, testing each with the tap of a knuckle at its base before setting them to cool on racks.

"Let Martin try," she said to Adam. "Come on, kiss it first."

Self-consciously, Martin did as he was bidden. Surprised by the soft touch of the dough at his lips, he pulled back, smiling, then he leant over the dough, pushing at it with bunched fists.

"Not so hard," Marina said. "It's alive. It wants to breathe. Be gentler. Try tucking your thumbs into your palms, like this."

After a few more awkward movements, Martin found the rhythm of the task. In the warm smell of the kitchen his body swayed to the roll of the dough. His big hands gentled at its living touch. And for those quiet moments he was untroubled by thoughts of Cripplegate or Africa, of his own father or of Adam's, and briefly forgetful even of the puzzling young woman who stood watching him. Then Grace said, "That's enough now." She offered him a knife to slice the smooth dough into three parts, each of which he lifted into its own greased tin. Grace covered them with a towel. "They need to rise again before I put them in the oven." She looked up, where sunlight glanced off the snow outside, brightening the kitchen's white walls. "It looks lovely out there now. Why don't you boys take the dogs for a walk?"

With the dogs bounding far ahead, plunging into drifts and clambering out again, pink-tongued, to shake their coats, they walked out under a sky that had cleared to a crisp, unblemished blue. Mostly they were silent, each absorbed in his own thoughts, but as they stood on a ridge of outcrop rock capped with frozen snow, Martin asked Adam about his time in Africa. Adam spoke at length about his childhood, how he and Marina had grown up there with their nanny, Wilhelmina Song, and their friends on the school compound, who taught them the traditional lore of animals and birds, of reptiles and insects, of witches, ghosts and spirits. Caught up in his memories, Adam went on to tell of a trip he had taken by steamer up the River Kra with Emmanuel and Hal. They were on their way to the forest city where the Olun of Bamutu, the most powerful of the colony's paramount chiefs, kept court. He remembered watching crocodiles glide away through the brown water, and the lean men who stood on their reflections, spear-fishing from pirogues. He remembered the sound of monkeys chattering in the trees as the forest drifted by in a haze of sunlight, and how villagers had gathered in crowds to stare in wonder at this white child each time he stepped ashore. By the time the steamer docked at Bamutu, the Olun's ceremonial durbar was already in full swing. Adam saw the chieftains carried high on their palanquins under flouncing parasols. He saw platoons of warriors gesturing with spears and muskets as they shouted and danced to the beat of drums and gongs. What he did not share with Martin, though it came vividly to his mind, was his memory of fainting that day. He had been carried through the excited crowd on his father's shoulders, and they were approaching the space kept clear before the Olun's pavilion when he saw the palpitating belly of a goat tethered on the ground. He could feel the sweat from his father's brow beneath his hands, his own shirt sticky at his back. Unable to blink, he had watched a fetish priest draw a knife across the goat's white throat. In the same instant, the fringes of the sun, which only moments before had been a glaring yellow, seemed to career into a livid green. Then the sky had turned inside out, revealing the darkness hidden there.

Listening to Adam's stories in the frosty air of that Pennine moor, Martin contemplated the banality of his own life. But when he remarked on it, Adam merely said, "Count yourself lucky. At least you were spared the bloody awful misery of the boarding school they sent me back to when I was a bit older. Hal said it was a good place to learn to know my enemy, and he was right about that. But I'd rather have stayed in Africa among my friends."

"Was your school really bad?" Martin asked.

"As you see," Adam answered, "I survived."

Later in their friendship Martin learnt more of what lay behind that dry response. After the heat of equatorial Africa, Adam had shivered in the winds that thrashed around the unheated rooms of Mowbray College. The dismal morning ritual of queuing naked on duckboards over wet floors before plunging into a cold bath left him with chilblains and chapped lips and a permanent, snivelling cold. But it was only when he was made to fag for a prefect called Hedley Bingham that he had begun to grasp what his father had meant.

Bingo was a notorious bully who saw in Adam's shy independence of spirit a thing to be broken, and in himself just the man for the job. Having informed the frightened boy that he was no better than a savage out of Africa who would one day thank his tormentor for teaching him civilized ways, he turned Adam's time at school into an ordeal of misery and humiliation. Adam suffered in silence for as long as he could, but Bingham was too randomly cruel, and he himself too proud. Eventually he mutinied. When he refused to boil a pile of dirty jockstraps that the prefects dropped at his feet one afternoon after rugby, Bingo took out his cane. Three mighty swipes across his naked buttocks later, Adam was still refusing to obey. Three more strokes were administered. The skin broke and began to bleed, but still he would not pick up the jockstraps. Cursing, Bingo lifted his cane, but was stopped by the house captain, Tom Hardesty. "Put him in the Hole," Hardesty said with a bored sigh.

The Hole was a small cupboard that had been made from a blocked-up lancet window four feet up the rough flint wall of the house's attic staircase. It took three prefects to manhandle the scrawny boy into its narrow space and lock the door on him. Trembling, Adam crouched in the dark niche, with barely room enough to bang a fist. He heard Bingo summon Laurence Stromberg – a podgy boy who had already endured a year of this grim culture – and order him to stand on the stairs throwing a tennis ball against the cupboard door at head height until the mutinous fag howled for release. Then the prefects lounged against the wall listening to the dull thud of the ball for ten minutes or so before going down to their study, demanding to be called when Adam broke.

Still the boy held out. The tennis ball pounded against the cupboard door, and the reverberations of its planks shook inside Adam's head until he began to wonder whether the next thud must drive him mad. He was given a vision of hell then – an eternity confined inside a cramped space with only the pounding of a ball to mark the passage of time. The thought occurred to him that if he held his breath for long enough he might suffocate and die, and the pounding would stop and the whole school would be so shocked by the discovery of his corpse that no one would ever be allowed to suffer such torment again. For a few moments there was something almost voluptuously consoling in the prospect of a martyr's death, but despite the contortions of his will, his mouth burst open and his lungs sucked at the air. He told himself that, sooner or later, someone must come along to drag him out of that hell-hole before he had the chance to die. Meanwhile his nose was bleeding and the pounding went on.

Almost an hour later, young Laurence Stromberg finally persuaded Adam to climb down. "For God's sake, Brigshaw," the boy said, "it can only get worse if you don't toe the line. Don't imagine you can beat those evil bastards. You'll have to cave in sooner or later. Besides which, this is pretty bloody shitty for me too, you know?" Another thud shook the door. "Better be crafty than crazy, don't you think?"

The suggestion struck Adam with the cool, refreshing force of reason. He saw that neither courage nor principle lay behind his resistance – merely the brute stupidity of a frightened dog. Now his head was clearing. He saw that there was no justice among men, and very little mercy. For the first time he understood the rage and ardour with which his father believed in the absolute need to change the way the world was run. "All right," he said, "tell them I'm coming out."

When he fell stiffly from the opened cupboard, he blinked up in the sudden light, and saw Hedley Bingham standing over him with the cane in one hand and a jockstrap dangling from the other. "Lick it," Bingham smiled, "lick it clean for me, there's a good chap!"

Out of the corner of his eye Adam saw Laurence give him an encouraging nod. A moment later Adam leant forward on his hands and knees, put his tongue to the sweat-stained cloth and stared into the eyes of his enemy.

His stream of thought had never run colder or more clear.

"There were times when I hated Hal for sending me to Mowbray," he said now, as he and Martin turned to walk back to High Sugden, "but I'll tell you something – I came away from that awful place with a much sharper understanding of just why he's so passionate about freedom and justice."

*

In the quiet time before dinner, Martin was lying on his bed when he heard a soft tap at the door. Marina came in and stood across from him with one hand held behind her back.

"I was wondering whether to come and see you," he said, sitting up, "but I couldn't see how."

"Just as well you didn't. I've only just finished this. It's for you." From behind her back she brought a small sheet of cartridge paper. "Because I'm sorry about being bitchy with you last night."

He sat on the edge of the bed, waiting for her to approach. Marina remained where she was, at a deliberate distance, extending her arm so that he had to get up and cross the room to see what she was offering. He held her gaze for a moment before glancing down at what she had given him.

"You painted this for me?" he said, and when she nodded he looked back at the picture of a young man in doublet and hose riding on the back of a fox. With one hand the youth gripped the red fur of the fox's neck, while the other was lifted from a slashed sleeve to clutch at his extravagantly plumed hat. Martin saw at once that it was an illustration of the story he'd told the previous night – the fox carrying the prince over hill and dale from one magical encounter to the next. A moment later he recognized his own features in the young man's startled face.

"I made him look like you," Marina was saying, "because if you ever find your princess, it will probably be by doing the wrong thing at the right time, like him."

"I didn't know you were an artist," he said.

"I'm afraid that hind leg went a bit wrong."

"No, the whole thing's brilliant. It's just how I imagined it."

"You're to promise not to show it to anybody."

"Not even Adam?"

"Not to anybody."

He looked up into her insistent eyes. "I think Emmanuel knows."

"Of course he does. But he's relaxed about it. He won't say anything. Africans are sensible about these things."

"Anyway, I shall be gone tomorrow."

"Lucky you!"

"Shall I get to see you again?"

"If you come back."

This was less encouragement than he'd hoped for. "I'm not sure Adam will invite me. He didn't bargain on having me around for this long. I think I bore him."

"That's just his stupid way of trying to stay superior. Actually he's intrigued by you. And I think you might be just what he needs. He needs a good friend – one who won't let him get away with anything."

Martin stood, wondering at her utter absence of doubt in her own wisdom. "What makes you think I'd be any good at that?

"Because I think you're honest. You say what you think and you seem to mean what you say – which is probably why you rub him up the wrong way sometimes."

"What about you?" he asked hoarsely.

This time it was she who glanced away. "You've never been in bed with a girl before, have you?" When he did not answer, she gave a little laugh, though it was not unkind. "I don't suppose it'll be long before it happens again."

"With you?" he dared.

Glancing about the room, she spoke not to his face but to the angled reflection of his face in the full-length mirror set into the wardrobe door. "That depends."

"On what?"

Marina merely shrugged, smiling, and pushed back a strand of hair behind her ear. "But in the meantime," she said, "you're not to go chopping off any foxes' heads!"

Grace went to bed early that night, complaining of a headache. Hal relaxed from the wider anxieties pressing on his mind by provoking Martin into debate. It began with literature, shifted to ethical issues, and was soon, as Hal had always intended, centred on politics. Emmanuel and Adam sat back, exchanging discreet smiles as Martin abandoned position after position under a dialectical assault conducted with such skill that he felt enlarged rather than quashed by each defeat. At one point, however, he looked up and caught a quick, swiping glance of disdain on Marina's face. More might be at stake, he realized, than he had so far seen.

"You don't question his premises?" she challenged.

"What's wrong with my premises?" Hal smiled.

Marina turned a cold stare on her father. "I didn't say there was anything wrong with them." She swept her eyes back across Martin again. "But if he's got a mind of his own, he needn't just accept them as if they were written down on tablets of stone."

Hal smiled across at Martin. "So do you think I'm playing God?"

"You don't believe in God, so why would you?"

"Words!" Marina snorted with contempt. "It's all just words, and I'm getting a bit sick of them. Suppose man isn't the perfectible animal you take him for, Hal – what then? Suppose all your theories are based on too high a view of him altogether? Suppose we just need to be bad sometimes, to be wicked even, to refuse to grovel under your high-minded moral imperatives. What if there's a dark part of us that would rather risk passion and tragedy than settle for a boring state of economic equity and social justice?" She was warming to her own eloquence. "Perhaps it has a bloody-minded preference for drama and turmoil and suffering? And suppose there's a good evolutionary reason why wickedness should flourish like the green bay tree? What if the real revolutionaries aren't utopian lefties after all, but diabolical angels who come whistling out of the dark with whips and tongs and temptations to shock the world out of complacency?"

Taken aback by this onslaught, Hal was about to answer when she added, "And don't patronize me by telling me I'm just being perverse."

"On the contrary," Hal coolly lied, "I was going to say that it's an interesting line to take."

"Suppose it's not just a bloody line," Marina shouted, exasperated by his mandarin composure. "Suppose I'm speaking for myself. Suppose I actually like chaos. Suppose I prefer sinfulness for its own perverse sake. How about that then? Suppose I tell you to take all your theories and schemes and good intentions, all your carefully worked-out positions on this, that and everything, and most of all your intellectual condescension, and…"

"Marina," Hal raised his voice over hers, "that's enough. This is Emmanuel's last night here. If you're not interested in taking part in a civil conversation, you'd better go to your room."

Marina got to her feet, staring at her father in silence. Then she scorched Adam and Martin with the same gaze and walked out.

"What was all that about?" Hal asked in helpless dismay as the door banged shut behind her.

"I think perhaps we are all tired," Emmanuel offered.

"She can be insufferable sometimes," Hal said.

Adam took a split log from the wicker basket and threw it onto the fire. "It's the lightning in her," he said. "One of her more spectacular displays, I thought."

"It wasn't coming at you," Hal complained, aggrieved and angry still. "I can't say I understand why I got hit this time."

"When was lightning ever rational?" Adam answered, stirring the fire to a blaze with the brass-handled poker.

"Does she have the mark still?" Emmanuel asked.

"I imagine so," said Hal. "I think it's there for life."

"People born in a storm can be touched with prophetic fire," Emmanuel reflected. "One must be patient with such a destiny. Sometimes it will shock and burn us, of course, but one day it may lighten our darkness."

"It's just as likely to bring the roof down round our heads," Hal muttered with a muffled fury that might have been directed as much against his friend's optimism as against his own difficult daughter.

Emmanuel smiled, undeterred. "That might be the way of it. But back home we say that a wise man does not trade blows with the lightning; first he waits for the fire to burn out, then he tills the ashes."

Grunting, Hal poured more whiskey. "Emmanuel has a proverb for every occasion!"

"In any case, my friend" – Emmanuel was laughing now, a low, mirthful, African laugh that was still laced with a peasant farmer's sense of irony – "you should be thankful that you are only her father and not her husband!"

"Heaven help him, whoever he may be," Hal sighed, coming around a little in response to his friend's good humour.

Shortly afterwards the two men drank the last of their whiskey and retired to bed, leaving Adam and Martin sprawled before the fire. One setter snoozed beside Martin, the other propped its head against Adam's thigh. A wind had risen, and the fire flapped and hissed in its iron basket. The night felt volatile still. Martin lay with his head on a purple cushion looking up at the mask over the fireplace. Balefully it glowered back through the empty slots of its eyes, leaving him uneasy under its black stare. When he glanced across the room, Adam's lean features were so disfigured by shadow that his face felt almost as impenetrable as the mask. It was like being abandoned in the company of a sinister stranger.

He considered things from a cold distance now. What a fool he'd made of himself here at High Sugden! He was hopelessly vulnerable to Marina's moods. Adam was obviously bored by him. And could he really have been manipulated so easily by Hal? A log shifted in the grate, quickening a constellation of sparks in the dark chimney. The dog at Adam's side kicked and panted in its sleep. The wind picked up the wildness in Marina's words and blew them about until the pageant of freedom fighters that Hal's zeal had earlier conjured in

Martin's imagination collapsed into a bloody carnage of riots, executions and atrocities. He saw torture, bomb blasts, massacre and counter-massacre. Perhaps Marina had put her finger on the dark pulse of things. Perhaps his own father had not been so wrong after all: politics was a dirty business, and if there were rare occasions when the tumult of human conflict was exalted by high-minded idealism, more often it proved to be a murderous Jacobean drama of betrayal and revenge.

Then he heard Adam saying, "Is there something going on between you and my sister?"

"What do you mean? Why do you ask?"

"It just feels a bit odd to me, that's all."

"What does? What feels odd?"

"The way you're both behaving. As if there's some sort of love-hate thing going on, and the rest of us keep getting snarled up in it."

"I hardly know her. I think it's your imagination."

"If you say so."

"You don't believe me?"

"It's just that I'd rather know," Adam said, "so that I can make allowances."

"Know what?"

"If something's going on."

"Well, there isn't." Martin recoiled from the partial lie into greater heat. "I don't want you making allowances for me."

"You're very defensive all of a sudden!"

"Why shouldn't I be? I mean, from the moment I turned up here you've all been having a go at me one way or another. Everyone except Emmanuel."

"Perhaps you've invited it?"

"Sure, that's why I came – to have my head messed up!"

Stroking the ear of the sleeping dog, Adam studied his friend with a mild air of disappointment. "I'm sorry you see it that way," he said.

"How else should I see it? I don't think you realize just how high and mighty you lot come across. You go on and on about changing the world, but I think there's a few things that could do with straightening out here first!"

"I'm sure you're right," Adam said quietly.

Accelerating on his own steam now, Martin heard only sarcasm in his agreement. "There you go – polishing your bloody ironies again! Can't you just try saying what you mean for once? Or are you just too clever and superior for that? Do you have to be proving something all the time?"

"I don't know," Adam said. "Do you?"

Confused by the swift return of his own arrow and by Adam's suddenly wounded manner, Martin faltered in his stride. The African mask stared down at him. Glumly he said, "I came out here thinking we might be friends."

"That's what I wanted," Adam answered, frowning. "Why else do you think I invited you?"

"Then why can't you show it? Why does everything have to be so complicated? I mean, for God's sake, things can be a lot simpler than you make them out."

"Some things only look simple," Adam countered, "because you haven't yet seen how complex they are."

"Do you think I don't know that?" Martin answered. "I'm not a complete fool, you know. And I only have to listen to you lot to see how you can think yourselves into a hell of a mess. I tried to tell you what feels real to me that first morning. Nothing I've heard since convinces me I was wrong."

"So we're back to the stones and the wind?"

"You can stand on stones. You can breathe the wind."

"But we're not wild animals," Adam retorted. "And we've moved on a bit since we were bare-arsed cavemen. We don't just inherit the world as it is. We have the ability to improve it."

"You mean with factories and mills? Have you checked out the state of the Calder lately? You mean with laws and politics and police forces? Like Siberia?"

"If you change the terms a bit and say the power of human invention and the principle of justice, yes, I do mean that. And if that sounds too abstract for you, well I'm afraid we can't all just be hermits holed up in the rocks. We live in the plural. We're responsible to one another." Adam was breathing quickly now, speaking with untypical agitation. "All right, you may not think much of me and my family, but what about Emmanuel? Think about what he's doing, and why. Can you honestly tell me it would be better for millions of oppressed people if he listened to you and gave up everything that he and Hal have always stood for?"

Frowning, Martin fell silent. He was trying to recover the ground on which he felt most securely himself. Like the snow-clad hill out there, that ground was far older than history, more deeply nourishing to the soul; but throughout the weekend he had felt its radiance fading from him, veil by veil, like a dream of innocence. It was as if he'd come out to this lonely house only to find himself confronted by the tumult of the world crying out for justice. And far from inciting Martin to defect from his family, Hal Brigshaw was demanding that he render it a more active loyalty, that he take up the challenge of the cry in his family's name, for their sake, and for the sake of millions like them. So even now, as he strove to hold on to a vision of a universe that spoke the language not of politics but of poetry, Martin heard himself being summoned elsewhere.

Meanwhile, Adam was also undergoing a silent crisis of belief. For yes, he did know how vilely the river in the valley below had been fouled by the power of human invention. He knew too how the principle of justice was honoured more frequently in the breach than the observance, and he had a shrewd idea how short the journey could be from democracy to demagoguery to dictatorship. Closer to home, he often worried whether a driven egotism lay behind his father's political ambitions, and he had been more disconcerted than he had shown by his sister's outburst. But he was pressed more closely still by the uneasy knowledge that, for all his advocacy of Hal's ideas and Emmanuel's dreams, he himself was not, and would never be, a man of action. When it was merely a question of debate, he could filibuster for hours at a time, but the thought of entering the public arena, of having to act on his opinions and endure the consequences of action – that thought filled his heart with dread. And a still more insidious pressure was building now, for during the course of their walk that afternoon he had begun to see that he might be resisting Martin's mystical vision of things precisely because of the draw it exercised on his own imagination.

"I didn't really mean it," he heard Martin saying now, "the stuff I just said…"

"It's all right. It's been a weird time. I understand."

Martin glanced up from his apology. "I know that a lot of what Hal has to say is true and real and important. But what I can't accept is that human beings are the only source of meaning in the world. Some of my most meaningful experiences have had nothing to do with people – things like staring up at the night sky, listening to water in a crag, walking through a wood and feeling the hairs prickle at my neck. You won't convince me that such experiences aren't real."

"I wouldn't even try," Adam said. "I've had the same feelings myself, many times. But I don't know what you mean by calling them meaningful. Powerful, yes. Charged with a primitive sense of awe and wonder. But I don't see that they carry any intelligible meaning." He looked up at Martin, not quite with disdain, both amused by such unguarded earnestness and discomfited by it. "Or if they do, it's regressive, the kind of animist superstition that's kept Africa in the dark ages. Like that mask up there. Yet here you are going on about them as if they were divine. Why can't they just be a kind of vestigial sensitivity left over from our animal nature? From a time before we had language, before we were conscious enough to find our own meanings in the world?"

"All right, maybe they are in part," Martin conceded, "but why should that diminish them? Perhaps the animals are saner than we are."

Yet, sick at heart behind his ardour, embarrassed by his own naivety, he was thinking, *What if he's right, what if he's right about this too?*

Now Adam was staring into the darkness of his closed eyes, listening to the wind in the chimney gusting out of empty spaces, coming from nowhere with nowhere to go. It echoed on a chilly atheism long since seeded in his soul.

"I'd like to believe it" – he might have been speaking aloud to himself – "I really would." Then he opened disconsolate eyes. "But there's just too much evidence that the universe is entirely indifferent to us, that it's absurd, and we remain absurd inside it – except in so far as we affirm the possibility of meaning on our own human terms."

Not sure that he wanted to hear the answer, Martin said, "What kind of evidence?"

For a time there was silence between them. The world might have been turning on that silence until, without stirring, Adam said quietly, "All right. Listen to this. It's a story my father told me. A story from the war. Something that happened to a friend of his in France."

This man had been a contemporary of Hal's at university, a principled and intelligent high Tory to whom he had never been particularly close, but for whom he felt the respect that one man accords another of differing but sincerely held views. Some time after the outbreak of the Second World War, the friend had volunteered for service behind enemy lines in occupied France, where he worked under cover for three years before his network was blown. Arrested by the Gestapo, he was questioned under duress without betraying his identity. Finally he was sent to a concentration camp. Somehow he survived and came home after the war, severely emaciated, to a hero's welcome.

"Have you seen pictures of the camps?" Adam asked.

"A few," Martin replied.

Adam crossed to a bookcase, searched along one of the shelves, took down a book and moved the oil lamp so that Martin might study the pictures more closely. The photographs were pallid and murky, as though the camera itself had winced in recoil from what it was required to record, so it took a moment before the twisted, almost abstract shapes resolved into a pile of naked bodies in a pit. In other photographs the dead were stacked like wattle hurdles. There were pictures of survivors too, prostrate on rough bunks or wandering the camp with barely the strength to stand upright, and between these portraits of the living and the wasted relics of the dead lay no more than a splinter of light in famished eyes, the merest thread of breath.

"The huts were festering with dysentery and diphtheria," Adam said. "They say there was the smell of excrement everywhere, of helpless human filth. And over that the smell of burning, the death smell." Martin looked up from the book into his friend's face. Adam shrugged and added, "This was – what? – a dozen years ago. You and I were four or five at the time."

Martin stared back at the pictures in silence, trying to connect with the feelings they aroused: on the one hand, a self-protective sense of distance from the squalid improbability of it all; on the other, a sickly feeling of culpability, as if he were somehow responsible. He remembered hearing that Germans who lived near the camps had been forced to file past such scenes, to stare at what they had chosen to ignore, and bear shameful witness to what had been perpetrated in their name. What must have they felt then, if he felt what he was feeling now?

"It's enough on its own to make my point," Adam resumed, "but there's something else. Something that happened in Rouen while Hal's friend was being interrogated there, something that finally broke his faith. I've never been able to get it out of my mind." Adam threw another log among the embers. One of the setters lifted its heavy head at the sound, then slumped back into sleep.

"The man's radio call sign was Dog Fox," Adam said. "He published his war memoirs under that name, so that's what I'll call him." He stared back at the fire as though watching his story played out among that sudden hot shift of ashes. "As a matter of routine, Dog Fox was searched when he was first arrested. Among his bits and pieces, they found a fifty-franc note in his wallet with a telephone number pencilled on it. Obviously a contact number for another member of the network, right? So the number was traced and its owner brought for interrogation to Gestapo headquarters. When he protested ignorance of the whole affair, that he was innocent, a quiet family man, a man who minded his own business, they began to torture him."

Adam prodded the fire to flame. "The two prisoners were brought together in the hope that they might incriminate each other," he went on. "Dog Fox had never seen the other man before. He had no idea who he was. Only when one of the interrogators referred to the number written on the banknote did he realize how the man had come to be there. But the frightened, bewildered face with the damaged eye and the electrode burns around his lips was that of a total stranger. The two prisoners were connected only by the outrageous misfortune that an ordinary fifty-franc note had passed through many hands before Dog Fox slipped it into his wallet without even noticing that a telephone number was scribbled on it."

Adam paused there, struggling to focus on the metaphysical implications of events which had become for him the stuff of nightmares. "Think about it. Because of a trivial coincidence, an innocent man was plucked out of his life, arrested, tortured and finally sent to a concentration camp where he may or may not have survived. And the poor devil was just a proxy for whoever the Gestapo had been after. Someone arrested as a proxy, tortured as a proxy, exterminated as a proxy. End of story." Adam stared across at Martin. "Of course, it's just one terrifying tale among many – no worse than what happened to millions of innocent Jews and gypsies. But imagine something like that happening to you. What comfort do you think you'd find then in wind and stones and stars? Do you seriously think they'd help you to write poetry that can out-stare that kind of horror? As far as I can see, no other kind will do any more."

The two young men sat on before the dwindling fire, each aware of the other struggling. Martin could find no adequate answer, and there was no triumph in Adam's eyes – only a bleak acceptance of the facts of the case as he saw it.

Eventually Adam sighed and said, "Martin, it's cold and dark out there. I wish I could believe in the universe as the enchanted place you seem to take it for. All I do know is that terrible things were done while we were children and there's no way past them into innocence again. If there was a God, he must have died of shame at his creation then."

Martin sat in silence, aware of the mask gazing down at him, its slotted eye sockets opening onto vacant space, and he saw that what was truly terrifying was the emptiness it masked. Hanging above the dying fire, it was as devoid of devils as of a god. Not only did it give no light, it offered nothing but a bleak refutation which left him speechless.

"And how about this for a final solution?" Adam added wryly. "At the very moment when our species was proving itself capable of murder on an industrial scale, it also devised the perfect instrument of its own total destruction. Death is what we've got really good at these days, don't you think? So isn't the real question now whether we actually deserve to live at all?" He glanced across at Martin, saw how his friend was assenting at last, but he took no satisfaction in the knowledge. It filled him rather with a huge, wearying sadness, like a loss. "And the mercy seat's empty," he said. "We're on our own. There's no saviour to ransom us. No guarantee of meaning in a world where things like that happen. All that counts is what we do, whether we know what we're doing or not. And all the time, for better or worse, it's entirely up to us to choose."

6
Lightning

On the point of leaving High Sugden late the next morning, Martin came out of his room and saw Marina on the landing in her dressing gown making her way to the bathroom. They stared at each other uncertainly for a moment, ill at ease, discomfited by their proximity.

He said, "I was just about to go." When she only nodded, he glanced away. "Anyway, I'm glad to have seen you before I leave."

"I'm sorry about last night," she said. "It wasn't you I was quarrelling with."

"Forget it," Martin shrugged. "I hope I'll get to see you again."

"I'm sure Adam will invite you back."

"That would be great, but..."

"And Hal's obviously taken to you."

But too much remained unsaid and unresolved inside him. "Do you want to go out some time?" he rushed. "To a film or something?"

"The three of us, you mean?"

"If you like. But I was thinking..."

"We don't want to upset Adam."

"No."

She left him there for a time, feeling the blood in his cheeks, wishing he'd kept his mouth shut. He saw it then: Marina was doing the impossible thing she had asked of him – behaving as though that intimate exchange had never happened and was best forgotten. *For everybody's peace of mind*, she'd said. But it was her own peace of mind she meant. He'd been a fool to think otherwise.

Yet to think about her at all – that fragrant warmth in the darkness – was to flood his heart with an aching blend of pleasure and pain that must soon become addictive.

Then, "Write something," she said, as he turned to leave. "Write me a poem. Write one that shows me who you really are."

"Sure," he said, without conviction. "I'll try."

But it was as though that visit to High Sugden had shocked him through into a foreign land, where he felt like a displaced person with no stable identity. He was no longer sure what he was for. And Marina had chosen this moment to ask for a poem disclosing his true nature. Had she commanded him to sprout wings at his shoulder blades and fly, he would have been as eager to comply, and no more able. Yet some hours later, as he walked down the bleak steps into the basement at Cripplegate Chambers, he was remembering the inciting light of challenge in her eyes.

He found his mother there, crouched before the hearth, sealing the chimney with an open sheet of newspaper to draw the fire she had just lit.

"You're back then," she said. "Did you have a nice time?"

The room felt cold. Only a drear light fell from the window's frosted glass. He watched the shadows move across the pane as people walked by on the pavement outside. "Yes," he muttered, "it was good. It was different."

Without turning she said, "Will you fetch me another bucket of coal, love?" Under the black-leaded cowl of the fireplace the newsprint glowed with a ruddy glare, while the chimney roared.

Martin picked up the metal bucket and went back out into the further reaches of the basement, past the bathroom door and the door to what must once have been a wine cellar. It was empty of everything except cobwebs now. At the end of the passage lay the sooty vault where a ton of coal had been tipped in a sloping pile between the flagged floor and the lid of the chute outside. The lumps were too big for the fireplace, so he had to break them up with the old hammer laid ready by the door. The pieces split beneath the blows, exposing new surfaces that glimmered with a sleek and glossy sheen, as though a dim carboniferous light had been shut up in there for millions of years awaiting this chance to break.

He stared at that blackness in fascination before reaching for the shovel. Coal clanked into the bucket, shedding its dust. This was what his father did, day in and day out. The task required neither skill nor intelligence, nothing but brawn, and it was performed at the lowest level of operation, in the grimy dark of the boiler house at Bamforth Brothers' mill. And here was Martin now, at the turn of the year, in the cellar of Cripplegate Chambers, underneath the prosperous offices of what he had just learnt to think of as the bourgeois world, shovelling coal.

After the airy spaces of High Sugden he felt buried alive.

By New Year's Eve the night sky was thawing in a cloudy mist of stars. Snow had been pushed back from the streets of Calderbridge into dingy heaps at the kerbstone edge. The pubs along Eastgate were crowded and loud. Shortly after eleven thirty Martin left Frank Jagger and his other mates blowing their fists under a gas lamp and made his way across the town to the house of his Aunt Violet. For as long as he could recall, the whole Crowther family – his father's four brothers and three sisters, along with their husbands, wives and children – had gathered there, in what had once been the family home, to celebrate the turning of the year. They would stay up carousing far into what they called "Old Year's Night", joking, playing cards, sharing memories of past times and singing the music-hall songs they had learnt when they were adolescents and children during the First World War. Jack Crowther had made it plain that he expected his son to be there before midnight, and by the time Martin arrived, the house was crammed with noise.

Auntie Vi's balding mongrel bitch, Judy, came panting to meet him at the front door. "Here's our Martin," called out Uncle Wilf, still buttoning his flies as he came out of the lavatory. "Come on in, lad, get thiself a drink." A twelve-year-old girl in a gingham frock ran squealing into the hall chased by one of the older boys. From behind them in the front room came a rowdy chorus:

Show me the way to go home,
I'm tired and I want to go to bed.
I had a little drink about an hour ago
And it went right to my head.

Martin walked into the bitter-caramel smell of stout and cigarette smoke that wafted through crepe-paper trimmings. He was greeted by faces he hadn't seen for many months. One part of the family had bussed across the frozen moors from Lancashire to be there, others had walked or ridden motorbikes and sidecars from outlying areas of Calderbridge. The younger children were already packed off upstairs – so many of them that they would have to sleep six to a bed, warm as puppies, boys and girls together, three at the top and three at the bottom. Martin and his cousins had done the same when they were small, and it had been no secret that, soon after they'd been tucked in, they would throw back the blankets and creep out, barefoot in pyjamas, to sit on the landing, listening to the din round the piano downstairs.

"*You will always hear me singing this song,*" they were singing now, "*show me the way to go home.*"

Smiling in her high-backed chair, Aunt Violet, grey-haired, in her late fifties and lame since she was a girl, blew him a tipsy kiss. With a sherry in her hand, she swayed her narrow shoulders from side to side as she began to sing 'Roll out the Barrel'. At once the others joined in, Martin's mother clapping her hands and crossing to hug him with a warm kiss when they reached the rousing final lines:

Now's the time to roll the barrel
Now the gang's all here!

A moment later his cousin Kathy, who had been his childhood sweetheart, was offering him a choice of beer or whiskey, a bottle in either hand, while she asked with a teasing smile whether he'd been out after the lasses that night.

"Nay, they've been after me."

"Oh aye, now you've got a place at Cambridge University I bet they just can't keep their hands off you!"

"I've said nowt to 'em about it," he grinned at her, "but then a good-looking lad like me doesn't need any other advantages!"

"Oh, I can see you're going to be as full of yourself as a Cheshire cat from now on!" Kathy said and turned to Martin's mother, who was approaching across the room. "Auntie Bella, come and help me bring this brain-box here back down to earth."

"Now then, Kathy," Bella Crowther said, "you're not to poke fun at our Martin. He were first in our family to stay on at school after he were fifteen, and now he's off to college and we're dead proud of 'im, aren't we, Jack?"

"Just so long has he doesn't let it go to his bloody 'ead," Jack Crowther answered. "Does anybody know what time it is?"

Martin glanced at his watch. "Just coming up to five-to."

"Come on then, get your glasses filled up everybody."

"Who's letting it in then?" asked Uncle Wilf. "Must be my turn this year?"

"Our Martin's tallest and darkest now," Jack Crowther declared. "He'll do it."

"I've only just come in," his son protested.

"Then you can just get back out again." Jack laughed, and turned to the piano, demanding, "Where's that New Year stuff got to?"

But his wife had already gathered up the ritual objects and was offering them to Martin. "Here you are, love," she said, putting the crust of bread, the cob of coal and the silver florin in his hands, "bring us all some luck."

Reluctantly Martin followed his father out into the hall. He could smell a mix of beer and spirits on his breath as the man frowned up at him, saying, "You took your time. I thought we were going to have to let that bugger Wilf do it!"

"I said I'd be here, didn't I?"

"Aye, well… Make sure you get them words right when yon door gets opened for thee. We don't want you letting no bad luck in!"

Martin glanced away. "I've heard 'em often enough."

Even at that moment, when the year was turning and the world changing with it, and both father and son might have yearned to reach out to each other from their separate worlds, there was this baffled shock of hostility between them. But then Auntie Vi came into the hall, where in a couple of minutes she would open the front door of her house at the midnight knock. With a stick in one hand and a welcoming glass in the other, she was already singing in her thin contralto warble:

O the lamps were burning brightly
'Twas the night that would banish all sin,
For the bells were ringing the old year out
And the New Year in.

And the moment had passed before Jack Crowther could find a way to say what was plain in his gaze: that he knew his son stood on other thresholds now, and this might well be the last New Year that the two of them would welcome in together. Instead he put a stubby-fingered hand on his son's shoulder and said, "All right, let's have you out there."

Then Martin was out in the night, stamping his feet against the cold. In one of the houses he could see the monochrome flicker of a television screen. When he looked up, the stars shivered over Gledhill Beacon. He tried to see them for what they were in Hal and Adam's uncompromising view of things – titanic accidents of stone and gas explainable by physics and chemistry and mathematical calculations, otherwise random and meaningless. The night smelt of alcohol and old snow.

He ran the words of the family's ritual greeting through his mind. *Here's a piece of bread for the staff of life, a piece of coal for the warmth of life, and a piece of silver for the wealth of life. And here's a kiss for the love of life.*

He was the stranger at the door. It was his role to usher in the New Year that was bearing down out of the dark on all of them, and who knew what promises or menace it carried on its wings?

Well, he had ventured beyond the mills and pubs and churches of this grimy town, beyond the humdrum activity of spinners, carders and slubbing dyers, of fat solicitors and sarcastic teachers. He had glimpsed intellectual horizons that reached across the Pennine summits, round the curving earth, out into the brown river mouths and steaming green rainforests of West Africa and beyond. History was on the move. The whole world was changing. And he too could change. For even though Hal had seemed to admit him to the order of manhood, those days at High Sugden had shown Martin how little he had so far grasped of life and its possibilities. It was a time for resolutions now. As the midnight strike of the Town Hall clock was answered by a peal of bells across the freezing air, he vowed that this year he would seize life with both hands.

Invited out to High Sugden again, he went in renewed pursuit of Marina. She proved friendly enough but elusive in the little he saw of her. Adam, however, seemed glad to welcome him back. Both he and Hal were eager to share news of Emmanuel's return to Africa, where he was now under arrest. Left restless by his own distance from events, Hal turned the visit into an informal seminar, and under his Socratic tutelage Martin was encouraged to observe both local affairs and international diplomacy with critical attention, to analyse motivations, to reason things out, and at every significant turn to demand to know, "Who gains from this?" Meanwhile he began to understand the kind of courage it took to act with radical purpose in the world – as, by early February, Emmanuel was daring to act from his cell in Makombe Castle; as the crowds of students, trade unionists and market women dared to riot for his release on the streets of Port Rokesby; as Hal's ambitious plans for a free Equatoria dared to offer a template by which things might be made new.

As also, more perversely, Marina's rebellious spirit had begun to break out from under the weight of her father's ideological authority. Quite early in the year Martin was dismayed to learn from Adam that she was infatuated with Graham Holroyd once more. Most weekends they went out together, driving across the county in his scarlet sports car, drinking too much at extravagant parties with a boisterous crowd who all seemed to be the sons and daughters of mill owners, property developers and consultant surgeons.

For a time Adam affected to despise the sister he adored. Hal was out of all patience with her, while Grace could only worry over her daughter's hectic veering between explosions of bad temper and a blithe disregard for anything that might interfere with her pleasure. Compromised by loyalty to Holroyd's circle of friends, Marina declared that she now shared their disdain for the increasingly vocal campaign against nuclear weapons, of which Hal was a prominent spokesman. As Easter approached, her resistance to joining her family on the march to Aldermaston became intractable.

As it happened, Grace fell briefly ill around that time, so only Adam and Martin travelled by coach to London, where Hal was already closeted with the other leaders. On their elated return four days later, Marina became aware that she had denied herself an important experience. She listened in glum silence as Martin and Adam reported on how a crowd consisting of no more than a few hundred good-humoured protesters had set out through the streets of the capital, only to grow in strength day by day, until the gathering outside the Nuclear Research Establishment at Aldermaston broke on the nation's consciousness as the most powerful demonstration of popular dissent since the Jarrow march. Filled with admiration, Martin described how Hal's bluff, charismatic manner had drawn many people into vigorous debate along the route as he articulated ways in which the aims of the march were related to the wider political and economic problems of the planet.

Among his listeners was the writer Miriam Stallard, whose controversial first novel, *The Mirror Room*, had attracted much attention that year. Her name was only one among a list of radical celebrities with which Adam later taunted his sister, but at its mention Marina could no longer conceal her regret for everything she had missed. "What was she like?" she asked Martin.

"She was brilliant," Adam chipped in, to Martin's astonishment. "I can't remember when I last met such a fascinating person. More fool you, Marina, for not having come! But as you don't have much time for us pathetic lefties any more, I suppose it hardly matters."

A few days later, Marina came back to High Sugden in a filthy mood to announce that she and Graham Holroyd would not be seeing each other again. About the reasons for the breakdown of the relationship, and the events surrounding it, she would say nothing. She withdrew inside herself, demanded the use of the haunted bedroom as a studio, and began to splash out her emotions on sheets of hardboard in collisions of carmine, purple, orange and black. If she had been volatile before, her moods were turbid and sulky now.

Martin arrived at High Sugden one Saturday to learn that she had been shut away inside the haunted room for three days. "She won't talk to any of us," Hal frowned. Having returned from London the day before, already tired from a difficult and ultimately unproductive bout of negotiations between representatives of Emmanuel's People's Liberation Party and delegates from Ambrose Fouda's conservative opposition, he had been further exasperated by Marina's refusal to respond to his approaches. "I'm just about at my wit's end with her. This has been going on long enough. I think it's time we called the doctor in."

"Shall I try to talk to her?" Martin offered.

Hal shrugged, and Martin went uncertainly upstairs. He stood on the landing for a time before tapping at her door. At his third knock she said, "Oh for God's sake go away." He cleared his throat and was about to say, "It's Martin," but saw that his name would alter nothing. Then, out of nowhere he heard himself saying, "It's Jonas Cragg! That's my room you're in."

Martin strained his ears at the silence for the best part of a minute before he heard the bolt drawn on the other side of the door. He pushed it open, prepared for a ruinous mess of paint and bed sheets, but the panelled room was tidy enough, its air only slightly tainted with the smell of turpentine and linseed oil. Marina stood with her back to him by the window, barefoot in her blue dressing gown, staring out across the valley. She neither turned nor spoke as he entered.

"Haven't we been here before?" he tried, and when she didn't answer, "Or somewhere very like it?" But the words elicited no response. He gazed at the loose fall of her hair above the belt of her gown, feeling his heart reach out at every accidental detail of her appearance. However stubborn this sullen mood might be, it was the simple, marvellous actuality of her being in the world that stirred his heart whenever they were alone together. Surely she must feel the longing in him? Surely she would respond?

"You wouldn't have let me in if you didn't want to talk," he said.

Still she was silent. He cast about, looking for ways to provoke a response. "It's Holroyd, isn't it?" he asked. "Has that selfish sod done something to hurt you?" He wanted her to look at him, to see that he was her gruff knight, the angel of retribution, standing ready at her command, her worried and unhappy friend.

"No," she said, without turning, "it's nothing like that."

"Then what is it like? Talk to me, Marina. How long are you going to let that crowd mess up your life like this?" He saw the blue cloth at her back begin to shudder then. Thinking she was about to cry, he wondered whether to move at once and take hold of her, but she dipped her head and crossed her arms over her breast so tightly that he could see her fingernails whiten at the curve of each shoulder. "I just wanted to be normal!"

"What do you mean?" he asked, bewildered. "You *are* normal. At least most of the time."

"Ordinary, I mean," she snapped back. "Satisfied to be ordinary. Like them."

"I see," he retorted. "Well, there's not much chance of that, is there? You're not ordinary. There's nothing ordinary about you. It's not your fate to be ordinary. You're special. You've always been special. You always will be. In fact, you're probably the most special person I know."

When she snorted at that, he let his outrage show. "What do you want to be like that lot for? That's not living, that's just squandering and foolishness. It's pretending that nothing really matters because, as far as they're concerned, nothing does count for much, except money and having a good time. If you ask me, you've been throwing yourself away on them. You're worth more than that. There's such life in you, such special, extraordinary life..."

"I wasn't asking you," she whispered.

"But I'm telling you anyway. I'm telling you what I know."

"You don't know me."

"I think I do," he came back at once. "At least, I once knew *somebody* who lived here, and she wouldn't turn her back on life like this. She might lick her wounds for a bit, but then she'd come out fighting."

Not a muscle of Marina's body moved.

"So what about it then?" His voice was hoarser now. "Are you going to stay walled up here? There are people downstairs worried sick about you, you know."

"Just leave me alone," she said.

"You've been on your own long enough. I think you should put some clothes on now. I think you should come out on the tops with me and Adam and the dogs. It's where you belong, out there. Not cooped up like this."

After a time, ignoring the continuing strength of her resistance, he heard himself say, "I'll see you downstairs then," and left the room.

As he went back into the kitchen and the others turned to him with anxious faces, Marina's voice came angrily down the stairs: "Come back here a minute."

He stood by the newel post, looking up where she stood on the landing, gleaming with fierce pride. "Just so you don't get the wrong idea," she declared, "I was coming down soon anyway."

"That's all right then" – he too held his head high – "I'm glad."

"But thanks for trying." With a quick, unrepentant smile she reclaimed the power between them. "You're my friend, Jonas," she insisted. "My good friend."

Later, the three of them set out together, following the dogs across the moor until they stood above the steep hollow of Sugden Clough, where the ruins of a burnt-out mill hung reflected in its own small dam. As they gazed down from an outcrop rock at the surface of the water shimmering in the breeze, Adam said, "Grace used to bring us swimming here. When we were kids."

"When she still took an interest in things," Marina frowned in reply. "She hasn't been up here for years."

"Too busy worrying about you, I should think," Adam retorted.

"Don't," Martin put in, sensing their imminent collision, "it's too good a day."

"The poet's right," Marina declared. "Let's swim instead."

But Adam and Martin only stared at one another in uncertain disbelief. High above their heads, a skylark scaled the blue air with its song.

"Come on," she urged, "why not?"

"Because for one thing," Adam answered, "it'll be bloody freezing. And for another we haven't got our swimming things. And you won't catch me jumping in there stark bollock-naked."

For an instant, as though her brother's resistance had left her questioning the impulse, Marina hesitated. Then she turned to scoff at Martin. "Seems you don't know much about wild things after all." With a contemptuous sniff she spurned both of them, jumped from the rock and ran down the slope with the dogs bounding beside her. Halfway towards the ruined mill house, she skidded to a stop and turned her head to glance back where Adam and Martin stood unmoving, hands in their pockets, not looking at each other, as a cloud passed briefly across the sun. Again she looked at the dam where the setters were drinking in snatches with their clumsy mouths. Through shadowy water she could make out the dim shapes where, half a century earlier, blocks of masonry and the cogged ironwork of machines had been tipped into the depths. The cloud moved on, and the surface glittered again.

"It's a dare," she called, tying back her hair, "a double dare."

"She hasn't even got a towel," Adam muttered, as Marina walked towards the dam. But his sister was already stepping out of her clothes, her slender back and limbs pale against the blackened beams and stones. At the brink of the dam she looked briefly back at them, waved, and then turned again, lifted both arms high in the air till her body strained at full stretch, and plunged into the water.

Long seconds passed before she broke the surface, shouting against the cold grip of the dam, shaking her head in a spray of light. Furious with himself for lacking the nerve to join her, Martin knew that the image was imprinted on his memory for ever.

On each visit to High Sugden, Martin learnt more of the truth of what was happening in British Equatorial West Africa than was to be found in the pages of *The Daily Express* which his father brought home each day. The campaign of civil disobedience begun by Kanza Kutu and other leaders of the People's Liberation Party after Emmanuel had been detained was now disrupting life right across the colony. Just as Hal had predicted, Governor Dawnay's efforts to choreograph an orderly movement towards independence around the conservative lawyer, Ambrose Fouda, failed to attract popular support, and the riots and demonstrations organized by the PLP throughout early June proved so effective that the British government wearily considered sending in troops. Before they could be mobilized, the dockers came out on strike, demanding the immediate release of Emmanuel Adjouna. When the copper miners of the Central Region joined the strike two days later, it became clear that the colonial era would end on terms set by the energetic new breed of African politicians, not by the old guard in Port Rokesby and Whitehall.

From the first hour of his imprisonment Emmanuel Adjouna had become the living symbol of a people clamouring for liberty. Belonging to neither of the great tribal factions, he was the only politician who could command loyalty among activists from both the Tenkora and the Nau. Only his PLP party was able to mount an effective majority in the newly constituted parliament, and only his release could end the current stalemate in the colony's affairs. So, with events progressing exactly along the lines that Hal and Emmanuel had foreseen, it was now only a question of time before a new nation was freed.

*

Jack Crowther bought a television set that year. Even though he had once vowed that he would never allow such an unsociable thing inside his house, he was swiftly mesmerized by its passing show of images. As soon as he came home he would switch it on and, as often as not, he would still be watching when his wife declared that she was going to bed. Sometimes he would wake with a start, hours later, dragged from sleep by the whine of the box, to find himself staring at a blizzard on the screen.

Having taken in the headline news one night, he was about to switch channels when Martin heard the newsreader's reference to Port Rokesby in British Equatorial West Africa. "Wait," he said, and the command was so urgent that his father's finger withdrew from the switch. "It's Emmanuel," Martin cried, pointing to a figure on the small monochrome screen. "I know him."

Jack Crowther frowned at his son first, then at the screen. "What do you mean, you know him?"

"It's Emmanuel Adjouna. I met him first time I went to Adam's. He's a friend of Hal Brigshaw's. He's a friend of mine."

"You said nowt about it." Jack frowned. "But then tha' never says owt to me."

But the truth was that Martin could hardly recognize the gangling figure who emerged from the gate of Makombe Castle amid a din of gongs and drums and singing from the adoring crowd outside. Blinking in the fierce light and still wearing a prison uniform with its pattern of arrow heads stamped on the smock, Emmanuel looked more like an escaped convict than a national leader. But a moment later, in full view of the crowd, the gaunt African pulled the smock over his head and wrapped his lean body in the folds of the traditional cloth which one of his supporters handed to him. Raising both arms above his head, he shouted out a single word – *Freedom* – and the shout was taken up by a crowd that had seen its own destiny made visible in that simple act.

Listening to the commentary, Martin realized how little personal knowledge the reporter must have of Emmanuel Adjouna. After only a weekend in the African's company, he was sure he knew more about the man himself.

"Sounds like more bloody trouble," his father muttered.

"You know nothing about it," Martin answered.

"Oh aye? You've been to Africa, have you?"

"No, but…"

"Well, I have, lad! From Cairo to bloody Cape Town, and I know a troublemaker when I see one."

"He's a brilliant man."

"That's what got him put away, was it?"

Father and son were not looking at each other as they spoke. With the memory of earlier quarrels hot inside them, neither wanted a pointless debate about distant matters, so Martin bit back his answer. Jack Crowther snorted, as if registering a small triumph. "Just 'cause you passed your Advanced Levels and got into that college, it doesn't mean tha' knows owt about life."

By now the brief item out of Africa was over, and Martin's mind was already elsewhere. The black-and-white pictures he had been watching might have been grainy and small, but they had magicked Emmanuel into his home from a country three thousand miles away. Such was the power hidden in that box of tubes and wires. Then it occurred to him that if his father had bought a television set, it surely couldn't be long before there was one in every sitting room. The journalists and cameramen behind the screen were reaching into homes where books were rarely opened. They could widen the horizons of millions of other people as his own horizons had been widened by his visits to High Sugden. He remembered the challenge that Hal had put to him there: *the people need intelligent men like you to get out into the world and tell the truth about what's happening.* Was this then how it might be done?

Martin felt everything on the move around him. In that moment he sensed that he had been granted something more than a glimpse into the success of Hal's plans for Africa. He had also caught sight of a career that might, with ambition and a touch of luck, take him out of this gloomy cellar into the heat of action in a rapidly changing world. Staring at a garish show on the little grey screen, he felt the future knocking at his heart.

Only a few days later, Martin and Adam felt an oppressive shadow lifted from their own heads. Both of them had been obliged to register for National Service in the armed forces that year. Hal had advised them to apply for deferment until they had completed their time at university. "Chances are the whole nasty business will be over and done with before you take your degrees," he said. "You won't even have to make a stand as conscientious objectors." And now, like a further sign of freedom in the air, their notice of deferment came through.

So they were free that summer to make the easy passage from sixth-formers to undergraduates, taking off with Marina and the dogs across the moors and through the crags. They were times of uncomplicated pleasure, enjoying the air, the midsummer warmth, the taste of water drunk directly from the troughs and becks. They played word games as they walked, argued the respective merits of traditional and progressive jazz, talked intensely about books and politics, about films and modern art. They drove to Manchester to see a major exhibition of Van Gogh's paintings, where Martin watched Marina studying the texture of the canvases with the same rapture as he had seen her watch the distant lightning-riven clouds of a thunderstorm across the hills.

Once they walked out on a midnight hike, listening to the pour of water among the boulders in the clough, hearing a curlew call as first light broke before they made their return, exalted by dawn, over the high tops. Then they took trips by car to the coast, eastwards to Whitby, west to Morecambe Bay, and increasingly, for Martin, each occasion felt vivid with the possibility that at any moment Marina might turn and recognize that their lives were irrevocably bound to each other. Yet that moment never quite came. However much they laughed together, or gazed in wonder at the raw beauty of things, the promise he had sensed in those hours went unrequited and, because he couldn't bring himself to speak of them, the hopes they encouraged seemed as unreachable as the landscape of a dream.

Then, one day, he came home from the library to find Marina standing in the porch of Cripplegate Chambers, sheltering from the rain. "I had an hour to kill," she said. "I decided it's time you showed me where you live."

"You weren't invited."

"I know, but I'm here."

She smiled at his frown.

He said, "I wish you hadn't done this."

"Adam said you'd say that. I couldn't persuade him to come. He said it was a bit pushy."

"He was right."

But Marina merely smiled and shrugged. When he didn't move, she walked past the polished brass plaques, pushed open the inner door with its frosted-glass panel and stepped through into the hall. She was gazing up at the elegant twist of the staircase through three floors as he came in after her. From behind a closed door to the left came the muffled whine of an electric drill. Marina feigned a wince as she read the brass shingle, which announced THEODORE NASH, *Dental Surgeon*. She smiled at Martin again. "Now which way do we go?"

From upstairs there came the sound of a door opening and an exchange of conversation as someone left the solicitor's chambers. Seeing that Marina would not be gainsaid, he glowered at her. "You'd better come down then. I think my mother's in. She'll be a bit flustered. She's not expecting you."

Marina watched him lift the latch on a door at the far end of the hall and followed him down the dark stone steps into the basement. He bit his lip at the vague smell of damp as they came out into a lime-washed passage that led one way to the bathroom, the other to the coal hole. It was lit by a single bulb.

Her eyes were caught by the varnished case of numbered bells high on the vaulted wall. "I suppose that's how they summoned the servants," she said.

"It's disconnected now."

"Good thing too."

He shrugged and opened the door onto the basement living room, where his mother stood at the old butler sink filling the kettle. Without turning she said, "I was just making some tea. Do you want a cup?"

"We've got company," he answered, putting his books down on the table. "This is Marina."

Bella Crowther made a small, regretful noise in her throat as she put a hand to the dark frizz of her hair. Above the sheen of the linoleum the furniture in the room stood very still.

"Oh, Martin, you should have said. I'd have got in something special!"

"I didn't know she was coming."

"I'm sorry to drop in on you like this," Marina smiled, "but I was just going past the door and I've been looking forward to meeting you for a long time."

Bella put the kettle down on the gas stove and wiped her hands on the towel hanging there. "Well, you'd better come in then. Sit yourself down, love. You look wet through. Frame yourself, Martin – take her coat before she catches her death. Just let me get this kettle on and I'll put a match to the fire."

"There's no need. I'm not cold," said Marina, unbuttoning her coat. Martin watched her glance take in the table with its hand-embroidered cloth, the sideboard and mantelpiece where two china figurines – a Regency dandy and his crinolined belle – stood at either side of the electric clock. "It's really cosy here." she said. "I don't want you going to any trouble."

"No trouble." Bella Crowther's eyes were assessing the young woman across from her as she added, "It's not every day our Martin brings a girlfriend home."

"She's not a girlfriend." Only in that moment did Martin fully realize how much he had come to loathe the garishly patterned wallpaper of the room. "She's just Adam's sister."

"Well, you know what I mean." The gas jet popped to the struck match. "Lucky I did a bit of baking yesterday. Do you like scones and jam, Marina?"

"Very much," Marina nodded. "Is there anything I can do? If you'll show me where the knives and plates are, I'll put them out."

Over tea there was talk of baking and shopping, of which stalls on the market were good and which were not, and other chatter about small matters of domestic life. Martin took no interest in it except that of watching an older woman and a younger woman discover more about each other through their trivial conversation. As they carried the crocks back to the sink, his mother mentioned how many pint glasses she could hold in her hands at once in the days when she worked as a barmaid. Marina listened wide-eyed as the older woman went on to tell her more about the pubs in those days before television, and how they were so busy most nights that ale swilled from the pumps across the floor of the bar.

"By the time the bell went for last orders," Bella said, "the soft shoes I wore were ruined. We had to get a fresh pair every night. They were cheap enough. And you should have seen the hem of my satin skirt. It hung round my ankles stiff as cardboard."

"I bet the men all fancied you like mad," Marina said.

"Funny you should say that," Bella smiled, pleased with herself. "Jack used to get right worked up about it. Still does sometimes, I'm glad to say."

When Jack Crowther came home from work, the two of them were laughing together as they peeled carrots and potatoes at the kitchen sink. Unprepared for company, Jack unbelted his raincoat to reveal his blue boiler suit beneath, though the hand he held out to shake Marina's was well washed. He appraised the smile on her fresh, slightly freckled face. "So you'll be Harold Brigshaw's lass," he said. "I were thinking it's time our Martin brought you home for us to see. Come and tell us summat about yourself."

Again Martin looked on, slightly askance, while Marina began to chat with his father as if she'd known him all her life. In those days Jack Crowther was still worrying about losing his job, but Marina's presence seemed to lift his spirit. Soon he was teasing her. She cottoned on at once and gave as good as she got. Within minutes, across the gap of a generation, they were flirting easily.

Martin said almost nothing. The whole room felt odd about his head, as if a new order of things had been announced while his back was turned. Even the quality of the light felt different, more buoyant, refreshed by company. And how strange to have Marina there, taming his father without a hint of falsity or condescension!

Most astonishing of all was the revelation that she knew enough about horse racing to convince his father that she shared his passion for the sport. Their talk was of horses and courses and jockeys, of classic flat races and steeplechases, of favourites and outsiders. Delighted by her enthusiasm, Jack taught her about the more complex aspects of betting in doubles, trebles and accumulators, and then he turned, grinning, to his son. "Well, you've found a lass with a bit of sense about her," he said. "If *you've* any sense you'll hang on to her."

Had Jack got his way, Marina would have stayed to eat her evening meal at his side but, explaining that she was expected at home, she got up to leave.

"You'll come and see us again, won't you?" Bella pressed. "It's been lovely having you!"

"Course I will," Marina smiled, and kissed her warmly on the cheek.

Martin accompanied her back up the stone stairs in silence and stood at the front door of the Chambers, chewing his bottom lip. "Well, you were a hit, "he said. "I didn't know you were such an expert on racing form."

Marina tilted her chin at him. "There's a lot about me you don't know. And as for you, Jonas Cragg," she said, unsmiling, "your mother's lovely and your dad's a poppet. So you've got nothing to be ashamed of. Nothing except your own snobby nonsense, that is." Then she turned on her heel and walked away down the damp pavement of Cripplegate without once looking back at him.

Martin went out to High Sugden for the August Sunday of Marina's birthday. After the recent developments in Equatoria, where the move towards independence was well under way, Hal had come home for the weekend. His impatience for the politic moment when a call from Emmanuel would officially install him as Special Advisor in Government House was evident enough, but he was determined to make this a happy family occasion. Having seen little of Marina in recent weeks, however, he misjudged her mood.

When the time came for presents, he produced an elaborate boxed affair wrapped in candy-stripe paper and professionally tied with a silk ribbon. Marina, who had been squally and restless since Hal's return from London, tore open the wrappings and found herself looking at a midnight-blue dress which would have made her eyes glitter only a few weeks earlier. Now she barely concealed her scorn for it as she muttered her desultory thanks.

"Well, that was a bit of a damp squib!" Hal complained. "I thought it'd be perfect for nights out on the town when you're at art school."

"Not really my taste," she answered, "not any more."

"I see. Well, I'm beginning to wish I hadn't bothered. Anyway," he grunted, leaving the room. "I've got bigger things to worry about."

"That seems a pity," Martin frowned at Marina. "It looks as though your dad went to a lot of trouble."

"Actually," Marina said, "I don't think *he* gave it too much thought." But she was watching her mother pour a large sherry. Grace had already lifted the glass to her lips when, with a vague, self-reproachful smile, she saw that she was watched. "Would anyone else care for a drink?" she asked.

Marina glanced across at Adam. "I need to get out of here. Let's walk the dogs."

Half an hour after they had left, the sky blackened westwards across the Pennines. Already in a grumpy mood, Adam turned back towards High Sugden, striding out to beat the coming rain, with the dogs bounding ahead of him. Martin kept to Marina's slower, pensive pace, though she hardly spoke to him as they made their way across the rough slope of the hill. She stood for a time on a high jut of whinstone, staring at the turbulent sky where dense rain clouds trawled the summits three or four miles away.

"Come on," Martin eventually called to her. "We're going to get soaked."

"Who cares?" she answered. "Go on if you want."

He shrugged, sensing her impenetrability, despairing of it. "It's up to you," he said, and began to walk on. But when he turned to look back, he saw that she was following him. Angry with her, at a loss, he stopped to let her catch up.

"Bloody awful birthday," she said.

"Was it? I'm sorry."

"Not your fault. It's me. I'm impossible. I loathe myself."

"No you don't. You love yourself. You just like giving us all a hard time."

"You don't really believe that?"

"Why shouldn't I?"

"Because you're my friend?"

"That's just it."

"Just what?"

127

He frowned down at the blowing tussocks. "If you don't know, it doesn't matter." He walked on, aware that she had come to a halt behind him.

"Anyway," he said, "it must be obvious by now." But he was resolved not to turn as he spoke, and the wind that was bringing the rain might easily have scattered his words before it. So they walked on in silence for a time. Then the light changed, and the rain was on them, a sudden squall, cold and drenching, almost as sharp as hail on their ears and hands. Martin looked up and saw the old stone cattle byre across the field. The grass was slippery under his shoes as he ran for the cover of its slates.

He was in amongst its warm smell of hay and dung and moulding leather harness, shaking the rain from his hair, when Marina joined him. She stared at him from the doorway, where the slope of coarse pasture glowed luminously green at her back. Her hair gleamed against the sky's bruised grey.

"I don't want this," she said.

"What? What don't you want?"

"You – mooning over me like this. You're supposed to be my friend. It's best that way. I don't want you loving me."

"Sometimes I wish I didn't."

"Then don't." She looked away. "I'm not even sure it's me you want."

"What do you mean?" he said, astonished. "Who else could it be?"

"Oh, I don't know!" she snapped impatiently.

Two seconds later she was standing in front of him, wet, smelling of rain. Holding his eyes in her gaze, she put her hands to his arms as if she was about to try to shake some sense into him. Then she pulled him closer and pressed her lips to his.

He held her close, and they were both trembling now. With his cheek pressed into her damp hair, he was whispering, "You're beautiful, you're so very beautiful," but she lifted her fingers to his mouth as if to forbid the next dangerous thing he might say.

Refusing to be silenced, he pulled back to confront her more earnestly. Shaking his head, he said, "It's not just mooning, Marina, it's really not."

"I know it's not," she answered. "That's why."

"Why what?" The eyes looking up into his were vulnerable and uncertain, but not forbidding. When his question went unanswered, he kissed her again, more gently now, and felt her move so tamely into the embrace that, for all her protestations, he knew she wanted to be there with him, like this, just as urgently, and with the same passionate trepidation, as he wanted it himself. Heartened, he pressed a hand to her breast. She lifted it away, looking round at the stalls and rusty mangers. For a moment he thought he'd lost her; then she led him to where a bale of straw had spilt across the flagstones.

They lay down side by side, hot and nervous, holding one another, almost as if in mutual protection from some mighty force that must soon overwhelm them. He could smell the rain in her hair. His eyes opened on the birthmark between her breasts. He lowered his mouth towards the fern-like blemish, hearing the intake of her breath, though whether she sighed with pleasure or impatience at his timidity he was unsure. But when, less tenderly, he reached down to dislodge her clothes, she raised a hand to push herself free, saying, "I can't, Martin. Not now. Not yet."

He wanted to protest, yet all that came to his lips was her name, uttered both as a plea and in acceptance, because he had sensed that she too was afraid. So they lay on the stone floor for a time in silence, watching the rain twist and shine in the changing light.

He wanted to speak, he wanted to tell her that he understood, that it was all right, that so long as they loved one another they had all the time in the world; but none of the words felt adequate to the strength and complexity of his feeling. So he lay with his eyes closed, taking in the musty smells, the sound of the beck falling down the field outside and the murmur of the summer rain on slate.

Thunder broke across the distant summits first. At its low, rumbling diminuendo Marina pulled herself up from under the weight of Martin's arm, tilting her face to listen more intently. He shifted his head to look through the open doorway, where the whole afternoon was streaming through the greenish light. Thunder rolled again, much louder this time. "There must be lightning," she whispered.

"There's no need to be scared." He had sought to console her, but almost before the words were out Marina was on her feet, pulling her clothes together and walking to the door. Ruing the sudden loss of her warmth at his side, Martin watched her step out into the rain. She had just passed out of sight when a detonation of thunder immediately overhead brought him to his feet with ringing ears. The whole sky shuddered and rocked above the cattle byre. The clouds might have been no more than a floor of rotten wood on which a chariot rolled by with iron wheels. Then all the daylight he could see was dazzled by a fierce glare.

When he got to the door, he saw the slight figure of Marina twirling on the bare slope with her arms stretched upwards and her head thrown back, inciting the sky. Her mouth was open, but the discharging barrages of thunder were still so loud that he couldn't tell whether she was shouting something or swallowing the light and rain.

Martin stood in the doorway, rain blowing in his face, staring out at Marina, expecting to see her hair catch fire at any moment, and her frail form charred to cinders while he watched. He wanted to shout out into the storm, to warn her that she should come back inside, but he sensed that her drenched figure stood far beyond recall. And so, with the storm flashing and growling above their heads, he gazed at her from the shelter of the byre, awed by her courage, afraid for her, almost afraid *of* her...

Like a razor stropped against the leathern sky, lightning crackled down again. For the duration of its glare – a fleeting, incandescent fraction of a second – he glimpsed again how vast were the distances that would always stretch out between them, however long they lived. Yet he knew he had no choice now but to strive to cross those distances – and if, as seemed likely, he must fail, then one day he must simply die for love of her.

Thunder sounded above their heads and travelled in a breaking roll across the valley. The storm was moving away. Marina stood, soaked and unscathed, rejoicing at its distant flashing in the gloomy smithies of cloud.

When she turned to smile at him, her skin was shining in the rain.

7
Lorenzo

Halfway down the track to Marina's cottage I saw the image of a black man coming towards me through the dusty light. A grizzled farmer wearing the traditional blue-and-white striped smock of the Mdemba, he was walking down a dirt road between shelled buildings, impervious to the smell of burning tyres and diesel oil and to the litter of shrapnel and unexploded ordnance. His smock was spattered with blood. Blood had dried almost black down the side of his face. Someone must have brought a cutlass down across his head with enough force to snap off the handle and leave the blade lodged like a fixture in his skull. Such force would have stunned him for a time, and when he came to his senses among the bodies of his family and friends, he would have seen that he was lying on the floor of hell. So now he was walking away from there, a survivor, with nowhere to go and no help for his condition, and the dirt road into the forest had brought him straight inside my head. He stopped in his tracks and stared at me for a time, not reproachfully, but beating the back of one hand against the palm of the other in a silent gesture of supplication.

Trembling, I stood in the heat of the Umbrian afternoon, waiting for the flashback to fade.

The door to the cottage stood ajar. Sure that I'd locked it and put the key back under the plant pot before I left, I looked across to the wall beneath the bamboo awning and saw a lean young man in a white singlet and blue shorts sitting at the table. He stopped picking his teeth with his fingers at my approach and turned his head towards the house, muttering something in Italian. I was about to ask who he was and what he wanted when he shook his head and pointed at the door, gesturing that I should go inside.

My grip on reality was still shaky. After the glare of the afternoon, it was gloomy inside the cottage, where a figure sat at the desk, examining the contents of the open drawer. He turned his head as my shadow fell across the floor. "My dear old thing, how very improbable you are, turning up like this!" Then he smiled at me over the rims of his glasses. "I've just cracked one of Adam's more palatable reds. Come and join me, do."

I hadn't seen Laurence Stromberg for years, and he had put on a lot of weight. His familiar features were dewlapped now, and his eyes thickly pouched. His lips seemed wearier in their sensuality, but the voice, measured and mannered as ever, was unmistakable.

"Hello, Larry," I said, "what are you doing here?"

Shamelessly he closed the drawer and proffered me a glass of wine. "Waiting for you, old soul. I feel sure Adam would want us to celebrate, don't you?" He swirled the wine in his glass and savoured its bouquet before taking a sip and chasing the wine around his palate. "Ah yes! Well met again! And in Fontanalba of all places." His eyes frisked me from head to foot in sceptical appraisal. "But I see you're still looking formidably *grim* behind the rumpled charm."

Contriving a smile, I said, "Does Adam know you're going through his things?"

Stromberg widened his eyes. "Does he know *you* are, old soul? After all, I can't imagine he invited you here. Not unless something quite marvellous has transpired. Has it?"

"Just the opposite, I'm afraid."

"Oh dear, not more dismal news from your lips!" Stromberg sighed his way out of a feigned chagrin. "I've been trying to recall exactly when and where you last left me distraught. It was on King's Parade, if I'm not mistaken. You affected black in those days – a black shirt, black jeans, rather displeasing black shoes. On a smarter man it might have been quite sinister."

"You've forgotten the crush bar at the theatre where Adam gave his last performances. You were still fishing for compliments on your *Tempest* as I recall."

"What a slanderer you are! Though I must admit there was a touch of flair in the way I released the actor in Adam. What a magnetic Ariel he made!"

"I don't recall you being thrilled with my Stephano however!"

"Well, we do what we can with what we have. And you've made rather a good living out of the voice I taught you – even if you've barely spared me a thought since then. Come, don't deny it. I can tell."

"We weren't exactly best mates, Larry."

"I'd much rather you called me Lorenzo, if it doesn't come too hard. That's how they know me here."

From a house somewhere up the hill came the sound of a woman beating a carpet over a clothesline. She called irritably to a child every now and then: *Tomassino, Tomassino.*

"But just look at you, dear man!" Stromberg smiled as I sat down across from him. "How much kinder the years have been to you than to me, for all your exploits in the gloomy places of the earth." He slipped me an arch glance. "Oh yes, I've kept track. But then how could one not with your face on the screen so often, persistently ventilating the planet's woes? Terribly intimidating, old soul! What *do* you think you're about? Reminding comfortable folk like me that there's a shit storm blowing out there, I suppose?" I caught the sly edge of his smile, and remembered that he had grown up in white South Africa under a regime with which he had so little sympathy that he exiled himself at the first opportunity. "The difficulty is," he said, "that your forthright way of spreading dreadful news across our TV dinners forces us to look *at* the horrors of the world without assisting us to see *through* them."

"I can't imagine you've ever eaten a TV dinner in your life," I smiled. "Anyway, would you rather have evil go about its business unobserved?"

"Now I suspect you're wilfully misunderstanding me. But you shall have the benefit of the doubt. After all, you were ever the noble ape. How else could you have endured those dreary hours of schismatic wrangling among the lefties? Yet the passion you brought to it all! Adam admired it in you. I rather worried over it myself. I felt it could only bring you to grief. Didn't I tell you as much once? Was I right or was I right?"

I remembered the occasion well enough – a late-night altercation in Adam's rooms, fuelled by a bottle of brandy. Adam had tired of our point-scoring and gone off to bed, leaving me to pit my political zeal against Stromberg's metaphysical despair. But it was as though Adam's assent had been the real trophy of our wrangle, and once he had gone we were left only with a sense of its futility.

I said, "For a few minutes you almost had me convinced that the whole political world is a mere illusion – "an evil dream of night" I think you called it."

"Yes, well I was probably quoting someone." Stromberg picked up his little book of *Umbrian Excursions* from the desk and leafed through it. "The question is," he said, "how are we to waken from that dream? I rather fear that your distressing expeditions into reportage serve only to darken its depths – particularly when you flirt with the camera in that fetching flak jacket!"

"But then," I said, "we never agreed about anything that matters, did we, Larry?"

"You know that's not true," he protested. "Didn't we once agree that we both love Adam, for all his little faults? However, I suppose I've taken far better care of my loyalties than you ever did of yours."

"Is that why you're here? Are you living here these days?"

"I come and go, dear man, like the swallows."

Outside, in a voice coarse with frustration the woman who had been beating the carpet scolded her child. I said, "Because Adam's here?"

Stromberg held up his little book. "Were you to browse in *cette petite folie de jeunesse*," he reproached me, "you would see that I was in love with Umbria long before the Brigshaws fled here. *Umbra santa, Umbra mistica, la terra dei santi e della negromanzia*. Was ever a place more richly endowed with sacred art, natural beauty and unspoilt young men such as Giovanni – who is, I trust, still sunning himself out there like a cougar? It has long been my heart's home. Let us not dispute precedence here."

"Yet here you are in Marina's house," I pressed, "and neither she nor Adam here. I can't help wondering what's going on."

"But don't imagine I shall say a word till I have a clearer idea of what you're doing here yourself."

"There's no secret about that. I've come looking for Adam and Marina. Their father's very ill. He may not have long to live. He wants to see them again."

"Am I to understand you're acting as the ogre's envoy?"

"You shouldn't believe everything Adam says about Hal."

"Now your loyalties come clear! Of course, of course! But I don't have to rely on Adam's opinion of his father. I found the man insufferable when he visited Adam at school. I mean, the hypocrisy, my dear! 'Were you to be true to your noble principles,' I goaded him once, 'you'd put this place to the torch sooner than suckle your son on its mouldy patrician titties.' His riposte escapes me – though I recall some effort to patronize me from the barren and truly *wuthering* heights of his egocentricity."

"I'm sure you left him speechless."

"Well, I wasn't about to let him bewilder *my* good sense with his preposterous ambitions. Grace, his poor wife, on the other hand, I found enchanting – though even in those days the shadow of that man's undeveloped soul fell hard across her. I visited them once, much later, in that dour fastness in the Pennine fells, and what a cat's cradle of fraught emotion I chanced upon in my innocence!"

Fetching a sigh, Stromberg lifted himself out of the chair and wandered the room, wineglass in hand, peering at the frescoes. He gestured to where a lion glowered down from a promontory of rock with a devouring glitter in its gaze. "Do you recall that line from Wallace Stevens?" he said. "Something about a lion roaring at the enraging desert? Long way from High Sugden this, wouldn't you say?"

"They are Marina's work then?"

"Yes. From some time ago, of course."

"But not at all like the canvases in her London show."

"I suppose not." He sighed and glanced my way. "So the flesh has scuppered Hal at last, and he wants to gather his children at his bedside? I wonder what Adam will make of that!"

"Not too much of a meal, I hope."

"But you can't expect him simply to shake off a lifetime's rancour and trot back home with you? I mean – really, Martin! – with *you*, of all people?"

"I don't expect it, but I live in hope."

"Then may you live long, for you may have to." Stromberg looked up from his wary inspection of a fresco in which a wild woman stood draped in her hair. He shrugged when I said nothing. "Well, who would have thought you'd still be dogsbodying for Hal after all this time? I don't recall ever meeting *your* old man, by the way. Is he an amiable cove?"

"Actually you did meet him once. On Graduation Day, though you didn't speak to him, and I guess he was more likely to remember you than you him – you and that colourful chum who was hanging on your arm that day. But no, I doubt you'd have found his company congenial. And by the way, he's dead."

"Oh dear, I'm sorry to hear that. Mine too – God rest his disagreeable soul!" Stromberg's wanderings had brought him to the piano. He opened the lid and flexed his fingers above the keys before trying a chord. "They keep this pretty little machine in tune, I see."

With conscious irony, he explored a few bars of Schumann's *Träumerei*, then stopped, sat down at the stool and began again with deeper commitment. As he leant his body into the phrasing, the room filled with yearning for things irretrievable – dead parents, lost lovers, broken friendships, the hopes of youth. Remembering how such music used to drift down his staircase in college, I felt again the insidious, salad-days spell of that Cambridge high culture to which I was no natural heir and which I had both coveted and affected to despise.

"Still, God forbid that we should be so poor in magnanimity as to lay all our troubles at mummy and daddy's door," he mused. "We have to forgive them their trespasses against us, don't you think? Far better that we salvage a little wisdom from the misery they cause us – and as much love as we can, not so?"

When he lifted his hands from the keys, the instrument resonated for several moments in the silence. "So you don't know?" He swivelled the stool to face me. "You know nothing of Adam and Marina's recent history?"

"There didn't seem to be any point trying to keep in touch. Not till now. What's been happening? And where is Adam by the way?"

Stromberg considered me with narrowed eyes. "But surely Gabriella must have put you in the picture?"

"How did you know I was with her?"

"This is a small village, my dear. The moment a cock pleasures a hen on one side of the hill, it becomes the gossip of the coops on the other. I know exactly what time you turned up last night, what time the Contessa came to check you out this morning, and how long you spent at the *Villa delle meraviglie* this afternoon. The only thing I didn't know was what a fool's errand you are on."

As if a different thought had crossed his mind, Stromberg looked at his watch. Raising his voice, he called to Giovanni, who came to the door and lolled against a jamb, glowering at us from the depths of his boredom. They spoke together in swift Italian from which I learnt nothing. Giovanni muttered something else and then went back outside.

"Well, you know now," I said. "So are you going to help me out?"

"Not sure I follow, old thing."

When I told him how cagey Gabriella had been about Adam and Marina, he seemed unsurprised. "It's not any of my business what they're up to here," I said, "and I don't care very much. I just want to do what I came to do and get back. So fill me in: what's the latest word from the chickens on their whereabouts?"

Stromberg glanced down at his feet – they seemed tiny in their thonged sandals under the overhang of his belly – then he looked up at me again, taking the pressure of my smile. "Even supposing I could help you," he said, "I'm not at all sure why I should."

"For old times' sake?"

"Old times indeed! Why would we want to wallow through that mire again?"

"We had some good times together, didn't we? You, me and Adam, I mean."

"Now you're being disingenuous. Even if Adam were here – which incidentally he is not – I can't imagine he'd want to speak to you. Besides, he'd have no time right now. As for his sister… well, you may have thought the Marina you knew formidable enough, but the figure she has become might verily shake your soul. And with good reason, I may add. No, dear man, I really don't think you want to see them again."

At that moment my mobile phone rang from the pocket of the jacket I'd hung over the chair. "That's probably Marina now," I said, but it was Gail's American voice that came crackling across the ether.

"So what's the story?" she demanded.

"Hang on, I can hardly hear you. I'll just take this outside."

Stromberg waved me casually away as he poured himself more wine. Under Giovanni's silent gaze, I sat down at the table and turned my back on the door, beyond which, I felt quite sure, Larry had his ears pricked for gossip. "I rang this morning," I said. "Did you get my message?"

"Yes. So what are your plans?"

"Still uncertain," I prevaricated. "Apparently Adam's not here, but there's a chance I might get to see Marina. Gabriella's discussing the situation with her. In fact, I thought it might have been her ringing."

"Who's Gabriella?"

"The woman I told you about. It turns out she's a contessa."

After a moment she said, "What's to discuss?"

"It's possible that Marina won't want to see me."

"But this contessa knows why you're there?"

"Yes, but…"

"So why can't she tell Marina what it's about?"

"She's going to, but…"

Now Gail's impatience declared itself. "But what?"

"Someone has to impress on Marina just how bad Hal's situation is."

"Sure." The syllable parched the air across the hundreds of miles between us.

I'd been vaguely aware of the engine noise of an approaching motor scooter. As it turned off the road now, onto the track to the cottage, Giovanni got to his feet from where he was lounging on the wall and walked to meet it.

"There's every chance I'll be on a plane tomorrow evening," I said.

"Have you booked a flight yet?"

"Not yet, no."

"So there's every chance you might not. Not while you get to spend time with this contessa. Not while there's a chance Marina might come through. We were supposed to be on our way to the Cascades right now, remember? We were supposed to be fixing up our life."

A young woman in a scarlet crash helmet and a white cotton dress had parked the motor scooter on the lane. She and Giovanni were exchanging hasty Italian sentences.

"Gail," I tried after a moment, "I thought we sorted this before I left."

"*You* sorted it," she said, "your way."

"I still don't see what's brought this on."

"You, Martin. You've brought this on. You're what you don't see."

With a bag hanging from one shoulder, the young woman was standing just a few yards away, half-listening to what Giovanni was saying but staring at me as if trying to work out who I was.

"The way I figure it," Gail was saying, "I'm coming in a slow third on your priorities right now."

"Then you're figuring wrong."

"Sure, like I figured wrong over Nancy Calloway during the Gulf War? Like I would have figured wrong over the French doctor who just got back to Paris from Equatoria an hour ago and thought she'd give you a call."

Now things came clear.

"I thought we were through with all that," she said. "It wasn't going to happen again, right? So why am I surprised? When was it ever different?"

"Look, this is bad timing right now," I protested, watching the woman in the white dress lift off her crash helmet and shake loose her hair. "I should be back tomorrow. Can't we?…"

"Did you hear what I just said?"

"Yes, I heard you." Mildly embarrassed now by what she could not help overhearing, the young woman turned away as I added, "I'm sure we can sort this out once and for all when I get home."

"That's what you said last time."

"Gail, there are people here. I can't talk now."

"I've had it, Martin. I can't take any more lies."

At that moment Stromberg appeared in the doorway of the cottage emitting a loud sigh of exasperation and glaring at Giovanni as the newcomer turned to greet him. "Hi Lorenzo, I'm back. Sam and Jago are coming the day after tomorrow. Is Adam about?"

"Give me a break, Gail," I was saying. "There's no need for this."

"You want a break?" Gail snapped back at me. "Here's a break. Let's make it permanent this time." And she shut down the phone.

"You're English?" the young woman had turned to look at me. There was no trace now of an Italian accent in her voice. I nodded in silence. Again came the shocking sensation of time folding back across itself, smoothly like linen.

And if I was silent it wasn't just because Gail had cut me off in mid-sentence. I was left briefly wordless by the dislocating experience of seeing Marina as she could not possibly be now, but as she might have looked almost thirty years earlier. I was still trying to come to terms with this trick of time when the woman smiled at me and said, "Hello, I'm Allegra. You must be here for the gathering."

8
Allegra

Though she was certainly not aware of it, Allegra and I had met once before, and that meeting had been fraught with all kinds of anguish. At that time Marina had been carrying boxes full of her things from her room to the rusty van parked in the yard outside High Sugden. It was the first time she had been there since her mother's death, and within the hour she would be driving away for the last time, taking her infant daughter to Italy, where they would begin a new life together. Marina had already told Hal that this was the last that he would see of either of them. To me she said almost nothing at all.

More than a year had passed since we had seen each other, and she had not expected to run into me that day. When I tried to approach her, she rejected my offer of help with cold disdain. Then Allegra began to howl from her basket in the van. Having fed and winded her, Marina brought her into the house, where she was still unsettled. So, without consultation or thanks, merely using me as a convenience that freed her to return to the work of clearance, Marina handed Allegra over into my arms. I must have stared at the baby then with something of the same awe that I stared at this young woman now, wondering if the child was mine.

When I first learnt that Marina was pregnant, I had sent a message asking that question, but no answer came. I knew there were a number of artists and musicians hanging about London and the West Country whose claims were as strong as mine, for in what had been a bad time for her, Marina had taken many lovers. My message had said that I was there for her and the child whether or not I was the father, but she had long since decided to have nothing to do with me.

That afternoon I asked again whether the child I was holding was mine. Marina merely said, "Even if I knew, do you think I'd tell you?" and then turned away.

Now I stared at Allegra once more, looking for signs that this striking young woman was my daughter. I saw only her mother's features mirrored there.

In the meantime, Larry Stromberg had been introducing me as an old friend of the family. "Though I'm not at all sure," I heard him sighing, "that Marina would want you to have anything to do with him."

"Really?" Allegra asked, intrigued rather than deterred. "Why not?"

I mumbled vaguely about a rift. We gazed at one another in mutual curiosity. Allegra was already a year or two older than her mother had been the last time I saw her, that uneasy day at High Sugden, and the more closely I looked the more I noticed other differences. Marina's hair had never been as blonde and finely spun, and she lacked the relaxed, sensual grace of this young woman, who had been nurtured in a warmer culture and a different, less inhibited age.

"It all feels like a long time ago," I said, as though in explanation.

"I'm sure it must," Allegra replied without malice or mercy. In that moment I felt sure that what she saw across from her was a man some way past his best, shabby with dust and heat, his hair much greyer than black these days – the kind of figure she would have passed without a glance had he not emerged unannounced from her own prehistory.

Her gaze shifted away. "So where's Adam got to?" she asked Larry.

"He's been on retreat in the mountains, but..." Then he broke into Italian, not for the benefit of Giovanni, who sat on the wall sulky and impatient, but for my exclusion. I picked out names

– Adam's, Gabriella's, Marina's – and little else. Allegra's eyes darted my way every now and then as he spoke. Eventually she turned to me and said, "I understand that my grandfather isn't well?"

"He's had a stroke. A bad one, I'm afraid. He can hardly move or speak."

A frown of dismay shadowed her face. "I'm sorry," she said. "But the sad truth is I've never given him much thought. He simply wasn't part of our life... of my life."

"You're right," I said, "it is very sad."

She glanced away towards Larry. "Is there any more of that wine, Lorenzo? I think I could use a glass."

"I'm not sure this is wise," he replied. "I really think you should talk to Marina before you..."

"Just bring me some wine please. I need to sit down."

Allegra placed her helmet on the blue table and pulled out one of the chairs. As I sat across from her, she looked away in thoughtful silence to where the late sunlight burnished the poor soil of the olive groves with its glow.

"I'm sorry," I said, "this must be confusing for you."

She answered with no more than an uncertain shrug as Larry brought out my glass along with hers. "If your mother kicks up about this," he fussed, "I absolutely insist it's not my responsibility."

"I'm not a child, Lorenzo," Allegra sighed.

"No, my darling, but you've been off the scene. You've no idea what a muddle we're in. And Adam should be here. I can't imagine what he thinks he's doing. We expected him back last night."

"Well, he's not about to let us down, is he? Do relax."

Again the restrained asperity of her tone seemed disturbingly familiar.

"Your hair's much fairer than your mother's," I said, "but everything else about you makes me think of her."

"Mine's been lightened." Vaguely she fingered a strand that dangled by her ear. "You know I can't even picture my grandfather. I used to imagine him as a lonely giant living in a gloomy cave."

"That's not so far away from the truth right now," I said, "though he wasn't always like that." I began to see how this unexpected encounter might be used to some advantage. "Listen, I know your mother's had a very hard time with him, but Hal's a good man. He may have made mistakes, but his whole life has been about building a better world. Your generation is the future he was building it for. It broke his heart being cut off from you and your mother."

"But then after what happened he can hardly have imagined that…" Allegra stopped herself there. "The trouble is, I don't really know what happened. Just that my grandmother died before I was born and that there was a rift in the family. It must have been very bad to make Marina and Adam break with him as completely as they did."

"If you really want to know, you should ask your mother. She's going to have to think it all through again anyway… if I ever get to talk to her myself, that is."

Sensing that much had been withheld, Allegra said, "Are there reasons why you shouldn't?"

"Gabriella seems to think so. I'm afraid there's a lot of history."

"Between you and Marina?"

"Yes."

"Bad history, you mean?"

"Mostly, by the end, yes."

Allegra shook her head. "This is so weird," she exclaimed. "It's like coming back and finding myself in the dark." There was exasperation in the way she frowned at me. "As if the darkness had leaked out of the past," she said, "out of the time before I even existed. Yet I'm caught up in it, not understanding."

"That sounds like a pretty good description of history," I smiled back at her. "Hal would enjoy talking to you about that."

Another frown, then, "I've just remembered," she said after a moment, "I almost did get to see him once. I must have been fourteen or fifteen I suppose, and I'd had a furious row with Marina... *This really is weird!* I'm not even sure what the whole thing was about now, but I told her I was leaving home and going back to England to look for my grandfather – to see if he would have me. I said it because it felt like just about the worst thing I could say to her." Allegra gritted her teeth in a wince of contrition. "Oh God, I can still see the expression on her face! And if I'd been a year or two older I might have done it, just for the hell of it. But it blew over, of course, the moment passed... I'd forgotten all about it till now."

"It's almost a pity you didn't go," I said. "It might have mended the breach."

"Is that what you're trying to do?"

"Yes, but it's beginning to feel like a waste of time."

"Then go home, old thing." I turned my head and saw Larry Stromberg leaning against the cottage doorway. "I mean, what's to gain from hanging on here? We're well apprised of the situation. Marina must make up her mind what she wants to do, and I fail to see the point of risking further bitterness. Why not join me for a meal tonight in a rather good place I know and then hop back on a plane tomorrow? Let old Lorenzo spoil you a little."

In that conclusive moment, Larry commanded all the logic in the situation. His smile said as much, and I had no answer. I looked at Allegra. "Will you come with us? There must be hundreds of things Hal will want to know about you – what you do for a living, what kind of education you've had, how you feel about the big questions, what gives you pleasure. He'll want to know everything about you." But there were other reasons why I was reluctant to let go of her company. "Anyway," I smiled, "having caught up with you again after all this time, I don't want to let you slip away. And there must be things you want to ask me too," I added in flagrant contradiction to my earlier reticence. "About the past, I mean."

Allegra stared thoughtfully at her wineglass. For a moment I thought I'd hooked her. Then she sighed and shook her head. "Thanks, but there are things I have to do. However I will take your advice and talk to my mother." She drank the last of her wine, pushed back her chair and got up to go. "I think it's been good to meet you," she smiled, "though I'm not entirely sure."

I got to my feet, saying, "I can't tempt you?" But for the moment it was clear that I couldn't. "Well, at least I can tell Hal he's got a beautiful granddaughter, one I'm sure he'd be proud of." She reached for her helmet. Watching her tuck her hair under the strap, I decided to risk a last push. "You know he'd love to see you."

"If there's love enough," she replied, "it might happen. You never know." She pulled the buckle tight under her chin but, even as she turned away, all three of us became aware of someone approaching the house on foot through the dusk. Taking a half-smoked cheroot from between his lips, the figure called, "*Buonasera*, Allegra, I saw your Vespa by the road and felt sure you must be here."

Allegra smiled with delight. "Fra Pietro, how lovely!"

Stromberg leant in through the doorway to switch on the outside light. Its glare heightened the yellowish cast to the newcomer's skin, which shone like vellum. Dark eyes glimmered within its wrinkles. He was in his late sixties, I guessed, his grey hair tonsured, his thin body robed in a brown habit.

"If you're looking for Adam," Allegra said, "I'm afraid he's not here. In fact…"

"No, it was you I wanted. I have been working on the *canzone* since I saw you last. I wondered if you would care to sing tonight? The air is soft. It promises to be a beautiful evening." With a shy nod he acknowledged my presence, then his smile broadened as he said, "*Buonasera*, Lorenzo."

"Perhaps later," Allegra said. "Maybe I could ring you?"

"Of course." As the newcomer stubbed his cheroot against

the wall, he studied her mildly flustered face. "Something has discomposed you?"

"No, not really," she answered uncertainly. "It's just that there were a couple of surprises waiting for me when I got back."

Allegra glanced my way, introduced me briefly and explained why I had come to Fontanalba. Fra Pietro listened gravely as she answered his tactful, concerned questions. "This is distressing news," he said. "Perhaps the time has come for reconciliations?"

"I was hoping so," I said.

"And Marina? She too must be concerned."

"I haven't had a chance to talk to her yet," Allegra said. It's part of what I want to sort out tonight."

"Then of course the singing must wait for another time."

"The other thing," Allegra frowned, "is that Adam has disappeared."

"Disappeared?"

"Well, nobody seems to know where he's gone or what he's doing. I was sure he'd be here when I got back, and the more I think about it…"

At that moment every one was startled by the trilling of my mobile phone on the round table. Even as I drew in my breath and answered "Yes?" I realized it was unlikely to be Gail – there had been no prospect of swift contrition in her voice – but I was thrown into further confusion when a voice asked, "Is that Guerino il Meschino?" Then I remembered the story.

"Contessa?"

"I have spoken with Marina."

"What did she say? Is she there with you now?"

"You are in too much of a hurry still. She is here but…"

"Let me speak to her please."

"One moment."

As I looked up from the telephone, all the others glanced away except Allegra. I waited until Gabriella said, "Marina says you have either nothing further to say to one another or a great deal. In any case, she would prefer not to speak by telephone."

"So what does she propose?"

"She will eat with me at the villa tonight. If it is truly important for you to see her at this time, then you may join us."

"You will be present?"

"If that is what Marina wishes."

"I see. What time would you like me to come?"

"Shall we say in about two hours?"

At that moment Allegra stepped closer to me and said, "Do you think I could have a quick word with my mother?"

"I'll be there," I said into the phone. "Can you tell Marina that Allegra wants to speak to her?"

"Allegra? She is with you?"

I handed over the phone and turned to where Larry Stromberg studied me through dubious eyes. "I confess I'm amazed," he murmured. "I doubt I'll ever begin to understand Marina! You're quite sure you know what you're doing?"

"I'm sure I don't," I said, "but it has to be done."

I was less preoccupied with his question, however, than with my efforts to eavesdrop on Allegra, who was quietly saying, "No, of course I didn't, not a word."

Fra Pietro favoured me again with his long, donkey-headed smile. "Will you be staying with us in Fontanalba for some time, Mr Crowther?"

"I'm afraid not. I have to get back."

"He thinks I should talk to you about all that," Allegra was saying. "Now I come to think about it, I'm astonished I haven't done so sooner. Anyway, what I really wanted to talk about was..." But Allegra was halted by an interruption there.

"A pity!" Fra Pietro smiled. "I myself have not been to your country for many years. Tell me, are there Beefeaters at the Tower of London still?"

"I suppose so."

"But I fear they will soon be quite mad, alas," he mourned, "like your English cows!" He took in my briefly puzzled frown. "The beef – is very diseased, yes?"

"Yes, all right, if you say so," Allegra said, then returned the conversation to her own priorities. "But Lorenzo tells me Adam's not back yet. Yes, he's here – with Giovanni. Adam was on retreat, wasn't he – in the mountains?" As she listened, her blue eyes shifted restlessly – to me, to Stromberg and back down the darkening valley.

"So sad!" Fra Pietro lamented confusingly. "I admired their bright clothings very much."

Marina must have overheard his voice because Allegra said, "Yes, he's here too. He was hoping to make music tonight... I'll ask him if you like. But are you sure you want us there? I mean, if you're going to do some serious talking... Okay, if you'd rather. I'll see you soon."

Allegra snapped my phone shut and returned it. "It looks like we're going to have the chance to interrogate one another after all." Then she smiled at Fra Pietro. "You're invited to dinner at the villa. And you're to bring your lute."

The Franciscan reached for one of Allegra's hands and held it gently in his own. "Now I am so happy," he said, "You see, all is for the best."

"Except," Allegra said, "I get the feeling that Marina's more concerned about Adam than she's letting on."

"Oh you shouldn't worry your head too much," Larry said with unconvincing nonchalance as he crossed to speak to Giovanni, "Adam was always one for the enigmatic gesture."

"Don't tell me you're not worrying," Allegra replied. "He should be here, and we've no idea where he is. Anything might have happened to him."

"I am sure Lorenzo is right," Fra Pietro said reassuringly. "I think you will understand me if I say that your uncle is one of God's fools." His sallow face was gentle with affection. "So wherever he is, and whatever he is doing, you may rest assured he is safe in God's hands." His smile looked to me for agreement, but as a confirmed atheist I was not the likeliest source of assent, and amazement must have shown plain on my face at this improbable description of the friend who had long ago taught me to share his disdain for God-botherers everywhere.

Adam might certainly have been a fool in his time. But one of *God's* fools?

Surely not in a million years?

Not long afterwards the others dispersed, leaving me alone in the cottage. From its arid rock on the sitting-room wall the painted lion glared down at me. The wild woman stood gowned and wimpled in her long white hair.

I thought about ringing Gail, but decided it was too soon. Better to wait until she'd had time to cool down. Meanwhile there were other calls I could make, but they felt arbitrary and futile, so I picked up Larry's little book again and took another look at his essay on the oracular springs at Clitumnus. Citing lines from Virgil it told how the hides of oxen were reputed to turn white when they were bathed in those waters, and went on to relate this legend to the myth of the Apis Bull, which was born from a cow impregnated by moonbeams. According to Larry, all this had something to do with the lunar nature of prophetic insight. I was fast losing patience when I saw a heading that caught my attention:

THE REVENANT OF FONTANALBA

Beneath it Larry had recorded a local folk legend that he'd heard from the lips of Angelina Tavenari, the wife of the village barber. According to the story, a young shepherd once took his flock up into the mountains to the high pastures, and during the lonely summer weeks he became obsessed with the mystery of where the sun goes at midnight. Determined to find the answer, he climbed onto a high ridge through the late evening light, lost his balance as he strained to peer down into the dark gulf where the midnight sun was vanishing, and fell to his death on the rocks below. A year later he returned to his homestead at dawn, radiantly transfigured into a woman. When this magical creature struck the ground with a shepherd's crook, a fresh fountain of spring water bubbled from the barren rock. Hence the name of the town that grew near that place: *Fontanalba* – the Fountain of Dawn.

I can't say that the tale made much impression on me. In comparison to the tales from Grimm that had so enchanted me as a child it seemed thin and colourless. But Larry saw it differently:

On first hearing this story eloquently told by a simple woman who had learnt it at her mother's knee, I was immediately struck by the familiar motif of the midnight sun. Where had I come across it before? In the mysterious eleventh book of The Metamorphoses *of* Apuleius, *of course, that ancient picaresque novel, more commonly known as* The Golden Ass, *where we are given the fullest account we possess of the secret rites of Isis as they were once practised in the Graeco-Roman world.*

Driven by his desire to acquire the powers of witchcraft, Lucius, the narrator and central character of the story, is transformed by mistake into an ass. Only after many scabrous adventures is he restored to human form by the goddess Isis, into whose sacred rites he is subsequently initiated. Though the narrative does not disclose the exact nature of those rites, Apuleius does permit Lucius to make this cryptic revelation: "I approached the boundary of death and returned from there, having crossed the threshold of Proserpine and been carried through all the elements. I saw the sun shining at midnight with a brilliant light, and stood in the close presence of the gods below and the gods above to worship them."

Now, to an African such as Apuleius (he was a citizen of Madaura in what is currently Algeria), the Arctic phenomenon of the midnight sun would have been quite unknown. His narrator Lucius is alluding, therefore, to an experience outside the usual realm of the senses. A transformative experience. An experience of rebirth such as is obtainable only at death's door, and which evidently depends on the reconciliation of opposing principles.

A moment's thought will show us how the story of the Revenant of Fontanalba moves along a parallel trajectory to that followed by the ancient mystai of Isis in the course of their initiation. The philosophical shepherd is preoccupied with the mystery of light at the heart of darkness. Where, he wonders, does the sun go at midnight? To solve that mystery he climbs upwards to the sky only to fall to his death in the earth. When he is reborn it is in female form, and from his death flows a new access of the waters of life. A transfiguring mysterium has been performed. As surely as was the case with Lucius the Ass, the shepherd has undergone a rite which ushers him beyond the blind world of the senses into the midnight light of spiritual vision. Considered in that light, what might otherwise be dismissed as a mere fancy of the peasant imagination emerges as a faint, but faithfully preserved, folk memory of rites that were once performed in the sacred places of these Umbrian hills. That those rites were Isiac rites may further be adduced from the town's abiding devotion to the icon of the Black Madonna which stands in its little Romanesque church – African Isis comfortably ensconced as a curiously androgynous Virgin Mary!

I snapped the book shut. My head felt heavy: sleep tugged at me again. Yet my mind was turbulent. Larry might be excited by fantasies of seeing the sun at midnight, but my world was still thick with darkness at noon. In place of Larry's comforting black Madonna, I saw a woman in a yellow turban howling over the small, mutilated body of her child. Around her lay the dead in the streets and compounds of Fontonfarom, toppled among hibiscus bushes and canna lilies, dumped in the storm drains, wallowing in the sluggish waters of the Kra. I saw the peevish flap of vultures against the heat haze overhead.

When I dozed, I dreamt fitfully of Gail, unable to tolerate any longer the pain of living with me as I was – going away, beyond recall, leaving me lying on our bed in Camden with rain falling through the ceiling onto its rumpled sheets.

A sense of utter loss then – my life bereft and desolate – from which I woke briefly only to be pulled back into sleep, where I found that my mother had moved out of the cellar in Cripplegate to live on some remote landmass. I needed to visit her there, but the journey meant crossing a wide desert like no desert I had ever seen – a torrid, undulating plain composed of some igneous ruby-red substance, as though the hot melt of lava from a volcano's mouth had covered the surface of the earth and congealed in its flow before the colour could fade. It was like walking on vitrified fire. When I reached my mother's house and looked back, I saw a vivid light drifting across the mountain range beyond the desert, tinting all things in its progress until the whole world was rinsed in its rainbow tide.

Waking, I lay with my eyes closed, yearning to be back in that vanished country; but my heart felt lighter when I rose. I showered, changed, decided to ring Gail, sure that I could talk her round. There was no answer. But it was about Marina I was thinking as I drove out to the villa.

Oddly, I felt more optimistic than at any time since my arrival in Umbria.

9
Music

Far to the east the evening sky was shot with silent lightning as I parked the car at the villa. Orazio took me through to the terrace, where I sat over a gin-and-tonic, watching the bats scud through silky air. He had made it plain that the Contessa would shortly join me. Meanwhile, a moonflower fragrance on the dusk left me feeling closer to Africa than England.

After a time I heard the engine rasp of a motor scooter echoing through the valley. Gabriella had still not appeared when a rowdy bray of laughter came from the house. Turning my head to look for its source, I recognized Fra Pietro chatting with a large woman in a dress of shiny black bombazine. The fat shimmied on her arms as she waved him away. Smiling bashfully, the friar stepped through the arched doorway and came to join me at the table.

"It sounds as though you were having fun," I said.

"Angelina, Angelina!"

I saw a scrap of tissue unpeeling on his chin where he must have cut himself while shaving. "She is the cook here. I think she was born beneath a laughing star. She calls me Fra Asinello, which is to say Brother Donkey! I cannot think why!" He widened his eyes. "But now I am at last here to keep you company, Mr Crowther – Martin, if I may?" While he was speaking he unslung a leather case from his shoulders. "Allegra is with the ladies." He made primping gestures with his hands. "Soon they will astonish us with their beauty."

"I see you've brought your guitar. Do you and Allegra make music often?"

"Not a guitar," he corrected me, "but a lute. And no, we do not play together so often as I would like. But whenever Allegra is here in Fontanalba."

When I asked if I might see the instrument, he threw the clasps on the case, took out the lute and held it out before him like a parent presenting a new child for admiration. Wide-necked, deep-bellied as a pear, it was painted a dusky blue fretted with stars, and felt so delicate and expensive that I held up a hand declining his offer to let me hold it. With an amused shrug, he sat down, strummed his hand across the strings and began to tune them.

"It's good that you are here." He glanced up at me as he twisted a peg. "I think Marina will be very happy that you have come."

Not sharing his confidence, I said, "But there's no word of Adam yet?"

"Not that I have heard. In his own time he will arrive."

"I hope he won't take too long about it. I'd like to see him before I go." I took in his amiable nod before adding, "May I ask you something? You called Adam one of God's fools earlier. I've been wondering what you meant by that?"

Fra Pietro stroked the crown of his head while he considered how best to answer me. "Are we not all God's fools," he smiled, "when we think we understand ourselves and our place in His world?"

"I had the feeling you meant more than that," I pressed. "Something particular to Adam. I'm interested because I've known him a long time and I've often despaired at his talent for throwing his life away."

Again Fra Pietro widened his eyes. They were long-lashed, a little troubled now. He said, "You speak as though you saw in him only some kind of failure."

"Does that surprise you?"

The man's bony shoulders shrugged beneath his habit. "Perhaps you mistake his scorn for the things of this world," he suggested, amused by my air of perplexity. "It can be extravagant, yes. But his heart is also large. He has a big capacity for love." Putting the lute aside, he reached into the wallet at his belt for a box of matches and the half-smoked cheroot he'd stubbed out earlier. "I think perhaps he is making his heart big enough that it can hold the soul? And in ways which have pained him many times." He lit the cheroot and contemplated the brilliance of the risen moon. "Perhaps they have also made him seem a failure to those who have not understood the true nature of his seeking?" If a reproach was intended, his voice softened it. "No, I do not believe that Adam has thrown his life away like a wasted thing, but perhaps he wishes to *give* it away, which is very different."

"To what?" I asked. "To whom?"

"Perhaps that is the question that most torments him?" .

"You're very fond of him."

"Of course. I have also much concern for him."

"Despite what you said to Allegra?"

"Perhaps because of it. God may have a special affection for those who go the Way of the Fool, but it is sometimes a hard and dangerous way."

"Can you say more?"

And he too furrowed his brow. "How shall I explain? It is to undertake the..." – he sought and found the word he wanted – "the ordeal – yes? – of the spiritual quest without the protection and discipline that comes from membership of an order? That is what I mean by the Way of the Fool. On such a way one can get lost many times. One may come to harm."

"And you think that's what may have happened to Adam?"

Fra Pietro meditated over the burning tip of his cheroot before answering. "Sometimes I see in him an avidity to make himself a sacrifice," he said quietly, "such as one finds more frequently among the young. But Adam has arrived there – how shall I say it? – after a maturity of pain. Perhaps he is still seeking the proper manner of his sacrifice? Perhaps also its occasion? And not as an escape from pain, I think, but as its only consummation."

"That sounds very gloomy," I said, wondering into what kind of language I would translate any of this for Hal.

"Yet he would like us to rejoice for him in the end. I trust that we shall. Also I pray for it."

The last words seemed uttered as an afterthought, for we had both heard the sound of women chatting as they came along the corridor and Fra Pietro was already stubbing the cheroot and pushing back his chair to stand. Allegra came out of the house first, followed by Gabriella and a white-haired woman in a simple, lavender-blue dress, who tilted her head towards the stars as she breathed in the fragrant night air. I got to my feet, expecting to be introduced. Only then did I see how the neckline of her dress revealed the coral-pink blazon of a birthmark.

Fortunately she had not looked my way. In contrast to Gabriella's dark, henna-tinged curls, that astonishing white fall of hair made Marina seem the older by at least ten years. I reminded myself that she was, by now, some five or six years older than her own mother had been at her death, and that Grace's dark hair had only ever been lightly sprinkled with grey. But Marina had always been her father's daughter, in appearance at least.

"Hello, Marina," I said, "it's good to see you again."

She turned her head my way and nodded in calculated, mute acknowledgement, like royalty, before responding warmly to my companion's greeting. "*Buonasera*, Fra Pietro," she said. "Tell me, how is Fra Rufino? Is he quite recovered yet?" They moved away in conversation together. From inside the house music floated across the air. I guessed at Cimarosa or some other composer with a heart more serene than mine. Orazio, who had brought out a tray of drinks, muttered something in Italian to Gabriella. I saw her glance at her watch as Allegra sat down in the ornate chair next to mine.

"You look as though you've seen a ghost," she said.

I remembered that night long before at High Sugden, the muffled sounds along the landing, the haunting radiance through the door cracks.

"Your mother sometimes has that effect on me."

"Must be guilt," she smiled. "Particularly as you have her at a disadvantage. You knew you were coming to Umbria, after all. She had no idea."

"You mean *I'm* the ghost at the feast."

"You're not a ghost," she replied, "you're a guest. And Marina's promised Gabriella that she'll be polite."

I glanced across to where Marina was laughing with Fra Pietro, indifferent to my presence, or wilfully oblivious of it. "If not exactly friendly?" I said.

"That rather depends on you, I suspect."

"So, Mr Martin Crowther," Gabriella said, approaching us, "welcome again to my house. I see you are already enchanted by my god-daughter?"

"She's been putting me in my place. With great charm, of course. I hardly felt a thing!"

Gabriella arched her brows at Allegra. "You must beware of this man. He has stories to tell that will make your heart sore. Also he has much to prove."

"I thought Guerino was the one at risk," I said.

"But it was not he who was rejected."

"Who are you talking about?" Allegra asked.

"Another adventurer," Gabriella explained, "a wretch who came to Umbria on a quest for the lost father."

"Gabriella also has stories to tell," I said.

"But my stories are true."

"Especially the part about the snake."

"Oh yes," she answered, "especially that." At that moment we heard a car pulling up at the front of the villa. "Ah, that will be Lorenzo at last. I think he takes longer than me to make himself beautiful. I understand he too is your friend?"

"Sort of," I said. "I didn't think he was coming."

"Oh yes, he very much insisted to be here with you."

"He invited himself?"

"He is an old friend here also. He understands this house very well. Lorenzo is always welcome."

Stromberg embraced everyone else on the terrace, and halted before me with a demonstrative gesture of his hands, as though his bulk had just materialized on the evening air. Then he puckered and smacked his lips in emulation of a kiss. "*Here will we sit*," he announced, taking the seat to my left, "*and let the sounds of music creep in our ears. Soft stillness and the night become the touches of sweet harmony.* Don't you so agree, old soul?" And before I could place which of Shakespeare's plays he was quoting, he turned away and began to speak to Marina in Italian.

I drank too much at dinner, listening to a conversation in which anxiety over Adam's absence was carefully suppressed. From the opposite end of the table to Gabriella, Larry kept it moving with such verve that I guessed he'd been invited for just that purpose. I had been placed on Gabriella's right with Allegra beside me and Fra Pietro directly across the table. Marina sat between him and Lorenzo, avoiding all contact with my eyes. She drank little, lifting her gaze every now and then to the ceiling, where a rousing scene from classical mythology had been painted – the rape of the Sabine women perhaps? At moments when our eyes might have met she seemed to stare right through me, and for the rest of the time her gaze drifted away from mine. I didn't know whether I was more hurt or affronted by her studied refusal to countenance my presence.

Meanwhile Larry and Fra Pietro were lightly engaged in dispute. Stromberg was saying, "But my dear fellow, the Bible is such a relentlessly *solemn* read. Surely there must have been a celestial paroxysm of relief when you Franciscans came along and dared to make God giggle?"

"Lorenzo, you are disgraceful," Gabriella sighed. "In which circle of the Inferno will you end up, I wonder?"

"Fairly deep, I should think," he pondered. "Somewhere among the fortune-tellers and fraudsters in the dingy pouches of Malebolge perhaps? Certainly not so deep as those who betray their friends."

"I should hope not!" Gabriella exclaimed.

"Besides," Marina added quietly, "that place is already reserved for someone else at the table."

Like an event long dreaded and finally arrived, her remark brought silence. With it came an uncertain stillness in which everyone looked at her, only to find her gaze fixed on the wineglass she had hardly touched.

Allegra dispelled the silence. "I don't think I believe in hell."

"Oh but you should, you really should," Lorenzo rallied in protest while enjoying my discomfiture. "By refusing to believe in hell, we give it leave to prosper everywhere. It becomes hell on earth, my dear, absolute hell on earth! Martin will tell you that. He's one of its principal cartographers."

Turning to me, Fra Pietro said, "You must explain for me what Lorenzo means by this."

"I'm a journalist," I answered, "mostly covering wars. For television."

"Ah, now I understand." As though I had confessed to an illness, Fra Pietro studied me with a troubled and compassionate gaze. "Then you have indeed come close to the Inferno, my friend."

"Things like that don't happen because people no longer believe in hell," I said. "It's because they no longer believe in man."

"Which is another way of saying the same thing," Marina said, with such cold authority that again the table fell silent round her. She put down her napkin, pushed back her chair and got to her feet. "I'm sorry, but Martin and I have to talk.

Will you excuse us, everyone?" Without so much as a glance my way, she walked across the marbled tiles of the floor and out of the room.

Excusing myself, I followed her through onto the terrace, watching the white sway of hair at her back. The breath felt constricted in my chest, and I was glad of the night air when Marina stopped at the balustrade and stood with her back to me, tapping the stone with her fingertips. I felt a sudden access of affection for the familiar line of her spine in the backless dress, though every instinct advised me against speaking first.

We stood in silence. "Marina," I finally said, "you have to understand why I came."

"I know about Hal," she answered, without turning. "I'm thinking about it."

"I just didn't want you to think…"

But she rounded on me then. "Don't." And before I could speak again, "Why should I be surprised that you're still as devious as you ever were?"

"I may have my failings," I said with a nonchalance I didn't feel, "but there must be better uses for this conversation than insulting one another."

"I want you to leave Allegra alone. I won't have you using her against me."

"I didn't know that I was."

"Oh yes you did, you bastard."

I released a tense breath. "Look, we can stand here trading accusations all night if you like, but what will it change, what good will it do?"

Marina tossed her head as if about to retort, then changed her mind. "All right. Let's walk," she said. "Don't say anything. Not yet. I want to take a few minutes to clear my head."

I followed a few paces behind as she walked along the gravelled path towards the hidden door leading down to the garden. The stair was narrow and dark; she felt her way down through the damp smell, which seemed ranker by night, and the garden itself was a warren of shadows through which water threaded its sound.

Marina sat down on the marble steps of the temple, holding the fingers of one hand in the runnelled cascade. No light reached us from the house, but the darkness was drenched in moonlight. We waited, as bereft of speech as two nocturnal animals of different species, as wary of each other, until at last she said, "This feels a long way from High Sugden."

"Yes."

"The weird thing is I was dreaming about the house last night. I was trying to fit together the words above the door. They wouldn't sit right. They seemed to be saying *This place hates peace, observes crimes, loves wickedness, punishes the virtuous.*"

"You left out *honours laws.*"

"The dream left it out."

"Because those aren't the laws it honours? It's a lonely place now, Marina."

"It always was."

"But not like this. Things are desperate there."

Her retort was immediate, "Do you think Grace wasn't desperate?"

Only the water spoke in the long ensuing silence.

Before I could think how to answer, Marina turned away, breaking the tension, though some unrequited appetite inside her was still hankering for the worst. "You've just come back from Equatoria," she said.

"This time last week, yes."

"How far upcountry did you get?"

"I got through to Fontonfarom just after the massacre. It was bad everywhere."

"Are any of Emmanuel's family left?"

"I don't think so. I couldn't trace them."

"They should never have gone back."

"Young Keshie felt that something of his father's vision might be retrieved." I heard a sound that might have been a sigh or a snort, a grief suppressed in the darkness. "I know," I said. "And with the army divided and Mouhatta's Action Brigades against him, and the UN wringing its hands at a standstill because no one would commit their troops... he never stood a chance."

"No, I don't suppose he did." Marina released a long, shuddering breath. "I haven't heard from Ruth Asibu in a long time. Is she dead?"

I might have lied, but Marina knew that her friend had been lucky to survive for as long as she did. As a radical lawyer, famed for her courage in taking on the corrupt and despotic regimes that followed the overthrow of the First Republic, Ruth's name had figured high on the death-wish list when General Obanji Mouhatta unleashed his bands of irregulars. I could imagine the volatile young men I'd seen careering the streets in a Datsun pickup truck breaking into her house, stoned out of their minds, carrying cutlasses and Kalashnikovs, one of them sporting a strawberry-blond wig. She too would have stood no chance.

"Wilhelmina Song?" Marina asked after a moment. "Old Joshua? The Diallo twins?" At each pause I shook my head before saying, "I tried to find them but... there were a lot of mass graves."

About one significant name, I noted, she made no enquiry, and it was not a name that I felt ready to raise. Out of the bleak distance I said, "I've brought a videotape with me in case... but I can't imagine that you'd want to see it."

Her voice was compressed with pain as she said, "I dreamt about it. Night after night, at the time it was happening. No faces, just nameless figures, killing and falling. At first I thought it was just me, my nightmare, but..." She looked up and must have remembered who she was talking to. "I have no use for your film." I flinched at the derision in her tone. "And what about you?" she demanded. "What does looking at that kind of thing do to you?"

"Nothing good," I admitted. "I used to think that bearing witness had to make a difference. That if we looked the horror in the eyes and showed people things they'd rather turn away from, things would change, that we'd learn something, that we might use the evidence against ourselves to some advantage. But the fact is we're far too comfortable with the way things are to be serious about change. Sometimes I think all we've done is turn the sitting room into a private amphitheatre – a cosy little peep show where we can get off on the visuals while indulging our compassion. Or we can just reach for the remote and change the channel. Either way we delegate the suffering."

"It will come back," she said. "One way or another it comes back." She got up and turned away with an impatient sigh, shaking her head. "Gabriella thinks you're in shock. So much in shock that you don't even know it."

"I see. Is that what *you* think?"

"I've no idea. I don't know who you are any more. I suppose it's possible. But as I reminded Gabriella, you're English and, what's worse, a Yorkshireman, which means you're probably so thick-skinned you might as well be in deep permafrost as far as feelings are concerned."

So here it was again – the old, judgemental arrogance. What did this woman know about my feelings? What had she ever known about anyone's feelings but her own? I waited in silence, denying her the satisfaction of a response.

"So was this just another war for you?" she asked.

"There's no such thing as just another war." I said quietly.

"But you'll go back to it, won't you? When you're finished here, I mean. You'll go looking for the next disaster?"

"I don't know. It's what I do. It's what I'm good at."

For an instant I glanced back across the landscape of my life as she might have seen it: a burnt-out zone of craters and wreckage, of flak jackets and body bags, where coming out alive was rarely compatible with nobility of soul and, as often as not, courage itself was no more than a half-demented talent for enduring the intolerable. Perhaps she was right. What kind of monster would take pride in competence with such atrocity?

Frowning, I said, "I was planning to take a break. I was going to rethink my life. I should be on my way to the Cascades right now."

"Then why are you here?"

"You know why. I came because Hal asked me to come."

Her voice hit me from the darkness. "If your only reason for coming here was to let me know about Hal you could have left already. Gabriella has told me all I need to know. There was nothing stopping you leaving for the Cascades, wherever they may be. I don't see why you needed to meet me again."

"Because I thought I should tell you myself. I thought that's what Hal would want. I'm here for his sake. He's…"

"Don't talk about Hal. Talk about you."

"He's had a stroke, for God's sake. He can't speak for himself."

"I know that. I've known it for several hours. What I don't know is why you're still here." I saw then that she was not, as I'd first thought, shying away from the painful truth about her father. Nor for all the unyielding detachment of her demeanour was she indifferent to his condition, though she might not yet have decided how to act in response to it. No, for the moment, this was between me and her. "So you're still his creature are you?" she snorted. "You thought you could do what he always did – argue your way into getting what Hal wants, what Hal must have and what must therefore be right for everyone else in the world? But you can't really have imagined that anything *you* could say would make the slightest difference to my feelings?"

"There was a time when it could, Marina."

"There was a time when I respected you."

She moved away a little. I saw her white hair glittering in the moonlight.

"Do you think I wasn't expecting this?" I countered quietly. "You don't think it would have been a lot easier for me to leave the message and walk away?"

"Then why didn't you? What do you want here? Why did you come?" For a few seconds longer she stood across from me; then, with a brisk sigh she turned away, saying, "Why did you have to come?" And it was no longer the same question.

I should have spoken then. I should have found the heart to say what I had come to say. But I was already far gone from the moment, gone from the midnight garden, plucked back to that desolate town in Africa where I stood across from a woman in a yellow turban who was holding her dead child out to me and my cameraman, cradling the loose dangle of its head in one hand, and crying, "What for you come to this place? Why you are here? Why?" – as though our presence there was not merely bearing witness to her suffering but feeding off it – and not innocently like the vultures scavenging in the heat haze at her back. The question was an accusation. It made me complicit with all the forces that had come together to wreck her life.

The camera was running, I was wired for sound, but the image of that woman holding the torn neck of her child and demanding to know why I was there would never travel out across the airwaves, never reach into the draught-excluded sitting rooms back home. Nor would it be erased from my memory – that human face disfigured by every atrocious thing that had happened to her world, leaving her half-crazed and speechless but for that unanswerable question.

As for me, I couldn't think, couldn't feel, couldn't act. I didn't know why I was there. I couldn't remember why I had come. And was there ever, I wondered, a less negotiable question than the question *why*? I was no more capable of answering Marina than I'd been able to answer the woman in the yellow turban. Who? When? Where? How? Those were the questions I could deal with, answerable questions. They were how you got the facts as straight as you could. When the river was shoaled with corpses, to ask "why" might have been part of my brief: but it was nothing I could answer, nothing I understood.

When I looked up, the tilt of stars was swarming round me. My mind felt as dizzily black and empty as the spaces between their flashing points of light. Perhaps Gabriella was right after all: I wouldn't be the first tired journo to have buckled under stress. And what was it Conrad's Marlow had said on returning from his journey far into the heart of darkness a century ago? That it wasn't his body that needed nursing but his imagination. And what hope for a man whose imagination was now so sickened and corrupt that he dragged his long-dead father's body through his dreams? No hope. No hope at all.

But in the next moment a waft of music descended from the terrace above us, commanding silence, and seconds later came the sound of Allegra singing to the accompaniment of Fra Pietro's lute.

As the girl's voice scaled the soft air, I recognized the note from *The Merchant of Venice* that Larry Stromberg had sounded on his arrival earlier that evening. For on such a night as this had Portia come home to her palace at Belmont, and this was the kind of music that played in her moonlit garden then – a music that presages those rare moments when justice has been done, and the sad and comical misprisions of the heart have all been sorted, and true friendship is restored.

I listened. My senses brimmed with sound. The music had already jump-started the heart. Now it released my tears.

In the midnight garden the song drew to its close, and was followed by a long-drawn breath of silence reaching deeper than applause. Though my weeping had been noiseless, Marina turned my way as if sensing how deeply I'd been moved. Meanwhile, from above our heads came the quiet sounds of a world where people lived pleasurably together, making music, drinking wine, enjoying the happy fact of each other's existence. A world in which, for the moment, Marina and I had no part.

"Hal didn't know how to cope with your hostility," I said. "And neither did I. You never gave me a chance, Marina."

But her own mood must have been altered by the sound of Allegra's singing, because her voice came more softly now, though still her eyes avoided mine. "I gave you rather more than that. But I didn't know who I was giving it to, did I?"

"I think you did. You knew exactly. It's just that you stopped believing in him."

"Why should I have believed in someone incapable of the truth?"

"I never lied to you, Marina." I protested. "Not once. But the truth…"

I hesitated there, pulling back from the hot ground I saw opening up beyond that word. Once again, after all the years that had passed since I had last confronted her, I felt stymied into silence under the force of her accusation.

"What about the truth?" she asked.

To speak or not to speak? In those moments it might have been possible to disclose everything I'd kept from her for thirty years. I was on the brink of doing so. And why not? Hadn't I paid the price of silence long enough? But then I thought of Hal, old and lonely in that desolate room in High Sugden, and could not bring myself to wreck whatever chance might remain of fulfilling this last mission with which he'd charged me. So once again I prevaricated.

"I've been a journalist too long to believe that truth is ever a simple thing."

"Then perhaps you should take up a nobler profession," Marina answered, retreating into such dense shadow that I could barely see her. "I remember when you were a poet. Giving up on that was one of the many things you got wrong."

"We were children in those days. Weren't we bound to get things wrong?"

"Unfortunately, Adam and I were Hal's children."

"Will you go and see him?" The question met with a silence so protracted it became unbearable. But silence was not yet refusal. Reaching back through time to an occasion I was sure she must remember, I said, "Perhaps I should dare you to? Perhaps I should double-dare you?"

With no hint that she shared either the memory or my affection for it, Marina declared, "I've never been afraid of Hal."

"I know," I answered. "But I'm wondering whether you're afraid to *see* him because you might find you've blighted more than half your life with this stubborn pretence that you hate him."

"You're quite wrong," she said calmly. "I stopped hating Hal a long time ago. I stopped hating him when I realized he had no interior life to speak of, that for all his rant about freedom he was the rather pathetic prisoner of his own narrow convictions."

"Then pity him," I said. "I don't share your view of him but, if pity's the best you can manage, maybe you can pity him enough to go."

"I wouldn't insult him with my pity. He'd rather be dead than endure that."

"He'd rather be dead anyway. But he wants to see you first, and he wasn't making any conditions. He just wants you to come. Both of you, if possible."

"Adam isn't here right now."

"I know. I gather he's on retreat somewhere. But he'll be back soon, won't he? Anyway, you can answer for yourself. You always have."

Marina stood quite still in the night, her head tilted upwards, attentive to the stars, as if navigating her way. But when she spoke, the question was to me. "What about your own father? Don't you remember how hostile you used to feel towards him?" She released a sigh into the darkness. "But then perhaps it's easier to forgive the dead?"

"I don't know. I'm not pretending any of it is easy." Then I heard myself saying a strange thing. "But if we don't try to get things straight with them while they're still alive, perhaps they find it hard to forgive *us*? The dead, I mean."

As soon as they came out of my mouth the words bothered and astonished me. Marina too must have been surprised, because her response came like a demand. "Why do you say that?"

"I don't know," I shrugged. "It was just a thought."

"No," she came back, "it was more than that. Something about the way you said it. Something in your voice. It felt personal. Where did it come from?"

Uneasily I said, "It's not important – just something that must have come out of a dream I had."

"What dream?"

"On my way here, I had a bad dream about my father."

"Tell me about it."

I hesitated, uncomfortable on this dubious ground. "Other people's dreams are boring. It's nothing really."

"Tell me," she repeated.

So I told her how I had pulled up in the car to watch out the storm over Lake Trasimene and about the dream that came while I dozed. "He was dead in the dream," I said, "but I was dragging him along with me. He wouldn't let me go. It was almost as if there was something he still expected of me."

"What? What did he expect?"

"I don't know," I shrugged again. "Nothing was said."

So what did you do?"

"That was all of it. I woke up then. Like I said, it was just a dream."

"Yet it's stayed with you."

"I wouldn't have thought about it again if you hadn't mentioned my dad."

"But you said what you said."

"Only because I was trying to get you to think seriously about seeing Hal."

With a small sceptical grunt of dissent, Marina stepped away into a place where the moonlight outlined her otherwise shadowy figure. The others must have fallen silent, or gone inside without our noticing, for there came only the sound of water running through the darkness. Out of nowhere it brought back the time when Marina, Adam and I had made a midnight hike through the crag below High Sugden. We had followed the river for much of that night, and by dawn all three of us felt almost as freshly minted as the breaking light of day, on the edge of a future vast with possibilities. Now, with more than thirty years of anger and pain between us, I stood in Umbrian moonlight, observing the sheen of Marina's hair, listening to the sound of water, aching with loss.

"Anyway," I said, "that's the real point. I think you should go and see Hal. He's old and broken and lonely." I glanced up in what felt like a final appeal. "And we're all fallible, aren't we? All in need of forgiveness? Isn't that about as close as we can get to love these days?"

But if she had an answer I didn't get to hear it, for at that moment both of us were startled by the urgent sound of Larry's voice high in the darkness.

"Marina, where are you?" he called. "I think you should come. It's Adam. He's in rather a bad way."

She had lifted her head at the call, now she turned it from side to side as if trying to get her bearings. In her haste to reach the door at the foot of the stair she bumped into the edge of the marble table. I heard her small gasp of pain before she hurried on with one hand held out before her as though fearful that the night might be filled with obstacles. I followed her through dappled moonlight to the door and heard her footsteps climbing quickly beyond the turn of the stair. When I came out into the courtyard she was confronting Larry with an urgent demand to know where Adam was.

"Orazio and Fra Pietro are helping him in," Larry answered. "He seems quite dazed. There was blood on his head. I've no idea what he's been up to. And look at you, for goodness' sake, wandering about down there in the dark. We could have ended up with both of you hurt."

"Don't fuss me!" she brushed past his offered arm, making for the house. "I'm perfectly all right."

Larry glanced at me reprovingly, then shook his head. "Well, I suppose it can't make that much difference to her."

"What doesn't?"

"The dark of course. Surely you've realized?" he said. "She's quite blind."

Then he was gone from my side, following her into the house, and I was left standing like a stone in the midnight garden.

As I walked back towards the house, the sound of a heated exchange came through the open door to one of the rooms. From the shadows of the terrace I saw Larry Stromberg and Fra Pietro sitting alone, each with a couch to himself.

Shoulders hunched, his big hands held open in mild protest, Fra Pietro was saying, "This may be so. You have known him longer than I have, but for me Adam is looking for his life still. His true life. The life that will bring rest and satisfaction to his soul."

"To the best of my knowledge," Larry retorted, pouring himself more brandy, "Adam already has perfectly adequate spiritual resources of his own." Looking up from the decanter, he saw Fra Pietro glance shiftily away. "You have the look of a guilty thing about you, Fra Pietro," he accused. "Do you know more about this than you've been letting on?"

Both men were so intent on their altercation that neither was aware of me. Larry's voice was cold, and his eyes were sharply fixed on Fra Pietro, who lifted his doleful donkey head to study the painted ceiling as though some glimpse of divine guidance might be found there. "We have talked a little, he and I," he prevaricated.

"About?"

"Many things. For example, about a member of our order who was canonized some years ago. Also about the nature of sacrifice, and such matters."

"Such matters indeed!" Larry peered over the rim of his glass. "What else?"

"About the Poverello, of course, and how he received on his body the marks of the stigmata when he was alone on La Verna."

"I see." Larry narrowed his eyes in accusation. "Have you been trying to convert him, Fra Pietro? Have you been urging poverty and chastity on him, and obedience to the Pope's authority? Do my senses entirely deceive me or is there a distinct whiff of Creeping Jesus in the air?"

But this was too much for Fra Pietro, who got up, gasping, "*Basta*, Lorenzo, *basta*!" and headed for the door. He blinked to see me standing there, then brushed past me, saying "Excuse, excuse" as he took a fresh cheroot from his wallet and went out onto the terrace muttering to himself in Italian.

"Ah, of course!" Larry sighed as I walked through into the room. "*You're* still here!" From the tone of his voice I might have wilfully neglected a convenient opportunity to take a flight out of Italy that evening. Then he must have seen from my face how shaken I was, because he glanced away uncomfortably and said, "I suppose I'd better fill you in with what's happening."

He told me how a man had driven up to the villa and startled everyone by shouting for attention. He was a hill farmer who claimed to have found Adam staggering down a remote mountain road several miles away. At first he'd thought him drunk and would have swerved his van past him, but when he noticed the bloody shirt and the wound on Adam's temple, he'd stopped to pick him up. Blurry but resolute, Adam had insisted that he be taken not to hospital but to Gabriella's villa. Between them, Orazio and Fra Pietro had helped Adam from the van. His clothes smelt of sheep and his face was white, but he was smiling vaguely as if amused by his own condition. Mumbling that he was all right, he told them they were not to worry, he just needed rest. Gabriella had arranged for him to be put to bed at once and then telephoned her doctor. The farmer had left just a few minutes before I came in, having refused all reward except a glass of wine and Fra Pietro's blessing.

Still dazed myself, I said, "Did Adam take a fall or something?"

"I don't know. Nothing's quite clear yet."

"What was he doing up there in the mountains on his own anyway?"

"As you may remember, Adam is sometimes a law unto himself."

"So why are you giving that poor monk such a hard time?"

Larry frowned into his brandy snifter. "He's not a monk – he's a friar – and I rather fear he's been poking his nose where it don't belong. I do hope you're not going to do the same. I've got too much on my plate as it is just now."

"Too much to warn me about Marina's blindness evidently!"

"Yes, well, your feelings don't rank very high on my priorities. Besides, I'm sure I recall saying something about what a formidable figure she's become."

"You know damn well what I mean."

Larry heaved another impatient sigh. "Why don't you go home, dear man? Go home and tell Bully Brigshaw that his daughter is blind and his son has just cracked his head in the mountains, so neither is in much shape to visit his sickbed – even if they had the remotest desire to do so." He knocked back the last of the brandy. "Now, if you'll excuse me, there are things I must sort out with Gabriella," he said, and left the room.

Hearing Fra Pietro's lute strumming a wistful little tune out on the terrace, I poured myself a brandy and tried to come to terms with the intolerable thought of Marina's blindness, and of Adam in much the same state of confusion and dishevelment as he had been when I had found him on King's Parade at the time of his breakdown at Cambridge.

Freezing sleet had been blowing about the streets on that winter night, shortly after the start of a new term in our second year. Adam had come back to college a week early after a disastrous Christmas vacation at High Sugden. I hadn't returned until later, so he must have been brooding on his own for days before he cracked and went out wandering the streets. With some difficulty I got him back to his room, where I lit the gas fire to warm him up. Ignoring the cup of coffee I brought him, he sat at his desk, shivering, vaguely shaking his head when I tried to make him talk. He seemed resentful of my efforts to help him. When I saw I was getting nowhere, I decided to let him sleep. Telling him that I'd call in the next day, I cycled back to the hostel across the river where I was living at that time. But I'd lain awake most of the night, worrying over what was happening.

I knew that things had been going badly for him at home. He and his father had been at loggerheads since Hal came to speak at Cambridge ('Does Freedom Have A Future?' had been the title of his talk) and I'd been caught uneasily between them. By the time of my New Year visit to High Sugden, they were no longer speaking to each other, and both were shaken by a row so bruising that neither would speak about it to anyone else. Marina was too taken up with the hectic complexities of her life at art school to show much interest in Adam at that time, and Grace had already begun to retreat into drink as a refuge from her own pain and loneliness. So I found Adam holed up in his room, preparing for an early return to college.

Typically, he sought to hide his feelings with the same dry nonchalance with which he'd concealed his occasional fits of depression at Cambridge. I tried to talk to him about those black moods once, but he fobbed me off with the bleak, deliberately excluding remark that no one with any sense of moral decency could be happy in times like these.

When I went back to his room the morning after his crisis, I found only his bed-maker there, sorting out a muddle of smashed crockery and books. It was she who told me that Adam had been taken for observation to the mental hospital at

Fulbourn. Later I learnt that Grace had driven down urgently from Yorkshire, but I saw nothing of her while she was in Cambridge. Within the week she had taken her son home to recuperate. Adam did not return for the rest of that term. When I saw him again at Easter, he still wouldn't talk about what had happened.

Thinking how that might have been Adam's first breakdown but certainly not the last, I was drawn by the sound of Fra Pietro's lute to the door of the terrace. I saw the tip of the friar's cheroot glowing where he sat propped against the pergola. Unaware that he was observed, he stopped playing, carefully stubbed the cigar, put it back into his wallet and gave himself over more intently to fingering the strings. Moments later I heard a soft chuckle from further down the terrace, and the plump figure of a woman in black bombazine flowed from the gloom into the moonlight as though she were an eddy of the night. When the light fell on her thinning silver hair, I recognized Fra Pietro's friend from earlier that evening: Angelina, the cook, who must also, it now occurred to me, have been the source of Larry's story about the Revenant of Fontanalba. I was wondering whether some crazy notion about that legend might have driven Adam to take off alone into the mountains, when I saw Orazio come out onto the terrace. He stood beside Angelina with one hand gently resting on her shoulder, both of them evidently entranced by the music, which seemed to still the whole night to a state of tranquil attention.

After a time I became aware of Allegra standing a little behind me. When I made way to give her a better view, she moved to stand at my side. Moments later the piece came to an end. Fra Pietro glanced away shyly from the applause before Angelina engaged him in conversation.

"Doesn't he play beautifully?" Allegra said quietly.

"Almost as beautifully as you sing."

"Thank you." The response was neither coy nor casual. With one hand she pushed back her hair. When I asked her how Adam was, she said, "The head wound doesn't look too serious. More of a graze than a knock, I think. He's asleep by now, I guess. He was quite exhausted."

"Is the doctor on his way?"

"Not till tomorrow. He seemed to think a night's rest was the best thing."

"Not just for himself, I hope?"

"Gabriella wouldn't have let him get away with that. It's just precautionary. We need him in good shape for this weekend."

"For the gathering you mentioned this afternoon?"

"Yes. We're expecting a number of people. I just assumed you were one of them." The sound of banter between the three Italians drifted on the air. Angelina chuckled merrily again; then Allegra turned to me and said, "So how did your conversation with Marina go?"

"It got better, I think, towards the end. Your singing helped. But I would have appreciated it if someone had thought to warn me that she's lost her sight."

"You didn't know?"

"How could I? Apart from anything else, she hardly looked at me all evening. How long has she been like this? How did it happen?"

Allegra considered me a moment and took in my distress. "It was a few years ago," she said. She was walking the hills with Gabriella when she looked up and thought it was snowing. By the time they got back she was blind. It's a disease. A deterioration of the cell structure in the retina. She must have known something was wrong before then, but she was working on a big mural at that time and she did nothing about it. Afterwards she said she'd been frightened, of course, but she was determined to finish the painting." Allegra's pragmatic tone of voice was matched by a philosophical shrug. "That's my mother for you!"

I questioned her more closely. Was the condition really irreversible? Surely something could be done? Weren't there specialists in the field? But the best eye surgeons had been found, they had done everything that could have been done, and Marina's sight was gone. "She accepted it a long time ago," Allegra said, "and now she copes so well that it's not surprising you didn't notice."

"But painting was her life."

"Yes. And now there are other things."

"God knows how I'm going to break this to Hal."

"You're his friend, aren't you? And isn't it your job – bringing bad news to the world? Isn't that what you're good at?" But she must have seen the pain in my face. "I'm sorry," she added. "It must have come as a shock."

"I keep thinking of her shut up in the dark this way."

"But she's not. She's not shut up anywhere. In fact, my mother is one of the most alarmingly free people I know."

I was still trying to gauge the force of that adverb when Allegra said, "Look. I think Angelina's going to sing for us."

The cook was standing on the terrace with her hands clasped at her bust. She took a deep breath as if inhaling the fragrance of the night, and gave her whole big body over to unaccompanied song. In contrast to her earlier merriment, the refrain was filled with plaintive lament, and as her voice faded on the air, the others responded to its sadness with audible sighs. Then Angelina opened her arms, tilted her head, jiggled her index fingers to change the mood once more, and led them into the chorus of a jollier song. Orazio took up the first verse in his husky baritone and, after a repetition of the chorus, Fra Pietro grinned his way into the second, before Angelina brought the song to its climax. Allegra joined in the final rousing chorus and clapped her hands in delight as it came to an end amid laughter and mutual congratulation.

But my own feelings were still too bewildered to share their levity. Glancing at my watch, I said, "It's late. I should be getting back."

"What's the hurry?" Allegra asked. "Why not stay here tonight? Gabriella wouldn't mind, and you could talk to Marina again tomorrow. She might have second thoughts."

"I don't think so."

"Well, what about me? You're part of my past too, aren't you? I find that interesting. I think you know things I need to know. And didn't you say you wanted to know more about me – things that you could tell Hal?" Our eyes met in a stare of mutual assessment, from which I was the first to glance away. "I'm puzzled by you," she said. "You seem very nice, but everyone keeps warning me against you. Are they right?"

"If they were, would I say?"

A capricious glint brightened her eyes. "Tell me," she asked, "were you and my mother lovers once?"

After a moment's hesitation, I said, "A long time ago."

"I rather thought so. Did you break her heart?"

Again I paused before speaking. "Yes, I think I did – though it was the last thing on earth I wanted to do. And in the process my heart got damaged too." Then with a quick ironical smile I added, "I don't think it ever quite recovered."

"She was your first love?"

"My first real love, yes."

"Ah, this is interesting. So now there are two reasons why you might be here!"

"You know why I'm here. I told you this afternoon."

"I know why you came," she said, "but not why you're still here. After Marina's outburst at dinner I thought I knew. I thought it must be out of guilt. Guilt over something you'd done a long time ago perhaps. A guilt that you came here hoping to expiate in some way. The bad history you talked about earlier, right?"

She eyed me shrewdly, waiting for a response. When none came, she said, "But now it looks more complicated. I think maybe you're still in love. But not just with Marina. With the whole family. With Hal certainly, otherwise you would never have come at all. But with Marina too? And what about Adam?" Without giving me room to reply, she added, "You've never been able to let go of any of them, have you? Why should that be, I wonder?"

"I do have a life, you know. A rather full one, as it happens."

"With the woman you were speaking to on the phone this morning? Is she your wife?"

"No. There's not a lot of room for a wife in the kind of life I live."

She tilted her head from side to side, as though examining a portrait, looking for flaws. "Being the intrepid reporter, you mean – wandering the world in search of violent action? So what happens for you personally? In your emotional life? When you're not dodging bullets and bombs? Do you just get it together with someone for a time and then move on?"

"I'm not as cold as you make me sound."

"No, you don't feel cold to me. But it does seem a bit lonely. As if somewhere along the line you missed your own real life and ended up filling it with other people's disasters."

"Don't you think that's a rather large assumption?" I answered with studied lightness. "But I can see you're blessed with a romantic imagination, so I forgive you. In any case, there's a simpler explanation for why I'm still here – one you don't seem to have considered even though you suffer from it yourself."

"What's that?"

"Curiosity. I haven't seen either Adam or Marina for years, and neither of them seems to be the person I once knew. Marina's work has changed out of all recognition – the paintings she did before she lost her sight, I mean. It's as if they were painted by a different person. And Fra Pietro had some rather strange things to say about Adam. So it's not surprising I'm intrigued. I'd like to know what's been happening to them and what they're both doing these days. This gathering you mentioned earlier, for instance – the one that's got Lorenzo in such a state – I'm wondering what that's all about."

"That would be hard to explain," she said, "even if I was free to do so."

"Who's stopping you? Larry? Gabriella? Your mother?"

"All of them – and none of them. They would tell you the same thing."

"That all sounds very mysterious."

"Yes," she answered, "that's the right word."

I was about to press her further when we heard Larry's voice complaining in the hall outside. "But Gabriella, darling, you can't insist on putting me out like a cat at this ungodly hour. Especially at a moment like this. After the amount I've had to drink I shall certainly drive into a tree, and then how would you feel?"

Glancing across to where Allegra and I stood together, Gabriella, who was holding a green ring binder, said, "Fra Pietro will lead the way on his Vespa."

"I'll drive you back, Larry," I volunteered.

"No," Gabriella shook her head, "you and I must have words, Mr Crowther."

Allegra said, "I've already told him you wouldn't mind if he stayed the night."

"That will be convenient," Gabriella nodded, and I was left with no more room for argument than Larry, who was ushered out to where Angelina and Orazio chatted with Fra Pietro. A few minutes later he drove off, muttering as he followed the Vespa's tail light into the night.

When we came back into the house, Gabriella suggested that Allegra must be tired after her journey from Rome that day – perhaps it was time she went to bed? Allegra was about to demur when she saw from the glint in Gabriella's eye that she wanted her out of the room. Moments later Gabriella and I were alone together.

Arching her brow, she said, "I see that you have quite charmed Allegra."

"On the contrary, it's she who has charmed me."

"Well, perhaps it is so. And perhaps your luck is changing after all. It seems that Adam is eager to meet with you again."

"He knows I'm here then? How is he?"

"He is weary and a little dazed, but yes, he knows you are here."

"Does he know why?"

"He knows that his father has asked you to come, yes."

"And what did he say? Will he go back to see Hal?"

"That is not yet decided. But I think that Adam may be well disposed to you."

"I'm relieved to hear it. Marina was very edgy with me still."

"Perhaps she has good cause?"

"I think you know that she does."

Gabriella smiled at me. "That is commendably honest, Mr Crowther. I wonder if Lorenzo is wrong to be so mistrustful of you. But then he tells me that he liked you much better in the time before you became a journalist."

"What about you?" I asked. "Are you still wary with me?"

She gave a little shrug, wry but not unfriendly. "My feelings are not so important. But let us say that you interest me. I shall like very much to see how you will respond to what Adam has asked me to show to you. Then I will know better what kind of man you are." She tapped the binder she held at her chest. "He wishes you to read what he has written in these papers."

"What are they? Do they explain what he's doing here?"

"Some things, but not all. He hopes that they will interest you." Gabriella handed me the file. "Maybe this will help you to understand us all a little better."

I opened the file on what seemed to be some kind of mission statement:

    HEARTSEASE
    1. Our lives are as we imagine them to be.
    2. Imagination is the agency of change.

3. Change in the collective begins with change in
   the individual.
4. Compassion is an act of the imagination.
5. Let us re-imagine our world.

Turning to the next of many pages, I came upon a single
word:

CLITUMNUS

"Read this and sleep on it," Gabriella said. "Tomorrow we
shall see."

10
Dance

That September, Martin was preparing to leave home for his first year at university when, unusually, his father came home from work one evening in the Bamforth Brothers' lorry. The driver unbolted the back and helped Jack carry into the house an old steamer trunk that he had bought from the manager of the mill. They put it down on the floor at Martin's feet in the small sitting room.

The trunk might have been half a century old or more and had seen better days, but it was strongly bound with studded woodwork, its corners were reinforced by leather and steel, and it was still in sound condition. Across the curve of its lid were glued the remains of ancient labels telling of voyages around the world – by Union Castle to South Africa, P&O to Malaya, and on the Cunard line, across the Atlantic, to America. The name of the previous owner had been painted out, and Martin's own name and address stencilled in white across the black patch.

Looking down at his purchase with suppressed pleasure, Jack Crowther said gruffly, "I thought you'd be needing summat like this for carting all your books and stuff."

When Martin did not immediately answer, his mother said, "It looks like a good'n, Jack."

"It'll last him the rest of his life, if he can be bothered to look after it."

Aware of the pride and sadness in his father's face, and of the hidden trepidation too, Martin flushed and muttered, "You never said owt about it."

"I didn't think there were any need." Then Jack Crowther risked a step further than the usual wary exchanges between them. "Well, do you like it then?"

Refusing to encounter that earnest gaze, Martin bent down to examine the trunk. Already amazed by the unanticipated way this battered veteran of the imperial past had crossed the oceans of the world to fetch up at last in his own life, he swallowed and said, "Yeah, course I do." Then for the first time he glanced directly into his father's eyes. "It looks great."

"You'd better open it up then," Jack nodded, "and have a proper look."

Martin felt his heart jump at the sound of the catches. He lifted the heavy lid and saw a shallow upper tray lined with fading pinstriped paper. When he removed it to reveal the empty chamber beneath, a dry exotic odour of camphor and sandalwood scented the air. It was like opening a box in which the past had evaporated to make room for his future, leaving only this scent of far and foreign places behind. The cabin trunk's memory traces of distant continents and oceans filled him both with nostalgia for the world he was about to leave and with the urgent yearning to be gone.

Around that time too he felt more poignantly than ever the draw of the hills, moors and crags around Calderbridge. His love for them had in no way diminished, but during that summer they had receded from the foreground of his awareness. Now, as the time to leave approached, he would catch himself gazing up at cloud shadows shifting over Gledhill Beacon and feel an aching sense of the transience of things.

In such a mood he took to his bike one afternoon and cycled out towards High Sugden. Though he had received no answer when he rang the house from a telephone box before leaving, he hoped that Adam or Marina might be back by the time he arrived. Best of all he might find Marina alone there, so that he could be granted space to declare his love for her, and to do it with such incontrovertible conviction that she could no longer evade him as she had done on every occasion since that afternoon of the storm.

In any case, he wanted to be out on the tops, breathing wild air, easing his unrequited heart. Yet the harder he pushed on the pedals, the more the landscape seemed to recede around him. He stopped to rest above Sugden Foot, and watched a sudden burst of sunlight pouring through a gap in the cloud to brighten the hills across the valley. The day glinted hard and clear about him. Unaccountably heavy-hearted, he pushed his bike up to the ridge and freewheeled down the slope towards High Sugden.

When he arrived at the grange, he found Grace alone with the dogs.

She opened the door at his knock. "Martin, my dear – how lovely!" she said, and looked at him with an air of puzzlement in her pale-blue eyes, as though having trouble identifying him.

"I thought there might be nobody here," he said. "There was no answer when I rang. I just called in on the off chance."

She frowned, silently tapping the panelled door with her fingertips, "I must have been out with the dogs. Adam and Marina have gone shopping in Leeds – things they need for the start of term. Didn't they say?"

"I haven't seen them for a few days."

"No? Well, they won't be back for hours yet. They said they were going to take in a film. And Hal's in London as usual. So it's just me I'm afraid."

He stood hesitantly in the porch. Could he ride away without seeming rude? Did she want him to leave anyway?

"I just came out for the air," he tried. "I wouldn't want to disturb you."

She gave a small, unexpected laugh and pushed back her hair. "Actually, I was feeling rather dull here on my own. Why don't you come in? Would you care for tea?" She turned away before he could decline, leaving the door ajar for him to pass through. Her voice reached for levity as she added, "Or we could have something stronger, why don't we?"

Uncertainly he stepped inside. She came to a halt at the sitting-room door and turned to look at him. Her eyes fell to his ankles, where his flannel trousers were still bunched in the grip of his cycle clips. "I was in here," she smiled. "Come on through."

Martin bent to pull off the clips and stuffed them in his pocket. Then the dogs came bounding out of the opened door and were all over him, their flanks shivering with delight.

"You know where to put your coat," Grace called as he fussed them. "I'm having a gin-and-tonic. What about you?"

"The same," he called from the coat cupboard, and cleared his throat. The smell of the house was familiar, but he had never spent time alone with Grace before, and he felt a little ill at ease.

"Are you sure? There's everything here. Beer? Sherry? Whiskey perhaps?"

"Gin's fine," he said, and pressed his hand to the head of the owl on the newel post as he crossed the hall into the sitting room.

Grace must have kicked off her shoes earlier, for she stood in her stocking feet at the sideboard where the drinks tray was kept. Her long back was turned to him. A blue cashmere sweater hung over her pleated skirt. As she skewered a twist of lemon on a cocktail stick, he glanced away from the line of her hips to the couch, where a book lay splayed open on its pages.

"Tell me if this isn't strong enough," Grace said, proffering the glass. "And do sit down."

By contrast with Grace's slightly distracted air, he felt more adult than usual. Composing himself in a studded leather armchair, he lifted one leg over the other and held its shin with his free hand. The light danced in his glass.

"I can't remember if you smoke..." said Grace.

"Not really." He lowered his foot to the floor again.

"...but do if you must."

"I don't."

"Very well." Grace crossed to the couch, lowered her back to the corner cushion and lifted both legs along its length. She raised her glass to him, said, "Here's cheers!" and took a sip. "I'm so glad you dropped in. Don't at all care for drinking alone, though I sometimes do of course." She sighed, smiled and glanced away.

"I suppose Hal has to spend a lot of time in London?"

"More and yet bloody more, it seems."

"You don't like to go with him?"

"Occasionally I do. But the flat's usually so crowded with Hal's chums that it can be quite exhausting. And then... well, he doesn't always want me there. Why would he?"

Martin smiled at what he took to be a self-deprecatory joke. "Independence Day isn't far off," he said. "There must be a lot happening."

"Oh yes, the action's certainly hotting up over there. Meanwhile," she added, "it's rather quiet here at High Sugden."

"I like that quiet," he said. "It's such a beautiful place. Hal's lucky to own it."

"It was actually bought with my inheritance. Didn't you know that? Hal's never had two pennies to rub together, but he did have the sense to marry money. I'm a Fairclough, you see. You must have heard of Fairclough's Fine Pennine Ale? You've probably drunk your share of it. And Daddy wasn't at all thrilled when his favourite daughter fell for a hard-up radical socialist, I can tell you. Having stumped up for my education as a lawyer, he assumed I'd marry a Tory Lord Chancellor or something like that. Funny how life turns out, isn't it? I mean, look at you – off to Cambridge. I bet your father never thought that would happen, even though you passed all your exams! Is it a good thing or not that you and Adam aren't going up to the same college, I wonder?"

"We'll still see a lot of one another."

"Yes, I suppose so. Though I expect you'll find things rather different up at Cambridge. People change, you know, once they're away from home. Anyway, the thing is," she said, changing the subject, "I was reading this novel before you came. *The Mirror Room*. It's by Miriam Stallard. Do you know it?"

"Oh that! No, I haven't read it. In fact, I felt a bit stupid when we met her on the Aldermaston march. Not even having heard of her, I mean. Marina seemed keen on the book. What's it about?"

"It's a book that asks to be taken seriously as a study in the absurdity of existence," said Grace, "but actually it's about sex."

"Oh, I see…"

Grace shook the ice in her glass. "Though to be fair, you can't really separate one from the other these days."

"I suppose not."

"Oh, so you know about these things? You must be a man of some experience. So have you contrived to get my daughter into bed yet?"

Floundering he said, "I didn't mean to suggest…" and could see no way to take the sentence further.

"Of course you didn't," Grace smiled in reprieve. "Take no notice of me. I'm in a tiresome frame of mind this afternoon. Anyway, it's perfectly evident that Marina is still a virgin. In fact I rather suspect she must be the most awful tease. Which is why the Holroyd boy finally gave up on her, of course – though that was a blessing if there ever was one!" Grace gazed across at Martin as if seeking his agreement, but he was staring uncomfortably at the dogs. "And what about you?" she said. "Let's hope Marina hasn't got your little man in too much of a pickle. Do you find it hot in here? Shall I open a window?"

"I'm fine," he lied, but Grace was already crossing to the casement. "Then I was forgetting," she said as she opened the window, "you're a poet after all. Perhaps a degree of erotic frustration is necessary to your art? Hopeless love and all that? You are still writing poetry, aren't you?"

"Not for a while."

"Oh that's really too bad! She's had the opposite effect, I see. I wish I could have warned you off earlier. Marina always was a difficult child, and I begin to think she'll be an impossible woman. Not that it's all her fault! She's inherited Hal's imperious spirit, of course, but I'm rather afraid she'll also be driven to live out all my own unlived life."

Still unwilling to look at her, Martin said, "You almost make it sound as though you don't like her very much."

Grace raised her brows. "Well, you know, I'm not at all sure that I do. I love her – which is quite a different matter, and beyond all choice – and probably much closer to hate at times than to mere disliking. But we're a passionate lot, you see, we Brigshaws. Even Adam, who's so deeply in awe of his own feelings that he thinks it's safer to pretend he doesn't have any!" She sighed, adjusted the hem of her skirt at her knees, and studied her guest's troubled face. "Dear Martin! You really should be more careful of us. Particularly Hal, who will charm your ego and flatter your youthful idealism, then run you ragged at his beck and call." Grace finished her drink. "But once again I fear I speak too late. And like Cassandra I shall certainly go unheard." Straightening her arm, she held out the empty glass to him. "Get me another, darling. I'm suddenly depressed."

When he came back with her drink, Grace took the glass without thanking him. "Shall I tell you why I dislike that book?" she said.

"If you like."

"Because it has a calculating heart. Because it does dirt on life. And if that's not reason enough, it may interest you to know that its rather pretty, twenty-eight-year-old author is fucking my husband."

Never having heard the word used by a woman before, Martin was doubly shocked by the dry, matter-of-fact tone in which it was uttered. "I don't think that can be right," he mumbled in confusion. "Surely Hal's got much more important things on his mind?"

"Oh do wake up, Martin! That kind of thing doesn't only happen in books, you know." She held him in a critical glare. "They've really turned you inside out, haven't they? Hal and Marina, I mean. I remember what you were like the first time you came to High Sugden. Here's someone rather special, I thought. Someone who might think the way a poet thinks, rather than this endless flatland wrangling between left wing and right. And now look at you – so infatuated by Hal and Marina that you really don't know who you are any more.'

Martin put down his glass on a side table, stood up and muttered, "I think I should go. I'm only upsetting you. I'm sorry. I shouldn't have come."

"I see." Grace drew in her breath. "You think I'm just an unhappy woman who drinks too much and cares only about her own injured feelings. Well, I'm not a hysteric, and I'm certainly not a fool. I care about my husband, insufferable man that he is, and I care about my children too. I care about all three of them very deeply, even though they don't think twice about walking all over me."

Again he said, "I really think I should go," and turned towards the door.

"Don't go," she whispered. "Don't leave me this way."

His hands hung heavy at his sides. "I don't see what I can do."

"That's what I mean," she answered. "Your heart needs educating. You might learn to respond a little." Grace got up from the couch and stood with her weight on one hip, twisting the silver bracelet she wore on her wrist. His gaze shifted to where, through the casement, the breeze was blowing light about the fell.

"Oh do come here," she said, and when he did not move: "It's all right. I won't bite you."

Her voice had made it seem an act of cowardice to stay where he was, so he took a few steps towards her. Grace reached out for his hands and pulled him closer. He stood a head taller than her, and when he looked down into her eyes they were filled with an amused but reassuring concern. "What am I going to do about you?" she sighed. Feeling him about to pull free, she said, "Marina tells me you're not a very good dancer."

This was unexpected. He flushed and said defensively, "I can waltz a bit."

"Well, I can help you to do better than that," she said. "In fact, I think that might be quite the best way to start putting you back inside your skin." Grace freed him from the grip of her gaze and glanced briskly round the room. "We should just about have space enough if you push the chairs and couch to the wall and roll up that rug, while I find us some music."

He watched her cross the floor to crouch before the radiogram. "Who do you prefer," she asked over her shoulder, "Joe Loss or Glenn Miller?"

"I don't know. I don't think this is…"

"Don't stand there twitching like a rabbit," she reproved him. "It'll be fun! You'll see. Let's have Glenn Miller." She took a record from its cover, placed it on the turntable, and was about to lift the stylus when she saw that he hadn't moved. "Dear me, you are slow!" she teased. "Come on, I'll give you a hand."

Reluctantly, he helped her to clear a space on the parquet floor. Grace slipped into her shoes and lowered the needle onto the record. The preliminary, dance-band strains of a quickstep filled the room. She came back to him saying, "Okay, hold me like this. Relax a little, for goodness' sake! Now, on the beat, lead with your left foot." Swaying, they moved off into an instant collision of feet. In the same moment, both dogs bounded towards them, open-mouthed, eager to join the dance. Martin groaned an apology. Grace laughed at the ridiculous leaping dogs. "I'd forgotten about these two," she said. "If there's hugging going on, they have to have some. Hang on, I'll put them out." She ushered the setters to the door and came back.

"Marina's right," he grimaced. "I'm not good at this."

"It's no harder than swimming or riding a bike. You just have to let it happen. Look, I'll show you." Grace stood beside him, waited for the music, and then moved her feet to its rhythm, speaking out the beat. "See, it's easy. Do it with me. These are the man's steps, look. Just follow my feet. Slow, slow, quick quick, slow. Slow, slow, quick quick, slow. That's the way. Listen to the music. It's telling you what to do. Just go with it. That's good! Now let's try it together." She moved round to stand in front of him, offered her arms and stepped in closer. Martin caught the waft of her perfume. He stopped breathing as he put his hand to her back.

"Loosen up a bit," she smiled. "I'm not an ironing board, and you're not a tin soldier. And there's no one watching us. It's just you, me and the music. You lead, I'll follow. Like I showed you. On the beat now – go."

Within ten minutes or so he had grown used to the responsive proximity of her body and begun to enjoy himself. He was pleased that he'd managed to cheer her up so easily. They laughed often, his confidence grew, she was patient with his errors, at pains to release him from his mind and put his body at ease. After half an hour had passed, he was dancing competently.

"All you need is practice," said Grace as she took off the record and returned it to its cover, "but to make a real dancer of you we should take you to Africa. They'd loosen you up there in no time."

"God, I'd like that!"

"It's not impossible. It won't be long before Emmanuel wants Hal out in Equatoria, and I'll have to go with him. The kids will be in college, and I'd go crazy here on my own. I'm sure Hal's already thought about flying you out there with Adam and Marina one vacation."

"Do you really think so?"

"I don't see why not. You must have realized he has long-term plans for you. Though whether that's a good thing is another matter." Grace frowned. "Anyway, I'm probably speaking out of turn. You're not to say anything."

"No, of course not."

Then Grace said, "You've never made love properly yet, have you?

Taken unawares, he looked at her wide-eyed.

"Well?" she pressed.

"Not with Marina," he said, "if that's what you mean."

Grace's expression softened, became more searching. "Not with anyone."

It was a statement, not a question, but it insisted on a response.

"No," he admitted, "not with anyone."

"That's better. Best to be truthful about these things. Would you like to?"

"I thought I just was."

"What?"

"Being truthful."

Her arched brows reproved his obtuseness. "Make love, I mean." With the palm of her hand Grace brushed back a lock of her hair. "It happens quite often in France, you know. But then in most of the important things they're much wiser than we are." Then she added, after a pause, "I'm talking about an older woman initiating a younger man." She crossed the room to stand close to him. "It's not so different from dancing." Lifting his right hand, she pressed it to her breast.

Martin felt as though he was swaying inside. A voice – his own, but hoarser – spoke his thought out loud: "You're doing this to get revenge on Hal."

Grace shook her head. "No, Martin. That's not what it's about. Hal will never get to know. I shan't tell him, and I'm quite sure you won't. This is between you and me. I'm doing it for you. I want you to understand that you're an attractive young man who still has important things to learn. I can teach you some of those things and would like to do so. In fact, it would give me a lot of pleasure."

Smiling, Grace put her hand to his chin and turned his face back to look at her. "So are you going to stay," she said, "or would you rather get on your bike and ride away, wondering for the rest of your life what might have happened if only you'd been a little more adventurous today?"

11
Clitumnus

(from the papers of Adam Brigshaw)

These events began just a couple of weeks after I first came to live at my sister's house in Fontanalba. I was still in poor shape at that time, but Marina decided it was safe to leave me for a while and took off to Rome for a few days. Neither of us knew that Laurence Stromberg had been invited to take part in a weekend symposium at Gabriella's villa, so he found me alone in the cottage when he dropped by one afternoon. Apparently he'd been thrilled – his word – to hear that I was in the neighbourhood. But he threw up his hands at the state I was in.

"My dear Adam, this will not do," he protested. "Paradise may be lost to you, but there is more to life after the Fall than festering in your shell like a hermit crab. You must rejoin the human race at once. I insist on it!" And so on, until I reluctantly agreed to go out to the villa for drinks that Saturday evening.

I found him among a gathering of scholars, poets, astrologers and shrinks who had been invited by Gabriella to pool their wits in splendour. Their theme – *De divino furore* – was taken from a letter written to a friend by the Renaissance thinker Marsilio Ficino, in which he'd shared his thoughts on some of Plato's ideas. I learnt that papers had already been given on three kinds of divine frenzy: love, poetry and – Larry's own offering – the mysteries. That evening, an American professor was to speak on the fourth: prophecy. Larry introduced me to her as a resting actor and his most precious friend. Having embarrassed me on both counts, he left us to chat.

Meredith Page turned out to be an intellectually vivacious woman in her late thirties with a fine scorn for the leather-bound condescension of established academics. Under question, she outlined her own countervailing vision of a world held together by intricate lattices of meaningful events from which, she assured me, guidance can be derived about the appropriate course of action at any given time.

I responded with a weak joke about my own poor judgement and bad timing, and said that my life had taken so many unexpected turns that I'd long since given up all hope of second-guessing the future.

In her mild Californian drawl the Professor pointed out that I was confusing prophecy with prediction. "But don't get me wrong," she added. "The future can be foreseen through the power of the prophetic imagination – though you'd better believe the variables are always on the move! But its divine function is to push us into making something new for life by disclosing the secrets of our hearts."

I must have pulled an uncertain face at that, for Professor Page looked at me with concern. A moment later she was drawn away by her chairman, a portly Swiss astrologer with a benevolent air, who wanted to discuss arrangements for the talk. I was left staring into my wine glass when Gabriella joined me, saying, "Has Meredith put you under an enchantment already?"

"She's certainly an interesting woman."

"Yes. She was a sibyl, I think. In a former life."

"You don't think one life is enough?" I said.

"With so much to explore? How could it possibly be? Surely more than one life is essential? Even in a single lifetime."

"This is a very confusing conversation."

Her onyx brown eyes widened to a stare, then she whispered, "*The great Divine commands me to speak, and my words pour out, perfect and purposeful, once they are put into my mind.*" She smiled at the incredulity on my face, then laughed out loud. "Those are not my words." Briefly she rested the fingers of one hand on my wrist. "I was merely quoting an ancient sibyl. No doubt Meredith will have much to say about her. Forgive me, I would invite you to stay and hear, but such things are delicate. A new presence can disturb the balance of the group, you understand?"

Of course I understood, she wasn't even to think of it. Across the room I saw her husband, the Count, conceal a yawn behind the back of his hand. Seeing himself observed, he smiled my way – a friendly, melancholy smile that seemed to invite me into a conspiracy of bored amusement.

"But I have another idea," Gabriella offered. "When you are free one day, I shall take you to the *fonti del Clitunno*, where the waters of the spring reflect not only a person's outward appearance but also the inward soul. There you will be able to experience the power of oracles for yourself."

I didn't like to tell her I'd already been to the Springs of Clitumnus and been disappointed by the place... I'd gone because I'd read Virgil and Propertius and been intrigued by the ancient belief that oxen grew mysteriously white from drinking the pure waters of the spring. But now, as far as I could see, it was the grisly sort of spot where day-trippers stop off for a stroll and a pee. There were snack bars in the glades. People fished for the wretched trout kept captive in concrete tanks onto which a hose pipe sprayed illusory rain, and in a grove where oracles were once cast, you could buy T-shirts quoting Pliny. If the gods had ever dwelt in that place, the twentieth century had surely seen them off.

In any case, I'd already decided not to take this conversation seriously. It was happy-hour chit-chat, no more, and the invitation was a casual gesture of the kind that gets made in one instant and forgotten the next. So I said, "My dear Contessa, that would be very nice," and thought, gratefully, that I would soon be gone and nothing would come of it.

At that time I did not know Gabriella very well.

Several days elapsed before I saw her again. Larry had left by then, and Marina had not yet come back. I stayed holed up in the cottage, reading, writing unsendable letters, fighting despair. Things were made worse by the return of Captain Midnight, who came in late most nights, on active service again. I had no idea whether it was the same woman he brought back with him each night. What lay beyond doubt were his appetite and energy.

Then Gabriella arrived about ten one morning. I was still in bed.

"You see, I have not forgotten," she announced as I came down, tucking the tail of my shirt into my jeans. "Today we go to the *fonti del Clitunno*, you and I."

"How do you know I don't have other plans?" I grumbled.

"I do not know. Neither do I care. Today nothing could be more important than that we go to Clitunno."

Annoyed by her imperious manner, I said, "I've been there already. There's nothing worth seeing. The place affronts me. It's a disgrace."

For a long moment she contemplated me in silence. "No," she said at last, "you are the disgrace, Mr Adam Brigshaw. You lie in your bed too long, you have not shaved for some days, there are stains on your shirt, I can smell the smell of your sleep, you neglect your body as you neglect your soul. Do you think Venus will ever return to your life when you allow Saturn to dull you so?"

"I was at pains to get Venus out of my house some time ago," I snapped back. "I can't imagine why you would think I want to let her back in."

"Because she brings the fragrance of life with her," she answered. "Because if you try to keep her out, her boar will break into your house and gore your manhood. Is that what you wish?"

A retort was at my lips. I did not utter it. She saw the wince flicker across my face. She read my silence. "Or has it happened already?" she demanded. "Yes, of course. It is inevitable. Then it is all the more urgent that you come to Clitunno and inspect your soul."

"You can't really believe all that stuff?" I scoffed. "Or perhaps you can – you and Larry and that cosy coven of fakes and obscurantists who were guzzling your wine last weekend!"

"*Basta così!* Is it not bad enough that you diminish yourself without insulting those who trouble over you? You corrupt your own spirit so. You defile your intelligence. I will not hear it. Are you the only actor ever to have a catastrophe of identity? Do you think you are the first to lament that his destiny cannot be as he has dreamt for himself? You have suffered an humiliation. Of course you are in pain! No one denies it. But do you think your pain so particular that you are licensed to accuse the universe? *Basta! Basta così!*"

My indignation was contending with an unhelpful sense of the ridiculous as I started to turn away, but: "*Vigliacco!*" she exclaimed, smacking the palm of one raised hand with the fingers of the other. "Do not dare to turn your back from me. It is time you made something new of your pain rather than permitting it to make something contemptible of you. I intend to see that you do so. Immediately. I shall take you first to the *barbiere* for a shave. When you are decent once more, you shall make your offering at the *fonti del Clitunno*.

"So," she pointed to the stairs, "you will shower now, and put on a clean shirt and trousers, please. Prepare yourself. *Vieni. Subito. Andiamo.*"

It was the first time I'd ever let anyone else shave me. Composing myself in the chair, I watched Giorgio, the village barber, finish stropping an open razor and lift his glasses from his neck to his nose. He pressed my head firmly back against the leather rest and twisted it by the chin from side to side, appraising his task. In the mirror I glimpsed Gabriella sitting on a plastic chair across the little shop, smiling with approval. I squinted back at Giorgio. Only then did I notice the large cataract in his right eye. But already he had dabbed shaving soap around my mouth and jaw, and was working it to a lather with a brush. Every now and then, as he worked, he glanced up at the game show on a black-and-white TV set perched on a shelf in a corner of the room.

When my face was bloated with foam, he swept the blade across my cheek before wiping the razor clean and lowering its edge again. For many precarious minutes, the blade twitched and slid across my face and neck. A pimple bled and was cauterized. His left hand pushed and pulled with surgical authority, lifting my earlobes, distorting my nose, and tightening my throat until he was content that the skin was frictionless. Then he towelled me dry and applied a lotion of such venomous astringency that I thought for an instant I might faint. Giorgio smiled, smacked his hands together and anointed my chin and cheeks with a fragrant cream before proceeding to pinch and pummel my skin. Lastly, having dusted me with talcum powder, he whipped the towel and sheet from my shoulders and, in a single continuous gesture, stepped back, smartly clapped his palms, and opened his arms in an expansive gesture.

"*Ecco*," Gabriella cried, "now you are beautiful again! Now you are ready to meet the god."

She brought me first to the odd little temple that stands butted against the hillside below the level of the road, a few hundred yards up the lane from the springs. We walked round to the front of the building and stood before a low arched portal at ground level, gazing up at six carved columns. They supported an entablature and pediment that might have been pagan Greek, but it was carved with a Christian inscription.

"Of course, your rude remarks were correct in part," Gabriella conceded. "Things are changed since Plinio was here. This *tempietto* is a pretty monster put together out of pieces from an ancient shrine that was destroyed. As you can see, even the water is now moved away. But once it was the source of power in this place. Look at the columns! See, these two are carved like fish's skin. And these two at either side of them – the lines in the stone – they are..." – she spun her index finger in the air – "*ondulate?*"

"They swirl?" I suggested.

"Yes, swirl. They swirl like water, no?" She huffed at my hesitation. "*Andiamo.*" She led me to the side of the building and up a flight of stone steps into the cool atrium. The area around the altar was recessed like a shallow apse. Frescoes had been fading for centuries round its curves, and a small empty niche was let into the wall above the altar, which seemed an improvised affair: no more than a slab with an inset piece of rosy agate, perched on a fluted length of pillar.

"It's such a hotchpotch," I said. "It feels more like a folly than a church."

She liked the term. "A hotchpotch, yes! The *tempietto* is a hotchpotch consecrated to San Salvatore da Spoleto. But I think we are inside what was once a sacred machine." I puzzled over the word, but she pressed on. "Now is time to use your imagination." Gabriella flapped a dismissive hand above the altar. "Take away this affair. Replace it with a noble statue of the deity."

"The god of the springs?"

"Clitumnus, yes, the oracular god of the springs."

"Wouldn't you rather have a goddess there?" I smiled.

"Listen to the name." She had not answered my smile. "Clitumnus?"

"Well? Can you not hear it speak of something which is at the same time both male and female? A secret thing?"

"Are you saying what I think you are?"

She nodded. I saw she was quite serious. "The name is latinized from the Greek. The root is *kleit*, as in *kleitoris*, yes. I like to think also that the end comes from the Greek *hymnos*, which means in Italian *inno*, a sacred song."

"A hymn, yes."

"So – to the Romans – Clitumnus. The name of the god is the voice of the spring singing her sacred song. As you will discover, this is a place of oracles."

"But you said 'her' – of the spring, I mean. Why not a goddess then?"

"The ancients used to say that oracles are like seeds," she smiled. "What they have to say is not made plain at once. Rather it is planted in the imagination to grow in the fullness of time. So you must not come to the oracle as to the railway office looking for informations or a ticket. Or if you do, you must not be surprised if you come away with a poem or a dream. Nor must you complain." Abruptly, she turned away to tap the back of the niche with her fist. "What is behind here?" And when I shrugged, she said, "I will tell you. It is the hill."

"So?"

"So." She raised her arms to the niche, crossed her wrists there and opened her hands into a splay of fingers. Then she brought them down towards the altar in silent imitation of a cascade. The descending hands parted at her hips. Her palms turned outward, and came to a halt with each outstretched index finger pointing to the floor. Looking down, I saw what I had not observed before: on either side of the altar two square cavities had been cut into the wall down at floor level. Both were now blocked off.

"Come, we shall pass below again," Gabriella said, and took me back into the lower storey, where I saw how the waterfall would have been channelled down into this chamber and out through the arched portal to flow as the shining stream that once sprang here. The quirky little temple had suddenly become a vestibule between the dark world hidden under the hill and the world of light outside. And the god – manifest as water – was at home in both.

When I looked back at Gabriella, her lips were pursed, her brows raised. "A machine," she said, "powered by water. A sacred machine."

"For what purpose?"

"For what I have invited you to imagine – the invocation of the god."

In the hills outside Assisi there is a little hermitage once frequented by St Francis. As you approach its gate through scented woodland, a sign warns that you are entering a ZONA SACRA – a sacred zone. It occurred to me afterwards that such a sign should have been placed at the entrance to Clitumnus Springs that day. Instead, we found a coach party leaving as we arrived – bored men in sunglasses with slouched bellies walking ahead of their chattering mothers and wives. At the gate an official was about to close the Springs for lunch, so Gabriella asked me to wait while she spoke to someone in the Tourist Office.

After a few moments she rejoined me. "It is as I hoped. We shall have the shrine entirely to ourselves."

I thought she must be referring to some other relic of the pagan world left standing, bereft and enigmatic, amid the degradations of our century, but there was no such building. We passed through the gate, the keeper locked it behind us, and we walked in silence round the edges of the lake. There was no one angling at the trout tanks. Almost no sound of traffic filtered through from the motorway. The poplars stood unruffled in the noon heat. A rowing boat idled at its mooring by the wickerwork embankment. Only the wake of swans rippled across its reflection. As Gabriella had said, we had the shrine to ourselves.

She chose a willow-shaded place far from the entrance, and we sat down together there. The sun was high, the day hot. Distantly, among the glossy panes of shadow shafting across the brownish underwater plants, were stretches that glittered with a vivid turquoise sheen. I slipped my sandals off, dangled my feet in the pool and gasped to find the water achingly cold.

Gabriella asked if I was hungry. I said yes, having had no breakfast before we came away, and not having bothered to cook the night before. In fact I hadn't eaten properly for days, and – now she mentioned it – I was very hungry.

I suppose I had some vague hope that she had brought things for a picnic and left them in the car. But all she said was, "It is good you have fasted. It would have been better with intention, and for some days more, but this must do. Your senses, they are quite sharp, I think?"

"I can smell sulphur on the air."

"It rises with the water," she said, "from the Inferno."

"But the water's cold!"

"It will cool your brain. Now I shall tell you our procedure. First is the ablution." She contemplated me with pursed lips. Did she seriously think I was about to skinny-dip in these chilly springs? "This you have already endured," she said. "You are well showered this morning, and Giorgio has made you smell more sweet. I approve of your white shirt and trousers, and you have not eaten, which is good."

"So I pass muster? Am I presentable? Acceptable?"

"Ah! Presentable, yes. Acceptable? We shall see."

"So what comes next?"

"After ablution comes confession."

"Confession?"

"Soon I shall ask you to look down into the water with great concentration. When you are ready, you will begin to speak. You will tell the story of your troubles these past years, omitting nothing important, however discomposing or painful it may be to you, however hard it comes to say the words. You will tell all that is to be told. However there is one rule you must respect: *it is forbidden that you speak of any other persons with blame.* Not your mother, not your father, not your sister. Not your enemies, not your friends. Not your lovers, not your wife. *Nessuno,* no one, no one at all. But about

207

yourself you must have no mercy. You will assume complete responsibility for all that is wrong in your life. If you speak of others, speak only of your own failures to deal wisely with them. This way you will collect all your troubles here and make them your own again. You will know you are guilty and there is nothing left but to confess. Do you understand this?"

"Of course. It's very clear." She was about to say more when I added, "But I don't see why the hell I should do it."

"You will see. I promise."

"I can't see how."

She smiled. "You have smelt that the water has also passed through the Inferno to come to this place. Maybe it will show you how!"

The water had me by the ankles in its cold grip. I withdrew them, stood up and looked down where Gabriella sat with outstretched legs, as relaxed as a sunbather who had asked nothing more difficult than passing her the suntan lotion. Her eyes were shaded by smoky black sunglasses, and she wore a silvery-blue headscarf knotted under her chin. Her face seemed quite impenetrable. The grass prickled the soles of my feet.

"Meanwhile," she continued, "I shall listen and say nothing until you forget the rule. In that case I will say 'no' or 'please'. Nothing more – unless you persist, of course. In that case, I shall reprimand you. Perhaps if something important is not being said I may also ask you questions. Maybe if it is too much I will say basta! – and we shall have failed. Otherwise, you will have only my silence. *Silenzio e massima discrezione, naturalmente.* It goes without saying."

I stood over her, saying nothing. Out on the water, a swan lifted its wings and smacked its way to shade across the startled lake. I watched as, moments later, the glassy span slid back into shape again.

"You are thinking it will be difficult," she said. "You are right. But, for a man of imagination, not impossible."

"And if I don't feel like subjecting myself to this?"

"You are free to go. We shall have passed a pleasant morning together. But I shall have lost interest in you."

"And I shan't see you again?"

"Perhaps you will. But there would be no meaning."

"Isn't that a touch extreme?"

"You prefer the ordinary, the trivial? Why come to me?"

"It wasn't me who came looking for you this morning."

"No, that happened some time ago. Today I am honouring your quest and advancing it a little. Perhaps you lack the courage to do the same?"

After a time I said, "Why should I trust you?"

"It is not me you must trust."

Unconsciously I put a hand to my face, and was surprised to find how smooth the skin was. It was like touching something unshelled and delicate. Giorgio's razor had planed the stubble more sheerly than any blade had done before. Touching my face felt like lifting my hand to the sun.

"Me," I said. "I have to trust myself."

"Ah! Now you begin to understand how it is difficult."

"And if I try and succeed?"

"Then we shall proceed to the next rite."

"Which is?"

"Oblation."

"What kind of oblation?"

"Let us take one thing at a time,"

"So – ablution, confession, oblation. And that's it?"

"Already that is a great deal."

"But not the end?" I guessed.

"Perhaps not. Though if you get so far – make no mistake – something quite tremendous will have begun to happen. Qualcosa di irrevocabile. Do you understand this?"

"Something irrevocable, yes."

"Then shall we see?"

After a time I swallowed and said, "All right, let's see."

For a moment longer she studied me in silence as though testing the quality of my resolve, before she nodded and said, "This will take time. I think first you must drink."

I had already seen where a rill of fresh water poured through a narrow cleft in the pinkish rocks above the pool. The present source of the spring? Surely that was the place to drink. So I walked the few yards along the bank to where it cascaded in bright sunlight. The sound of falling water pacified the heat. As I leant closer, its fresh smell lifted on the air. Reflections marbled the stones. The cleft was mossy and wet. I dipped my fingers into the little torrent, let the water sleeve my wrists, and then cupped my hands to drink. When my thirst was slaked, I walked back again and sat down beside the pool.

Pure living water. Water issuing from its own dark sources deep beneath the hill, yet shining so clearly that it might have been a condensation of the light. For a long time I stared at the pool in silence, waiting, and found it hard enough just to gaze down into its shallows without glancing away from the sceptical ghost of my own reflection, out across the glassy surface to the companionable trees and sky. My mind was restless, its attention caught by the prismatic glitter of light and the surface clip of damselflies. And some moments later by the sleek approach of a trout that sensed my shadow and twisted away into greener depths. So there were still wild trout swimming here! I presumed they must be the source of the bubbles rising through clumps of weed towards the light. Then I was looking down into the eyes of the spring.

I saw one of them blink open on the gravel bed, releasing a simmer of bubbles through blue-green moss and ferns. As they dispersed, they left a cloudy twist of sand in their wake, which swiftly cleared as the bubbles reached the surface to expand across the pool in bangles of light. It happened once, close by me, then again, a few feet away.

After a few seconds, I made out more bubbles rising here and there through other budding apertures in the bed of silver sand.

The longer I looked, the more I realized how frequent these brief ascensions were – yet they never seemed to break from the same place twice. Only gradually did it occur to me that each tiny eruption was feeding the spring, that these were its secret sources, exhaled from the underworld as if on the watery breath of an invisible school of naiads. Then, above them, I made out my own reflection, quivering at every touch. No more than a flickering sway of light and shadow against the reflected sky, and laying no claim to boundaries, fixity or permanence, it was deeply immersed in – finally inseparable from – the seamless flow of being all around.

A moment later, my mind was on a rolling boil. As if for the first time I saw that if we actors are always questioning our own existence, it is because we are nervously aware of the void inside us. Others may feel free to fill that space with a substantial self, but we players have no such self (except as a more or less viable social strategy, which is itself an act), because that space must be kept clear for invention. And now, staring into the spring, I saw how deep my need for that essential vacancy was, no matter how often it filled me with dread and terror. It was the velvet bag from which doves and coins were conjured. It was the black hole where the stars go through. And, if Gabriella was to be believed, it was the pool of the living god. Without it, all the rest was imitation.

Such thoughts were breaking at the surface of my mind when I remembered why I'd been brought to that place. Then I was staring at a stretch of water where a person might drown. When I closed my eyes, the pool deepened to an abyss, dizzy and sheer. I could smell the sulphur there. I was thinking of what was forbidden by Gabriella's rule. I was thinking that there could be no scarier condition than to be held accountable for all the ills in your life. It made no sense to deny oneself the simple justice of blame, let alone its consolations. What business did Gabriella have meddling in my life like this?

I opened my eyes again. I opened them on calm sunlight and shining water and living green depths. I opened them on the rowing boat and its perfect reflection; on the low rustic bridge that passed from one bank to another; on the poised white splash of a swan's back in the shade of trees. The afternoon composed itself into attentive silence.

I looked back into the pool where, as they had been doing since Pliny was here, and for millions of years before that, the bubbles were still rising through the gravel to break like light across the surface of my mind.

After a time, almost of its own volition, it seemed, my reflection opened its mouth and began to speak.

I don't know how long I spent in that trance of speech, or how much time elapsed in silence as I sought a route past each softly interjected "no" or "please". Certainly there were moments of self-consciousness when I became aware of the absurdity and, therefore, of the possible falsity of this strange procedure. But there were also times when I heard thoughts passing through me with a fluency different from the old, worn-out record of my woes. Insights as fresh and sudden as the water pushing through the gravel bed uttered themselves in clear words. And as long as I stayed inside that zone, the process proved less difficult than I'd imagined.

I heard myself speaking first of the recent death of a friend from university, a fellow actor who had borne with patience the ravages of an incurable disease. No one was responsible for his death. Everyone who knew him had been prepared for it, yet we were all devastated. So I began with lamentation   a low, raw cry of grief for someone I had loved and admired, and whose premature passing seemed a denunciation of the way things are down here beneath the moon.

Perhaps the absoluteness of death gave me perspective. I began to review the occasions of failure, betrayal, loss, hurt and humiliation that had knocked me off my feet during the past year. And though it had all ended with me losing my lover, my home and the last of my money, and though I'd been railing against a hostile fate for months, I found it possible now to acknowledge the fault as mine, to take my bow and let that crazy theatre go dark.

I moved on back. Things got harder. Several times Gabriella cautioned me for berating colleagues and friends who had let me down. Soon, as I approached what I thought of as the lost years, that drug-intoxicated delirium of time that began with the most catastrophic events of my life – a time which I had no wish to recall and of which I had even less desire to speak – I was openly defying the rule.

"This is too hard," I recoiled at last. "You have no idea how painful this all was."

"Then do you wish to stop?"

Perhaps I was fearful of her contempt. Perhaps, more positively, I had a dim sense of possibilities that would be extinguished once and for all if I refused this challenge. Either way, I shook my head, though I could glimpse the enormity of what lay in wait. But I said, "I just don't see what you expect me to do with it."

"Only to accommodate the pain," Gabriella insisted, "to own it as your own creation."

And so, for as long as I could, I pressed on, staying with the tension of each remembered crisis, doing my best to own as mine each clumsy failure of the heart. For a time, I spoke as nakedly as I dared about some of the black places to which my mind had taken me – as a man in London and elsewhere; as an undergraduate when things first slipped out of control at Cambridge; as a terrified boy at Mowbray College, and earlier with that frightening experience as a child in Africa. At last – it seemed like hours later – I tried to speak about that devastating year in which all things seemed to conspire to overthrow my sanity. The year in which my marriage ended; in which I was betrayed – unforgivably, I believed – by my closest friend; in which my mother was driven to her death; and in which I saw my father as the egotistical monster I had always feared him to be.

Staring into the waters of Clitumnus, I stared again into that dark chamber of the mind where I had remained too lucid to let madness rule my life and too cowardly for the act by which I might put an end to it. But as I tried to speak of these things now, the effort proved more than I could bear. I broke off, lifted my head, opened my eyes. "I'm sorry," I said, "that's it, that's as far as I can go."

The sun had moved across the sky, lengthening the shadows of the poplar trees. The gate to the gardens must have been reopened, because people were now strolling across the other side of the lake in ones and twos. Gabriella was seated where she had been throughout, a little behind me, out of sight. She had not spoken for a long time. Now she said, "Do not be sorry. You have achieved much."

"But I failed at the end. I kept expecting you to interrupt me."

"It was not necessary."

"Even though I kept breaking the rule?"

"If we do not break the rules sometimes, then how shall human life progress?"

Puzzled, I turned my head to study her.

Evidently untroubled by contradictions, she added, "Also, when one attempts the impossible, it makes no sense to speak of failure. Only of more or less gain."

"When we began," I reminded her, "you said this was difficult – not impossible."

"If I had said it was impossible, would you have begun?"

"Have you ever done this before?" I asked with sudden mistrust.

"Like this? No. Never before."

"Then I don't understand. Why pick on me?"

"Because something was necessary. We were all agreed."

"We?"

"Myself. Lorenzo. Marina."

"Marina was in on this?"

"Of course. But the responsibility is all mine."

I glanced away, beginning to see just how much preparation might have gone into this encounter. I imagined conversations assessing my condition. I remembered puzzling things that Marina had said, and Gabriella's provocative remarks at the cocktail party. Then I was wondering whether Meredith Page had also been involved, whether the astrologers had even been asked to study my horoscope. I felt the hot afternoon swirl around me. It was stationary and swirling at the same time, like the columns on the *tempietto* that were carved to resemble water. What had seemed the impulsive events of an extraordinary day were now revealed as a carefully staged operation to transform my life. And if the intention had been benign, the methods now seemed humiliating.

"Is that supposed to make me feel better?" I said. "It just leaves me feeling manipulated. As if this has been some kind of experiment for you. A game, even."

"Do you take me for so capricious a person?" And when I did not answer, Gabriella said, "If you have sensitivity as an actor, you will know the difference between those times when you have ceased to pretend and have become instead an instrument through which the play performs itself. I mean the times when the god has entered you. Today, for a while, I think you were more even than such an actor. You were also the author here. You were the play itself. And in that sense you are right – it was a game. But a serious game. A game of transformation. In any case, I think it is as I said."

"What? What did you say?"

"That a tremendous thing might happen here. *Qualcosa di irrevocabile*, yes? I think already it has begun."

"As far as I can see, all that's happened is that my ghosts have come back and I don't know how I'll ever lay them at rest again."

"No," she said, "I think that is not all. You have numbered the ghosts and owned them as yours. You have seen that these ghosts are of your choosing, that they are the needful occasions of your suffering, not the cause of it. For that we must search deeper. For that we must ask who is the one that has chosen them. The question now is whether you can remember who it was who made these choices, and why they were made, and whether you are yet ready to be worthy of them." She pressed on before I could protest. "You have already risked much, but you must continue to be truthful with yourself, or all will be in vain. Now you must discover whether you are worthy to be possessed by the god, or willing to become so? If so, then everything can change. If you are not," – she shrugged without glancing away – "our business here is done."

She lay stretched on the grass, slightly tilted away from me. This woman was crazy, no question about it. Crazy as a hare. Yet her voice, its edgy absolutism, filled me with an almost sensual appetite for change.

I gazed back down where the bubbles simmered upwards in the spring. Perhaps this was a game after all, a game playing itself out at many levels. A game such as the one Marina and I had played with friends as children, that game called "Truth, Dare, Force or Willing", the object of which was to push us beyond safe boundaries, sometimes merely into pranks and scrapes but, more scarily, into saying or doing things we secretly wanted to say or do. It was a game that brought desire and fear very close together, a game that made real things happen; and it always carried an undercurrent of excitement.

"Suppose I turn out to be worthy, as you put it," I said, "what then?"

Alert to the change in my eyes and voice, she smiled before saying, "I think you will find that a number of astonishing things become clear."

216

"Such as?"

"If I try to say more, it can make no sense to you. Also I do not presume to speak for who you might become."

"Then speak for yourself. What difference do you think it might make between you and me?"

"As I said before," she insisted, "we should take one thing at a time,"

"Surely we're not thinking in straight lines here? If I understood you correctly, the oracle isn't a railway station. It doesn't keep timetables."

"Nor is it an express." She countered my smile with her own. "Sometimes we must be patient for answers. Besides, you have not yet made the oblation."

"Tell me what it is."

"An offering. An offering to the god."

"Of what?"

"Of yourself. But you must make some sacrifice as a sign of it. You must surrender to the spring something that is precious to you."

"I haven't got anything. Nothing of value. That last disaster stripped me bare. I came here penniless. I've been living at Marina's expense. That's what I'm reduced to. That's the ignomiy of my condition."

Firmly she shook her head. "Everyone keeps a thing that is dear to them if they can. For you I think it was possible."

"There's nothing," I insisted.

Sighing, Gabriella got to her feet. "Then we must wait until you have something that you do not wish to lose. Come to me again when you have such a thing." She brushed down her skirt and replaced her sunglasses. "I will drive you back to Fontanalba," she said, and began to walk away.

She must have gone six or seven yards before I called, "Wait."

She turned, tilted her head at me.

"There is one thing," I said. "But I don't think I can part with it."

"What is it?"

"A coin."

"You are attached to money?"

"Only to this coin."

She stepped back towards me, held out her open hand. "Let me see."

Without moving, I stared back at the black lenses masking her eyes.

She said, "You do not trust me?"

"It's not that. This thing was given to me by my mother. A long time ago. It's all I have of her."

"Your mother is dead. A coin cannot buy her back."

"That's a hell of a thing to say!"

"Marina is my friend. I care for her very much. We are speaking also of *her* mother, yes?"

"I see. Did Marina tell you about the coin?"

Ignoring the question, Gabriella looked out across the shimmering span of the pool, then back to where I sat at the water's edge. "Come. You had this coin from the dead. Is it not time that you gave it back to the dead? It will make a suitable oblation."

"I can't. I feel that as long as I have it..."

"Yes? What then? What is the magic of this coin? Do you think you have your mother in your pocket?"

"It was precious to her as well."

"Then return it to her."

I got to my feet, but stood unmoving, remembering that snow-bound Christmas long ago at High Sugden, how Grace had given me the ancient silver coin, knowing how long I'd coveted it. I remembered how I had vowed to treasure it always, and had done so for a time, then put it away and forgotten it until the time of her death. Since then I had carried it with me everywhere.

"Come, let me see this coin," Gabriella said. When I still made no move, she glanced at me almost in disdain. "Don't worry, you shall have it back. I cannot make the sacrifice on your behalf." So I took the battered leather purse from my trousers' pocket and fished out the coin. Gabriella held it up to the sunlight to inspect its eroded inscription. "Ah! *L'imperatore Adriano*," she exclaimed, turning the coin over in her hand. "And here, on the other side, his lover, for whom he grieved so much that all the world was made to honour him as a god. Antinous. Was that not his name?" She glanced back up at me. "But do you think even an emperor can keep a loved one from death by locking memory inside a piece of metal? Even if it endures two thousand years?" When I failed to answer, she closed the silver coin in her fist and held it to her breast. "About Antinous," she said abruptly, "tell me: do you know how he died?"

Still I said nothing.

"I think you must know that he drowned in the Nile," she said, "while all around him the Egyptians were mourning the day of the death of Osiris. I think you must also know that Antinous was a fine swimmer. That it would have been hard for him to drown in the mud of the Nile, unless..." She removed her sunglasses again. "His clothes were found folded on the bank. Earlier he had made a sacrifice in the temple of Osiris. It seems he had already decided to make a sacrifice of himself." She opened her fist, stared down at the coin, and then tossed it across to me. I snatched out a hand to catch and grip it. "Release her," she said in strict tones that shocked me with their coldness. "Free yourself. Give this silver back to the underworld." Almost as if my hands had been pressed against my ears to shut out every word she said, I could feel the pressure building inside my head. "Do it," she said quietly. "Be done with her now."

"My God!" I gasped. "Do you have no feelings at all?"

"Yes, I have feelings."

"Well, right now I'm finding it hard to believe. You seem to have made up your mind to take away every last thing that matters to me. I don't understand any of this. What do you want from me?"

"Everything that can be taken from you."

I stared at her in silence, beginning to understand just how absolute her claims were. I turned away to stare down into the pool. The coin was gripped in my hand. I turned it over and over, feeling its substance, its worn surfaces and edges, its obstinate ability to survive. I remembered how often, at moments of uncertainty or stress, I had tapped it for solace without conscious thought. It was the single holy thing in my unholy life. I could not conceive of parting with it.

At my feet the surface of the water rippled and shone.

"Make the oblation," Gabriella said quietly at my back.

"You don't know what you're asking."

"Do you wish her to haunt your life for ever? Let it go."

"I can't imagine what I'd become if I did."

"That's exactly right," Gabriella answered. "You will become that which you cannot yet imagine."

Her presence was no more than a chilling whisper inside my head, a voice that might have been that of the water of Clitumnus, rising fresh and clear in each utterance of bubbles after its long journey through the underworld.

I must have held out and opened my fist, but it felt as though the coin my mother had given me delivered itself of its own desire to that clear spring. I saw it turn and sway and shine. I saw it drowning as it fell. Then it vanished in a blur of mud and light.

Eventually my eyes cleared and my breathing slowed. I stared at the water into which I had poured my life. In the stillness between my face and the reflection of my face I became a moment of pure vacancy. Time slipped by. And then, to a sound that might have been the throbbing of the universe, there came the inrush of the god.

12
Decision

I came awake to a soft knock and the sound of the bedroom door swinging on its hinges. A crack of daylight split the room. My eyes opened on the green binder of Adam's manuscript lying beside me. The bedside lamp was still lit.

Lifting my head, I saw Angelina carrying a breakfast tray towards the bed. Her chirpy "*Buongiorno, signore*," was followed by a mutter of disapproval at the sight of me sprawled across the brocaded counterpane, still wearing my clothes from the night before. With a shake of her head, she put the tray down on the bedside table before swaying across the tiled floor to throw open the shutters onto the loggia. The morning light wafted into the room on a wave of heat.

I drank a strong espresso, took a shower and lay back on the half-tester bed in a borrowed bathrobe. Then I reached for the folder and glanced quickly through its pages, trying to decide once again why Adam had decided to inflict them on me.

I had read the document the previous night with growing unease. At first I was amused by Adam's satirical description of the gathering at the villa and his account of the visit to the barber. But amusement soon gave way to disbelief – not so much at Gabriella's behaviour at the *tempietto*, which seemed quite consistent with her tales of oracles and omens and the scaly-legged sibyl in her underground boudoir, but at the outrageous demands she made once she and Adam had arrived at the springs. The guarded young man I'd first met at High Sugden would have run a mile sooner than submit to such an ordeal of self-revelation. Yet Adam had gone along with it.

Knowing that I must be implicated in any disclosures he made, I had prepared myself for more, and for worse than his account obliged me to feel. He hadn't even mentioned me by name in what was, admittedly, no more than a brief summary of the most painful crisis of his life. I featured only in passing as the friend – the *closest* friend – who had betrayed him. Who had betrayed him *unforgivably*. But brief as the reference was, that last word had pierced me. It did so again as I reread it now. Was this Adam's way of telling me that if I had come to Umbria looking for reconciliation I was on a fool's errand? But what else did I expect? Hadn't I said as much to Hal back in High Sugden?

Or had Adam's intention been more challenging? Evangelical even? *You may have made me suffer abominably*, he seemed to be saying, *but I have transcended all that. I have re-imagined my life. Dare you do the same?*

I looked again at the first page with its questionable five-point manifesto. Well, if this flaky talk of gods and oracles and sacrificial rituals was Adam's way of re-imagining his life, of putting his fugitive heart at ease, then he was welcome to it. I wanted no part in it. Again I wondered why I hadn't trusted my own judgement enough to refuse to come looking for him here in Umbria. I would certainly have preferred to live without the knowledge that he had so foolishly relinquished the rational powers of a mind I'd once admired. Or that his will had been so far corroded by despair that he was incapable of resisting a woman who was – he acknowledged it himself – as crazy as a hare.

And what about Marina? I'd lain awake half the night, yearning for all that had been lost between us. But it was clear from everything I'd seen and heard and read in this place that the people I'd known and loved no longer existed. They had changed so much it felt as though we no longer lived in the same universe. So why was I wasting my time here when my own real life was elsewhere?

Throwing the pages aside, I fished for my mobile phone in my jacket pocket. I'd switched it off during the previous evening's dinner party, and had been so eager to read what Adam had written that I'd forgotten to check it afterwards. Waiting for me was a voice message from Gail, a message filled with reproachful hesitations.

"Look, I'm sorry I was short with you earlier," she began, "but I was feeling... well, you know what I was feeling. I think we've reached the end of the road... Anyway, I can't sit around here waiting for you to come back and hurt me again. So I'm taking that flight after all... I don't expect you to come after me. In fact, I don't *want* you to come after me. I really don't... And I won't be back, not this time... Let's face it, Martin, we're through. We've been through for quite a while now. We just didn't want to admit it, did we?" After a longer silence she sighed, "Oh what the hell!... Believe me, Martin, not all the memories are bad..."

After a time I went out onto the loggia. A fine haze hovered across the wooded hillsides and the plain, veiling the scene with a filmy, insubstantial air. I stood, suspended in beauty, wretched and bereft, staring down at the ornate fountain and the clipped hedges of the parterre. Then I began to boil with rage.

All this should never have happened. I should have been hiking the trails of the Cascades with Gail right now. We might have reconnected with each other again under that clear sky. Instead I'd let the Brigshaw family wreck my life once more.

I was bracing myself to go downstairs when a door opened at the far end of the loggia, and Allegra stepped barefoot onto the tiles. She was wearing a white, calf-length cotton nightdress. Her hair was loose and tousled about her shoulders. She rubbed her eyes with both hands and then blinked across at me, saying, "I hope you slept better than I did."

"I doubt it," I answered. "I lay awake most of the night."

"Something on your mind?"

"Lots. Too much. Mostly what a big mistake I made in coming here."

Surprised by my tone, she said, "That seems a pity. Are we a disappointment to you then?"

"Not you."

"Then who? My mother? It can't be Adam – you haven't spoken to him yet."

"Marina's response to me was pretty much what I expected."

"So Gabriella then?" Her eyes subjected me to sharper scrutiny. "Did you quarrel with her last night?"

"Why would you think that?"

Allegra shrugged and gazed back at the view. "I don't know. I just thought I picked up some sort of tension between you."

"Perhaps because I don't accept her at as the fount of all wisdom."

"That sounds rather bitter! Did she get under your skin?"

"Not bitter," I said, "merely sceptical. As I am about most aristocrats. I don't care for the casual way she confronts people."

After a moment she said, "But then you don't know her very well."

"Well enough, I think."

"Then you should know there's nothing at all casual about Gabriella."

"Irresponsible then. Altogether too convinced of her own righteousness."

"I rather think she has rattled you a bit," Allegra smiled. "Her manner can have that effect at first. I've seen it happen before."

Now it was my turn to look away. "Well, I'm sorry to disabuse you, but I can't say it bothered me very much."

"You've changed," she said quietly. "Since last night I mean. You feel different to me. Something not good must have happened."

"You might say that."

224

"Are you going to tell me about it?"

"It's nothing that concerns you. Nothing to do with anyone here."

She stood, leaning on the balustrade, waiting for me to say more without demanding it.

Eventually I said, "I just picked up a message on my phone. My partner has left for the States. She made it clear she wasn't coming back this time. It seems I'm a single man again."

"I'm sorry to hear that," she said.

"We've been through a lot together. I wasn't ready to let her go."

"But it wasn't just your choice, was it?" She held my cold stare for an instant, then gave me a wry smile. "Or perhaps it was?"

"I see you like to speak your mind. You're like your mother in that."

"I would hope so," she said, then added, without looking at me, "Did she really break your heart? What happened between you and Marina?"

"I'd rather not talk about it. Anyway she'd only tell you I was lying."

"Why would she do that?"

"Because that's what she believes. Because life is sometimes so unjust it's more than possible for two well-intentioned people to do each other harm without either of them being wholly in the wrong."

"You're speaking of some sort of misunderstanding?"

"Worse than that. I'm suggesting that there may be something perverse at the very heart of the way life operates."

"I don't believe that," she said firmly, and glanced away as if losing interest. "So what now? Will you be leaving today?"

"I don't see any point in hanging around."

"Even though Adam wants to see you?"

"I doubt that he and I have anything much to say to one another these days."

"Are you quite sure about that?"

"Sure enough."

"He'll be disappointed," Allegra said. "And I would have thought a good journalist would take more care to establish the facts of a situation before rushing to judgement. But it's up to you." Then she turned away with a nonchalant shrug and went back into her room.

I was left fuming at myself, frustrated once more by the trick women have of walking away as if they've won an argument when not a word they've uttered has carried any logical force. I turned back into my room and threw myself onto the bed. I closed my eyes, and was filled with the dreadful certainty that if I opened them I would see the dead body of my father lying beside me, cold as clay, not a motion of breath from his slack mouth, the flesh wasted under his cheekbones and ribs.

A sense of absolute moral defeat accumulated inside me. And then I remembered how once, many years earlier, my father and I had wrestled across the stacked bales of cotton waste in the warehouse of Bamforth Brothers' mill. For lack of paid work elsewhere, Adam and I had been taken on among my dad's team of casual labourers during our first long vacation. Along with a feckless old Irishman called Paddy, a tubby Polish refugee nicknamed Piggy and two young Pakistanis, Mohammed and Saleem, we'd unload the lorries when they came in, stack the bales of cotton waste in the warehouse and cart them to the mixing chambers and machine rooms as they were needed. One hot day, Adam and I had fooled around in the lunch hour, trying our strength against each other across the bales. Comical figures in our baggy blue overalls, we were wrestling in a jokey way that suddenly turned into a serious contest. But I was bigger than Adam, more solidly built, and when I came out on top, my father – who had been watching us fight – challenged me to take him on.

I tried to laugh the moment away. Retorting that I was afraid of getting beaten, he pushed at my chest. I pushed him back, and then it was as if all the years of mutual bafflement and hurt swooped down on us in the dusty arena of the warehouse, and we were struggling, each gripping the other's hands, puffing and blowing as we moved unsteadily across the stack of stuffed tares.

I could see the resolution in the grey-green irises of his eyes, the certainty that he was strong enough to knock me over and pin me down. My back began to bend as he strained his sinews to throw me. We both tried to laugh, just once, as we swayed together there. I could feel his breath warm at my cheek, the coarse skin of his hands gripping mine, his muscles flexing. Gathering my strength, I broke free and made to turn away, wanting to put a stop to it; but he grabbed me by the shoulder and pulled me back again with a taunt.

We were no longer laughing as we staggered across the bales. I was inches taller than him, younger, stronger in the lungs, less worn. I had him gripped by the wrist while my bent right arm pushed at the top of his chest, just below his throat, forcing his body backwards. Quite suddenly I knew I was going to win. In the same instant I saw the light in his eyes falter. His knees buckled under him, he slipped and collapsed back onto the rough tare. I followed him down into the rising dust, pinning his hands back near his shoulders as my weight slumped across his chest. I held him down, vanquished, unable to move anything but his eyes. There was a smell of hemp sacking in my nose. White flakes of cotton clouded the air. My eyes were fixed on his. I took in the mix of pride and pathos there, and the heat of triumph surging through my body instantly expired.

When I turned away, I saw Adam staring down at us in dismay.

I had recalled that moment on the hot June afternoon of my father's dying as I sat listening to the rasp of his breath beside his bed, where he lay deep in his morphine dreams, no longer aware of the raw bedsores at his back. And now it was as if his poor body was stretched at my side again, on this high Italian bed where I lay, feeling impotent and defeated. I heard a car arrive in the courtyard. A murmur of voices rose off the terrace below the loggia.

I lay there for a long time, and even as the knowledge that Gail was gone out of my life coursed through me, I knew that I was aching for Marina. Hadn't Gail anticipated the ease and speed with which my feelings would make that shift? But was it a sign of my faithlessness or of my fidelity that they should do so? And, if the latter, which Marina was it that I ached for? The girl who had come into my bedroom at High Sugden all those years ago and listened with rapt attention to the story of the Golden Bird? Or the one I had once watched dancing to the flash of the thunderstorm on that Pennine hill outside the cattle byre? Was it the woman whose love I had finally won one night in London years later and then almost immediately lost again? Or was it the blind woman with whom I'd talked last night in the dark garden, the figure in whom all the previous Marinas were resumed, and who still, after all this time, seemed to want as little as possible to do with me and would be glad enough to see me gone?

After a time I heard a splutter of gravel outside as the car which had arrived earlier drove away. Then I heard my father's gruff ghost growling that I couldn't just lie on that bed for ever, that I should shape up and make a better bloody fist of things. So that was what I did.

Dressed in the clothes I had slept in, I went out onto the loggia. The voices I had heard were those of two gardeners: an old man, tanned like shoe leather, in a green apron, and his younger assistant, who was snipping with shears at the hedges of the parterre. The doors along the loggia were all closed. I found the way back down the staircase into the atrium, and saw no one. The thought occurred to me that I could just walk out to where I'd parked my car and slip away. In the circumstances it was probably the wisest thing to do, but I would have despised myself for doing it.

I stepped into the courtyard at the back of the house. That too was deserted, but as I crossed the terrace the sound of voices lifted from the lower level beyond the boxwood hedge. The women were down by the pool. I heard Marina's voice, and then Allegra's. I stopped in my tracks. All my earlier anger had evaporated, leaving a sediment of grief for everything that had gone wrong in our lives, a grief that threatened to overwhelm me when I thought again of Marina's blindness amid this blaze of morning light. Unready to face her yet, I decided to walk round the courtyard before going down to the pool.

The path took me along the pergola, past the boxwood screen towards the shady tunnel in the centre of the rear wall. Under the small, railed balcony that looked down from a door above the arched entrance, an iron gate now stood open.

My footsteps echoed in the vault. At its far end the tunnel narrowed to a damp, encrusted grotto with a grating let into the floor. To the left the carved-stone figure of a brawny satyr held a nymph in his embrace. Both of them brandished full wineskins. On the right, a Nereid proffered a conch shell, while her Triton-like lover carried a fat dolphin. The figures were open-mouthed and bare-breasted, their gaze less riotous than lewd, as they pointed the way through to what lay beyond.

I came out into a sunlit place more like a Jacobean stage set than a secret garden. Ahead of me lay the straight edge of a marble pool, in which golden carp were swimming. The far side of the pool followed the same elliptical curve as a high, elaborately ornamented façade. Two muscular wild men supported a dark archway at its centre. At either side the wall was carved into niches, each housing a smaller nymph-like figure. Birds, animals and grotesque masks were festooned in the panels between. Above them, on the moulded entablature and tympanum, men in armour sported with garlanded women, while at the apex of the pediment stood a single, meditative statue of ambiguous gender. The wooded hillside rose steeply behind the wall, looming so close that it seemed the arch could open only onto a thin recess. Yet as I stood gazing at this fantasy of the baroque imagination, I heard a door thud shut in there, and Gabriella stepped out into the light. She was followed by Orazio and a bare-chested workman in oil-stained jeans. All three stopped in surprise to see me standing by the pool.

Gabriella turned and muttered something to her servants, who immediately came either way around the marble edge of the pool to brush past me with a nod as they entered the tunnel. Gabriella remained centre stage at the far side of the pool, as though guarding that dark entrance. Her reflection swayed and fractured in the bright water.

"I came to say goodbye," I said, "and to thank you for your hospitality."

"You are leaving?"

"I've done what I came to do."

"And you will not wait for Marina?"

"If she really wants to see Hal, I think Allegra should take her. My presence would only complicate things."

Gabriella nodded. "But you have not yet seen Adam."

"I'd only disappoint him," I answered. "As no doubt I've disappointed you."

Her shoulders gave a little shrug. "I have no such feelings."

"How is Adam, by the way?" I asked.

"He is resting still. Dottor Galletti has seen him, and is not concerned."

"I'm glad to hear it. Perhaps you'll remember me to him."

"I don't think he forgets. He will come down soon. You will not wait for him?"

"I think it's better if I just go."

Nodding again, she said, "You have read what he has written?"

"Yes, I read it."

"Ah!" she said. "And that is why you are leaving? Very well. I understand." She gestured to the stone extravaganza at her back. "So you will miss to see the operations of my *teatro d'acqua* after all."

"Another time perhaps."

"No, I don't think so. Such things are offered once only." She drew in her breath, shook her head. "And Marina? Allegra? You have said goodbye to them?"

I watched the water light flicker over the reddish-gold back of a carp. "I wonder if you might do that for me."

Gabriella gave a small derisory laugh. "Marina said that you have betrayed her hopes for you before, and that you would do so again."

"I don't remember it that way," I said. "But it doesn't much matter now."

"No," she agreed. "So you will carry your heavy ghost back to your young American *innamorata*. What a shame you are afraid of us, Mr Crowther! You who are not afraid of bombs and guns and wicked men."

"I'm afraid of them all right," I said. "But of you? No, I don't think so."

"Oh yes," she smiled. "I think it is perhaps because I chose to show you my scales."

"I think I made a mistake coming here at all." Then I added, "But I shall remember you, Contessa, with a rather weird sort of pleasure."

"I shall remember you too, Mr Crowther, as a *meschino* who might have been something more. Go then. I will speak to the others for you. I wish you well. Goodbye."

Sick at heart, I drove to the cottage, threw my things into the grip, stopped to look at Marina's frescoes for the last time, and then locked the door behind me. Franco Gamboni and his brother stood in the track watching me place the key under the flowerpot. Their dog panted beside them.

"*Ci vediamo presto*, Signor Martin," Franco said, and then asked me a question.

"*Inghilterra*," I answered speculatively.

"*Arrivederci allora*," he said solemnly, watching me climb into the car.

I waved and started the engine. He felt like the one friend I'd made in Italy. As I reversed to the junction, the dog danced round my wheels, barking.

I made a left at the shrine, and was adjusting the sun visor above the wheel when I saw a habited figure waving as he ran down the lane from the *convento*.

"Signor Crowther," Fra Pietro called. "*Aspetti! Un momento,* please."

Reluctantly I braked. He stood panting at the window of the car. "There has been a telephone call," he said. "From the villa."

"I've said my goodbyes."

"But not to Adam, I think. He has given me a message for you. He said... *un momento*... I have written his words here." Fra Pietro opened the scrap of paper in his fist. "*Dog Fox got it wrong,*" he read. "*I got it wrong with less reason. Forgive me. Let's talk.*" The monk peered at me. "You will understand this, I think?"

"Does anybody understand Adam?" I said after a time.

Fra Pietro shrugged. "God understands him."

"Which god, Fra Pietro?"

The friar gave me a worried frown, then said, "God, Signor Crowther. There is only the one God."

"Not in Adam's world." I smiled at the friar's perplexity. "You were more right than you think when you called him a fool."

Fra Pietro shook his head and said, "But you will talk with him as he asks?"

I reached for the handbrake. "Just give him my regards."

In my rear-view mirror I saw him bless the swirl of dust left in my wake.

*

I could have been gone, clear of it all, high on the far side of the clouds, had I not seen the sign that said "Fonti del Clitunno". Even then I might have ignored it, but in my current state the sign also said, "Check me out. Satisfy your curiosity. You have nowhere else to go right now."

A few day-trippers wandered the springs under the afternoon sun. The sky had a murky brown cast to it where clouds were piling up for a storm somewhere to the east, yet the air around me felt kindly and serene. I watched people fishing in the trout tanks for a time. Then I went to look at the bubble-blowing naiad carved in relief on the monument to the poet Giosuè Carducci. Eventually I decided to do what it seemed I had come to do. Settling for a quiet place on the bank, I looked down into the eyes of the spring.

I did not like what I saw reflected back at me there. So little did I like it that I thought about every thing of consequence that had been said to me during the previous two days. I thought about Gail, and knew that she had done well to break away from me. I thought about how Adam had sat there before me, looking into the waters of the lake. Had I judged him too quickly after reading what he had written? His last line about the inrush of the god certainly bothered me, yet what had he done but look at the most disastrous events of his life, and do it without blaming others? And if in doing so he had tried his best to exculpate me, then perhaps this mission to Italy might not prove hopeless after all. Perhaps I needed to see him and hear him more clearly. Perhaps I needed to do the same with myself. So wondering whether I might summon the nerve to do what Adam had done, I too tried to confront the various injuries and losses of my life.

I can't say that the waters of the spring spoke to me. Certainly I felt no god rushing in. But something did change during the course of that afternoon. For a time at least, the grief that had raged inside me was dispelled by the tranquil light, by the way the living water surfaced quietly from its depths and dispersed into itself, as thoughts surfaced and settled throughout my mind.

I recalled my past fondness for Adam and winced to remember the harm I had done him all those years ago. And it seemed that, despite all discouragement, my love for Marina remained as undiminished as it was unrequited. And because that love refused to accept the case that circumstances had conspired to make against its continuing existence, I knew by the end of the afternoon that, whatever might be waiting for me there by way of shock or revelation, recrimination or reproach, I had to go back to Fontanalba.

13
In Equatoria

The BOAC turbo-prop liner had landed in Zurich first, and then, briefly, for refuelling in Barcelona, before taking off on the last long stage of the journey. Gazing down in wonder at the changing world, Martin Crowther saw the blue-green glitter of the Mediterranean break in surf against Africa's northern coast. He watched the plane's cruciform shadow traversing the Atlas Mountains before falling prostrate on the Sahara's floor. Then, for hour after hour, with Adam asleep in the aisle seat beside him, he looked down on a contour map of silent plateaux and parched wadis until the desert yielded at last to savannah lands, through which the Niger twisted its brown coils. By the time he glimpsed the green welter of rainforest far below, declining sunlight had begun to redden the clouds.

He was flying into Africa as into a possible dream, and if he felt a knock of trepidation at his heart, it was not because this was the first time he had flown; nor because this opportunity had come to him at such short notice. All of this felt exhilaratingly new to him, as new almost as the country to which Emmanuel Adjouna's government was bringing such radical change. But whatever else awaited him down there, Martin knew that he would be obliged to spend time in close company with Grace Brigshaw, of whom he had chosen to see little since their encounter at High Sugden two years before – and that thought worried him.

Yet his doubts fell away as he stepped off the plane into the shimmer of heat lifting off the tarmac. He was remembering his first conversations with Emmanuel and Hal, the way they had enlarged his vision, showing him how a man's destiny might lie in his own hands if only he found the courage to seize it. And here he was now, in the land they had liberated. Didn't this prove that everything was possible, no matter how steep the odds? He was taking his first steps into a new world. The air smelt differently here, of spices and flowering trees, of wood smoke and fetid vegetation. Martin drew it into his lungs, and with it a strong premonitory conviction that he too had begun to find his destiny.

Meanwhile, "Oh God," Adam was grumbling at his side, "I'd forgotten just how bloody hot it gets over here!"

A burly African, affable with them and officious with everybody else, waved them through the crowd in the customs hall, and out to where Hal leant against a shiny Opel saloon, smoking a cigarette. He and Grace had been in Equatoria since the celebrations of independence a year earlier, so he was browner than Martin remembered, and his unruly hair shone silvery now. Also he seemed even more grandly built, as though he had grown in stature with his controversial appointment to the office of Political Advisor to the President.

Stubbing the cigarette under his foot, he opened his arms to receive his son. Martin looked on while Hal and Adam hugged each other warily. Neither had forgotten their terrible row two Christmases ago – and perhaps, Martin thought, Hal must still feel guilty at having left his son behind in England so soon after his breakdown at Cambridge. But, "It's so good to see you again, my boy," he was saying, as the driver put their bags into the boot. "And you're looking well." Then he turned to Martin with a grin. "And you too, young man. It's a pleasure to have you here with us."

"It's a privilege to be here, sir."

"Well, I wish my sniffy daughter thought so too," Hal answered with a wry tilt of his brows. "But as she wouldn't deign to join her old mum and dad this summer, I'm glad you could come in her place. And the name's Hal, remember. No need for this 'sir' nonsense just because Emmanuel's made me his Grand Factotum. Now come on, into the car with you both. I can fill you in on the latest news while Samuel drives us home."

They drove through downtown Port Rokesby to the noise of car horns and shouting, and tinny Highlife music wafting from luridly lit bars. Hal pointed out the white walls of Makombe Castle, where the slaves had been herded in while they waited for the ships to arrive; and when they came out onto palm-lined Atlantic Parade, Martin caught glimpses of high-crested combers breaking against the seaward wall of the corniche. He felt his shirt sticking to the seat. Through the car's window came hot smells of charred meat and open drains, and then the warm salt wind off the sea. His senses were so quickened that he found it hard to concentrate on Hal's brisk chatter about the government's progress and Adam's enquiries about old friends. But the more they talked, the clearer it became that both father and son were eager to forestall what might otherwise be a hostile silence.

Then a sentry in khaki drill and a scarlet tarboosh was raising the striped boom of a roadblock and stamping into a smart salute as they drove through into the Government Residential Area. The Brigshaws' bungalow stood in its own large garden, with bougainvillaea and poinsettia rampant against its walls, and a heady scent of moonflowers on the night air. As soon as the car drew up, a uniformed steward came out to fetch the bags into the house, and then Grace was at the door, the breeze off the sea blowing at the skirt of her pale-blue cotton dress as she opened her arms to embrace Adam, saying, "Oh thank goodness you've made it safely, darling! It's so lovely that you're here. I can't begin to tell you how much I've been missing you."

"This is a bit grand, isn't it?" Adam said, disengaging himself and gesturing at the house. Then he smiled at the steward. "Hello, Joshua, I'm glad to see you're still in charge of things!"

The African beamed with pleasure. "Yessah, Master Adam."

Grace glanced across at Martin with a quizzical look. "And here you are too, young Mr Crowther! Welcome to Africa. Whoever would have thought we'd meet like this? I have to say it's a pleasure to see you again."

Martin pecked her quickly on the offered cheek. "Thank you so much for inviting me."

"Oh it was all Hal's idea," she said, "once Marina had made it clear she'd rather stay in London – though of course I was delighted that you could come. It's been rather a long time, hasn't it? You're almost a stranger these days." Before Martin could think of a reply, she turned to Hal. "I'm afraid Government House has been on the phone again. Emmanuel wants you over there chop-chop."

"Oh damn it!" Hal exclaimed, though with no great heat. "Didn't you tell him I was meeting the boys off the plane?"

"It was his secretary who called. She said it was urgent – Emmanuel wants all his Cabinet there."

"When was this?" Hal frowned.

"Nearly half an hour ago. I got the impression it was some issue that Kanza Kutu had raised."

"I'd better get over there." Biting his lip, Hal turned to Adam. "Look, I'm really sorry about this. Your mother and I had planned a slap-up dinner for us all, but... Well, you know how it is..." He took in his son's sidelong shrug, gave Martin an apologetic grimace and glanced at his watch. "Anyway, the two of you are here for weeks. We'll have plenty of time." He looked back at Grace, "I'll ring if it looks as if I'm going to be late." Then he called for Samuel to get back in the car.

Two days later, Martin and Adam were sitting on the rear terrace of Government House when Emmanuel came out to greet them wearing a cloth toga-fashion over shorts and traditional leather sandals. They had spent the morning touring various ministries, to which everyone had free access these days – not least, Martin had observed reflecting on his own position, the many relatives and friends of those whose loyalty to the PLP had won them positions of power and influence.

"My dear chaps," Emmanuel exclaimed, "I'm so sorry to keep you hanging about. I've been stuck for half the day listening to the Cultural Commission arguing over *names*, for goodness' sake! The only thing we managed to agree on is that Port Rokesby is far too colonial a moniker for our capital, and ought to be changed."

"Sounds like a good idea," Adam said. "What are the options?"

"Well, most of them were a touch embarrassing."

"Don't tell me," Adam said, "they wanted to rename it Port Adjouna?"

"Something along those lines." Emmanuel wrinkled his nose and then laughed. "But I wasn't having any of it. There's already too much of a cult of personality gathering around this harassed head."

"What was the place called before the British came?" Martin asked.

"Makombe – but that's part of the problem, I'm afraid. The Nau are all in favour of restoring the name. But it was a king of theirs called Osa Bassoumi who let the traders build the slave fort here – for captives he'd taken during the tribal wars."

"So the Tenkora are opposed to it in principle," Adam put in.

"Exactly." Emmanuel shrugged his narrow shoulders. "It's the old tribal rivalry rearing its ugly head again. The PLP was always a tricky coalition. I sometimes think I'm only allowed to be in charge of this place because I'm just a poor bloody Mdemba and we're too insignificant an ethnic group to upset the rest! Anyway, enough of our neighbourhood squabbles!" He drew in his breath, gazed with a distracted frown at where a gardener was hosing a bed of canna lilies, and then turned back with a grin. "Well, come on, out with it, tell me all your news: about Cambridge and what the girls there are like – terribly intimidating, I should think! Look, we could do with more beers, couldn't we?" He signalled to the steward who stood at a discreet distance with a tea towel over his arm. "Hal should be with us in a little while. And then he and I have to put our heads together with Hanson Osari, my extremely able Minister of Finance. So let's make the most of this, shall we? Oh, and by the way, Adam, have you been in touch with Ruth Asibu yet? I hear she's devastated that Marina decided not to come. And what about you, Martin my friend?' he said. "Hal has been talking to me about your plans for the future. I think there may be things we can do for you. What do you say?"

"So tell me," said Grace some hours later, swirling the ice in her glass, "how is my daughter these days? Adam has been somewhat tight-lipped about her."

Martin was also annoyed with Adam, who had drifted off without apology or explanation, leaving him alone with Grace on an evening when Hal had been called away to another meeting. "Doesn't she write to you?" he asked uneasily.

"Not often," Grace answered, "and her letters are very sketchy. I get more news from Jim Lumb about how the poor dogs are doing!" She got up to let down the blind. "Anyway, I was rather hoping you'd tell me that I needn't worry."

"I'm sure Marina can look after herself."

Grace took a cigarette from a silver case, lit it and relaxed back on the couch. "So when did you see her last?"

For a moment Martin relived his bleak visit to the London flat only a couple of weeks before – a distinct smell of cannabis in the air, two students arguing listlessly about something in the other room, while Marina played handmaiden to a lean, bearded man in jeans and a leather jacket, who was several years her senior, and probably – Martin guessed – one of her tutors. Presumably it was he who had arranged the illegal abortion she had recently undergone in a doctor's surgery in the Elephant and Castle area of south London.

"Some time ago," he said.

"And how was she?"

"She looked in good shape."

"And is there anything else I should know?"

"Such as?"

Grace uttered a small dissatisfied grunt. "I see you're going to be no more use to me than Adam." Sighing, she looked up where the blades of the ceiling fan languidly stirred the night's humid air. "And what about him? He's so evasive with me these days I hardly know what to think about him."

"Wasn't he always a bit like that?"

"Not with me. He used to be clear as a stream to me. But ever since... well, you know... that bad time he had..."

She faltered there, paused, glanced back at Martin with firmer resolve. "What I really want to know is, have his nerves really been all right since then? The doctor seemed confident enough. But does he resent my leaving him to come here with Hal?"

"I'm sure he doesn't. He just wants to get on with his life."

"Yes, but how? I don't even know what's important to him any more."

Worrying whether Adam was still somewhere in the house and able to hear this conversation, Martin said, "He seems very serious about his acting."

"Acting?" For a moment Grace failed to conceal her surprise, then she said, "Yes, I suppose that makes sense... so long as he enjoys it, I mean. Have you seen him in something? Was he any good?"

"He's very good," Martin reassured her. "He has a terrific range – comedy as well as the serious stuff. He was brilliant as Touchstone. Someone in the Third Year had already bagged Jaques. Everybody loved it. Didn't he tell you?"

"Well, he mentioned it, of course, but I hadn't realized..."

"Though he's less committed to politics than he was," Martin added.

"Well, that's no bad thing."

"I'm not so sure about that."

"I am. He badly needs to get out from under his father's shadow." Again Grace fixed Martin with her gaze. "But what about girls? Is he showing an interest?"

"You do realize," Martin answered, "that for every girl in Cambridge there are at least five lonely men?"

"That isn't quite what I asked," Grace pressed.

"Then what are you asking?"

"Don't be difficult, Martin."

"I'm not being difficult," Martin glowered, "nor am I your informer, Grace – especially about Adam. He's my friend."

Now the woman looked hurt as she glanced up from her gin. "But I rather felt that you and I were also friends," she said, "however little effort you made to see me. Before Hal and I left England, I mean."

"It wasn't deliberate," Martin lied. "I was very busy."

Grace drew on her cigarette and flicked away the ash.

"I don't remember you smoking in England," he said.

"Does it bother you?" As Martin shook his head, she turned her face away, adding, "Hal says I lack the aptitude for happiness. Do you think he's right?"

"It doesn't really matter what I think."

"It matters to me. After all, you're the only man with whom I've seriously attempted infidelity." She smiled at his startled eyes. (*If Adam is listening to this*, he was thinking, *then there's no hope now*.) "Does that surprise you? It shouldn't. I'm not at all like Marina, you know. She's got Hal's devil-may-care attitude about such things. Perhaps that's the best way. Are you following his example? You seem to be taking after Hal in every other way."

"I admire him," Martin said, reaching for safer ground. "I think it's extraordinary what he and Emmanuel are achieving here." But he was thinking uncomfortably of that afternoon at High Sugden as he added, with a regrettable air of condescension, "They're not just playing at politics, you know."

"I do know that," Grace said, and poured more gin into her glass.

"I mean, the schools and hospitals and roads they're building – they're going to make a huge difference to real people's lives. And the openness of government... Look what an example they're setting... People are watching all over the continent, and much further afield. I'm sure Hal's right: given time, this place could alter the whole balance of power in the world."

"And you think they'll be allowed that time?"

"Why not?"

"Wake up, Martin... Even an idealist like you won't have to stay in this country long to realize that some of the forces at work around here aren't at all enamoured of their way of doing things. And those people are quite capable of pulling the plug when it suits them. Right now Emmanuel thinks he's invulnerable because everybody loves him. And so they should, but..."

"But what?"

"Oh I don't know... Let's see what happens when times get hard, as they surely will."

"Isn't that a bit Cassandra-like?"

"Cassandra spoke the truth, Martin – it was everybody else who got it wrong..."

A gloomy silence filled the room. Grace took two more puffs at her cigarette and then stubbed it out. "Oh don't take any notice of me," she said. "I'm just feeling old and depressed."

"You're not old," Martin protested.

"Well, it's a relief that you think so."

"You shouldn't be depressed either. I think it's great what's happening here."

In the ensuing silence the beat of the ceiling fan loomed loud, until Grace asked in an affectionate tone, "Are you writing poetry these days? No? That's very wrong of you. No one should betray their gift."

"I was never that good. If I didn't know it before Cambridge, I know it now."

243

"So you let all those ferocious minds discourage you?"

"They didn't have to – I saw it for myself."

With a shake of her head, Grace asked, "So what are you going to do with your life? Take my word for it, Martin, you'd be quite hopeless as a politician."

"Do you think I don't know that too?" He hesitated before adding, "Anyway, I'm pretty sure I want to work in television." He saw Grace blink as she sipped at her gin. "Why not?" he demanded. "I think that's where the future of communication lies. It's going to wake the world up to what's going on everywhere – all the poverty and injustice, and all the good new things that are happening too. It'll change everything." In the heat of the equatorial night Martin could feel the back of his shirt sticking to the chair. "Emmanuel says he can help. He's going to fix things so that I get some experience working with the government's film unit while I'm here. They're making a documentary about development projects in the regions. It means I'll get to see more of the country too. And Hal has friends among the British media people here. He's going to talk to them about me. He thinks there's a good chance one of them might consider taking me on, back home, after I graduate."

"I see. So you're giving up poetry in favour of propaganda?"

"Well, there's more than one way of telling the truth, and…"

"There's no call to be quite so smug," she interrupted, "particularly as we're also rather good at concealing the truth, you and I. In fact, we're rather better at it than poor old Hal, don't you think?"

Martin shifted his eyes uneasily away. "I'm not sure what you mean."

"Oh don't be disingenuous, Martin," she sighed. "It really won't wash."

Martin stared at her aghast. "You'd never say anything – would you?"

Grace took a moment to answer. "I can't imagine it would do any of us much good," she said at last, "so I don't suppose I will." But she left him worrying over that hint of uncertainty.

In the following days Martin was troubled too by the way Adam had begun to feel restless and distant, edgy at moments, perhaps even bored by his company. At first he'd put it down to Adam's uneasiness around his parents, but he felt it most strongly after they had spent an enjoyable evening drinking with Adam's friends. The group had all welcomed Martin warmly enough during their joyful reunion with Adam the day after his arrival in Port Rokesby, but in later meetings he was left feeling increasingly excluded by Adam's devotion to these people he had known since childhood and had not seen for years. When he decided to raise the subject, he was dismayed by the response.

"I don't expect you to understand" – Adam was staring out into the night as he spoke – "but there are things between me and Ruth and the others that you can't possibly share..."

"They're all fine with me," Martin protested. "It's only you who seems to have a problem."

"The thing is," Adam looked away as he spoke, "it's a bit awkward for me having to include you all the time. Everywhere we go, I mean."

"You mean you're beginning to wish I hadn't come."

"It's not that. It's just... there are some things I'd rather do alone."

"Well, don't let me stop you."

"That's the point. I don't intend to. Anyway," Adam resumed in the face of Martin's resentful silence, "you can't really complain, can you? Hal and Emmanuel are setting things up for you rather nicely. In fact, as far as my father is concerned, you're being treated better than I am. But then that's no great surprise."

"Perhaps if you were a bit less bolshie with him..."

"I don't really think I need your advice."

"That's fine by me."

"Good," said Adam. And then, after a moment, in a more conciliatory tone, "Look, I'm sorry but... well, there's stuff I just have to do... I'm going to Adouada tomorrow. I'll be staying at the Diallos' house for a couple of days. You've got the car – Grace or Samuel will drive you wherever you want to go, and it won't be long before you're off on your trip upcountry. You'll be fine."

"Don't worry about me," said Martin. "I can take care of myself."

He got up, leaving his beer unfinished, and went to his room, and when he came to breakfast the next morning, he found that Adam had already left the house. Grace was clearly upset by his departure, and Hal felt peeved because he had expected his son to attend a reception for the leaders of the recently organized Youth Brigade that evening, an event over which Emmanuel's eldest son Keshie was to preside.

"Oh well, it'll only be the two of us then," Hal said to Martin. "It's a relief that one of you takes an interest!"

Though the event ended late in the evening, Hal insisted that they should go for a drink in a nightclub bar which offered a cabaret of belly dancers. As they went in, Martin noticed that, apart from a couple of Africans, the clientele was entirely made up of European businessmen. Hal sat in silence over three straight whiskies before leaning towards Martin and saying, "You're an intelligent chap. Here's something for you to think about, okay?"

"Go on," Martin assented, by now slightly drunk.

"Conceive of this then," Hal began "and I'm only speaking theoretically, you understand." He waited for Martin's nod before proceeding. "All right, here's the thing. You've established a new regime firmly founded on the twin pillars of freedom and justice, and you've done it with an overwhelming democratic mandate. Are you with me?"

"Yes, but it doesn't sound exactly theoretical to me."

"Ah, but hang on a minute. Let's suppose that there are those who don't share your principles. People with no such democratic ideals. People who are quite prepared to take advantage of the freedoms of your regime in order to cause trouble. Political trouble. What are you going to do about them?"

"I suppose," Martin frowned, "it would depend how serious the trouble was."

"True. So let's suppose it's serious enough to be worrying. Serious enough whereby, if left undealt with, things might start to get very iffy."

"Iffy enough to threaten the stability of the regime?"

Hal nodded, and turned to where one of the dancers was jiggling her hips towards them. Reaching for his wallet, he took out a couple of the new currency notes and inserted them in the soft hollow between her hip bone and her belly. To the jingling of her shiny coin belts she swayed away, leaving a taint of sweat and perfume on the air.

"You did say that this was strictly theoretical?" Martin said after a moment.

"Absolutely. I like to think ahead. Call it contingency planning, if you like."

"Well, I'm not sure what to say. Have these people done anything illegal?"

"Let's say, not yet. Not as far as you know."

Studying his impassive face, Martin said, "Then I don't see what I can do. I mean, I can't just order them to be locked up, can I? Not if I really believe in freedom and justice."

Hal smiled at him. "So you're no Saint-Just?

"Who?"

"Saint-Just. He was a rather terrifying young man at the time of the French Revolution. He made a case that Louis XVI should not be given a trial precisely because such an event might presuppose the possibility that he was innocent. More to the point, he also declared that there could be no liberty for the enemies of liberty."

Again Martin took time for thought. "So you think I came to the wrong conclusion?"

Hal answered him only with a wry tilt of his head, and for a long time that night Martin lay awake wondering whether Hal's comment that he was no Saint-Just was a critical judgement on his limitations or an affectionate expression of relief.

The next morning he learnt that, whatever other cares were on his mind, Emmanuel had made time to speak to his Minister of Information, who had in turn contacted the head of the National Film Unit. Two days later Martin boarded a crowded river steamer headed upcountry into the Eastern Region. He was now assistant to a wry-eyed journalist, Joe Lartey-Quah, who was taking a cameraman and sound technician to film the progress of a new agricultural cooperative and a number of other development projects in Emmanuel's hometown Fontonfarom.

If the film crew was sceptical about the young supercargo's usefulness, they had the grace to show it only in sardonic comments on his ignorance, and such comments were invariably followed by good-natured laughter. They delighted in sending him on errands which turned out to be absurd, and in thwarting his efforts to learn the local language in ways that elicited cackles of hilarity from fat market mammies or blushes from young girls. Yet he took it all in good part, and soon began to tease them in return. He impressed them too by his willingness to learn, and learnt much about the country in the following four weeks – about the cheerful optimism of the people gathered round him, about their delight in celebration, their love of food, their reverence for the ancestors, and about the poverty of many of their mud-hut villages. He learnt the acrid taste of palm wine and the glutinous texture of fufu on his tongue. He learnt what was meant by the ravages of smallpox, dengue fever and bilharzia. And with each day that passed he seemed to learn more about himself, about his hunger for adventure and his lust for horizons wider than this African rainforest could open to his gaze. Under the amused tutelage of Joe Lartey-Quah, he acquired an alert eye for camera angles too, and quickly sharpened his skills in selecting images which best served an overriding editorial purpose. Above all, he became increasingly proficient at finding ways in which what he took to be the needs of others might be met through the satisfaction of his own priorities.

Thinking back over these times many years later, as he sat through three long nights with his crew and other frightened journalists in the cells of Makombe Castle, he came to see how much more might have been revealed to him then – about the world and himself – if he had listened with a mind less persuaded of its own cultural superiority.

Martin arrived back late one evening at the Brigshaws' bungalow, having stayed too long in a dockside bar, celebrating the success of the expedition with Joe Lartey-Quah and his team. Already looking forward to the forthcoming days when he would begin to learn editorial skills in the cutting room, he was eager to share tales of his travels with Adam, but he found Hal and Grace embroiled in heated discussion about their son.

"What good do you think shouting at him will do?" Grace was saying. "Do you want him to have another breakdown?"

"Of course I don't," Hal snapped back. "But you can see he's not thinking straight. Goddammit, she's probably the first woman the boy's ever had!"

As Grace turned away, she saw Martin standing by the sitting-room door.

"I'm sorry," he said, embarrassed, "I didn't mean to disturb you. Just thought I ought to let you know I'm back."

"Right," said Grace. "Thank you."

"Is Adam here?"

"No, I'm rather afraid he's not."

"Oh, right." Martin's fingers tapped the door jamb. "I'll be off to bed then."

"Hang on a minute," Hal ordered, and glanced back at his wife. "He's going to know soon enough, and he might just be able to help."

When Grace merely shrugged, Hal turned to Martin again. "The thing is, my damn fool of a son has decided he wants to give up Cambridge and stay here and get married. What do you think of that?"

Martin was so astonished by the news that he could think of nothing to say.

"And it's not as if I don't have quite enough on my mind as it is," Hal muttered, after a pause.

"Who to?" Martin asked. "I mean, who does he want to marry?"

"Efwa Nkansa," Grace said, "that primary school teacher from Adouada. The one who talks too much. Have you met her?"

"Only briefly, but…"

"But what?" Hal demanded.

"I quite liked her."

"Of course you did," Hal exclaimed. "We all like her. That's not the point."

"Oh for goodness' sake, Hal, this is hardly Martin's fault. He wasn't even here."

"No, but the lad needs to understand the situation. The point, Martin, is that Adam's got himself infatuated. He's lost his head. The girl's all over him, you see, and…" He faltered there, grunted, fumbled with a button of his shirt. "Well, you've seen her. I'm not saying she's not attractive. She is. But that's just the trouble." He glanced back at Martin, man to man. "You know what I mean."

Martin did indeed know what Hal meant, but at that moment he was doing some quick calculations. He had been away upcountry for only three weeks. Surely not enough time for Efwa to get pregnant and have it confirmed?

"As you can see," said Grace, who had now lit a cigarette, "we're worried that he's about to make a mess of both their lives."

"And he won't listen to you?"

"Worse than that," said Hal, "he even accused me of being a closet racist. Me, damn it, after everything I've bloody done for these people!"

"But that's absurd."

"Of course it's absurd. But I'll be damned if I can get a sensible word out of him."

Exhaling a smoky sigh, Grace said, "Hal made the mistake of suggesting that Efwa is the kind of girl it's okay to go to bed with, but not the sort you marry. Which wasn't the cleverest thing to say in the circumstances, even if it were true."

"Of course it's true," Hal insisted. "That's exactly the kind of girl she is. I just wanted to make him see sense."

"Instead of which you drove him out of the house."

Hal turned impatiently away from her. Grace drew cigarette smoke about her like a veil.

After a long oppressive silence, Martin said, "Do you think it might help if I talked to him?"

"Would you try?" Hal turned to him and beamed. "I think he trusts you. He might listen to you. And you know what? It couldn't hurt to have a private word with Efwa too."

From the moment they sat down in the neon-lit bar of the Adouada Beach Hotel, Martin knew that this conversation with Adam was unlikely to go well.

"It's obvious that Hal and Grace have set you up for this," Adam said, gazing out of the window, where breakers crashed onto the wide curve of the sand. "You're going to have to choose sides, that's all."

"I'm on your side, Adam,"

"Good. Then you're happy to be my best man?"

"If that's what you want. I'd be proud to. But..."

251

"But what?"

"I think your mum and dad are on your side too."

"Ah," said Adam with a sour smile, "here it comes. Do you really think I can't anticipate every weasel word you're about to utter?"

Martin ran his fingertip down the condensation on the green beer bottle in front of him. "I'm sure there's nothing I can say that you haven't already thought of."

Adam exhaled a long, frustrated breath. "Look, I'm sorry," he said. "I know I wasn't straight with you – before you left I mean. But you can see why now. None of this has been easy for me. Nothing except being with Efwa, that is. That's brilliant. That's perfect. But the rest... Well, I don't have to tell you what Hal and Grace can be like..."

"They're only concerned for you, Adam."

"I know that. Of course I do. But they don't know me. Neither of them. They've no idea what it's like to..."

"To what?"

But Adam turned away again in frustration. "Oh forget about it. I'm not looking for sympathy."

"I'm not offering you sympathy."

"What then? Just what are you up to?"

"In case you've forgotten," Martin said, "I'm your friend."

Adam made a self-reproachful grimace. "Oh shit!" he winced, "I'm sorry. Look, let's not talk about this. Why don't you tell me about your trip instead? Was it good? Did you have fun?"

"It was great," Martin said. "But listen, I'm worried about you. I'm worried you might be making a big mistake." He saw Adam open his mouth to speak, but pressed on. "Just listen to me a second, all right? Efwa's a lovely girl, Adam. I can see that. But what's the hurry? I don't understand why you have to give everything up to marry her next week. She seems to be crazy about you, so I'm sure she'll be happy to wait till you've got your degree. In fact, I bet she'd prefer it. At least there's a chance you could provide for her that way."

"You don't get it, do you?" Adam scowled. "This isn't a sudden thing. I've been sick and tired of Cambridge for quite a while now. As soon as I got back here, I realized that I was less than half alive there. Just a brain twitching among other brains, a mouth mouthing like all those other mouths. The only thing I enjoyed was the acting. At least there was something honest about that. It wasn't pretending to be anything other than acting. And don't look at me as if you don't know what I mean."

"There are phonies everywhere, Adam."

"Of course there are. But take a good look at the people here. It doesn't matter whether they're crooks or rogues or heroes, they're fully alive. Alive in a way that nobody I know in England is alive. Watch them dancing and making music. Listen to them laughing. Hear them howling when they grieve. That's what it means to be alive. Alive inside your skin. You must have seen it and felt it every day when you were upcountry. Well, that's what Efwa's given me. Not just a reason to be alive, but a whole new way of *being* alive." Shaking his head, Adam uttered a little, dismissive sniff. "You remember all those dark ideas that used to haunt my mind back home? Well, they're gone. They can't thrive in this light. They were just the kind of bad dreams that a brain's bound to have when it gets cut off from the body and the pulses and the real living heart stuff that throbs out of these people all the time. That's why I'm staying here. That's why I'm marrying Efwa. We belong together and we belong here. So if you've got any other ideas, you might just as well save your breath."

For a while Martin listened to the palm fronds tapping in the breeze, then he said, "So what are you going to do with yourself? For the rest of your life, I mean."

Adam shrugged the question away. "I don't know yet. I haven't made up my mind. This is a new country. There's plenty to do here."

"You think your dad will find you something?"

"I don't need him. Emmanuel will always help me out."

"You don't think he has larger demands on his time?"

"He helped you, didn't he? Anyway, if necessary I'll find something for myself. In fact, I think I'd rather."

Martin took the last sip of his beer. "And what about Efwa?" he asked a moment later. "What does she want?"

"She wants what I want, of course."

"Are you sure about that?"

"Of course I'm sure. That's why we're together. We want the same things."

"How long have you known her, Adam?"

"Since we were kids." Adam said confidently. "We were already very close back then."

Uneasily Martin said, "But she's not a kid any more."

"No she's not," Adam snapped back. "And neither am I, so stop treating me like one. Now do you want another beer or not?"

14
Deal

The Fiat was winding uphill through a steep stretch of forest a couple of miles outside Fontanalba when I rounded a bend and saw two women resting beside the road. Both wore khaki shorts and hiking boots, one was seated on a rock, the other looking down in concern at her companion. Two backpacks lay on the verge beside them. The car shot past them at speed, and it was only when I checked the rear-view mirror that I saw the standing figure waving both arms in the air to attract my attention. I braked and reversed back down the road. When I opened the door to speak to them, I heard the older, seated woman saying, "Dammit, Meredith, we're almost there! I can make it on my own two feet."

"I've been watching you limp for the last hour, Dottie," answered the other one. "We're hitching a ride while we've got the chance." Then she came across to the open door of the car. "*Mi scusi*," she began. "*Questa signora...*" – she indicated her friend, who was shaking her head, and then raised the foot of her own right leg, miming pain as she rubbed the heel. "*Noi può dare un...*"

"Where do you want to go?" I interrupted, already knowing the answer.

"You speak English!"

"I am English."

"Great! We're headed for Fontanalba. It's not far, but..."

"Okay." I got out of the car, picked up one of the backpacks by its frame and shoved it into the boot beside my grip, saying, "Can one of you take the other pack in the back seat?"

"Sure, no problem. Let me." The woman was in her early fifties and wore owlish glasses. Unaware that I already knew

255

other things about her, she tipped the passenger seat forward, lifted her backpack in before I could offer to help, and then climbed in after it. I pushed back the seat for her older friend, who lowered herself in saying, "This is very civil of you and kind of unnecessary, but thanks anyway." She would not see seventy again, and her face was flushed after a long day's hiking through the heat, but her voice was that of an unfazeable New Yorker who might have smoked a pack a day for thirty years before the Surgeon General started worrying in public. One of the shrinks, I guessed, who had been at the villa with the astrologers and poets on the night Adam had described.

"Dorothy Ziegler," she offered. "Glad to meet you."

I nodded and smiled, concentrating on the road, while the trimmer figure in the back seat leant forward at my shoulder and said, "Hi, I'm Meredith Page. I hope you were going to Fontanalba anyway?"

"I was."

"Well, it was just great of you to stop," she said. "Thanks."

"You want some candy?" Dorothy Ziegler offered me a chunk of the Kendal mint cake she had unzipped from her green leather bumbag. "It's English. Try it, you'll like it." I took a piece and put it in my mouth – an excuse not to speak. Meredith Page declined the offer and filled the silence. "We have friends expecting us there. They said we were crazy to hike from the railroad station. Guess they were right, huh?" I smiled at the face she made behind her glasses as she pushed back a strand of brown hair.

"You staying in Fontanalba?" asked Dorothy Ziegler.

"Yes. Maybe. Tonight anyway."

"We'll be around Fontanalba for the next few days," Meredith said. "We're here for an event that doesn't start till tomorrow night, but we wanted to arrive in time to freshen up after the hike."

"An event?"

"It's a kind of celebration."

"Sounds like fun."

Dorothy Ziegler looked back over her shoulder. "Meredith honey, did you think to pack some bug spray? I plain forgot mine."

"I don't use it, sweetie. There's sure to be some at the villa, if you can hold out till then."

Dorothy Ziegler grunted. "Won't get too much sleep tonight then. Not with these bugs gnawing at my cellulite. My own damn fault though." She shook her grizzled head at me. "Used to have a mind that worked pretty good."

"She still does," Meredith put in dryly. "Dottie's last book won a National Poetry Award."

"You're a poet?"

"Don't sound so surprised, Mister," the older woman answered. "We come in all sorts of shapes and sizes. And some of us have blisters."

I glanced into the rear-view mirror, where I saw Meredith Page shaking her head and smiling. "You're not a poet," I said.

"Nothing so special!"

"Let me guess," I said, "you're an academic," and watched her blink behind her glasses. "Classical studies, I'd say. Or archaeology perhaps? But then you sound west coast, not east like your friend here, so you might just be into something a touch far out."

"Where's this guy get off?" exclaimed the amused, throaty gravel of the voice next to me. "Reading so much into a lousy pair of glasses, which" – she glanced back at her friend – "didn't I always tell you, sweetheart? – you never ought to wear."

"Do I gather I'm right?"

"Close enough to be worrying," Meredith answered. "Is it that obvious?"

"Put it down to male intuition." I smiled into the mirror and returned my eyes to the road. A minute later I took a sharp bend round a rock face and saw the lights of Fontanalba strung along its hill.

"Guess you were right," Dorothy Ziegler said to her friend. "At the rate I was hobbling along it would have taken us another hour or two. And I could kill for a shower right now! What d'ya think? Do we owe this guy a meal or what?"

"You don't owe me anything," I said.

"Sure we do, Sir Knight. You just rescued us. That right, honey?"

"Why not?"

"Perhaps tomorrow," I prevaricated. "If I'm still in town. You must both be tired out right now. There's a crossroads coming up. Which way?"

Meredith Page leant forward between the seats and pointed. "Turn right at the shrine of the Madonna. The place we're staying is just down the road."

I saw the tall house that had loomed out of the fog on my first arrival in Fontanalba two nights before. Again the dog began to bark as I pulled off the road, but there was no sign of Franco and his brother. I got out, opened the boot, lifted out the backpack and carried it to the house. Dorothy Ziegler watched me from the open passenger door, where she was standing, while Meredith leant over to drag her own pack from the back seat.

As I walked back to the car, a woman's voice called out something inside the house, then a door was opened and the boy's mother stood in its light.

"*Ciao*, Assunta," Meredith said. "We made it at last."

The Italian woman greeted both her guests by name, evidently delighted and relieved to see them. While Meredith crossed the yard to exchange embraces with her, Dorothy asked me, "Do we get to see you tomorrow then?"

"Could be. You never know."

Before she could question me further, I was reversing the car onto the road. Glancing back as I pulled away, I saw the two women waving in the glare of light from the house, calling out their thanks.

I'd been thrown by the down-to-earth manner with which those two American women had defeated all expectations aroused by Adam's satirical description of the gathering at the villa. Yet it was with the sensation of being caught in a loop that I turned once again down the track to the cottage. No mist blurred my view this time, so I could see the drop at its edge and the crowns of the fig trees on the slope below. The cottage itself looked as bereft of life as on my first arrival. The yard was empty, the key lay under the stone, but when I opened the door and switched on the light I saw at once that things had changed.

Someone had rearranged the furniture in the living room to make space for an old-fashioned camp bed against the frescoed wall, and when I went through into the kitchen I saw that provisions for guests had been laid ready in the cupboard and the fridge.

I poured myself a glass of water and took it through into the living room. Then I noticed a postcard propped upright against the books on the desk in the little alcove: Giotto's picture of St Francis giving his sermon to the birds had not been there when I left. I turned the card over and read:

Dear Jago and Sam – It's great of you to lend a hand with the "backstage aspect of things at such short notice. I hope you'll be comfortable enough here for the duration. Lorenzo will sort out anything else you might need. I've marked the relevant pages of his book for you. Once everything's in place, please feel free to take as much part in the open proceedings as you wish. I know we can count on your discretion. See you soon.

> *With love,*
> *Adam*

Beside the postcard lay Larry's *Umbrian Excursions* with two strips of paper protruding from it. The first marked the passage about Fontanalba I had read earlier. This time the name of the woman who had told Larry the legend of the revenant leapt out at me: Angelina Tavenari, wife to the town barber – and now, I presumed, housekeeper and cook out at Gabriella's villa. I read the page again, more carefully this time. Then I turned to the second strip, which seemed to have been torn from a sheet of writing paper, because it bore the heading:

THE HEARTSEASE FOUNDATION
Villa delle Meraviglie Fontanalba Italy

The page it marked was from an essay on the ancient mysteries that I hadn't read before. This paragraph had been scored:

Is it not possible that the Sibyl and her ministers were fully conscious of their own manipulative part in the process while at the same time trusting the impersonal forces that worked through them? Perhaps it might help to think of their operations as a form of sacred theatre where the power of the performance depends on the willingness of the actors to be possessed by the god. When, today, we attend a performance of King Lear performed in that spirit, we know that we are only watching men and women, our contemporaries, act out that awesome pageant of suffering, and that soon the actors will change back into their everyday clothes and go home unharmed. But though the event may be illusory, its power is not. We are moved and transformed by it. We are imaginatively enlarged. For a time our sense of the world is altered. How much more potent then an event in which there is no distinction between audience and protagonist? How much more deeply might one be drawn beyond the quotidian confines of the mind into the realm where changes begin to happen? Already induced into a heightened state of receptivity, the willing participant in such rites descends deeper into the self even as the literal journey takes him deeper into the earth. And though the journey is always inward, the outward journey – down and through and out again – is indispensable, for it is down there, in the darkness of the underworld, that the sun at midnight shines.

I checked the back of the title page and noticed for the first time that the book had been published nearly forty years earlier, when Larry had still been in his middle twenties. A *folie de jeunesse*, as he himself had called it, characterized by the sententiousness of youth. Yet in those extravagant paragraphs some seeds had been sown that must have come to fruition many years later.

Wondering who Sam and Jago might be, I had just opened another bottle of Adam's red wine when my mobile phone rang.

"Martin?"

"Yes? Who is this?"

"Where are you?" Many things might have changed about Adam across the years, but his laconic voice was not among them. "Are you still in Italy?"

"I'm in your cottage."

"You did come back then! I rather hoped you might, but when you ignored my message ..."

"Fra Pietro wasn't exactly clear," I said. "Something about foxes and dogs. I couldn't make much sense of it."

"Dog Fox," Adam pointed out. "I was talking about Dog Fox. Don't you remember? The story I told you. Years ago, when we first met. The code name of the agent who went to Auschwitz? It's part of what I wanted to talk over with you..."

"Adam, you're not making much sense either. Are you all right?"

"I'm fine, I'm fine."

"I heard you banged your head, and..."

"Nothing to worry about," he interrupted. "My skull's still very much intact."

"What the hell were you doing up there in the mountains all alone?"

"Thinking. Centring myself. Communing. Not so different from what you used to do when you were younger. But something came rather clear to me when I banged my head. That's partly why I wanted to talk to you. I wanted to apologize."

For days I'd been wondering what it would be like to talk to Adam again. Anger, resentment, the bitterness of his contempt – for all of these I had prepared myself. Yet nowhere in my expectations had the possibility of apology figured. Not after all that had come between us.

"There's no need for that. I always knew there was a price for the choice I made."

After several moments of silence, Adam said in a colder voice, "I don't think you understand. I wasn't thinking about that. It's something else I need to get clear with you. Something that happened between us right at the start, in our first big conversation, that night at High Sugden."

"Oh yes? What was that?"

"I have the clearest memory of making you feel ridiculous because you had the courage to tell me what you really believed. I want to try to put that right. You were so open with me at that time, so lacking in all the defensive irony I'd got used to at home and at school. And what did I do? I set about turning you into the cold-blooded sort of sceptic they'd made of me, infecting you with the virus of my own disbelief. I watched it changing you then, and it got worse at Cambridge. It still bothers me to think about it."

I was frowning as I said, "That's not how I remember it."

"The truth is," he continued, as though I hadn't spoken, "I believed in nothing. Not even in that existentialist bill of goods I tried to sell you. Least of all in myself. That's why all that heady stuff about anguish and absurdity, about dread and nothingness and bad faith appealed to me so much. I was a prime specimen of all of them. As for *nausea* – I was sick to death of myself. Sick as only an adolescent narcissist can be. And there you were, holding on to the kind of dream I'd once had in Africa as a child – a dream of nature, of the sacred wholeness of things. You were trying to stay true to the claims of that vision, making poetry from what you heard. And I talked you out of it."

"That's not at all the way I see it," I said.

But his wry snort stalled me there. "I stopped you writing, didn't I?"

"Well, that was hardly the most grievous loss to English literature since the death of Keats!"

"Maybe not," he said, "but I killed off the poet in you, and that's a terrible thing to do. The minute you started paying attention to me, you stopped listening to the Soul of the World."

So strange was the assertion that for a moment we were at an impasse. I had no idea what he meant. I wished he was there with me in the room so that I could see what he looked like now, what kind of light was in his eyes. And why were we talking about this when so much else remained unresolved between us?

"That's your language, not mine," I answered. "Sorry to contradict you, Adam, but I really can't remember ever listening to the 'Soul of the World'. I don't even pretend to know what you mean by it."

"You knew back then. You didn't call it that, but you knew what it was all right. You were trying to speak its language until I convinced you it was a waste of time."

For a single, vivid instant it was like being dropped vertically down a shaft through time. I was back there, in the shadowy cleft of a crag, listening to the rush of water among ferns and stones, in a state of passionate attention such as I had never quite attained again. Briefly I felt an irrepressible pang of loss for all that was as nameless as it was irretrievable, and so far gone down the years that it resonated through me with no greater force than the muffled plop of a stone dropped down a well. Then I was back in the present, pouring wine into a glass with my free hand, wondering what on earth to make of this.

I said, "Adam, whatever else went wrong between us, you must know that I owe just about everything I've achieved to you and Hal. That's why I'm here. That's why I came – to try and get the two of you back together again."

Out of the uncertain silence down the line Adam said, "Marina tells me he's in rather a bad way."

"He's had a second stroke. He's lost the use of his right side, and his speech is barely comprehensible. But he very much wants to see you."

"Is he in hospital?"

"He was, but there wasn't much they could do for him, and they needed the bed."

"So who's looking after him?"

"Marjorie Cockroft. Do you remember her?"

"Vaguely. Big woman? Lived down in Sugden Foot?"

"That's her. And the District Nurse comes in to help. The point is, he wants to see *you*. Both of you."

After a further pause I said, "Adam, I don't know how long he's got."

"It's that bad?"

"Well, he's seventy-nine now... And with nothing much else left to live for. Not after everything that matters to him has gone so desperately wrong." I picked up the glass, took a sip. "I think it's only the chance of seeing you two again that's keeping him alive."

I heard Adam draw in his breath. "Marina's thinking of going."

"You wouldn't let her travel alone?"

"Allegra will probably go with her."

"That's good. But what about you? He wants to see you too."

"I haven't made up my mind."

"Surely you can forgive him after all these years?"

"Maybe. I don't know. But that's not it."

"Then what?"

When Adam's answer came, its coldness chilled me. "There are other calls on me."

"Oh, right, yes," I said in a voice still colder than his own, "I was forgetting that you seem to have become an important player in the snake-oil trade."

"Shall we not quarrel?" Adam said quietly after another pause. "I'd made up my mind not to lose my temper with you. I don't think either of us needs that now."

"Yes, let's not," I said. "I'm sorry I said that. But the fact is I'm having a hard time understanding what you're about these days. Marina's probably told you – I've just got back from Equatoria. I can't square what's happening there with the kind of life you seem to be living here."

"But then you don't really know what I'm doing, do you?"

"Just enough to worry me. So tell me: what is The Heartsease Foundation?"

"How do you know about that?"

"I read a note left for Sam and Jago in the cottage."

After several moments Adam took a decision. "Heartsease is an American philanthropic foundation. We're affiliated to it here."

"And it does what exactly?"

"Look, I don't really want to get into that right now, but its thinking is quite radical, believe me – particularly its interest in the way changes come about."

"Which could mean anything," I said. "So, all this mumbo-jumbo about the sibyls and astrology and the goddess Isis – what's that about?" When he didn't answer at once I said, "What the hell are you doing with your life, Adam? There was a time when you were as serious as anyone I know about what's going on in the real world. You'd have had no time for all this irrational claptrap."

He sighed at the edge of sarcasm in my voice. "Let's not talk about this over the phone," he said. "We have to talk properly or not at all."

"Sure."

"All right," he said. "I'm tied up all weekend, at least till Sunday evening. Can you wait until then?"

"Sunday evening! You expect me to sit on my hands for all that time while you and your friends play mystical charades and your father might be dying?"

Adam's response, when it came, took me by surprise. "Marina tells me that you had a dream on the way here – a dream in which you were dragging your father's corpse along with you. Is that right?"

"Yes, but I don't see what that has to do with anything."

"Just that it seems I'm not the only one being summoned by his father."

Disconcerted I said, "I wouldn't put it quite that way."

"Why not?"

"Well for a start, Hal isn't *summoning* you – he's *asking* you to come. And then your father's still alive, remember. Mine has been dead for a long time."

As if such considerations were of no consequence, Adam said in a calm and deliberate tone, "I think that you and your father need to talk.

Snorting again, I said, "I think you've just stolen my big line. In my world the living have more pressing claims than the dead. In fact, I can't quite believe we're having this conversation. This isn't about me anyway. It's about you, Adam, and whether or not you can bring yourself to care enough for your father to go back and see him."

"It seems it's about both of us," he replied. "It looks like we're in this together, just as we always have been. In fact I'm beginning to wonder whether we shouldn't strike a deal, you and me."

"What kind of deal?"

"A straight exchange. I'll talk to my father if you'll talk to yours."

I thought about that for a moment and decided to humour him. "Well, if it's the only way I can get you to go back to High Sugden..."

"We're agreed then?"

"Agreed. But I've no idea how I'd keep my end of the deal."

"Don't worry about that. I have. You can sleep at the cottage tonight, but it's needed for the next few days, so you'll have to move out in the morning. I'll speak to Fra Pietro and ask him if you can stay in the visitor's cell at the *convento*. It's the ideal place for you to prepare. You need a period of fasting and silent meditation. You need to reflect on your past – about your father and what he means for you. You might even try to write something about it – that would be good. But try to sidestep your ego. Go for some deep subjectivity."

"Sure," I said, "we journalists are famous for it."

"And I've just had another thought. While you're in the *convento* I'll ask Fra Pietro to tell you a story he told me – the one that finally provided me with some sort of answer to Dog Fox. It's a story about a different kind of proxy."

Again I went along with him. "That sounds interesting. But I'm wondering what happens after that?"

"I can't tell you."

"Why not?"

"Because it's the kind of thing that can't be told – only experienced."

"I see. So I get left on my own for three days with nothing to eat in preparation for some experience you're not prepared to talk about. Right?"

"That's about right."

"You can't seriously think I'm going through with this?"

"I thought we had a deal."

"In honest deals you get to read the small print first."

"This isn't a contractual arrangement. You're asking something of me; I'm proposing something in return – something you're at perfect liberty to refuse."

"Let's be straight with one another for a minute," I said. "As I recall, you were so full of hatred for me the last time we met that you could hardly bear to look at me. That's true, isn't it?"

"Yes, that's true."

"So how do I know I can trust you now?"

"You don't."

"Then why should I go along with what you have in mind?"

"Nobody's forcing you to go along with it. As I just said, you're free to choose. We can leave it here if you like. In fact it might be for the best. It's your decision."

But even as he spoke I realized that I wasn't thinking about him at all. Nor about my dead father. I was thinking about Marina, and where she might be in all of this. "If I stay," I asked, "what will *you* be up to for the next three days?"

"I can't talk to you about that. Not now. Perhaps never. We'll have to see what happens afterwards – if you stay, that is." After a pause he added, "I hope you do. I think Marina hopes so too."

And in that moment, whatever my doubts and reservations, I knew that what had happened between us in the past could be kept from the present no longer, and that the deal was already done.

15
Hal

The past is retrievable only through an act of the imagination. What survives is what we are able to make of it, and I should admit that the account of the early years of my involvement with the Brigshaw family is my own disputable version of those events – a stab at autobiographical fiction written long before my errand to Umbria. Even as I was writing it I understood well enough why that account dried up where it did, and why Hal had played only a shadowy role in its pages. But it's time to bring him out of the shadows now.

Hal Brigshaw then – six foot four inches tall, a big man with big ideas, and a habit, when under pressure, or when trying to articulate some difficult thought, of interlacing the fingers of his hands, raising them at full stretch above his head, and then lowering them slowly to his crown, as though compressing all the available oxygen inside his brain.

I was watching him do that on the night when he took me to see the belly dancers in the nightclub in Port Rokesby. I should have realized that the gesture betrayed more anxiety than his words disclosed. But I was infatuated by the glamour of this new country and ignorant of the reason why Hal had been called away to the meeting of the Inner Cabinet on the night of our arrival. I was young in those days, and idealistic. I didn't know that the government kept a network of informers in place, and I would have found it hard to believe that the author of *The Practice of Freedom* was contemplating the need for a Preventive Detention Act that would cause more unrest in the nation he had helped to found than its tentative grasp on

269

liberty could sustain. Not until later did I learn that Ambrose Fouda and his allies were already in covert negotiations with executives of the Anglo-Equatorial Mining Corporation and certain figures ostensibly attached to the US Trade mission in Port Rokesby, and that they were laying the groundwork for a *coup d'état*. Only then did I understand why Hal saw the necessity for such summary abrogation of their civil liberties.

Since our first encounter at High Sugden, I had always been in awe of Hal as a libertarian thinker and political philosopher. Now he impressed me as a man of action too, one entirely prepared to take whatever measures might be required to protect the stability of Emmanuel's regime. Not that this should have surprised me, because Hal's war record in both the Desert Campaign and the invasion of Italy had proved him capable of acts of extreme courage. I'd once heard Marina ask him just how many people he thought he had killed. "Enough," he had answered her curtly, "to do my bit in ensuring that you and your chums can enjoy the democratic freedoms which you choose to abuse in such trivial ways."

My admiration for him grew. So did my gratitude that so forceful a man should take the trouble to further my education and career. After all, the attitudes and opinions I first brought with me to High Sugden were entirely opposed in spirit to Hal's rational vision of the world. At that time I was often discomfited by his brusque way of sharpening my thinking against the steel of his own uncompromising mind, but it was clear from our first exchanges that Hal was on my side. At least, that was my positive reading of the interest he took in me, though there would be occasions when I wondered whether I had merely chanced along at the right time to be caught up in the strength of his gravitational field as so many other people were, and not always to their advantage. Perhaps I was just luckier than the rest of them, or perhaps his affection for me was genuine from the start? Whatever the case, Hal took me on board, licked me into shape and found ways to make use of me. And because it flattered me to be closely associated with such an impressive figure, I was ready to be used. Even to be used against Adam.

And maybe that was the real reason why I feared Hal as well as admiring him – not because of what he might do to me, but because of what, in an effort to secure his good opinion, I might do to myself.

That concern was already evident when I spoke to Efwa Nkansa at Hal's request. I liked Efwa a lot. She was quick to laugh and eager to please. Her face shone bright with African optimism, and because her attachment to Adam did not preclude a shrewd awareness of her own interests, she proved easy to suborn. Listening to her chatter, I remembered how dismissively Adam had spoken about the falsity of life in Cambridge and saw how Efwa's lack of interest in the life of the mind must have appealed to him as much as her spontaneous warmth and the casual grace with which her body moved. Because she was a woman who nursed no pretensions, Efwa knew where her true strengths lay and how to make the best of them. Like most men, I found it hard to resist her charm.

It quickly emerged that Efwa had ambitions of her own and that she was planning to set up home in the UK with Adam as soon as possible rather than remain in Equatoria for the rest of her life. "I think maybe we will live in London," she declared.

"London's very expensive," I said. "And the trouble is, Adam could have a hard time getting a well-paid job if he doesn't finish his degree."

"His father will help him," Efwa responded cheerfully. "He is an important man."

"In Equatoria he is – but not in the UK. Hal doesn't have much influence there. That's why he thinks Adam should go back to Cambridge." For the first time I saw her face fall. "Of course," I reassured her, "once he's completed his degree, he'll be able to take his pick among any number of good jobs."

"Then, when we go to UK," she said, "he must certainly do that thing."

"I'm sure you're right. But as a student he won't have very much money – not really enough to support you both. It seems a pity that you should have to struggle with financial hardship when he's only got another year to go." I left a pause for her to think about that before adding, "Adam is aware of all this, of course. I think that's why his mind seems made up to stay in Equatoria. He thinks you'll both be happier here. Perhaps you should talk to him about it?"

Afterwards, when Efwa succeeded in convincing Adam not to leave Cambridge, and Hal was thanking me for my part in the affair, I told him that I hadn't really done anything other than help Efwa to see her way a little more clearly. But I knew that wasn't the case. I had set out intending to get the result that Hal wanted, whether it was what Adam wanted or not. And though I happily accepted Hal's verdict that it was all done in the best interests of both Adam and Efwa, I was less sure of it than he was. But then who, at twenty, knows much about anything that matters in a swiftly changing world?

Adam and I flew back to England together near the end of that long vacation, sitting in silence throughout most of the flight. Did he suspect my involvement in Efwa's change of heart? I don't think so, because I had covered my tracks by letting her appear to reach her own conclusions. But not since the days preceding his breakdown had I known him so gloomy and reserved with me. He might have been flying into exile rather than returning to the privileged life of his college. And there had been more genuine warmth in Hal's farewell to me than between the bluff father and his taciturn son.

As for Grace, there was such grief and wistfulness in her grey eyes as she waved us off at the airport that I think our departure can only have increased her restlessness. At one point towards the end of our stay, I even wondered whether she was making up her mind to come back home with us, but Hal did nothing to encourage the thought; and neither, it must be said, did I. On the contrary, in the small amount of time that she and I were left alone together, I tried to suggest that Hal drew much of his strength from having her there with him at his side. Whether she believed me or not is another matter. Whether or not I believed myself is another matter too.

Somehow Adam got through our final year at Cambridge, visiting Efwa during the Christmas and Easter vacations. The high point of the year was Larry Stromberg's production of *The Tempest* in a darkly panelled Jacobean hall, which looked more like an alchemical laboratory than an island. Adam's elusive nature made him perfect casting for Ariel, and his was certainly the most exciting performance. My own role as Stephano made fewer demands, which is why I eventually came away with a better degree than either Adam or Larry. Larry was confident that they could make careers on the stage, so neither took the final exams with great seriousness. By contrast, I swotted into the small hours, knowing that even if I achieved an upper-second, my dad would want to know why I hadn't taken a first.

Towards the end of term, never thinking for a moment that she would accept, I invited Marina to my college's May Ball. As a buffer against rejection, I suggested that a bohemian artist such as she had become would probably have no interest in attending this bourgeois mating ritual, but I thought it worth a try. She came and appeared out of the room I'd rented for her in the Blue Boar, wearing the expensive midnight-blue dress which her father had bought for her birthday three years ago. When I told her that it looked stunning on her, she said, "It seemed a pity not to give it at least one outing."

"You've never worn it before?"

"And probably won't ever again."

"Hal would love to see you in it."

"Yes, but he never will."

"Oh come on," I protested, "I thought you'd have given up fighting him by now."

"I have," she answered, "but that doesn't mean I have to please him."

"Well, we don't have to please anyone but ourselves tonight. Let's enjoy it, shall we?"

"I mean to do just that."

And she did – the champagne, the food, the dance band beating out quicksteps and foxtrots in the hall, the jazz combo in the marquee, the string quartet playing Mozart and Vivaldi in the cloisters, the tall stained glass of the chapel windows illuminated from inside. Marina and I were as relaxed in each other's company as at any time since the night she'd come to my room at High Sugden – which is to say, of course, that she was more relaxed than me.

Over dinner we chatted about Adam for a time. On the few occasions she and I had been together that year, Adam had also been present, so this was our first chance to talk about him freely. What did I really think, she wanted to know, about his commitment to Efwa Nkansa, and how serious was her attachment to him?

I told her I wasn't sure on either count and that, for all I knew, it might be no more than a mutual infatuation that would burn out as quickly as it had flared up.

"That's what I'm afraid of," she said. "I don't understand why mum and dad didn't let Adam stay on in Africa. It would have given them time to find out whether it was going to work."

Later, as we leant on the parapet of the bridge looking down at the punters waiting for the firework display to begin, I risked asking her about her lover in London. "How does he feel about you being here with me tonight?"

"That's over," she said.

"By your choice or his?"

"His actions, my choice."

I nodded. "Can't say I liked him much. Wasn't he a bit old for you anyway?"

"That wasn't the problem – though he did turn out to be too like my father."

"In what way?" I asked, surprised.

"Full of big ideals about how the world should be run. Also a complete rat in his private life. Don't look so surprised – you must know about Hal's affairs!"

"Not really," I mumbled.

"Oh come on, Martin, you can't be that naive."

"Well, I'd wondered of course. I mean, he's very attractive to women, but…" I slid away from half-truths. "Anyway, what about your man? Is he married then?"

"He was. His wife had the sense to leave him. But he still screws around."

"And you were hoping for something else?"

"Yes," she said flatly, "fool that I am."

"I don't think you're a fool."

Marina turned to look at me, shaking her head. "You've never seen any of us very clearly, have you? Not me, not Adam, not Hal. Not even poor old mum, I bet, and she's the simplest of us all. You always think the best of us, don't you? But we're not like you, us Brigshaws. We're not straightforward, not any of us."

"Is that how you think of me?"

"Course I do. You're just about the most honest person I know."

Swallowing, I said, "Do you think it was honest of me to ask you here tonight as if we were just friends? As if I didn't still want you more than anyone I know?"

"Why do you think I came?" she asked. "Do you really want to watch these fireworks? Haven't you got a room in college?"

Marina and I in bed together again then, albeit my narrow single bed, and with a rowdy, drunken noise rising from the room below us on the staircase. I was trembling as I helped her out of the dress, but she smiled and said, "You've done this before."

She was right, of course. During my second year in college my confidence had grown, and a few of the girls who cycled in from Newnham or Homerton had proved responsive to my northern accent and a spurious air of knowing what I was about – an air that soon became more self-possessed. But that night with Marina was different. Our mouths opened softly as they met. My heart swayed as we slipped out of our clothes. Then we lay together on the bed and filled that intimate dark space with kisses and whispers, ignoring the noise from the floor below. Tenderly I gave myself over to love for her, and though it might have been nervous and unseasoned, love it surely was; so I dared to call it by its name.

"But are you sure it's me you love?" she said quietly.

"Of course I'm sure," I answered at once. "I'm absolutely sure."

"You might just be in love with love itself."

"I don't see how there can be a difference. I love being in love, yes. It makes me feel more real, more completely me. But it's you who makes it happen," I insisted. "It's only you I love. It only ever has been you."

So we kissed and held each other more closely still, but when I lay over her, lifting my hand gently to her face, I felt the dampness of tears on her skin.

"What is it?" I pushed myself up to gaze down at her. "Are you all right?"

"It's nothing," she whispered, turning her face away. "I was just thinking,"

"What were you thinking about?"

"I'm sorry. It doesn't matter."

"If you're crying," I said, "it matters. Tell me. What is it?"

In the half-light of the room she turned to look up at me again. Her eyes searched mine, her gaze more vulnerable than I'd ever seen it before.

"Tell me," I said again.

"I was thinking about the abortion."

Softly as that whisper came across the narrow space between us, it pierced right through me.

"I'm sorry," she gasped, "I shouldn't have said anything... It's not fair..."

"Yes, you should. It's part of who you are. It's part of what I love."

"You can't really mean that."

"I do. I do mean it – even though that must have been a terrible time for you."

I shifted my weight to lie beside her again, stroking her cheek with my fingertips, and felt the breath shaking through her.

"The worst thing," she began. "The worst thing was when I knew that..." But again she faltered there.

"What?" I asked, afraid to hear yet feeling her need to speak. "Go on."

"It was as if a presence I had felt inside me vanished. As if a spirit had been there for a while, for a purpose, then left."

Gently I tightened the fold of my arm across her. We lay together in silence, filled with mutual sadness, mourning her loss. Some time later, in the half-light of my room, to the accompaniment of the revellers singing a rugby song on the floor below, I found the courage to say, "Marry me."

"No," she answered at once, "I can't do that."

"Why not?"

"Because it wouldn't be right... Because we don't know who we are yet."

"I know that I love you. I know that I want to be with you."

"Oh God, it's so loving of you," she said ruefully, her eyes closed, "but think about it, Martin. We're still at the start of everything. I've already made big mistakes. If we give away our freedom now, before we've even begun to understand what it means for us, we might end up hating each other."

"I could never hate you," I protested.

"If we don't know who we are," she said, "we don't know what we might do."

"I'm prepared to take that risk."

"I'm not, Martin. Not for myself, and not for you either."

I would have pressed her further, but her voice was too firm. Also, even as I braced myself against it, a part of me, my inward observer, felt secretly relieved by her refusal. Then, for a time, we were overtaken by a further sense of loss – both of us, I think, though each in different ways. So we lay cradled in each other's arms for a long time, each with our own thoughts, uttering no more than a few hesitant sentences of mutual tenderness and consolation, until Marina said that she thought it best if I took her back to the hotel.

Nevertheless, I woke the next morning hoping that something permanent had begun between us, however long it might take to mature; but I was wrong. I didn't even see Marina again until some months later, and by then it had become clear that she was avoiding me. I suspected it already by Graduation Day. Hal and Grace had flown home from Africa for the occasion, but for reasons that were not at all convincing Marina decided not to come to Cambridge with them. Yet I was more relieved than disappointed by the decision, for with her mother and mine chatting together outside the Senate House, I could only look on, flustered and ridiculous in my hood and gown, seriously thankful that Marina was not there to complicate an already fraught situation.

Meanwhile, as my father gazed in wonder down sunlit King's Parade, he was telling Hal that he'd had no idea how cushy a life his son had been living for the past three years. And then, throughout lunch, undeterred by the fact that his experience was largely limited to seafront bars and bazaars, he regaled Hal with his wartime knowledge of Africa "from Cairo to the Cape".

Hal listened patiently enough, and deepened my affection for him by saying in his West Riding accent, "Well, unless I'm much mistaken, Jack, it won't be long before your Martin has seen more of the world than you and me put together." But then he glanced briefly across at Adam, who was furious with his parents for not bringing Efwa out of Africa with them, and added as he looked away again, "As for that lad of mine, I've no idea when he's going to shape up and frame himself."

Adam and I had booked a punt to take our parents along the Backs that afternoon. On the way to Mill Lane we met Larry Stromberg coming out of Fitzbillies, accompanied by a tall person of indeterminate gender wearing a velvet jacket and a pair of purple trousers. Larry paused to nod amiably at my parents. My father stared in amazement at the other person's tangled red hair and blue eye shadow as Larry congratulated Hal on the medium-term success of his efforts to bring the empire of the Philistines down about their ears. Then the pair sauntered off down Trumpington Street with Larry's arm draped round his friend.

When we arrived at the millpond, Adam grabbed the pole and stepped onto the counter of the punt, leaving me holding on to the painter. Hal handed my mother down to sit beside Grace, then he and my father settled themselves on the cushions at Adam's feet. Perched in the bow, I pushed off, scowling at the remote figure of Adam, who poled the punt downstream, safely above it all.

Having expressed her admiration for the woodwork of Queen's Bridge and the view of King's, my mother turned to Grace, remarking what a pity it was that Marina hadn't joined us. If truth were told, she admitted, she and Jack had hoped that something was quietly going on between the Brigshaws' daughter and me.

"Oh I believe there once was," Grace said, smiling. "But you know how these things are. I think they're just good friends these days. Isn't that right, Martin?"' She rested her hand on my mother's arm. "But I'm sure he'll have no difficulty finding a more reliable girlfriend than Marina. It's really her loss. Believe me, if I was twenty years younger I could quite fancy him myself!"

And the two women laughed together at the idea.

Was that the last time I heard Grace laugh, I wonder? I don't suppose it was, but when I look back across my later memories of her, it's a forlorn figure that comes to mind, bitter and pitiful, as though life had reneged on all the early promises it made, disappointing her at every turn.

Hal and Grace did not stay in England for long after that day, but it was long enough for Hal to antagonize both his children once again. I was briefly back home in Calderbridge for my cousin Kathy's wedding at the time, so I didn't hear about their big row until Adam told me about it afterwards. He was still fuming after Hal's renewed attack on his plan to bring Efwa to England and marry her. Marina had sprung to her brother's defence, and succeeded only in calling Hal's frustrated rage down on her own head. When he accused her of degenerating into some sort of artsy trollop with no morals to speak of, she retorted that it was he who had convinced her of the hypocrisy of bourgeois values – not through any of his high-minded rhetoric, but by his furtive escapades outside marriage.

Then it was open warfare between them. Even Adam had been shocked by Marina's vehemence, particularly when she dismissed Hal's involvement in African affairs as no more than a further twist in the history of white colonialism. Hal might have set himself up as an autocrat playing at politics in Equatoria, she declared, but he shouldn't delude himself into thinking that anyone took him seriously in the UK – least of all his own children.

Astonishingly the row ended with Marina standing her ground unshaken, while Hal stormed out of the flat into the London night, leaving Grace to repair the damage as best she could before making her way back to their hotel by taxi.

At her mother's entreaty, Marina had turned up the next day for a brief and uneasy show of reconciliation before Hal and Grace flew back to Equatoria. After they'd gone, Marina told

Adam she thought he was a fool to be contemplating marriage. Why was he mortgaging his whole life that way when it had scarcely yet begun? Had he learnt nothing from their parents' disastrous relationship? As for herself, she was a free woman and intended to remain so for the rest of her days.

Whether Adam noticed how upset I was by this absolute pronouncement, I don't know, but after hearing what Marina had said I paid little attention to whatever else he tried to tell me that day. Her declaration felt like a deliberate rebuff to my own hopes. How could she imagine that what I felt for her might amount to nothing more than an imposition on her freedom? Wasn't freedom the single most important value I'd learnt at the feet of the father she fought? In any case, if she felt that way, why hadn't she told me so directly, face to face?

I decided it was time I started to look after myself.

I took up the contacts in television that Hal had given to me. The people who interviewed me for NTV were impressed by the work I'd done in Equatoria. I was signed up for the company's trainee programme. My intuition that a whole new world of communication was opening up across the planet had proved sound, and I was in that world now, not too far from the start of it and ready to go. My ambition grew. What mattered was my career. Get that right and everything else would take care of itself.

Not long afterwards, Adam astounded me by announcing that he had decided not to chance a career on the stage after all. He was going to return to Equatoria and begin married life with Efwa there. I could make little sense of what seemed to me a waste of his talents. When I learnt later that he was taking a post in one of the new government secondary schools, two hundred miles upcountry from Port Rokesby in Emmanuel's hometown, Fontonfarom, I felt confirmed in that judgement. But by that time I was too busy pursuing my own career to spend much time worrying over the thought of my friend languishing in a bush town ringed by rainforest. If that was what his fugitive spirit wanted, who was I to argue? So I wished him good luck and promised to stay in touch.

I hadn't been at NTV long when news came through of political developments in Equatoria. On his return to the country, Hal must have decided that Fouda and his cronies did indeed represent a threat to the stability of Emmanuel's regime. Despite the qualms of the more tender-minded cabinet members, he and Kanza Kutu, the powerful Minister of the Interior, persuaded Emmanuel of the need to introduce a Preventive Detention Bill to parliament and get it quickly onto the Statute Book. As soon as the measure was passed, Fouda and four members of his party were arrested and confined without trial in Makombe Castle.

Predictably, the British press condemned what it saw as a shameless breach of civil liberties. Meanwhile, in Equatoria, the single newspaper not directly under the PLP's control ridiculed the inadequate legal safeguards built into the Act. For the first time since independence, grumblings of unease were heard throughout the country. They sounded loudest among the lawyers and businessmen in Port Rokesby and in the tribal councils of the Eastern Region, where opposition to the government had remained strong under the conservative influence of the Olun of Bamutu. Then discontent turned to outrage when the Olun's most distinguished spokesman was also detained for his alleged involvement in a conspiracy against the State. Rioting broke out in the streets of Bamutu, and more arrests were made.

Shortly afterwards, one of the PLP's Regional Commissioners was accused of amassing a private fortune by imposing fraudulent taxes on local farmers. In an effort to demonstrate the impartiality of the law, the man was arrested, tried and given a long prison sentence. But rather than appeasing discontent, this action encouraged complaints against corrupt practices right across the country. Too many local officials were half-educated party activists who had proved useful in rallying the masses during the struggle for independence, and were now reaping their rewards by abusing their positions of power. That it could prove unwise to challenge such "Party Hard Boys" became apparent when Kanza Kutu authorized further controversial arrests under the provisions of the Preventive Detention Act.

I remember trying to defend these measures to a hard-bitten old journalist, once a foreign correspondent, who was now desk-bound at NTV. I told him that Emmanuel and Hal were my friends, that they were visionaries, and that their project was too important to let subversive factions or a few corrupt party cadres endanger its achievements.

"It may be unthinkable to imprison anyone without trial here in the UK," I argued, "but you can't judge the new African nations by our standards. They're coping with the stresses of a whole new world, a whole new way of doing things. They're bound to get some things wrong."

"Nice line in loyalty, old son," he replied. "It looks good on you. Only thing is, you'd best wear it with a dash of cynicism, or this bloody job will drive you mad!"

I was far away, working on my first assignment in Vietnam, when I heard reports of the attempt on the life of Emmanuel Adjouna – an attempt which took place on the football field of his hometown, Fontonfarom.

I learnt later that Adam and Efwa were seated under a palm-thatched awning with the local dignitaries and representatives from the Secondary School when the President's open-topped limousine drove into the football field flanked by an escort of motorcycle riders and followed by a convoy of party cars. A big crowd had been waiting for hours, waving banners and flags as they listened to the public-address system crackling out party anthems at ear-splitting volume. The dry season was nearing its end, and the sky lowered thunderously mauve above them.

I'd been to Fontonfarom, and knew how the air always smelt of wood smoke and a hot swirl of ash from the refuse dump across the marsh outside the town. It must have felt as though the afternoon was burning on a long, slow fuse.

At the first sight of the presidential limousine, the tape on the loudspeakers stopped and the Police Band struck up the chords of the Founder's Hymn. Standing between the awning and the flag-decked rostrum on which Emmanuel would make his speech, the school choir began to sing above the shouts and cheering of the crowd. Policemen in their flowerpot tarbooshes strained to hold back the crush as the presidential limousine paraded around the ground with Emmanuel Adjouna holding his arms high above his head, twirling a white handkerchief in his right hand and beaming his famous smile. The words of the hymn may have proclaimed him liberator, saviour and redeemer of the land, but that day, dressed in his striped peasant smock – emblem of his identity with the common man – he was the favourite son come home to be honoured and embraced by those who loved him. His face revealed his appetite for adoration. He delighted in the tribute of flowers thrown by the market women, who jiggled in a dance of welcome. He must have been all the more astounded, therefore, when something else was lobbed out of the jubilant crowd – something small, dark and unidentifiable that broke open around his car in a flash of harsh, disintegrating light.

16
Convento

I did not sleep well that night in the cottage. Shortly after Adam rang off, Captain Midnight turned up with his latest woman and for what felt like a session long enough to flight-test all the sexual positions known to man the night was loud with their noise. After that my sleep was troubled by dreams, of which one in particular stayed with me.

I was sorting out a century of junk stacked in an attic room at Cripplegate Chambers – old ledgers, unsorted papers, broken furniture and Victorian engravings with cracked glass. Though I'd been warned the room was haunted, I didn't believe it, yet when I gave up on the mess in despair and tried to pull the door shut behind me, it felt as though the handle on the other side was gripped by strong hands. I couldn't see what held the door against my pull, but I could feel its strength and it frightened me. When I called for help, my voice wouldn't work properly. Yet some sort of muffled shout escaped me as I lurched awake in thin light.

I got up early, went outside, and was watching the swallows skittering in the early light above the wooded hill when the whole landscape around the cottage seemed to change its appearance. What had simply been a sunlit hill now struck me as a recumbent woman's pregnant belly. Beyond it, her breasts were formed by a higher saddle of twinned hills. The terraced groves to my far right covered the open curve of her left thigh, while her right thigh rose to the knee at the crown of the hill on which the village proper stood. The cottage lay cradled in her lap, and her groin was shaped by a bushy cleft of steep shadow, where some household rubbish had been tipped beyond the nearest stretch of olive trees.

Once having seen the figure, it seemed impossible not to have noticed it before. Shaking my head, I went back inside to get some breakfast, and when I returned to the blue table under the bamboo awning, the illusion was still intact. A few minutes later the brown-robed figure of Fra Pietro appeared round the bend of the track. I got up to greet him, eager to ask whether this illusion of a gigantic female figure in the landscape was common knowledge.

As I tried to point out what I'd seen, the friar looked around uncertainly, then he stared at me bemused. But we were both standing, and the view had altered with that angle of vision, so I persuaded him to sit at the table, gazing up in the direction I pointed, while I traced the woman's massive contours with my finger.

"Those far hills are her breasts," I insisted, "and that nearer hill is her belly. Then if you follow the slopes down you can make out her thighs. Don't you see? It's as if we're in the lap of a giantess, looking up at her."

Obligingly he peered into the sunlight. His head moved from one side to the other, then he turned to smile at me. I looked back at the landscape and saw only what he was seeing: the rounded contours of densely wooded hills banked steeply behind each other.

"I understand that you wish to come to the *convento*?" he said quietly.

"It's Adam's idea," I said.

Fra Pietro nodded. "I know something of the terrible things you have seen. I think that after one has suffered to look at such things, it is wise to come out of the world. For a time, yes? If not, the heart can – *soffocare?* – suffocate, I think." The fingers of one hand fluttered as if tracing the flight path of a moth. He shrugged and smiled. "In our *convento* you will have time to bring a little peace to the soul. Come," he said, "you have a bag? You will permit?"

As I drove him around the village walls, we passed no one except an old woman dressed in black who walked slowly with her back bent and her slight weight propped on a stick. In her other hand she held a posy of flowers.

"Serafina…" Fra Pietro smiled. "Two hundred years old, I think, and every morning she makes her offering to the Madonna!"

In the wing mirror, I saw the old lady stop to watch me pull up on a verge of rough grass across from the *convento*. The walls of the building glowed softly pink in the dry light. I switched off the engine. Except for the sound of water pouring into a cistern and the tap of the old woman's stick against the road, the morning was very still.

"Come, come," fussed Fra Pietro, "welcome." He opened a small door in the wall, ushered me through, and I stepped out of this world.

The day's heat had already begun to build, but there was respite in the cool, reclusive shade of the *convento*. I had expected to be affronted by the kind of overdressed religiosity a northerner associates with Italian Catholicism – a taint of incense in the air, a display of old bones and murky bits of cartilage encased in glass reliquaries. Instead I entered a bare, white-plastered hall with a vase of lilies on a simple table and low arched doors on three sides. Fra Pietro led me through the farthest door, where we stepped out into a cloister. At the centre of its courtyard a fountain shivered in the sunlight.

"Once this was a large community," the friar was saying. "But now only few of us remain. I regret that my brothers have no English, but Adam has told me that you wish to make a silent retreat and that you will not eat with us, so it's no problem. It is very quiet here. Come, I will show you the room we have for you."

I followed him round the cloister to where a flight of stone stairs climbed from the far corner, each tread so scooped by wear that I guessed some parts of this building were much older than its exterior suggested. At the top we came out into an upper corridor, where he opened the door on a narrow room and ushered me inside. Light slanted through Romanesque windows piercing the bare stone walls on two sides. Under one of them, a single bed occupied a corner of the room. Under the other stood a desk with an inkwell, three drawers and a chair. On the white-plastered inner wall hung a large icon of the crucifixion with a prie-dieu beneath it. The cell was otherwise empty, except for two wire coat hangers dangling from a spike next to a cupboard.

"Is very simple," said Fra Pietro, "but you will be comfortable, I think?"

The window above the bed looked down where the lane wound round the *convento* to dip towards a shady glen with a bridge. From there it climbed into the wooded hills towards Gabriella's villa. Not a breath of wind disturbed the trees. The other view, from the desk, looked south towards the distant plain, where a train sped silently along the tracks. I looked back at my quarters, wondering whether I could live with that crucifix for the next three days.

Fra Pietro had taken my narrow-eyed gaze for admiration. "It's wonderful, yes? A copy, of course. The original is in the Basilica of Santa Chiara in Assisi. I love how our Lord's arms are open as in an embrace, yes? An embrace wide enough, I think, to take in all the sufferings of the world. But come." He opened the cupboard to reveal a washbasin with a shaving mirror and shelf above it.

"The water is good to drink," he said. "From our spring. And when you wish to make a bath, then you must come this way." He took me out onto the landing and opened a door on a cubicle large enough to hold a lavatory and an open shower. "Through here," he said, gesturing me along the corridor towards another flight of steps, "you can come to the roof."

I followed him up the steps and out onto a flat roof terrace with a low parapet. Light blazed out of the immaculate blue sky. Turning my back to the sun, I saw the campanile rising from the chapel roof, and beyond, at the top of the hill, the walls of Fontanalba. As Fra Pietro gazed out across the parapet towards the hills, I heard my voice saying, "So what is this event they're organizing at the villa?"

Fra Pietro blinked at me in the heat. "It's a big conference which happens each year. For people that have a great interest in the art and philosophy of the Quattrocento – Marsilio Ficino... Pico della Mirandola... Botticelli. Also the music – *arie antiche*. Many poets and thinkers will come."

"I see. And Adam's never mentioned anything to you about the sun at midnight?"

He looked at me in surprise, puzzled by this arbitrary shift of attention. "The sun at midnight? Ah, you mean *La leggenda di Fontanalba*? Yes, of course, we have talked of this sometimes. But I think it is Lorenzo who is interested in this old story."

"The other night," I said, "before Adam came back, when you and Larry were talking about him – I got the impression he thought you knew where Adam was – what he was doing in the mountains?"

The friar shrugged and made a small, self-effacing moue.

"Yet you didn't seem to want to talk about it," I pressed. "All you said was that you and Adam had been talking about St Francis."

"Yes." Fra Pietro looked uncomfortably away. For a moment I thought he was about to say nothing further, but then he added, "Lorenzo and I... we do not see – how do you say it? – eyes to eyes? But Adam – he is a serious man. When we have talked together about the shepherd in the story, we have also talked of more serious things."

"What kind of things?"

"Mostly we have talked about the Poverello, and how he saw the presence of God in the beauty of the earth. We have talked also of the true thing – the historical thing – that has happened when he climbed into the mountains."

"Which was?"

Fra Pietro seemed mildly amazed by my ignorance. "At La Verna the Seraph came to him from heaven. Francesco was given a vision of a man crucified among his wings of fire. The *beata stigmata* appeared on his hands and feet at that time. Also the wound in his side."

"And you consider that history rather than myth?"

"Of course. They are God's wounds. Many people saw them. They were with the Poverello till death. What Dante has called *l'ultimo sigillo*. The final seal of his union with Christ. That he is become an instrument for God."

Scarcely a breath of air moved on the terrace. With a flattened palm Fra Pietro consoled the tonsured crown of his head. "The day will be very hot, I think. Shall we go inside?"

"Is that the story that Adam wanted you to tell me – the story of St Francis on the mountain?"

The friar frowned in perplexity. "Excuse me?"

"He said something about a story you'd told him. He wanted you to pass it on to me."

"Adam has said nothing to me of this."

"Must have forgotten. He said it was a story about a proxy."

Fra Pietro was already descending the steps. "I don't understand this word."

"Proxy? It means a person who does something instead of someone else. On their behalf."

"Ah yes! Proxy! *Una persona al posto di un'altra*. Now I understand. I think Adam means the story which I have told him about Maximilian."

"Maximilian?"

At the bottom of the steps Fra Pietro smiled up at me. "Maximilian Kolbe," he nodded. "He is the saint of Auschwitz. He is a saint who, like yourself, was also a journalist. Yes, I think perhaps this story will speak to you, my friend."

*

Back in the cell, I slipped off my shoes and stretched out on the bed while Fra Pietro settled himself in the chair by the window to share the story with me.

"It begins in Poland," he said, "in a small town called Zduńska Wola, not far from Łodź, which is a city of industry where clothings are made. A weaver called Julius Kolbe once lived there with his wife Maria. They are hard workers, pious people who are members of the Third Order of San Francesco, which is for those who must live in the world. Also each year Julius makes the pilgrimage to Jasna Góra – the Bright Mountain – where is the holy sanctuary of Our Lady of Częstochowa. She is the Black Madonna, who is deeply loved in *Polonia* – as also here in Fontanalba."

Fra Pietro went on to tell me that Julius and Maria Kolbe had been blessed with five sons. The second, born in 1894, was baptized Rajmund, though he was affectionately known to his mother as Mundzio. He had grown up as a normal, lively boy until he was ten years old, when his behaviour suddenly changed. He became much quieter and more withdrawn, spending an unusual amount of time kneeling before the family's shrine to the Black Madonna. One day, finding him there in tears, his mother insisted he tell her what was wrong.

"At last," said Fra Pietro, "the boy makes his confession. Some time before this day he has caused some trouble in the house because of his mischief, and his mother has said, 'Mundzio, Mundzio, what kind of man will you become?' Of course, always a mother will say such a thing when her child is a trouble to her, yes? But the question touches this boy in his heart. He kneels alone to pray for forgiveness at the shrine of Our Lady and asks the question to her. 'What kind of man shall I be?' he asks, and so innocent is his prayer that immediately the Holy Mother appears in front of him. She is holding in her hands two crowns. She explains to him that the white crown is for a life of purity and the red one is the crown for martyrdom. She asks him which crown he will choose for himself, and

Mundzio says, 'I will take both.' When he became a young man Mundzio dreamt to be glorious as a soldier fighting in war, like San Francesco, who was a knight in his youthful days. But his mother has persuaded him to follow the true path of the Poverello and serve God as a Knight of Christ. So he took for himself the name of Maximilian, a saint who was martyred in ancient days because he refused to become a soldier like his father and fight in the wars."

Fra Pietro was warming to his theme. Picking his way through the language, he spoke of a modest young man, both scholarly and zealous, and utterly devoted to the Virgin Mary. Despite his weak tubercular constitution, Maximilian resolved to create a new knightly Militia of Franciscan Friars consecrated to the service of the Madonna – the *Militia Immaculatæ*. Their mission would be to combat the evils of a world in the throes of revolution and world war – a war in which his own homeland had been the principal battleground of the eastern front. A war in which his father, who was a Polish nationalist, was captured by the Russians and hanged as a traitor.

Maximilian was in Rome at the time of his father's death, and it was there that he first became inflamed with missionary fervour. At first just six of his Franciscan brothers were inspired to action by his vision of an international Christian militia, but from this small beginning, he began to conceive of a crusade that would reach all over the world. In 1918 Maximilian was ordained as a priest, and only a year later, Benedict XV gave the papal blessing to his *Militia Immaculatæ*, which grew to become one of the largest and most influential religious communities.

"Soon they built a village in Poland. A newspaper was written and printed there, which was read by many people. There was a radio station and industries – not for making money, you understand, but to feed the community and to spread the word of Maximilian's love for the Immaculate Mother of his childhood vision. Then in September of 1939 Germany invaded Poland, and Maximilian and his Franciscan brothers were arrested by German troops because of their links with the Polish intelligentsia. After much suffering, he was sent to the forced-labour camp at Auschwitz.

"There are many stories of how he has given strength to others in the camp. Those who have come out of that place speak of him with love and wonder. They tell how always there are too many sick and hungry there, but Maximilian, who was never strong and often ill, would make others go to the hospital before himself. One man told how he had carried dead bodies to the fire with him. When that man shouted out against God, Maximilian said to him that hate could do nothing, for it is only love that creates." Fra Pietro held open his hands. "He was truly a man. A saintly man. A man who has understood that when San Francesco spoke of poverty he has meant for us not only to be poor in money and things of the world, but to be poor also in self. To refuse to possess even life itself when life requires it of us. Truly he was a man not like other men. Yet here is a question for you: is the life of such a man of value more than any other man?"

Evidently the question was not rhetorical: Fra Pietro was waiting for my answer. "It depends what you mean," I said. "In one sense of course it is. Why else would we be talking about him when there are tens of thousands who died in Auschwitz about whom we know nothing? But I suppose in another sense..." I faltered, thinking of the many people I'd seen die in wretched circumstances, unattended by any saving miracle or grace. "I don't know," I said. "I don't know how you make such judgements."

Fra Pietro nodded. "Perhaps only for oneself," he said, "only for the life that we are given. But when it was time to make such judgement, Maximilian had no doubt. It happened like this. It was July in 1941 and very hot. One day a prisoner has escaped from a *Kommando* working on the farm. The rule is that when one man escapes, a certain number of men who live in the same block must die. This man is from Maximilian's block. All day he and his comrades have stood in the sun. At last the officers come to choose who are the ones to die. They inspect the first line. An officer points to a man. The others move away and the next line comes forward. Another man is chosen. And it goes on until one man cries, "Oh my poor wife and children!" He is a soldier in the Polish army. Now he will die for nothing he has done, and who will care for his family?

"In this moment another man comes from his line. He wears glasses and is very weak, but he takes off his cap and presents himself before the officers. 'What does this Polish pig want?' one of the officers says. Maximilian Kolbe answers him: 'I am a Catholic priest. Take me in that man's place. I will die for him.'"

Fra Pietro released his breath in an expressive shrug. "If the number is right, the officers don't care if this man or the other man will die. Maximilian has offered himself. He gives himself as proxy, yes? For them better a weak man dies than one who is strong to work. So Maximilian and the other *condannati* are taken away to a dark place, under the ground, made of concrete. Like a cellar."

"A bunker."

"A bunker, yes. They have no clothings when they go in there. They will have no food to eat. When they go into that place they are already dead men. There is only the dying remains to do." He glanced across at me again. "In Africa we have seen such death, you and I. We know how it is slow, how it is full of pain. We have seen that such death has no dignity. But there is one thing that these men have. They have with them a priest. A priest who will pray with them and comfort them. A priest who has chosen to suffer with them, who gives his life so that another man might live, and who will be with them in the hour of their death. One by one they die, until only Maximilian is left alive. In the end they inject acid into him and Maximilian Kolbe dies on the fourteenth day of August in 1941. But I think, my friend, by the free choice he has made to die in the place of another man, Maximilian has already defeated all the powers of death."

For a few moments Fra Pietro sat in silence with his eyes closed and his palms together at his lips as though in silent prayer. Then he drew in his breath, lowered his hands and looked across at me where I lay on the bed.

"I think this is the story that Adam wished for you to hear. It is a noble story, yes? A story that answers the question some have asked about where was God in Auschwitz. He was there in the cell with Maximilian and his brothers. He was there because – just as Maximilian has said – God is everywhere."

"But as you've said yourself," I retorted, "people are still dying everywhere too – dying in terrible ways, in circumstances of extreme cruelty."

"This is true," Fra Pietro agreed, nodding his head. "But has not Maximilian shown us what we must do in the face of such evil? He has shown us once more how it is to love. He has shown us that we cannot rise over the evil in the world or stand aside from it as if it was not also ours. Rather we must go under it – is that how you say?"

"You mean *undergo* it."

"Yes, undergo. We must undergo it in the deep places of our heart and our imagination. We must undergo it as Maximilian has done, knowing that this evil also is human. We must try to pass through the *inferno* without falling asleep down there, or into despair. And we must trust that life will open once more into love on the other side." He looked at me as if for confirmation. "Is not this the only good way to live with what we have seen, you and I?"

Not long after that, having made sure that I had everything I needed, Fra Pietro left to go about the customary ritual of his day. I lay with my eyes closed in the silence of the bare cell under the mild gaze of the crucified Christ, conscious of many things, but the presence of God was not among them.

Fra Pietro had promised that a stay in his *convento* would bring peace to my soul, but I could see no chance of that. On the contrary, everything he had said had left my heart heavy and my head agitated by further questions. So, as Adam must have done before me, I juxtaposed the story of Dog Fox with that of Maximilian Kolbe and tried to balance the equation.

I couldn't make it work. Hours went by, hours in which I wallowed between spurts of wakefulness and longer bouts of sleep. I remember the tinny clang of a bell ringing somewhere. Two or three times I vaguely registered the noise of traffic outside, of cars changing gear as they negotiated the bend round the *convento* and sped off downhill. On one occasion – it might have been around noon, it was very hot – I got up to drink some water and saw a limousine with shaded windows making that descent. *Mystai*, I remember thinking, *travelling in style*.

Not long afterwards I fell asleep again. Disturbed by what I took for the syncopated thud of a helicopter's rotor beating the air outside, I looked at my watch and was astonished at how much time had passed. Yet the surprise was quickly folded back into sleep, for my dreams had claims on me, and their prolonged phantasmagoria seemed at pains to prove that, even with its senses shuttered and its circuits of consciousness closed down, the mind remains a restless, self-tormenting thing.

Around ten o'clock at night, I came fully awake, got up, drank some water, went to the lavatory, drank another two glasses of water, and knew that I wouldn't sleep.

Quietly, so as not to disturb any of the sleeping brothers, I went back out into the corridor and climbed up to the roof terrace. Beyond a streak of cirrus under an almost full moon, stretched the whole range of summer stars. The night was sweet and warm, less vast than I'd seen in Africa. Yet, standing alone beneath its dizzy reaches, I was struck by the mystery that finds us treading space between wonder that consciousness should exist at all and incredulity that it can be of any consequence when measured against such immensities. For the briefest of moments, my mind stood still. The boundary between exterior and interior space dissolved, and then the stars were neither lifeless globes of burning gas nor evidence for some celestial ministry of light: they were simply, and mysteriously, stars.

When I went back down to the cell, I sat at the desk and took some sheets of paper from a drawer. My senses were so heightened by hunger that I could smell the ink in its china well. So rather than reaching for the finely pointed fibre tip in my jacket pocket, I lifted the old-school pen from its slot in the desk, dipped its nib and began to write.

Not ready for the thoroughgoing effort of self-analysis that Adam had advised, I decided to sketch out a few notes about the events since my arrival in Italy – the cottage in Fontanalba, Captain Midnight, the Villa, my early conversations with Gabriella, Larry and Allegra. They were no more than thumbnail jottings, the sort of memoranda I used as a journalist to capture first impressions. Then opening lines of a poem emerged – a poem about the dream of my father.

> *Long after I had thought you safely dead*
> *you came to me in sleep, where we two*
> *walked together, side by side,*
> *trying the beer in certain pubs you knew.*

What followed was lame at best, but charged with feeling. I felt confident only of what I thought might turn out to be the four last lines:

> *I jumped awake at that, appalled to know*
> *You dead again with no one standing by*
> *To help or carry you away, and I*
> *Still shaking in my sweat, unable still to let you go.*

For some time I struggled to pull the rest of the poem together, but it resisted all my efforts, so I gave up in frustration. Then I lay, thinking about Marina, wondering what she was doing now, and feeling almost as cut off from her as if she had been swept out of my life once again, abducted by circumstance, or by powers stronger than mine, into some underworld region beyond my reach.

From my bed I watched the first light break. Eventually I must have fallen asleep to the plainsong Latin of the brothers chanting somewhere below, invoking hosts of angels along with sun and moon and stars to join them in their praise.

Hours later I woke up, famished and alert.

17
Emmanuel

When I came to discuss with Hal what had happened in Equatoria, he told me he had remained certain of Emmanuel's ability to hold the country together until the attempt on his life at Fontonfarom. Difficulties were mounting, of course. Factional struggles had broken out inside the PLP. The judiciary were growing restive, and the country's sterling reserves were depleting rapidly as much needed public spending on roads, health and education coincided with a fall in export commodity prices. All these problems caused Hal restless nights and loaded the opposition press with ammunition, yet Emmanuel's popularity was undiminished. Long after the initial euphoria of independence had faded, his status among the people remained more messianic than political – a benign, regal presence gazing down with care and compassion on the failings of lesser men.

Hal knew and loved his friend too well to share these illusions. He admired his strengths, which were many, while worrying over his weaknesses – the fits of depression that could undermine his customary geniality and exuberance, an irrepressible personal vanity which sometimes belied the humility with which he dedicated himself to the grand vision of a united Africa, and a tendency to dither over unpopular decisions. Being prey to all of these frailties himself, Hal was able to understand them, and stood in the shadows at Emmanuel's back like a corrective daemon, at pains to make sure they remained hidden from public view.

In this respect he had been largely successful. Though his opponents were shrewd enough to see beyond the mask, the majority of Equatoria's seven million people were still spellbound by their president's eloquence and glamour. But now an attempt had been made to kill him, and it had been done on his home terrain, where his support was strongest. Emmanuel had survived the attack, but five utterly innocent people had died around him, with many more badly injured. Everything was changed.

Yet the first reports to come out of Fontonfarom were reassuring. An immediate arrest had been made – that of a mentally disturbed man who had served with the British army during the war and had convinced himself that Emmanuel Adjouna was a traitor to the Empire. But then disturbing rumours began to spread. It was claimed that the poor devil had been talked into committing the crime by the local Police Commissioner, who was in league with Kanza Kutu. According to this version of events, the ambitious Minister of the Interior had planned to take control of the government when Emmanuel was dead.

Kutu vehemently denied the charge, and announced that his agents had uncovered evidence that the true mastermind of the plot was Hanson Osari, the Minister of Finance. Osari was conspiring to take over the government, privatize the various state enterprises which had been founded by the Adjouna regime, and realign the country's position on the international stage. All of this, Kutu claimed, was to be achieved with the covert backing of the CIA, whose agents had been active in Equatoria since the declaration of independence.

For a time Hal sat in the midst of this confusion somewhere close to despair. The only good news was that Emmanuel was still alive and under the protection of an army detachment in the hospital at Fontonfarom. But the party they had founded together was splitting apart along fault lines that were both tribal and ideological. Kutu was a tough-minded political leader of the Tenkora who had been given the Interior Ministry as a reward for his successful efforts to mobilize popular support for the PLP. By contrast, Hanson Osari was a sophisticated Nau businessman with a Harvard degree in Economics who had maintained strong international contacts on both sides of the Atlantic. Originally a supporter of Ambrose Fouda's National Congress Party, his political instincts had led him to switch allegiance to the PLP shortly before it became obvious that Emmanuel would lead the country to independence. In return he had been entrusted with the management of the Ministry of Finance, under close observation from Hal. But theirs had never been an easy relationship, and not only because of their ideological disagreements.

Osari resented Hal's strict supervision of his ministry. The two men had argued ferociously over the stringent provisions of the country's Exchange Control Regulations. As the economic situation deteriorated, their collaboration was increasingly soured by mutual mistrust. Now, in the confused hours following the failed assassination attempt, Hal was ready to be persuaded that Osari's shrewd, ambitious intelligence lay behind the coup.

With the government about to implode and Emmanuel still incapacitated by his wounds, Hal took matters into his own hands. A tense interview with Kanza Kutu confirmed his suspicions. The Minister of the Interior produced evidence of links between Hanson Osari's principal aides and known subversives who had almost certainly been suborned by the CIA. A state of emergency was declared. Restrictions were placed on the press, and three American diplomats were expelled. At the same time, the head of the CID was ordered to detain Hanson Osari and two of his close advisors. To Hal's relief the loyalty of the army seemed assured when the detachment stationed in Fontonfarom obeyed the order to arrest the Regional Commissioner of Police.

For the moment, therefore, everything was under control. But Hal understood that nothing could ever be the same again.

*

In a letter he wrote to me around that time, Adam tried to explain how the sight of three of his students and one of his colleagues lying in their blood while his friend Emmanuel was driven off at speed to the local hospital had convinced him that all political activity is a more or less explicit form of violence. "However deeply in history they may be buried," he insisted, "the roots of political authority always spring from acts of violence – the violence of one people against another, the violence of one class or caste against another. And violence always remains the final sanction. Some radical thinkers may glorify violence as a transformative rite in the struggle for liberation, as the means by which a subject people restores its pride – but not me, not after what I saw in Fontonfarom. And not because I'm squeamish, but out of revulsion at all the implications of what I saw that day. I feel certain now that we must look beyond politics for meaning and value in our lives."

Efwa's response was more pragmatic. The atrocity convinced her that she could live no longer in what she had always considered to be a mere bush town. She had never fully understood why Adam wished to live in Equatoria at all, and had been dismayed by his decision to take a post in Fontonfarom when his father could have secured him a job in one of the best schools in the capital. She would certainly have been happier there among her friends, enjoying the distractions of city life rather than enduring long days in a dusty town surrounded by dense rainforest. She had never felt quite safe there. The electricity supply seemed to break down with every storm. The noises screeching out of the trees at night wore on her nerves. She was disturbed too by the fetish priests of the area, who clung to customs of blood sacrifice that had long been disdained by her own people on the coast. And now the tedium of living among such people had been broken by a thing more terrible than any she had witnessed before. Who was to say that more horrors would not follow?

Efwa was adamant that she could not remain in Fontonfarom. She was going to return to Port Rokesby at once. Adam could join her at the end of the school year, which was only weeks away. They must talk seriously about their future then, a future which would unfold, if she had her way, not in Equatoria, but in the safety and comfort of the UK.

And Efwa did have her way. Worried about how well he would cope there, Adam took her to England that summer. A brief visit to his parents in Port Rokesby had ended in an acrimonious dispute between Adam and Hal, which left both of them bruised and regretful. Because neither would acknowledge it to the other, Grace was more deeply wounded by the row than either of the two men. Later, alone at the airport, she watched her son and his wife fly out of Africa in a jet plane painted with the scarlet-and-green insignia of the country's new airline.

Meanwhile, the arrest of Hanson Osari had left the Ministry of Finance in a state of chaos. The man appointed to replace him lacked both his experience and his contacts abroad; so Hal was required to spend most of his time worrying over the accelerating decline of the country's finances. He would return home late, gloomy and taciturn, only to fall into troubled sleep. On waking again, his temperament, always argumentative, turned ever more irascible, particularly in response to the emotional claims that Grace tried to make on him.

"As I watch events slip out of your father's control," Grace wrote in a letter to Adam some time after his return to England, "I keep recalling the day when we went sledging on the tops above High Sugden. Do you remember how a runner came loose and Hal and Emmanuel ended up in a snowdrift? At the time I joked that they should be careful their attempt to build Utopia in Africa didn't also end in farce. Now I'm worried that it will end in tragedy – and tragedy on a grand scale. Sometimes I wonder whether the world is incorrigible after all, and has always been so. Though I found it painful, I think you made the right decision in leaving Equatoria when you did. It gets harder each day watching Emmanuel and your father estrange themselves from values that the three of us once cherished. Perhaps there are other, less compromised and more durable values for which one might strive? But the truth is – and this is a dreadful admission for a mother to make to her son – the truth is that in these darkening days – war in the Congo, war in Vietnam, not to mention the ever-present threat of an all-consuming nuclear holocaust – I find it difficult to believe in anything very much – except, of course, 'the holiness of the heart's affections'. That at least we must hold dear."

Emmanuel recovered from his injuries, but his confidence was shaken. The days of open government were gone. Now he preferred to concentrate his efforts on the international scene, travelling across Africa and further afield, championing the non-aligned status of the newly developing nations rather than embroiling himself with intractable domestic issues. By the time he returned to Equatoria, shortly before the start of the treason trials, a newly formed Presidential Guard had tightened security around Government House. As far as the people who had brought him to power were concerned, Emmanuel Adjouna was becoming an ever more remote and reclusive figure.

Because Hal had neither the energy nor the inclination to keep her informed of his problems, Grace had no exact notion of the scale of the crisis that he now faced. In retaliation for the expulsion of its diplomats, the US government had reduced development aid to the country. The price of its principal exports was still falling, so public services could now be financed only through massive loans from foreign banks. Numerous corrupt officials had found ingenious ways to embezzle public funds, and the failure of various state-funded enterprises to break even, let alone turn a profit, compounded the government's problems. In these circumstances, Hal was forced to the conclusion that only a steep rise in taxation might retrieve the deteriorating state of the nation's finances. He knew that a drastic budget would be little understood and universally unpopular. Profiteering businessmen were sure to exploit its measures by upping the already inflated prices of imported goods. Peasant farmers would be hard hit and discontent among increasing numbers of unemployed workers might lead to rioting in the towns. But Hal had done his sums and could see no alternative.

The reaction was stronger than he had feared. When the public discovered how much more they were expected to pay for everyday items such as kerosene, cloths of Manchester cotton, shoes, flour, schnapps and beer, the outcry could not be silenced. For the first time since taking power, Emmanuel's party lost the support of the trade unions. The dock workers of Port Rokesby were the first to go on strike. Soon they were joined by the miners of the Central Region and railway workers nationwide. Negotiations towards a settlement broke down. A new state of emergency was declared.

Grace and I discussed this dark time when we met after she returned alone from Equatoria. "Consider the irony," she remarked. "Hal Brigshaw, avowed socialist and anti-imperialist son of a railwayman, whose freedom to think revolutionary thoughts had been financed by the inherited wealth of a brewer's daughter, was now calling on the troops to put down a bunch of African railway workers who were striking over the price of beer!"

"I don't see what else could have been done," I answered her. "The banks were holding the country to ransom. Politically motivated people were exploiting the situation for their own advantage. I don't think that Emmanuel and Hal had any choice."

"Not if you accept their premises," Grace replied. "Which only adds to the irony. They commanded all the instruments of power in a country which they'd founded on principles of freedom and justice, yet could only act in ways that made a mockery of both. You're quite right – they were trapped inside the unintended consequences of their own actions. I didn't get to see much of Emmanuel in those days but Hal... Poor Hal! He was like a man walking through a bad dream."

Hal saw things differently of course. "It was our rotten luck to be hit by so many things at once," he said when I visited him much later. "Yet I'm confident we could have handled all of it peaceably enough if Kanza Kutu's people hadn't been so bloody heavy-handed with the strikers."

That heavy-handedness cost the lives of two dockers and injuries to many more, but it drove the rest of them back to work. The deaths went unreported by the state-owned media, which headlined instead a vituperative campaign of blame against Hanson Osari as the man responsible for the country's financial crisis. The former minister was accused of embezzling government funds on a massive scale – funds now stashed away in private bank accounts abroad. This money had been used to finance the assassination plot and pay agents working to overthrow the government. So even before the treason trial began, Osari and his associates had been found guilty by TV and newspapers. All that remained was for the courts to punish them.

When I asked Hal whether he and Emmanuel had planned that press campaign, he denied it at once. "On the contrary. It was obvious that it might prejudice the outcome of the trial. But Kanza persuaded the Cabinet it was the best way of deflecting public hostility from the government."

"And you went along with it?"

Hal raised his arms and brought the linked palms of his hands down to the top of his head. "Any politician will tell you that there are times when you have to massage the facts if you're not to lose control of events."

Meanwhile Grace looked on in dismay at the way things were going. As a trained lawyer, she was outraged to learn that there would be no jury at the treason trial. Her outrage turned to disbelief when, for want of substantial evidence, the State

Prosecutor conducted his case entirely on the basis of hearsay, rhetoric and innuendo. Wary of her scorn, Hal refused to discuss the trial with her. His silence erupted into rage when she demanded that he publicly dissociate himself from what was happening. And then, to everyone's amazement, the Chief Justice ruled that the prosecution had failed to prove its case.

For a moment it appeared that, despite all the pressures applied against them, the forms of justice had been preserved. But even as the opposition leaders began to celebrate, a meeting of the Inner Cabinet was called. Kanza Kutu insisted it was imperative that Osari and the others be rearrested before they could leave the country. Hal persuaded Emmanuel to exercise his presidential authority by sacking the Chief Justice and appointing a more reliable figure in his place. Then an act was rushed through parliament modifying the constitution in order to give the president powers to overturn the verdicts of specially convened courts in the interests of state security.

"It simply had to be done," Hal insisted to me later. "The future of the country hung on it. If we'd we let Osari go free, he would have galvanized the opposition into disrupting government business. Our whole programme would have been thrown into disarray. Splits would have opened up along political and tribal lines. It was already beginning to happen inside the party itself. Everything was volatile. I was damned sure that if we didn't assert control there was a risk of civil war. Balance all that against the fate of a handful of crooks who had certainly been up to no good even if the case wasn't properly proved in court, and what are you going to do? We were in no doubt. They had to be found guilty. All of them. And yes, I don't deny it, the risks were high. But the alternative was unthinkable."

Hal had come back from Government House late one night to find that Grace had already packed most of her clothes and possessions and intended to leave the country on the next available flight. Though she'd been disgusted by his actions in government and had known for some time about the mistress he kept in one of the wealthier quarters of Port Rokesby, her reasons were neither political nor moral. After all the hopes and hardships and disappointments they had shared together, what she could no longer bear was Hal's refusal to communicate with her about the grave difficulties in which he found himself.

"He'd become unreachable," she told me later. "He was beyond my reach at any rate, and I couldn't live with him like that any more. I told him I was leaving, and that he was going to have to choose which was more important to him – his marriage and his family or his commitment to a political career that was now damaging his soul. I never doubted for a moment which way he would go."

So Hal and Grace lived apart for the following two years, she mostly alone with her dogs in High Sugden, while Hal worked on, striving to retrieve amid the growing unrest of a disenchanted people some vestiges of his vision of a free African commonwealth that might offer a hopeful model to mankind.

One afternoon he was sweating in the torpid heat of his government office when he heard an unusual grinding noise outside. Looking out of the window he saw military vehicles entering the compound of Government House. Then the sound of gunshots cracked along the corridor. Moments later a terrified secretary ran down the corridor screaming that his friend Emmanuel Adjouna was dead, shot twice in the head. In the same intolerable instant Hal Brigshaw understood that such faltering life as remained in the Democratic Republic of Equatoria had been extinguished with him.

18
The Jaws of Orcus

Awake and alert, as though a switch had been thrown. A dog barking somewhere. The tinny peal of the church clock counting five. My throat parched. Afternoon light glaring against my eyes. And hunger. Hunger shaking me between its teeth.

I must have slept for over ten hours, and it was now... which day? I'd flown out of Gatwick on Tuesday morning, slept in the cottage that night, then in the villa, then in the cottage again. And one night – or was it two? – no, I'd slept through most of two *days*, but only one night in the *convento*. Therefore: Saturday. It must be Saturday afternoon, which meant, if I stuck to the absurd deal I'd made, another whole day in this bare cell without food or company.

I pulled myself out of bed, crossed to the basin and drank three glasses of water before scouring my teeth. Lifting my head, I felt it swim.

Saturday afternoon. If the *mystai* had arrived on Friday morning and Adam was prepared to pick me up on Sunday evening, then it seemed likely that the climax of the ceremonies at the villa would happen tonight, quite soon, in just a few hours' time. And if that was when and where the action was, then the journalist in me insisted it was where I had to be.

I took a hot shower, then a cold shower and changed into the last clean clothes in my bag. Checking my phone for messages, I found nothing there. Then I scribbled a quick note of thanks to Fra Pietro, slung my bag over my shoulder and slipped from the room, resolved to leave the *convento* unseen.

I passed down the stairs, round the cloister, and was crossing the tiled floor to the front door when one of the other doors opened. A friar I hadn't seen before came out holding a brass candlestick. We both stopped in surprise. Full-bearded, burly in his brown habit, and built like a wrestler with enormous sandalled feet, he addressed me in throaty Italian. I caught only a greeting and his name: Fra Cherubino.

I smiled back, muttered, "*Mangiare*," and mimicked putting food in my mouth.

"*Ah, mangiare!*" He tutted, smiling, shook his head at the frailty of civilian flesh, crossed the hall with his candlestick and went through another door. A couple of minutes later I was switching on the ignition of my car.

Taking the bend round the *convento* past the walls of the town, I drove down to the hump-backed bridge across the stream, but when I turned up the hill through the valley I was confronted by a road block bearing the sign:

STRADA INTERROTTA

As far as I knew, this road led only to the villa. So was it privately owned? Or did Gabriella pack enough power to get it closed? In either case it seemed that the only way through would be on foot, and hunger pangs had me jumpy at the prospect of a three-mile hike uphill.

I was on the point of giving up and turning back in search of food when a figure appeared out of the pines. He wore a black uniform with a holstered pistol at his belt. Staring at me through sunglasses, he held a two-way radio in his left hand while, with a gesture like that of a man brushing dust from his suit, his right hand signalled for me to go back the way I had come.

A policeman? A private security guard? I didn't know, but the mere fact of his presence was enough to strengthen my suspicions. Before he could speak, I nodded, reversed the car onto the verge and drove back round the bend towards the bridge. Some distance down the lane, I parked on the verge and walked back to a track I'd spotted that might take me up the bank, through the pines, and on up to the next switchback curve on the road.

The track was steep and the ground rough. By the time I clambered the last few yards onto the road, I was sweating and short of breath. Hunger was driving me on, and all my senses were ablaze. Cicadas shrilled in my head. I could taste resin on the air and a hazy fragrance of rosemary and thyme. Clouds glowed in the evening sunlight.

After a couple of miles I came to a place where a stream trickled down the hillside. I knelt to drink, splashed my face and neck, and stood in green shade, thinking, while gnats danced around my head. If an armed sentinel had been posted on the road outside the village, then more guards were probably stationed at the gates to the drive. To avoid them, I would have to strike out across the hill and come at the villa from the cover of the trees. Checking my position against a mental map, I worked out that by following the stream up the hill, keeping my back to the sun, I should be headed in the right direction.

Half an hour later, I was leaning against a turkey oak, panting as I gazed down across the villa. Between my vantage point and the main house, a range of smaller buildings stood beside a large vegetable garden and a walled orchard. Smoke drifted from a slowly burning bonfire, but there was no one about. Nor could I see anyone among the large number of cars parked in the front courtyard of the house. It was well after eight. The light was starting to fail.

When I moved in closer, strains of music lifted across the evening air – a consort of stringed instruments playing a tune so melancholy that it might have been the sound of dusk descending over the hills. Then I saw some movement below – a stately procession walking in pairs by candlelight from the rear door of the house across the courtyard to the arched gateway of the water theatre. More and more people came out of the house, until around thirty of them must have passed under the arch. All of them seemed to be wearing antique dress – high veiled hats and lace-fringed doublets with bulky sleeves, the men in capes, the women in full skirts, like people from another time. Was Marina among them somewhere? I could hear nothing except the music and the sounds of woodland under the setting sun.

It looked possible to edge round the orchard wall closer to the rear of the house, but as I stole quietly past the end cottage, the strains of music faded on the air and a dog began to bark. The coarse din echoed back off the darkening hillside across the whole estate. I froze for a moment, and then decided to make for the cover of the orchard wall before anyone came out. But then another dog answered the first from somewhere nearer the main house. Voices clipped the air, not loud but urgent. An iron gate squeaked open and a uniformed guard came out of the courtyard with a brawny mastiff held on a leash. A second man appeared behind him. I heard a radio crackling, but almost immediately the noise was drowned by a new sound from beyond the courtyard wall – the clatter of many torrents of water cascading among stones. Light from unseen sources illuminated the space beyond the wall. Instantly came the noise of a cheering crowd, then cries of *"Bellissimo!"* and *"Bravo!"*

I guessed that Gabriella's water theatre must now be in operation, perhaps as a grand opening to whatever occult ritual had been devised for the company.

A soft breeze carrying a taint of woodsmoke drifted from the vegetable garden. Then the mastiff by the gate began to bay more loudly. I backed away in the direction from which I'd just come, but the dog that had first raised the alarm was still barking there, and I was caught between them now. Another exchange was followed by a staccato command to the dog. Seconds later the skid of gravel crunched the air behind me. Glancing back, I saw the mastiff hurtling out of the gloom. There was time only to make a half-turn and lift my left arm for protection as the dog leapt, struck me on the side of my chest with its massive paws and sent me flying. I hit the ground winded, scraping palms and knees against sharp gravel. When I turned my head, the dog's mouth was over my face, slavering as it snarled. Moments later the first security man arrived and I was shouting, "Get this fucking animal off me," when he pointed the nose of a pistol at my head.

An hour or so must have passed, during which time I was handcuffed, thoroughly frisked, questioned in halting English, then taken to a disused tack room behind the loggia at the front of the house. I was held there in total silence. The room smelt of leather and dry timber, and was empty except for a table and a few chairs. A deck of cards lay splayed on the table next to a tray, on which stood a moka and four small glasses.

Despite my protests, I was handcuffed to the chair and kept waiting, watched by a guard who spoke no English. My ankles throbbed from where my legs had been kicked apart, my arms were stiffening behind my back. The guard passed the time playing solitaire until his radio spluttered into life. He listened to some brief instructions, then folded the cards away, crossed the room and went out, locking the door behind him. Several minutes later the door opened again, and a huge figure came into the room dressed in a black velvet doublet with slashed sleeves and matching hose, like a character out of Jacobean drama. His hands were gloved, his neck swathed in silk scarves beneath a plumed hat, and the face was entirely concealed behind a mask that shone with an ivory lustre in the light from the bare bulb. Its tilted eye slots and solemnly pursed lips held me for a long moment in a remote, implacable gaze.

"You can take the mask off, Larry," I said. "Your weight's a dead giveaway."

Sighing, Larry shook his head and sat down in the chair across from me. Sweeping off his hat, he placed it on the table, brushing the white ostrich-feather plume with a gloved hand, but not removing his mask.

I shook the handcuffs behind my back. "You might at least have told them to get me out of these bloody things."

"Had to make quite sure it was you, old chum."

"Well now you're sure."

"Yes, and you've turned out to be exactly the sort of damned nuisance I anticipated. I can't think why the others were so insistent that you stay. Nor for that matter why you should choose to do so. I wouldn't have thought that this was your sort of thing at all."

"But I can see why it's yours," I retorted. "Occult hocus-pocus in fancy dress. Plenty of old money financing your production values! Not much mystery about what keeps *you* here." I took in the sardonic tilt of his head. "But the rest of it – heavies with guns and dogs and handcuffs? That worries me. That makes me question just what sort of fascistic shit you and Adam have got yourselves into."

Larry tutted ruefully behind his mask. "I'm sorry you should think so badly of us. And a little disappointed, I have to say! *Fascistic* indeed! No, my dear. Absolutely not. Occult we may be, fascists we ain't."

"Doesn't the one tend to lead rather quickly to the other?"

"Only in wicked or stupid hands."

"Then why the need for all this secrecy?"

"Some things shrivel in the light," he sighed. "But this is Fontanalba, old thing, not Wewelsburg. I assure you my friends and I have nothing in common with Heinrich Himmler."

"Are you sure your minions understand that?"

"My dear man, if you've been inconvenienced it's entirely your own fault. Adam did ask you to stay away from the villa until he sent for you."

"And because I didn't, that gives you the right to set the dogs on me?"

"Yes, well we're sorry about that, of course. This is the first time we've had to put such measures in place. You merely happened to trip the wires."

"So who are you protecting, Larry? "

Behind his mask, Larry glanced away across the room.

"There's someone here who brings his own security?" I guessed. Still he said nothing. "That's why you wanted to see me off, right? Because I'm a journalist? Because I might recognize someone in your little mystical coterie and blow the gaff on him? Who is it, Larry? A politician? A billionaire? Some celebrity or other? Royalty?"

"The real question," Larry said, "is just what we're going to do with you right now. You've already mucked things up for *me* this evening. Can't have you wrecking it for everyone else."

"Wrecking what, Larry?"

"Surely Adam's told you all you need to know? I thought the two of you had reached some sort of agreement? Not that I expected you to honour it."

"Does he know I'm here?"

"Of course, and in the circumstances he's decided it's best if you stay. So let's get those manacles removed and we'll fix you up with a room for the night. We have a very full house, so it'll be rather basic, you understand? Gabriella suggested we install you *in faucibus Orci*."

"Install me where?"

"*In faucibus Orci*. Have you forgotten your Virgil, old soul?"

"I never had your classical education."

"The *Aeneid*. Book Six. It means, 'in the Jaws of Orcus'."

"I'm no wiser."

"Orcus, one of the underworld gods. Another name for Hades, if you like. So don't be surprised if it's a bit hellish compared to your usual standards of comfort! But then, as I recall" – the mask concealed what I imagined must be a wicked smile – "you're not unused to basements."

I was prepared for something simple, but not for the room that Larry ushered me into – a windowless, dimly lit vault with painted walls somewhere under the main house. A glass and several bottles of spring water stood on a table no higher than a footstool. Apart from a large couch, there was no other furniture, so I assumed that the passage at the far end of the cellar must lead to a bedroom. Larry pointed that way. "The usual facilities are through there."

I went into the passage, saw one closed door ahead of me and another to my right that stood ajar on a small white-tiled lavatory and washroom.

"The flush works on a sort of pump," he said. "Makes a bit of a noise."

I tried the other door and, when it didn't budge, said, "Is this the bedroom door?"

"There's no bedroom. This is it."

"Just the couch? You've got to be joking."

"However, you'll find a pamphlet of mine which might prove of interest, and you do have the wall paintings."

Not an inch of the plastered stone was unpainted, but the single bulb in the room emitted such low wattage that I could make out no detail.

"How long do you expect me to stay down here?"

"Till we're ready for you," Larry answered. Then he slipped out of the door, which clicked shut behind him.

There was no handle on my side of the door. I banged a few times, but only a hollow echo answered. I went back through to the far door and knocked on that one too, with no better result. The cellars were built of stone. No matter how much noise I made, it was unlikely that anybody in the rooms above would hear me. The security man had taken my mobile phone when he emptied my pockets – though down here it would have been useless anyway – so until someone came to fetch me, I was cut off from all human contact. Nor was I even sure what time it was. My watch too had been confiscated.

It occurred to me then that no one else in the world knew where I was. Raging that they should dare to lock me up this way, and thinking up all kinds of vengeance, I picked up the pamphlet I found on the couch. Published by the Heartsease Foundation and entitled *KATABASIS: The Journey to Hades*, it had three epigraphs, one from Jung, another from T.S. Eliot, and the third – its presumption did not greatly surprise me – came from one of Larry's own works. It said: "Only a foolish mind fails to value reason highly among the instruments of knowledge; only a fearful one clings to it as though there was no other." Shaking my head, I scanned the pamphlet's opening paragraph:

Let us begin by acknowledging that we are mysterious creatures inhabiting a mysterious world whose nature we do not understand, and where, if we are honest with ourselves, we will admit that, apart from the inevitability of death, there is nothing fundamental that we know for certain. Despite our best convictions, we do not know who we are, we don't know why we are here or what will become of us. This is, and has always been, the radical uncertainty of the human condition. Out of that uncertainty arise all the stories and stratagems by which we strive as best we can to connive at life and shape it to our purposes, to seek to make a go of things, to try to become what we believe ourselves to be, while attempting at the same time to make sense of the others around us who are caught up in the same marvellous and fateful game.

I skipped to the next page, and was confronted by a lengthy disquisition on the name and nature of the invisible Greek god Hades, together with accounts of various mythological journeys to the underworld drawn from Sumerian, Akkadian, Egyptian, Sanskrit, Japanese, Amerindian, Classical and Christian traditions. Flicking quickly through a dozen more pages, I came to the concluding paragraphs:

Thus it can be seen that, whether we are conscious of it or not, our powerful culture is now far advanced on such a Hades

Journey. But as long as we continue to devolve the suffering on those less fortunate than ourselves, or to look for solutions in mere amelioration of the attitudes that precipitated the current planetary crisis, we will get lost on the journey and fall asleep in our own dark shadows. Yet to push on through will make severe demands on us. It will require a willingness to subordinate the ego's narrow ambitions to the wider claims of the compassionate imagination. It will demand more serious respect for those feminine – or lunar – values which, because they are not easily quantified or controlled, have been too long demeaned and neglected in our culture. It will involve a revaluation of the ancient wisdom of the ancestors, not only as found in surviving texts, but as a part of our genetic structure – the dead ancestors alive inside each of us, speaking through our dreams and genes. Lastly, and most comprehensively, it will require an honest responsiveness to the intelligence of the earth itself, of which each one of us is a living filament.

In short, only by undergoing such ordeals of self-divestiture will our Hades Journey be completed. The demands it makes will not easily be answered. But without a willing acceptance of its claims on us we may live and die in ignorance of who we truly are.

Impatient with such pompous rhetoric, I threw the pamphlet aside, and lay back on the couch.

After a time, as though someone was turning a dimmer switch, I sensed the room growing darker round me. I closed my eyes, shook my head and, when I looked again, could see nothing at all. The room was absolutely black, not a cranny of light anywhere, just this dense blackness pressing against my eyes, a blackness into which everything – the paintings, the walls, the vault, the couch on which I lay – had disappeared. And then, somewhere above me, a recorded voice began to speak.

After a moment I recognized the words as Latin verse, but I understood little of them until a second voice cut in over the first, and I was listening to someone translating Virgil's hexameters into English:

Here, at the entrance, in the jaws of Orcus,
Grief and vengeful Trouble make their lair.
Here too are foul Diseases and the miseries
Of Age and Hunger driving men to crime.
Here's Want that causes fear, hard Toil, and Death;
Death's brother Sleep, and every wicked Lust
The mind conceives. And at the door where Furies
Rage in iron cages, War brings yet more death,
While Discord binds with snakes her bloodied hair.

A glimmer of light returned, the room grew brighter again, much brighter than before, until the whole vaulted chamber became a radiant gallery in which the paintings glowed around the walls in lurid colour.

My first thought was that this must once have been a chamber where some ancestor of Gabriella's family had indulged his secret vices. But as my eyes took in more of the detail, I saw that many of the images were drawn from contemporary sources, that the work was recent, executed within the last decade or so, and evidently with an apocalyptic moral purpose.

I sat up under the gaze of an African woman who would have had all the solemn beauty of a Benin bronze had not one side of her face been eaten away, from eye socket to jaw, by the ebola virus. All about her were images that might have illustrated a medical encyclopedia – a horrifying freak show of frightening diseases. When I turned away from them, it was only to encounter the famished eyes, brittle rib cages and bloated bellies of starving men, women and children.

An entire wall was given over to the depiction of such suffering. Another to the obscenities of war – soldiers with stomach and

319

head wounds, helicopter gunships spraying fire, skeletal corpses crudely stacked or tipped in ditches, men dangling from scaffolds, bodies tangled in wire, frozen into rigid postures, mutilated beyond repair, with tanks exploding around them and cities in flames. Here and there I caught allusions to the work of other artists – the fiery landscape of Brueghel's *Mad Meg*, tormented figures out of Hieronymus Bosch, Goya's *Caprichos* and the mutilated corpses from his *Disasters of War*. But there were also people and places I recognized from photographs and newsreel footage – the man in the Balkans whose head was being sawn off by his grinning captors, the Chinese child with chopsticks pushed into her ears, the frightened eyes of the little Jewish boy with hands raised under the muzzle of a gun. Unquestionably I was looking at a late-twentieth-century vision of hell – the kind of inferno through which I'd been travelling for most of my adult life. And when I turned round to take in the wall at my back, I was faced with another kind of obscenity – a life-scale painting of an orgy in full swing.

Every conceivable mode of sexual congress, from the voluptuous to the worryingly sinister, was portrayed in shameless detail. People of every size, shape and race were bucking and humping, sucking, grasping and thrashing in a depraved, sometimes comical, more often grotesque tangle of organs, mouths and limbs. But the skin tones of these naked creatures gave off a weird bluish light, like that of rotting fish, so there was nothing remotely arousing in those images. If they were pornographic, it was a pornography that took no pleasure in its appetites and vices.

At the still centre of the orgy knelt an anomalous figure with her hands clasped at her breast. I recognized her immediately as another study of the naked woman kneeling in the desert – the figure I had first seen among the frescoes in the cottage, with silver-white hair gathered about her like a shawl. Her presence here confirmed what I had already guessed – that these murals were also Marina's work, that in the days before her sight was gone, she must have spent many gruelling weeks transferring this infernal pageant from her imagination to these underground walls.

What I also saw was that this figure was intended as a self-portrait. It was how, presumably in some grave crisis of revulsion at the entire human condition, Marina had seen herself. It left me grieving for her, and yearning for her too.

I have described the pictures in the cellar of the villa at Fontanalba as I first saw them. I have not yet conveyed their hallucinogenic impact over many hours on my isolated senses. During the grim nights of imprisonment in Makombe Castle there had been six of us thrown together in that squalid cell, all frightened by the hideous sounds along the corridor. Here there was no one else to turn to, and nowhere to fix the attention except on the hellish vision of a world where – in stark repudiation of all our claims to progress – the apocalyptic horsemen, Disease, Famine, War and Death, still marauded among us unchecked.

Through long hours I stared at the images. The images stared back at me, and when I closed my eyes it felt as though the usual roles were reversed and I had become the object of observation around which representatives of the mutilated, dying and dead people I had filmed over the past thirty years were gathering to pity and to grieve.

At moments, too, I seemed to sense other presences in the room. To my left lay Hal Brigshaw – not the vigorous figure I had known in my youth, but the crumpled victim of a stroke, stretched out on the bed I had seen in the sitting room at High Sugden, breathing only with difficulty, unable to speak a word. To my right, confined in the darkness of the starvation bunker, Maximilian Kolbe, saint of Auschwitz, knelt in prayer. Yet, when I opened my eyes and looked to either side, neither of those figures was there.

At other times I was surfing on a sea of memories in a state between sleep and waking, thinking of Marina and of everything she must have endured in order to be able to paint this terrifying vision on these walls. My heart ached to remember her as she had been in the early days – her passion for storms, her courage and candour, the easy way with which she had chatted to my parents on the day she had unexpectedly come to visit us in Cripplegate Chambers. Larry had joked that I had once been familiar with basements, and it was true enough; and here I was again, back in that cellar which had once been my home, believing myself to be some sort of underground creature, a troglodyte, living with the faint smell of damp and chilled by cold draughts blowing through the vaults.

Then I must have fallen asleep for a while, because I jumped up trembling from a dream that had shocked and frightened me. In the dream I was looking up at the dingy frosted glass in the windows of our cellar living room when I saw my father grinning back in at me, young, handsome and virile again.

"What are you doing?" I said. "You're dead. You've no business here."

"That's what you think" – an unnerving green glint shone in eyes tricky with mischief – "but I've not been dead at all, lad – just hiding. And now I'm back!"

I jumped awake. Did I dream I was shouting, "Why won't you let me go?" or was I actually shouting it? Only gradually did the shock of the dream abate. What remained was a heart-wrung awareness of everything that had been left unresolved in my life – of that and of the uncrossable distance between the living and the forever dead.

19
Trust Game

In Vietnam I learnt to inhabit a strict exclusion zone of the emotions. After being picked up from a firefight and flown by chopper through an electric storm, I named that condition my "Faraday Cage". It was where Crowther's Law prevailed while the intolerable voltage of warfare flashed outside. From there I saw what happens when villages are incinerated and mortar shells explode in close proximity to human flesh. I saw body bags filled with enough bits and pieces to make up the weight of a single son, and though I would never be inured to such sights, I no longer retched at them. But when news of Emmanuel's assassination caught up with me, it hit me hard.

That night I lay in sweaty fatigues, smoking dope as I listened to the stoical banter of a bunch of black infantrymen gathered round a radio. A rock band was driving a heavy beat across the airwaves. I took another drag on the joint and felt my brains scooped up and tilted backwards into space. Silently, with tears streaming down my face, I recalled each act of kindness the African had shown me, first in those snowbound days at High Sugden, and again, later, when he welcomed me as his friend in the Presidential Palace of Equatoria. I remembered his pride, his proverbs, his humour, his warmth. Yet the shock and pain of Emmanuel's death quickly blurred in the heat of the next day's action. I was twenty-eight years old then, and living in a world of phantasmagorical violence to which, with each adrenalin rush of terror and excitement, I was increasingly addicted.

Six weeks later I returned to a London in thrall to a delirium of its own. After Vietnam, the city's newly acquired taste for love and revolution felt about as likely to put right the structural injustices of the planet as might the revels of an unruly street carnival. But it did offer scope to indulge my hyperactive senses.

More than a month passed before I travelled north to Calderbridge. It was my first visit to my parents in a long time, but I'd learnt that Hal was back at High Sugden, having escaped out of Africa alive. It was him I wanted to see.

From the moment of my arrival, I felt restless and estranged in my parents' new home. Since my father had been appointed warehouse foreman at Bamforth Brothers' mill, they had moved out of Cripplegate Chambers into a terraced house with two bedrooms and a small garden, which they rented from the mill. My mother fussed over me, while my father preserved his usual taciturn air of judgemental detachment.

My mother now worked as the cleaning lady for a family in Heathcote Green, who thought of her as their treasure. Though she seemed to take pride in the title, I told her there was no call for her to work, as I earned more money than I needed, and would be glad to send some of it her way. She answered that she wouldn't know what to do with her time if she gave up the job, and she was sure the family's two teenage girls, for whom she had become a trusted confidante, would be lost without her. Meanwhile, my father remained entranced by his television set, watching out the evenings after work more or less indiscriminately. On fine weekends they had taken to driving about the local countryside in their ageing Ford Prefect, of which they were very proud.

"I don't know why you go gallivanting abroad," my mother said, "when there's all these grand places to visit round here!"

On Saturday nights, they joined their friends for drinks and Bingo at the North Vale Working Men's Club. I went with them and sat staring in rueful wonder at the warm, jocular world to which I'd once belonged, and which now regarded me with good-natured respect as a sort of celebrity: Jack Crowther's lad made good on the box. We played bingo and laughed at a comedian fallen on thin and boozy times, and the man in drag who impersonated an opera singer. Each time his falsetto voice hit a high note, the glass earrings he wore lit up with a fiendish green glow.

I drank too many pints of ale and lay on my bed that night, surrounded by the bits and pieces from my boyhood that my mother had decided to save when they moved: the hand-carved model of an Arab dhow brought back from Mombasa by my dad, the banjo I never learnt how to play, a shelf of children's books. I felt unappeasably sad, as though each gesture of my parents' affection was a reproach for which I had no answer. It seemed fraudulent either to speak their language these days or to refuse to do so. My voice sounded forced and alien in my ears. But I'd made up my mind to get away without arguing with my father or upsetting my mother, so next morning I agreed to stay for Sunday lunch, which meant going to the pub with my dad while my mother put the roast in the oven.

"I know she won't have said owt about it," he grumbled over his second pint, "but your Mam frets about you, you know. When you're abroad, I mean. She's worried you might get shot or wounded or summat. That's what upsets her most, but it's not just that. She goes on about what it's doing to your nerves."

"She shouldn't worry. I'm used to it by now."

"That's what I tell her. Think on what it did for me during the war, I say. The real war, I mean. Made a man of me, it did." Giving me a quick glance, he conceded grudgingly, "Happen this war might be doing the same for you."

I took in his barely qualified approval, wondering how he would have reacted if I'd admitted that for much of my time in Vietnam I'd been stoned out of my mind, and that my dreams still frightened me.

"I know a bit about what it's like under fire," he said. "Just you remember to look after Number One, right? I don't want to see your mother wearing black."

When I told him that I liked my arse well enough not to put its welfare at risk, he smiled and then changed the subject.

"The other thing she goes on about is wondering when you're thinking of getting wed?"

I told him that the thought was nowhere on my mind.

Nodding, he said, "We always thought a lot of that Brigshaw lass. She were genuine enough in my opinion. No airs about her. You coulda done a lot worse."

"Like I said, I'm happy as I am."

"Aye well, happen you're right. You can make a mess of things if you wed too young. Look at me – if it weren't for the war, I'd have had no life. I were glad enough to get out of your mam's clutches for a time."

"Who are you kidding?" I laughed. "She told me years ago that it was you who pestered *her* into getting wed."

"Nay, she never did!"

"Aye, she did that."

"Well, I couldn't let some other bugger nab her, could I? She's a good lass, your mam. I've got no grumbles there." He glanced at my empty glass. "Are you having another then?"

"Better not. I'm driving. Anyway, she'll be wanting to lift that roast."

"Don't worry about her. She'll be all right. Come on, it's my round this time." He fished in his pocket for cash and signalled the barman. And then, almost as if in reparation for all the years of taciturn derision, he said, "It's not that often we get a chance to chew the fat these days, thee and me, is it now?"

Later, after we'd eaten the roast and the rice pudding, I felt treacherous leaving my parents alone together in that small house, when I might have spent several more hours in their company. Their air of muted deference as I left seemed to acknowledge that I had more important things to do in the world than pass the time with them. To my shame, I left them believing it.

*

I found Hal relaxing on a sunbed in the garden. I'd last seen him three years before, and was troubled by the change in his appearance. He looked older than a man still in his early fifties. His hair was thinner: it straggled about his ears and neck in wisps as grey as beck water at a trough. His skin had a yellowish tinge, and he'd lost a worrying amount of weight.

To conceal my shock, I turned my attention to the two dogs as they bounded out of the house in greeting – and there was Grace, not far behind them, wearing a faded lilac shirt hanging loose over her slacks. She carried a tray of glasses and a jug of barley water.

She offered her cheek to be kissed, and told me I was looking well. "So are you," I lied, taking in the stresses left on her skin by the years in Equatoria. "And so's the garden, and I see the dogs are still full of beans." I looked back, smiling, at Hal. "Even this poor old thing seems to be on the mend."

"Yes," Grace sighed, "I suppose it can't be long before he's insufferable again." She looked down at us wryly and decided against joining us. "You two must have a lot to talk about." Glancing my way, she said, "I'll catch up with you later." Then she turned back to the house.

"A good woman that," Hal said after she'd gone. "Haven't treated her well, you know. Too preoccupied, I suppose."

"And not only with politics," I risked.

He eyed me suspiciously. For a moment I thought he was about to take offence, but then he sniffed out a smile. "The women, you mean? Well, what can I say? Guilty as charged, m'lud. But what the hell! A man has to have some pleasure, doesn't he? We can't be saintly all the damn time!"

"No," I said, "I guess not."

After a thoughtful silence, we began to talk more seriously, though I did most of the listening as he gave me an account of his last days in Equatoria. With the roads, ports and airports blocked by the military, Hal had been lucky to get out of the country at all. Helped by nervous old comrades, he was smuggled under a lorry load of Manchester cloths to a town near the eastern border. From there he had to walk through the forest. Over a week later, reduced from one of the most influential political figures in newly liberated Africa to a bedraggled refugee with a gastric infection, he turned up in England, having flown from Yaoundé via Algeria and Paris. He rang Grace at High Sugden, told her that he was ill and needed help and, with a meekness born of exhaustion and distress, asked her if he might come home.

"I didn't even get to see Emmanuel buried," Hal grieved. "Sometimes I think I should have stayed and got shot with him."

"I can't see what good that would have done," I said. "I don't understand why they killed him anyway. Why didn't they just imprison him or send him into exile?"

"I'm not sure that they planned the assassination," Hal frowned. "It was a young hotheaded colonel called Mouhatta who pulled the trigger. He claims it was to stop Emmanuel becoming a rallying point for resistance to the coup. But it wouldn't surprise me if Mouhatta turned out to be some sort of psychopath."

We talked about the military junta now ruling the country under martial law, those solemn young colonels whose politics amounted to no more than a military assumption that people should do as they were told.

"It can't last," Hal said. "The Equatorians will find their way round that staff-officer mentality, and when the soldier boys find they've bitten off more than they can chew, they'll hand the country over to Fouda's gang of crooks and opportunists. Either that or some half-crazed brute like Mouhatta will emerge from their ranks and turn the place into his personal fiefdom. That's what really frightens me."

Later we talked about Adam and Efwa, whom Hal had not seen since his return from Equatoria, though whether this was the way Adam wanted it, or the demands of his work as a supply teacher in Dagenham prevented it, remained unclear. I guessed that the first was masquerading as the second, but decided not to say so.

"His mother misses him too," Hal said. "I sometimes think you're more of a son to us than he will ever be." Shaking his head, he added, "He was a damn fool to marry that chirpy little looker, don't you think?"

Less comfortably still, and rather more briefly, we talked about Marina, who was estranged from us all as she pursued her own increasingly dissident life. "She's still living in my flat," Hal grumbled, "but she seems to spend a lot of time going back and forth between there and a commune some friends have set up in a Somerset farmhouse. She won't talk about it much, but as far as I can make out they claim to be some sort of anarcho-syndicalist outfit. Mind you, I rather doubt that many of them have read Kropotkin! This country's changing all right," he scowled, "but not in ways I'm sure I like. I hear a lot of talk among young people on the telly about freedom and love and revolution, but to me it looks like a feather-brained mix of self-indulgence and social irresponsibility. Or am I missing something?"

Finally we talked about me and my work. I told him about what I'd seen and learnt in Vietnam, and he ranted for a time against the dangerous stupidity of America's foreign policy. "I've watched some of your reports," he said, "and you're doing really well. In fact, I've been thinking about you a lot. Can't do much else but think these days! Anyway, however badly I may have cocked it up in Equatoria, I did make a lot of contacts on the world stage – politicians, diplomats, bankers, UN officials, aid workers with their noses to the ground, influential academics, military men, energy and health experts, not to mention various international wheeler-dealers and a few assorted spies. They're all contacts that might prove useful to you if you want them. Are you interested?"

Yes, I was interested. I was very interested.

"Good," he grinned. "Glad to see I might still be of some use in the world."

Later, Grace came to keep me company while Hal telephoned a few people on my behalf. Dryly she asked whether the two of us had put the world back to rights. I answered as dryly that these things take a little time. We exchanged uneasy small talk for a while, I fending off the possibility of closer communication, she not concealing her awareness that I was doing so. To fill a silence I said that I was glad to see her and Hal back together again.

"Together?" she answered. "Is that what you think? Well, it's true we're living under the same roof." Grace looked away, speaking more to herself than to me. "He was in such a woeful state when he came out of Africa that someone had to look after him, and in the generally unjust scheme of things I suppose it had to be me. But Hal's not really here you know – here with me, I mean. Yes, he's grateful to me for being the dutiful wife and taking care of him. He's even been apologetic about his mistresses and all the rest. But that's about as deep into feelings as he's willing to go. And there's no point asking for more. I only get upset, and he remains impervious. The truth is that his soul's in Africa still."

"Hal doesn't believe in souls," I said.

"No," Grace gave a rueful smile. "Perhaps that's the problem."

I didn't know what to make of that, so we talked about Emmanuel for a time, and I could see her biting her lip as she recalled their times together and the shock and pain of his loss. "For Hal," she said, stroking the ear of the dog that lay across the couch with its head in her lap, "it was like losing a son and a brother and a friend all at once. I doubt he'll ever get over it." She drew in a heavy breath and pulled herself back to the present. "He's also missing the children. Did he ask you to try and persuade them to visit us?"

When I shook my head, she said, "No, I might have guessed he wouldn't. The stupid man's too proud even to use a go-between.

But I'm not. Did you know he's got a birthday coming up on the sixteenth of next month? I'm sure if you gave Adam a prod, he'd come and celebrate with us, especially if he knew you were going to be here. Can you come?"

"The sixteenth?" I checked my diary. "I can't make that, I'm afraid."

"Oh dear, that's a pity. But you could speak to Adam, couldn't you? The two of you together might be able to get Marina here. Would you do that for us?"

"Of course I'll try."

"You could tell her that if she doesn't make some sort of effort to cheer us up, sooner or later they'll find two mouldering corpses in this house, each with a dagger in the other's heart. Mind you, I don't suppose that would upset her very much."

"That's a bit harsh," I protested. "She cares about both of you."

Grace shrugged with cool, remote deliberation. "Marina's always been angry with Hal, of course, but that's only because she's been half in love with him since she was a little girl – just as he's always been besotted with her. But she's been cold with me for years. I feel sure she blames me for everything that's gone wrong. Certainly she's holding on to something unresolved between us... Something I really don't understand. In fact, I sometimes wonder whether..." Grace turned to face me, her eyes forbidding mine to shift away as she said, "Did you ever tell her what happened between you and me all those years ago?"

"Hell no," I exclaimed, "I'd never do that."

For a long time Grace stared at me. Resolutely I held her severe gaze.

"Oh I rather doubt that," she sighed. "She's sure to get it out of you one day."

Once back in London, I decided it would be less difficult to talk separately to Adam and Marina, and more likely to succeed. So I phoned Adam first and offered to take him and Efwa out to dinner. I was worried that he might be overly conscious of the current discrepancy in our circumstances, and perhaps resentful of my success. But when they turned up in the Charlotte Street restaurant he was cheerful enough, evidently glad to see me, and tenderly solicitous with his wife.

Efwa was wearing a thick roll-neck sweater and a jolly, cherry-red beret which she refused to take off. "Is cold in this country," she explained. "This red hat is good for me here."

"It looks very good on you," I smiled, lightening the compliment by adding at once, "You should wear it everywhere – even to bed. Now what are we going to eat?"

I brought up the subject of Hal's birthday early, assuring Adam that his father had been chastened and mellowed by the catastrophe in Equatoria. "But he's not in a good way." I said. "The stomach bug he brought back with him hasn't cleared up: he's lost weight and his spirits are low. Seeing you might give him just the lift he needs. Grace tells me how much he misses you, but I could see it for myself."

"Our last conversation wasn't exactly amicable," Adam frowned.

"I know, and Hal regrets it. He must have been under a hell of a strain at the time. But he wants to put it behind him now – if you'll let him, that is. What do you say? It is the poor old bugger's birthday after all."

"I suppose it can't make things much worse to give it a try." Adam reached out to touch his wife's hand. "What do you think, Efwa?"

"I think is better we try. Maybe is good for all of us. Maybe it makes us happy again?"

"We're happy anyway," Adam answered, "but I guess we can give it a go."

The conversation moved on. He questioned me about my time in Vietnam, and I answered at length until I saw Efwa growing restless. When I asked about their life together, Adam spoke without enthusiasm about his supply teaching, through which

332

he was financing a much more satisfying involvement with a community-theatre project in Hackney. Efwa worked with him there, using her skills in music and dance. He talked eagerly about the role of imagination in grass-roots politics as opposed to the top-heavy ideological socialism that his father had tried to impose on Equatoria.

"That was bound to fail," he insisted, "right from the start."

"Only because the whole system of international capital was against it."

"Also because the whole concept had nothing to do with traditional culture," he came back emphatically. "It was an alien system. It had no roots there. Nothing that spoke to local needs in the way that the tribal councils of elders did, with their built-in checks against any chief who got the will of the community wrong."

I suggested that tribalism didn't offer much hope for the future, but when he countered with a reminder of the wretched condition in which Hal's policies had left the country, Efwa began to air her personal anxieties.

"I am worrying too much about my family in Adouada," she said. "Now even the price of yam and cassava is too dear. Also is hard for them to get kerosene and petrol. As for Adam and me, we don't get money to send for them. Sometimes I am feeling too too bad about it all."

The mood around the table had changed. Adam and I averted a political dispute which had nowhere to go, but now tensions between him and Efwa surfaced as she went on to complain about how hard-up they were.

"Soon I would like to have baby," she finally admitted, "but Adam says we don't get enough money yet."

"We just have to be patient, love," he reassured her. "It won't always be like this. When the grant proposal gets accepted, the project will take off. Then anything can happen, you'll see. Once we're better off, you can have seven babies if you like – one for each day of the week."

Efwa grunted dubiously, and he pulled a face at her. She put out her tongue at him, then burst into loud contagious laughter. I ordered more wine.

At least Adam had agreed to go to High Sugden. I felt sure I could use that as leverage on Marina, but our meeting was baffled on my part and distanced on hers. I scarcely recognized the stark, monochrome figure who came into the Brewer Street bar she'd suggested. Her hair was cropped short and dyed black. She wore a black leather jacket with black trousers, and was now wearing glasses with severe black frames. In the old days I might have teased her about such drastic changes, but her manner discouraged me. Even so, I tried to reach out to her, but our exchanges seemed fenced with razor wire. She asked about my work only to dismiss television as "a toxin for the public imagination". For the first time in my life I began to feel hostile towards her, and decided to get quickly to the point before we teetered into some stupid argument that might wreck any chance of persuading her to visit High Sugden.

She listened to what I had to say about Hal with a sceptical twist to her lips before saying, "There's no point. It will only go wrong again."

"Hal doesn't want that to happen," I countered. "Why should you?"

"I don't. That's why I'd rather not go. I don't need that kind of grief."

"What is it between you and Hal?" I asked.

She merely shrugged, stubbed out her cigarette and stared through a grimy bottle-glass window into the crowded Soho street.

I said, "Your mother thinks you only fight with him the way you do because you love him."

"I've never been impressed by my mother's grasp of psychology," she retorted at once. "In any case, how can you love someone if they won't accept you for what you are?"

"People can change."

"You certainly have."

"You too, Marina," I replied with equally critical force. "And so has Hal. Say what you like, but I don't think he's in any mood to pass judgement on you right now. He just misses you. He misses you very much."

But the best I could extract was a promise that she would talk to Adam about it.

"If I go at all," she said, "it will only be to help him out."

Looking – too late – for a way to breathe some warmth into our meeting before she left, I asked about the progress of her work. She told me that there was currently an exhibition of her paintings in a small East End gallery. "If you're interested," she said without enthusiasm, "go and look." I said that I might just do that, and we parted a few minutes later.

Though I concealed my dismay at her unresponsive manner, watching her walk away felt like surgery, part of me detaching itself and migrating to some other life. But if Marina had been chilly and distant in person, the impact of her work was fiery and immediate. Large abstract canvases blazed across the gallery in lightning strikes of crimson, smoky whites and magnesium yellows. Was this what had become of her passion then? Had it all been consumed by the power of an inward vision to erupt across these canvases in hot conflagrations of paint?

I wanted to buy one of the bigger pictures, but their scale was far too large for the walls of my flat. The smaller studies were less dramatic, but one of them burned with an intense smoky glow, like the opening of a furnace door. I wrote a cheque and took it away with me, a keepsake of the Marina I would always love.

Having observed the scope for disaster in Hal's reunion with both his daughter and his son, I had no regrets about missing the party at High Sugden. I was surprised, therefore, by Hal's description of it in a letter he sent afterwards.

"All things considered," he wrote, "the do went rather well – largely I have to say because of the way Efwa's bubbly spirit took the edge off things. I never really got to know the girl back in Port Rokesby, but I see now what attracted Adam to her. She's full of warmth and jollity – she has a great sense of fun – reminded me of everything in that marvellous continent that warms my heart. Things were much stickier with Marina, of course, but I was on my best behaviour (Grace's orders) and my tempestuous daughter managed to get by without starting a row. I can't say I thought much of the bloke she brought with her though – an opinionated lizard called Jeremy, who charitably gave us the benefit of his Olympian views on Art in words of such mind-numbing abstraction that Efwa almost collapsed in squeals of mirth. Too much brain, I thought, too little human feeling, and at least a decade too old. But if he makes Marina happy, who am I to carp? Not that I can quite believe he does – she looked withdrawn and peaky to me, and I don't think that was all my fault. Something not right there. But I suppose we ageing parents understand our adult children no better than they understand us! Anyway, I want to thank you for your part in making it all happen. I shan't forget it. If there's anything I can ever do for you, just say the word."

That letter, together with Marina's painting, was all I saw of the Brigshaws for some time after that. I was immersed in the demands of my work and caught up in casual affairs that had nowhere to go. I was beginning to wonder whether my efforts to help heal the rifts in that complicated family had spelt the end of my connection with them when Hal rang me one evening out of the blue. He told me he would be coming down to London more often, that he would be working with Emmanuel's son Keshie and his group of exiled Equatorians, and that he still had influential contacts on the world scene who wanted to keep in touch with him.

"Some interesting straws in the wind," he said. "We're not finished yet, old son. Not by any means. The thing is, because

Marina has colonized the family flat, I've got nowhere to stay. Any chance you might put me up every now and then?"

I was still sufficiently in awe of Hal to be gratified that he should call on me for help, and still sufficiently driven by secret guilt to feel I could refuse him anything. In any case, I owed my entire career to him, and that career took me out of the country for so much of the time that I had only occasional uses for the flat. So I was happy to give him a key on the clear understanding that he wouldn't hang about there when I got back.

The first time he came down to London we spent the evening together, and I was immediately impressed by how much better he looked. His stomach troubles had gone, he had regained his weight, and long hikes across the Pennine hills had built back his strength. His skin shone healthy and clear, the Viking glint was back in his eyes, and though his hair was wintering towards white, he might have been a decade younger than his fifty-seven years. Also, along with his vigorous good looks, his appetite for life had returned, so I wasn't entirely surprised when, at the end of his third brief visit, he said, "I was wondering how you would feel about my bringing a friend here every now and then?" He gave me his most raffish smile. "Shouldn't think it would bother you too much, would it?"

"A friend?"

"Just hypothetical. Probably never happen. But if the chance turned up?"

Predatory and amused, his eyes drew me into complicity. We were men together, weren't we? We understood one another.

"Of course there's no reason why Grace should know about it," he added. "Only upset her after all." And when I didn't reply: "Not that I'd want to upset you either. Don't mind my asking, I hope?"

"I was just thinking about the practicalities."

"Yes, of course." He angled his brow at me. "Well... what do you think?"

What *did* I think? I remembered every kind thing that Hal had done for me. I remembered what had happened behind his back some years ago. I thought that whatever Hal wanted of me, Hal must have. It was the price.

"It's up to you," I said. "But I'd rather not know too much about it."

"Of course," he agreed. "It would only happen while you're away, if at all. I wouldn't want to compromise you in any way."

We didn't discuss the matter again. For all I knew, he could have been sharing my flat with the city's most expensive hookers while I was out of the country, but he took care not to interfere with my privacy. When I was in London the flat was exclusively my own. I drank too much wine in those days, and smoked too much dope. Yet somehow I held my life together. Just.

I first learnt of my father's failing health through a routine phone call I made to tell my mother I'd got back home safely from the latest assignment. Almost as a dubious afterthought she mentioned that he'd been complaining about a nagging pain in his stomach.

"He says it's just a touch of indigestion," she said, "but he will keep going on about it."

I caught the trace of suppressed anxiety in her voice. When I heard that he'd been complaining about the pain for more than two weeks, I told her she should get him to see a doctor.

"You know what he's like about doctors," she said.

But the next thing I heard was that he'd been sent for an X-ray and then quickly admitted to the men's ward at Calderbridge General Hospital for an operation.

"They say it's a blockage," my mother said, "so it's just as well they're getting it sorted out."

The news did not reassure me. A colleague put me in touch with a friend who was a consultant at one of the London teaching hospitals. He described my father's condition in less euphemistic terms. I decided to go home that weekend, but by the time I arrived in Calderbridge, the operation was over. His belly had been stitched up to his satisfaction, and even though dark shadows clung around his eyes, he was looking forward to early discharge almost with an air of defiance.

Grey with worry by then, my mother had also lost weight, but she was relieved that it was all over. I left them alone together while I went to ask the matron how long it would be before my father could go home. She hesitated a moment and then said that it would be best if I had a word with the surgeon.

He too sized me up quickly before telling me that the tumour was already far advanced, and that he had found secondary growths. "We've done what we can for your father," he said, "but I'm afraid he doesn't have much longer to live. We'll be sending him home shortly. The district nurse will come in to see him every day. But I think your mother's going to need some support."

None of this was disclosed to my father by the hospital staff, and he was so cheered by the prospect of getting back to his life that I decided I could say nothing either. But my mother had to be told. She had to be told in time to get over the first devastating shock before he returned home. White-faced, I held her as she wept. Later I made some urgent calls. I was due some leave, and the company agreed to extend it on compassionate grounds.

Three weeks later my father died. By then he'd understood what was coming. "If anything happens to me," he said, "you'll take care of your mother, won't you?" I promised him I would. Soon after that, he was so far gone inside his morphine dreams that he no longer suffered from the bedsores on his back. In one of his rare moments of almost complete lucidity, I asked how he was feeling. He mumbled, "I'm as happy as the flowers in May." They were the last words he spoke.

He died on a stiflingly hot day in mid-June, three days before what would have been his fifty-eighth birthday. On her visit that morning, the district nurse expressed her concern at my mother's depleted condition. She asked how long I would be staying with her, and nodded thoughtfully when I told her I would have to leave for London soon. Since then I've often wondered whether she pumped a merciful overdose of morphine into my father's bloodstream before she left. Whatever the case, later that morning we heard a change in the sound of his breathing, and when I went upstairs to check how he was, I found him deeply unconscious, eyes half open, mouth agape.

Throughout that hot afternoon my mother and I sat in the parlour together, hearing the sounds of the continuing world outside, hardly speaking at all. Nothing we said could cancel out the sound of my father's breathing, like a saw dragged back and forth across wet wood. She sat beside me, wringing her tense hands, a slight figure in her floral housecoat, her face drawn, the skin around her eyes dark with exhaustion and grief. Already my father was elsewhere in some narcotic zone, where I imagined him dreaming himself back at sea on a long Atlantic convoy with a steep dark crowding from the Arctic at his prow. And here were my mother and I, left alone together again, as we had been left alone in my childhood when he was gone with his friends to the war.

I was astonished by the number of mourners who came to my father's funeral at Bridestone Royd. His surviving brothers and sisters and their families were all there, of course, but so were neighbours from the street, a few office workers from Cripplegate Chambers and many of the staff and employees from Bamforth Brothers' mill. Looking around the chapel, I also saw faces that were new to me – friends from the Working Men's Club and people who had enjoyed his company for years in pubs and clubs around the town. Tightening my arm round my mother, who wept shaking beside me, and humbled by the discovery that my father was held in such regard by so many people, I found myself envying – if one *can* envy the dead – his lifelong membership of this closely bonded world mourning his loss.

Hal and Grace came to the funeral too. Touchingly kind with my mother, they brought condolences and flowers from Adam and Efwa, who were unable to come because they were committed to an important event of community theatre that day. Sadly, Marina was out of contact, travelling abroad with friends. "But I'm sure she would have come if she'd known," Grace said to my mother, while Hal looked on. "She was very fond of both you and Jack."

For a man who thought he'd learnt to deal with death across the war-torn regions of the world, I did not cope well with my father's passing. Outwardly I remained more or less impassive. I told myself I was holding my grief at bay for my mother's sake, and perhaps in part I was. But a time came, just a few days after the funeral, when I had no choice but to leave her alone in that little house in Calderbridge. Even then, long after I was out of earshot, my feelings remained ice-packed in cold storage. No tears were shed. I turned instead to dope and drink, and found a shell-shocked sort of refuge there.

Then one evening, several weeks later, my phone rang, and Marina's voice came down the line. "I've only just heard about your dad. I am so sorry, so very sad. I can't bear that I missed the funeral. I was wondering... Perhaps we could get together? For a drink... or a meal even? If you'd like that, I mean."

I said, "I don't know what there is to say."

After a moment she said, "I really liked him, you know. I liked him a lot. I want to talk about him. I want to listen to you talking about him too."

We met in a pub by the river. Wary as I was, I found her as approachable and responsive as she had been cold and aloof the last time we'd met. We moved on to a quiet Chinese place she knew, where it was easier to talk.

When I told her how dismayed I'd been by our previous meeting, she said, "I'm sorry. It had nothing to do with you. There were difficult things going on at the time."

"Jeremy?" I hazarded.

She sat back in surprise "How do you know about him?"

"Hal wrote to me after your visit to High Sugden."

"I see." She studied me with ironical, suspicious eyes.

"He only mentioned it because he cares about you."

"You're pretty close, you two, aren't you?"

"I owe him a lot. He's always been kind to me."

Marina sat in silence for a time. "Anyway," she finally said, "I know he couldn't stand the sight of him. Didn't surprise me. I rather think that's why I took Jeremy to meet him. They're too alike, you see."

"In what way? Hal doesn't seem to think so."

"He wouldn't, would he? I mean, when would Hal ever admit that he's an autocrat and a bit of a bully and exploitative of women?"

"And Jeremy is all those things?"

"And more. And worse."

I waited for her to go on, but she was not ready for that. Instead she changed the subject. "Well, at least Adam's happy enough. And Efwa seems to be enjoying life over here. I have to admit I was worried when they first got married, but it looks as if it's working out a lot better than I expected."

"I hope so," I said less confidently, "but it can't be easy."

"I don't suppose marriage ever is. Not if my parents are anything to go by."

"Have you been in touch with Grace lately?"

"Not since we were at High Sugden. Why do you ask?"

"Because of something she said the last time I talked to her."

"Oh yes? What was that?"

"That she felt you were very judgemental of her."

Using the tip of a chopstick to make a lacy pattern with the remaining grains of rice on her plate, Marina said, "It's just that I can't stand the way she lets Hal walk all over her. I thought that when she came back from Equatoria she'd finally found the guts to make a clean break. But as soon as he turns up again, there she is, licking his wounds, doing his washing, cooking his food – and there's Hal, lording it over the place again as though nothing bad had ever happened."

"You didn't find that he'd changed?"

"He was making more of an effort, but…" She faltered there. "Look, you and Hal are friends. I'd rather not talk about him. Anyway, what about you? You haven't said much about yourself, about your feelings."

So she pushed me into talking, and once I had begun I talked for a long time, opening up to her again as once long before at High Sugden. I talked about my anxieties for my widowed mother. I talked less comfortably about my father, and how my feelings of grief at his funeral were less strong than my awareness that, unlike him, I belonged to no community, was no longer rooted in a world of shared values and unquestioned loyalties. I talked about how far I had been distanced from both my parents, at first by my education and then by my experiences as a foreign correspondent. Only when Marina pressed me did I talk about the state in which I returned from the world's war zones – the prolonged hangover of nervous tension, the avidity for renewed excitement that propelled me into frequent, meaningless encounters with women. Yet, even as I spoke, a part of my mind remained aware that it was precisely through such calculated acts of confession that I accomplished those seductions, and I saw that Marina understood this well enough.

"It feels to me," she said, "as though we've both got lost from ourselves. Perhaps we should try to help each other find a way back?"

We went together to the flat in Bloomsbury, and because I was still young then – younger in many ways than Marina, though there was only a year between us – and because I'd longed for her across so many years, and because I hardly knew myself at all, I thought it would be easy for us to make love. Since my return from Vietnam I'd grown used to approaching sex with cool, observational detachment, savouring its excitements while feeling little more than a mild erotic affection for the women who shared my bed. This night, I knew, would be very different, but my whole body began to tremble with emotion as we moved together. And then, thrown by the images assaulting my mind, it juddered and stalled.

Shaken, eyes screwed tight shut, groaning with misery, I pulled away in failure and recoil. Then Marina was over me, soft with concern, gathering my head to the fern frond of the lightning sign at her chest. I lay shaking in her arms, as a long overdue release of jammed feelings turned at last to tears.

"It's all right, don't try to stop it," she urged. "Let it all go."

Only then did I discover how congested with grief my heart had become, how much anguish and woe had been packed in there as the wretchedness of the world compounded my own, blurring with it, congealing there, freeze-framing each occasion of shock and fatigue till I'd scarcely dared to feel anything at all. Now, with all the fuses softly blown, the mess of thaw was pouring everywhere.

Through shallow gasps of breath, I struggled to say I was sorry, but Marina shushed and rocked me in her arms, reminding me how she too had been in tears the last time we'd tried to make love: now she was here for me as I had been beside her then. Though more deeply so, more completely so, I insisted, feeling the turmoil of her hair against my skin, wondering at the clear strength of her presence, its maturity of care.

"Let's just hold one another for a time," she quieted me. So I stilled my breath in her embrace, and felt the exhausted store of grief give way to a powerful new love for this woman whom I had already loved for so many years.

We lay talking for a long time afterwards, as we had once done long ago in the moorland silence of the night around High

Sugden. The noise and half-light of a crowded city surrounded us now, but we were exempt from its restlessness, and so deeply at peace with one another that we might simply have fallen asleep together there. But a moment came when she touched my face, saying, "I need to tell you how good it feels to be held by someone as if you are precious, as if you're soft and human and breakable." Perhaps only then, as we began to make love with a tenderness and passion that astonished us both, did I truly come to understand what she too had endured.

We woke early the next morning and lay, listening to London droning into gear, in awe of what had happened between us and half-afraid to believe. We were both well practised at escape by then. We each had separate, complicated worlds into which we could return. But I was determined that wouldn't happen to us this time. We had to get together again very soon, I insisted. Why not that night? Either at her place or mine. Wherever she wanted, I'd be there. But it had to be soon.

Marina hesitated. "I think I need to get used to the idea of this. I think we need to feel our way."

"That's all right," I said. "We can do that."

"It's going to take me time."

"We have time. Tonight. Tomorrow. The next day. Whenever. Tell me when."

"Don't rush me, Martin."

"I don't mean to. It's just that I don't want to let you slip away again."

"Is that what you think I'm going to do?"

"No, not really, but…"

"But what?"

"I didn't think so last time either… In Cambridge, I mean."

After a further moment of hesitation, she glanced up at me almost in contrition. Then she astounded me by saying, "I was afraid then."

"Afraid? What of?"

"It was hard for me. I was still feeling vulnerable and confused…"

"But I'd loved you and wanted you for years."

"What I mean is that I was afraid for *you*. I knew I wasn't ready for what you wanted. I don't believe that either of us was."

When she looked away from me, I said, "Are you still afraid?"

"No, I wouldn't say that." But her eyes remained elsewhere, looking down where she loosely creased the edge of the sheet between her fingers.

"All right," I conceded, "you may have been right back then. Perhaps neither of us was ready. But we know we're ready now, don't we?"'

Lifting her eyes back to mine, she said, "I think we're still finding each other."

"Consider yourself found. I found you a long time ago, Marina."

"And you?" she asked. "With all you've been doing out there in the world, have you found yourself yet?"

"I've never felt more myself than I did with you last night."

"But it's not just about making love, is it?"

"That's why I'm impatient for us to do other things together. Don't you think we've wasted far too much of our lives already?"

"It hasn't been a waste," she said. "It's been painful and hard, and we've both made mistakes, but it was all necessary, all part of the finding-out."

I studied her in silence before responding. What had happened during the course of that night was real and true and profound. I had no doubt about that. But did she share that certainty? Did she believe it too?

"Yes, but what about now?" I said. "After last night I mean… I don't understand why you're hesitating."

"I'm not. Not really. But, like I said, I don't want to rush this. I don't want to manage and tame it with arrangements either.

I want us to be freer than that. I want us to give each other the chance to find out how we really feel."

"I already know how I feel."

"You know how you felt last night, and you know how you feel right now. And so do I. But what I'm trying to say is that I don't want to kill this with expectations."

"You can't think that I do?"

"No, but…"

"But what?"

She looked up at me, bright with inspiration. "Listen, I surprised you by calling you last night, didn't I? And look what happened! Neither of us expected it. We surprised each other into this, right? That's why it feels so alive, so new. It's like a gift from life, not something we managed and contrived. So why don't we do it that way again?"

I looked down at her face in wonder, delighted to discover the impetuous spirit I'd loved since she was a girl. "If that's the way you want it," I smiled. "But I get to call you this time."

"No," she said at once, "that's too easy. Let's be wilder than that. Let's find some other way of surprising each other into meeting. What do you say?"

"You make it sound like a game."

"Why not?" she answered. "But it's a game about being truly serious. About allowing ourselves to come together without trying to control things, without tying each other down. It's a trust game. A trust game with life."

"Isn't that just a bit crazy? I mean, what if one of us tries to surprise the other and it doesn't work out?"

"If it's meant to, it will. At the right time it will."

Again I saw in her eyes the flash of intrepid light I recognized from the old days. We might have been out at the foot of the moor beyond High Sugden again, with me shaking my uncertain head, breathless with adoration, yet thrown by her sudden wildness as she taunted me to jump into the waters of the dam.

"Are you daring me?" I asked.

"Do you need to be dared?"

I saw then that I too would have to learn to trust once more.

"I just want us to be together," I answered, "whatever the rules."

20
Descent

When I came awake again inside that painted chamber I had no idea how long I had been there or what hour of the day it was. Someone was standing over me, dark against the soft glare of the electric light, saying, "Wake up, Martin. It's time." I made out Adam's face looking down at me, familiar but unaccountably aged. Strange to wake from sleep – a sleep that might have lasted hours or days – and see that face loom out of a past so distant it seemed almost another incarnation. A face not yet old, but decades older than I remembered.

"What time?" I muttered. "Time for what?"

"For what we agreed."

Adam walked back to the open door, waited for me to get up and follow him and led the way along a vaulted corridor, up a flight of stone steps and out into a moonlit night. Bats skittered about the eaves of the villa. The air smelt heady and fresh. Beyond the hypnotic whirr of the crickets I took in the sound of water flowing through the garden below.

"Where are we going?" I asked.

"To the House of the Dead." Adam turned towards me then. "If you're still sure you want to go through with this, that is. You can leave, if you prefer."

Already the night felt to be floating round me. His answer had added to the prevailing air of unreality, but I nodded my assent and followed him through the shadows of the pergola and out across the enclosed courtyard at the rear of the villa. As we made for the dark archway in the wall opposite the house, I heard a coarse peal of laughter somewhere above my head. Looking up, I saw the bulky figure of a woman standing on the little balcony above the arch. She bent forward from the waist, reached for the hem of her long black gown and lifted it high to her chest, revealing the naked white spread of her belly, thighs and groin.

The spectacle lasted only a fraction of a second before she laughed out loud again with an edge of mockery in her laughter and let the dress drop. Then she dissolved into the shadows at her back.

I said, "Was that Angelina?"

Adam offered no explanation. He pushed open the wrought-iron gates and stepped through into the dripping darkness of the arch. I hesitated, staring down the tunnel to the far end, where moonlight gleamed like frost on the surface of the pool. Adam turned to beckon me on, waited until I stood at his side, and then we entered the grotto together.

I glanced up where the larger-than-life statue of a satyr embraced a nymph on one side of the cave, and a Nereid reclined in the arms of a Triton-like figure on the other. The floor beneath my feet was no longer paved with flagstones, and we had taken only a couple of steps onto an iron grating when a grinding noise creaked out of a crevice in the rocks to our left. Adam stopped as if in surprise, putting a hand to my shoulder to halt me. Almost immediately fierce jets of cold water spurted from the carved wineskins held by the satyr and the nymph to our left, and from the conch shells in the hands of the other two figures on our right. The water splashed against our bodies where we stood. It was pouring from the roof above us and spouting from the mouths of fauns and dolphins carved into the rocks. By the time we dashed through the grotto and out onto the path around the pond, we were both drenched.

Orazio was waiting for us there, offering two large bath towels. Beside him stood Larry Stromberg holding what looked like lengths of white cloth folded over his arm. Smiling at my furious scowl as I shook water from my hair and clothes, he said, "Welcome through, old thing. Don't be too upset by our little *gioco d'acqua*. It's done you no harm, and serves a serious purpose. Now get out of those wet clothes, dry yourself down, and put on this spankingly clean tunic I have for you."

Before I could reply, Adam touched me on the shoulder again. I turned and saw him standing beside me, his lean body already naked as he dried his hair with the towel that Orazio had handed to him. If the drenching had been intended as a humiliation, then he had suffered it too.

He said, "The same thing happens to everyone who enters the water theatre for what we're about to do."

Larry handed him a white tunic, which he pulled on over his head. With my clothes dripping wet, I had no practical choice other than to strip and dry myself and do the same. The linen tunic fell to calf length, hung loosely at the left shoulder and was belted at the waist with a narrow cord. By contrast with Larry's buttoned and embroidered costume, it left me feeling like a spear carrier in an amateur production of a Jacobean play. I was about to ask Adam just what he thought we were about to do when I was silenced by a startling alteration in the light. The ornate façade rising beyond the marble pool was now brightly illuminated, and the sculptures carved into its panels and niches – wild men, armoured knights, garlanded ladies, various animals and birds – were all thrown into sharper relief. At the same time, the night air filled with a shushing sound, and water began to pour from chutes concealed within the stonework. Gathering force, it twisted and plunged in cataracts among the carved figures, which seemed animated now by the play of light on the water cascading round them.

The façade of Gabriella's *teatro d'acqua* had been impressive enough the first time I saw it, motionless and silent, on the morning when I left the villa, but gazing up again at that kinetic stage set, I felt something of the same wonder with which the hermaphroditic figure at the top of the pediment seemed to meditate on the shining spectacle at his feet. In that moment I saw that this fantasia of the baroque imagination was a portrayal of the legend of Fontanalba. The statue was the transfigured revenant returned from his search for the sun at midnight to see the spring breaking from the earth at his command. And this whole improbable artifice had been set in motion, on this occasion at least, for no one's benefit but mine.

"Our presence is required," said Adam quietly.

A female figure was now standing by the arch at the centre of the façade. Holding a silver staff, she wore a costume of deep carmine red cut in the High Renaissance style. The muslin-veiled hat, the full sleeves, frothy with lace, fastened to the bodice by ribbons stitched with pearls, and the richly brocaded skirt might have been worn at a Venetian carnival – not least because the woman's face was covered by a mask as pallid as the moon. For a hopeful moment I thought this was Marina, come to meet me at last, even if concealed behind a disguise; but the figure's height was wrong. My spirit dipped again.

Guessing it must be Gabriella, I said to Adam, "Sibilla, I presume!"

Without smiling, Adam said, "It might be wiser to keep your sarcasm in check."

"Against the voice of the *nihil*," Larry put in, "nothing is safe."

I gazed back at the glistening marvel of the water theatre, reflecting that the cascade must flow through into the garden and out to the fountain at the front of the villa. In Adam's account of Clitumnus, Gabriella had called the *tempietto* "a sacred machine", and it occurred to me that this house might have been built on the same principles, for it too seemed to be a vestibule through which water was conducted between the dark world under the hill and the world of light outside.

As we approached, Gabriella turned into the narrow arch and led the way under the vault of a short stone passage, through into a chamber with a half-domed ceiling, similar to the roof of an apse. After the baroque fantasia of the façade, the room we had entered was small, dimly lit by candlelight and almost shockingly bare. Covered only in brownish-pink plaster, the walls were featureless, apart from a small wooden door directly opposite the one by which we had entered. Even when that first door had closed behind me, I could still hear the murmur of the water plunging outside.

Gabriella led the way to the door at the far end of the chamber, took a candle from a basket on the wall and lit it from one already burning in a sconce. Adam and Larry did the same with the two remaining candles. The hinges of the door whinnied as Gabriella opened it. With the two men offering the shifting light of their candles at my back, I stepped through the arch into a narrow tunnel. The candle flames bowed to the suck of air as the door fell shut behind us. Under a low barrel vault of rock our shadows flitted along walls covered in rough-cast plaster. The stone floor slabs sloped downwards into the belly of the hill.

After ten yards or so, the tunnel opened into a wider natural gallery in the rock. From somewhere out of sight came the sound of falling water. We advanced up a steepish gradient before Gabriella mounted a flight of rough steps and vanished in the darkness at the top. Following her, I saw how the passage curved sharply to the right to dip through a narrow cleft in the rock face, which was shiny with damp. The candles illuminated splashes of ochre, pink, white, dun brown and amber-tinted calcite in the rock, but their light penetrated only a little way into the gloom.

Where the track inclined steeply down again, I saw Gabriella stoop to pass through a gap little more than four feet high beneath a spur of mineral-stained limestone. As I crouched to get through, my hair brushed against the underside of the rock, making me think of the massive tonnage above my head. The passage took a narrow turn. I found more headroom. The sound of water came louder on my ears. Then we were through into a wide chamber, where Gabriella used the flame from her own candle to light others fixed in sconces to the walls. Light leapt among the recesses of the cave. One wall was textured like drapery gathered into swags. Another formed a geological map of compacted layers. I made out the swirling patterns etched by some primordial whirlpool into the low roof of the chamber. I felt as though I had entered one of the organs of the earth.

Now the candle flames were reflected in the bluish-green water of a pool. A skiff floated there, tied by its painter to a stake driven into a gravel strand. An arch of rock sprang from the strand with the grace of a flying buttress, spanning the pool to meet the opposite wall of the cave. A torrent of water poured down that wall.

Despite Adam's earlier warning, I felt a strong need to break the silence. Smiling at Gabriella I said, "Is this Sibilla's cavern then? I don't see any pomegranates."

"You are letting your imagination wander inside the wrong story," she answered. "*La grotta della Sibilla* is in another part of Umbria. We have our own legend here in Fontanalba."

"So is this where the Revenant came to see the sun shining at midnight?"

"You have to go deeper still for that," Adam said. He handed me the candle he was holding, turned towards the skiff, hauled on the painter to pull it closer to the strand, and with a curt nod of the head indicated that I should sit in the stern. I hesitated, looking from his impassive face, beyond the buttress of rock, to the black hollow into which this underground river was flowing. Having come this far, could I just laugh it off, call a halt, say this was too much and walk away?

Adam, Gabriella and Larry were all studying me. Not one of them said a word. A flippant remark about Charon and obols, sops and Cerberus stuck in my throat. Thinking *What the hell!* and wondering why I was doing it, I boarded the boat. Adam climbed in after me, and fitted the oars into the brass rowlocks. Calling out something I didn't understand, Larry pushed us off towards the middle of the pool.

"What did he say?" I asked.

"He said *Tharsei*," Adam answered. "It's ancient Greek. It means *Take heart*."

A moment later we were floating under the arch of rock into the gloom beyond.

When we rounded a bend in the rock, the faint light from the candles vanished behind us. Moments later the prow bumped against stone as the skiff took another turn. I heard the creak of the rowlocks and the dip of oar blades into slowly moving water. Otherwise we were afloat on silence.

"Why haven't the others come?" I asked.

"You'd better not let that candle blow out. It's our only light."

"You don't have matches with you?"

"It's best if you keep quiet."

After a pause I said, "You might at least say where we're going."

"I already have."

"And you're seriously suggesting that my father's there?"

"Not only him."

"Who else?"

"One can never say."

"You mean you're taking me to some sort of seance?"

"I mean what I said. We're entering the House of the Dead. Now be silent please."

Apart from the small flame cupped in my hand, we were in complete darkness. Already nervous, it was impossible suddenly not to feel very scared.

Over countless millennia this underground river must have incised its way ever more deeply, gouging its passage through almost solid rock. A couple of feet above our heads, the roof had been worn smooth. Again it was like travelling through the entrails of a living organism, though when I closed my eyes it also felt as if I was being drawn on strong currents through the channels of my mind.

We rounded a number of bends before Adam shipped the oars. I saw how the passage had narrowed to a constricted throat of rock. Pulled by the current, the skiff was moving more swiftly. Nor was there room to turn the boat about and go back.

Minutes later the skiff grounded on another strand. Immediately Adam stepped ashore and held the prow steady as I climbed out, anxiously protecting the candle flame. Then he hauled the skiff farther up the slope to where the current couldn't pull it away, and pulled out two jumpsuits from under the prow. "We'll need these," he said. He slipped out of his tunic, put one of the jumpsuits on, and then took the candle from me while I did the same. The cloth, I noticed, was thickly padded at the elbows and knees. When we were both suited up, Adam led me across the uneven floor of rock beyond the strand. After ten yards or so he pointed to a dark pit in the floor ahead. Holding the candle close to the mouth of the shaft, he said, "Can you see the ladder? We're going down. You go first."

I stared down where the ladder vanished into darkness. "How deep is it?"

"There are twenty-two rungs. Count them as you go. The ladder's secured into the rock. Just hold on till you reach the ground."

"Is this really necessary?

"Yes. Now go."

I had made my way down a dozen rungs of the iron ladder when, without warning, total darkness shut down round me.

"What's happened?" My shocked voice echoed in the shaft.

"The candle went out." In the darkness I heard Adam swing on to the ladder. "Keep going," he ordered. I'm coming down."

"I can't see a bloody thing."

"Don't worry. You must be almost down."

"How the hell are we going to find our way back?"

"We don't have to. Are you at the bottom yet?"

The sole of my right foot landed on cold stone. It smelt ancient down there. The air tasted of damp, and the darkness was so thick I might have been surrounded by a crowd of people and unable to see a single one of them. I could hear Adam coming down the rungs, but he too was invisible. Shocked by the tense noise of my own breath, holding out my hands as if to push the darkness aside, I stepped away from the foot of the ladder.

If that place had ever known light, it had found no use for it. The darkness was intrinsic and eternal. It offered no way out or through. In that sightless place it felt as though my boundaries were leaking out into the blackness until there were no boundaries. I might have been drowning inside it.

I had known terror before – the terror of the battlefield, the dread of ambush or of stepping onto a mine, but such terror always had its rationale in the knowledge of a clear and present danger. This was different: it was the terror of absence, of being stripped of everything, even my shadow, and then confined inside a deep oubliette. I had no idea whether the space around me remained a narrow shaft with no exit or formed the atrium to some vast basilica of rock. No idea whether I stood within inches of a rebutting black wall that would never move, or on the brink of a drop.

All sense of limit and measure had vanished with the organizing power of sight. I no longer knew where the muffled lantern of my consciousness ended and the darkness began.

Startlingly close, Adam's voice said, "Where are you?"

"I'm here."

"Hold out your hand." I felt the fumble of his fingers searching for mine before my hand was gripped. Hollow in that dark recess, deliberately calm, his voice came at me again. "Okay. We're going to take five steps forward."

"Did you blow out the candle on purpose?"

"Does it matter now?"

In the black silence he tightened his grip on my hand. "Are you with me?"

"Five paces, right?"

"Let's go."

At the fifth pace he released my hand and told me to stretch it out in front of me. Immediately my fingers bumped against solid rock.

"Crouch on bended knees," he said, "and reach out again."

This time my hand met no resistance.

"That's the entrance to a narrow gallery. In some places it's not much more than three feet high. Better keep your head down."

I turned to stare at him in disbelief and saw nothing at all.

"You expect me to crawl in there?"

"The passage is about sixty yards long up a slight incline. And it twists. You're going to have to feel your way."

"If you think I'm going in there you're out of your mind."

"Stay here if you prefer."

A silence as dense as the darkness settled round me.

I said, "Are you still there?"

"If you go first," he answered, "you won't have my feet bumping into your face."

"What if I get stuck?"

"You won't. Just keep going."

"Where to? Where the hell am I going?"

"You'll know when you're there. Get down on your hands and knees. Keep your head low."

I lowered myself to my knees and explored the rough ground in front of me with both hands. Then I crawled through the fissure in the rock into further inhospitable darkness. Inching cautiously forward, I held out one hand like a probe to check the width and the height of the corridor through which I was crawling. In places it found nothing. For all I could tell, I might have been keeping my head low in a passage as high and wide as a tunnel of the London Underground.

Then my hand collided with a wall of stone directly ahead. I paused, stretching out both hands. Behind me came the sound of Adam's breath. Groping at black space, I found only one unobstructed direction. I turned that way. A few yards later I hit another turn. When I lifted my head it grazed against the roof. A sweep of my hand found a gap no more than a yard wide between two protruding rocks. The gradient of the floor was steeper there. My knees had begun to smart. I started at the unexpected touch of Adam's hand on my foot.

"This is getting bloody tight," I gasped.

His silence offered no reassurance.

I said, "Does anything live down here?"

"Why do you ask?"

"I don't know. It doesn't feel empty. It feels as if…"

"What?"

"Never mind."

"Push on," he said. "It gets steeper now."

I turned my head back in the darkness and groped my way through the gap between the rocks. Now there was so little headroom I had to squirm upwards along a narrow passage on knees and elbows like an infantryman under fire. Why the hell was Adam doing this to me? Why had I been singled out for this ordeal? Why had I agreed to go along with it? I wanted the whole thing to be over now. I wanted to be out of there, to be back in the pleasurable world of light and life.

As if to compensate for being deprived of all sensory input, my mind began to traverse a gallery of memories – brief, luminous flashbacks, many of them startlingly clear. I seemed to glimpse in quick splashes of colour the fairy lights and balloons of childhood parties, and the glow of the chapel windows illuminating the Great Court on the night of the May Ball. I recalled the garish, spot-lit glamour of award ceremonies I'd attended and the cocaine glare of parties in war-torn cities of the world. Conflagrations of shell fire and napalm began to combust in my imagination as mutinous reminders of the lost world of light. And, weirdly in this all-concealing gloom, I seemed to detect, at the periphery of my vision, bright rectangles of light. Yet the darkness remained absolute.

Then I reached out my fingers and met a dead stop.

Groping with both hands, I found solid stone ahead of me. Again at either side, mere inches away, there were only walls of stone. No way through. This space was too tight to turn round and go back. It couldn't be the right way. I must have taken a wrong turn. I was stuck here.

Trying to keep calm, I said, "We've hit some sort of impasse. I'm feeling for a way through."

No answer came.

"Adam?"

Darkness swallowed the sound.

"Adam," I called again. "where the hell are you?"

Still there was no response. To the terror of this black trap was added the fear of being abandoned alone inside it. But Adam couldn't just have vanished. He must still be behind me, concealed in this passage, keeping quiet, waiting to see what I would do, how I would cope. No other explanation made sense unless – the thought stopped my breath – unless there had been a forking of the ways that I'd missed in the darkness and I'd crawled on into this dead end. Fighting against the panic threatening to engulf me, I moved my hands upwards in the only direction I hadn't explored. Beyond the top edge of the rock stretched a flat plane. Not a blockage – a step. If I pulled myself up I might be able to slide along at its higher level.

By now strength was draining from my limbs. The effort of shinning inch by inch up a sloping chute began to tell. I was running on empty when I raised my head and banged the crown against a rock. A spasm of lightning zigzagged through my brain. Tears came to my eyes. That's what I was reduced to now – tears and the taste of terror in my mouth. Everything else was gone. Everything I'd been, everything I'd done, all the devices and desires of my unrequited heart, every last pathetic shred of what I'd thought of as my identity was sucked out by a final vortex of despair.

"Adam," I murmured, "for God's sake…"

Even though I knew he'd gone, that somehow he'd slipped away, leaving me alone there, I strained to listen for the sound of his breath in the dark. All I could hear was a noise like tinnitus in my ears. Distant water? Or just the hiss of darkness swirling in to fill this untenanted space?

I slumped back, lacking the energy to curse Adam, and not even thinking about him now, because I was thinking about my father as I had last seen him, all signs of life extinguished, lying on his deathbed in Calderbridge. I could see him very clearly there. It was all I could see, like the lit corner of a studio, in the dark. Then I remembered: Adam had called this the House of the Dead. Hadn't I been told that I would confront my dead father here? Here he was now, and with a frightened, mirthless chuckle I realized just what kind of trap this was. This was the real deadfall that had been lying in wait for me, and here I was under the stone. This was the House of the Dead, and my father was dead inside it, and the only way I could have met him here was by becoming one among the dead myself.

So was that what Adam wanted? Was it possible that he still hated me so much after all these years that he was willing to let me crawl into this impassable place and leave me here to die? Could that have been his intention all along? And what about Marina? Surely she could not have consented to this?

Whatever the case, it seemed that it was about to happen, because I was drifting away, outside my body now, back inside the landscape of the dream. Again I was walking the quarry path on the hill above the town, dragging my father's emaciated body with me, naked and limp and utterly devoid of life. And I knew that now it would always be like this. It could never change. The two of us, father and son, were forever stuck together in a mortal embrace. I could feel the silent presence of his corpse there in the darkness with me, another portion of the dark. He was there because I'd dragged him with me every gruelling inch of the way. Adam might have gone, but my father and I were together again, as close to one another and as remote from one another as we had been on those Sunday mornings fifty years earlier, when I was a boy and he used to insist that I keep him company at the mill.

All boundaries were blurring now. I no longer knew where I was. There was a slippage in time, a slippage of consciousness, and I was back in the days of my boyhood, days when my father used to go to work so early in the morning and worked such long hours of overtime that I hardly saw him at all during the week. The arrangement suited me very well, because it left me unaccountable to him for the things that mattered in my life. I preferred him gone, because my life was easier that way. But then he made up his mind to strengthen the bond between us by insisting that on Sunday mornings I was to go with him to the mill, where it was his job to light and tend the fires in the boiler house, so that there would be a sufficient head of steam to drive the machines at the start of work next day.

On those still summer mornings, the plume of smoke he sent billowing from the high chimney stack would drift slowly over the hills and moors, and out towards the cold North Sea. Meanwhile, across the whole town, nowhere was emptier than the mill. To me it felt like a penitentiary. I didn't want to be there in the hot grime of the boiler house with this stranger in baggy blue overalls who was heaving shovelfuls of coal from the bunker to the furnace mouth as he tried to make me talk. I knew he was doing his fatherly best with his gruff jokes and questions, and must have been baffled by the glum way I shied from each approach. I knew that he was reaching out for me, and I didn't want to be reached, because I didn't want his kind of life, and had only incoherent yearnings for any other. So as soon as I felt able to do so, I would slope away to explore the rest of the mill.

And I was back there now, walking up the yard from the boiler house, past the panelled room where the black-and-scarlet engine rested, its wheel and pistons sleeked in oil, the leather drive belts hanging slack and still. Up the stone stairs beyond that room lay floor after floor of dusty halls, where the air tasted of cotton, and skips filled with varnished bobbins waited beside the machines. To enter there felt like breaking into a museum, as though the cast-iron jennies and carders were arranged not for use but for study and inspection, like the artefacts of an ingenious culture that might otherwise get lost and pass away. On those Sunday mornings there was not a soul about but my father and me. I could hear the scrape of his shovel down in the boiler house, and knew that soon I would have to go back.

But they were too long, those melancholy hours I was forced to spend with him, and wearing on the nerves with their tedious fatigue of evasion and pretence. After a time, when my distaste for them became too plain for him to bear, he stopped insisting that I accompany him, and things turned cold and rancorous between us.

And now, having resurrected and brought him back this way, it was impossible not to relive once more the long night of his dying, his breath rough as the sound of an old saw biting through unseasoned wood as he dreamt his morphine dreams on the lonely bed upstairs. Down below, my mother and I sat silently together listening, both of us dreading and praying that the sound would stop. And when at last it did, I went upstairs to make sure that he was gone, and laid him out before the undertakers came, folding his arms across his chest, staring in guilty awe at the lax penis slumped at his thighs, waiting till his eyelids stayed shut at last beneath my shaking fingertips.

But he was back with me now, laid out here in the darkness at my side. He had never really gone away, and this black passage through the rock might as well have been the gloom of the boiler house, with me tongue-tied there, hating the demands he made on me, wishing to be anywhere else on earth but there.

"Why won't you just talk to him," my mother had often asked me, caught between us, loving us both, watching us hurt each other as, again and again, we both hurt her. But my father and I had never really talked, not even when we went out drinking together as adults. We preferred to conceal our mutual vulnerability behind bluff exchanges that passed for conversation, or the barbs of sarcasm with which each strove for ascendancy over the other. And he had never understood that my failure to respond to his gruff chatter about cricket and football and horse-racing was no deficiency of spirit on my part, but an act of passive resistance. What had he ever known about my sense of wonder at the landscape round me? About my attempts at poetry? About the idealism that fired my political opinions and my work? When could he and I ever talk about such things? Even towards the end, when both of us had known he was dying, we still found means to avoid the desperate truth of things between us. And when he was gone, hadn't some part of me exulted with relief? Yet it seemed that I'd dragged his dead body with me into this last desolate place, where there was no foreseeable future for either of us, no present except the featureless present of this impenetrable darkness – only the past, the unassimilated past, from which more figures crowded round me now, invisibly observing me, keeping me from sleep. Who were they?

They were the other figures from the dream that had come to me in the storm by Lake Trasimene – my mother and all the other women, invisible in their kitchens, cooking the food, lifting the roasts from the oven, waiting, while we men were still out there, doing what men do. And here was my mother now, standing by her own oven, looking across at me, shaking her head in troubled, exasperated love. "If you won't *talk* to him," she's saying, "you might at least listen to what he has to say." And I know she's speaking about my father, who is lying there beside me in the dark.

So what did he have to say? What did he ever have to say that I wanted to hear? Nothing. Nothing that mattered.

Then I remembered that there was one thing at least – the true thing he'd said that day when he'd come home from work, still in his boiler suit, and found Marina in our cellar living room in Cripplegate Chambers, and they'd chatted together, happily, knowledgeably, about horse-racing, and he'd looked up at me afterwards and said the one true thing with which I could wholeheartedly agree. "Well, you've found a lass with a bit of sense about her. If *you've* any sense, you'll hang on to her."

Then I was biting my lip, biting back the grief as I remembered the time in London when I'd said to Marina, "I just want us to be together, whatever the rules."

Lying in that underground passage, I repeated the words to myself, and even as the darkness absorbed them I was thinking, *Wasn't that the reason why I left Gail and came to Umbria? Wasn't that why I'd agreed to Adam's dubious deal and followed him into the underworld?* Hadn't all the accumulated energy of my life's unrequited longing brought me to this place where I lay, ruing the worst mistake I'd ever made, ruing the way my life had been lived since then, the life of a man groping through a moral darkness which had brought me down at last into this actual subterranean darkness gathered closely around me now?

And at that thought I realized that in one cruel respect Marina and I were already together, for the darkness in which she lived was co-extensive with this darkness in which I was confined. Her darkness and mine flowed into one another in much the same way as did the water I could dimly hear falling in the distance and the water rising at Clitumnus springs. My life now felt so completely exiled from the light that no distinction could be made. Down here it was all one.

But then I realized that there was a difference too, for Marina remained steadfast and undefeated in her blindness, whereas I had given up on everything. Depleted of all energy, I lay abject and helpless, panting like an injured animal in its lair, willing myself to cultivate an animal's acceptance of its coming death. But the body wasn't ready to die. Either that or the soul wasn't yet ready to desert the body. All I knew was that something restless was stirring inside my emptiness. It had a voice. It had my father's rough and grudging voice, a voice edged with the familiar derisive impatience I remembered from my boyhood, speaking in the millstone-grit accent of the Calderbridge streets.

"Is that it then?" he growled into the dead-end silence. "You're giving up, right? And when I didn't answer, "Come on, speak up. Have you nowt to say for yourself? You've had enough, have you? You're just going to call it a day?"

"You know nothing of what I'm feeling," I said. "You never have."

"That's what you think, is it? You think I know nowt about what you're going through. Well, let me tell *you* summat. I've been there, lad. I've been there and worse. I'm talking about when the old *Karima* went down in the Atlantic and I was in the water and I couldn't swim, and I had to hold on to a bit of wreckage just to stay afloat. It were night and black as pitch and these big waves kept coming at me out of the dark, and I've never been so cold or frightened in my life. But I didn't give up, did I? I hung in there. I hung in there for what felt like bloody hours, and I got lucky. One of the corvettes in the convoy put a boat out looking for survivors, and I got picked up. Afterwards they told me that if I'd been in that water five minutes more, I'd have been dead as a doornail. They said I'd done bloody well to hang on for as long as I did. And do you know what it was that kept me hanging on all that time? I'll tell you. What kept me going was thinking about you and your mam. I thought to myself, *I'm not going to bloody die here when I've got a wife waiting for me at home and a little lad I've hardly seen owt of yet.* So I hung on and kept on shouting in the dark till some bugger heard me at last, and this lifeboat picked me up. You want to think on about that and learn summat. Or are you telling me you're not man enough to do owt but lie there whinging like a Mary Anne?"

"I can't turn round," I said, "and I can't go on. What do you expect me to do?"

"You'd never let me in, would you?" he said. I could almost see him shaking his head in the dark. "No matter how hard I tried, you'd have nowt to do with me. But it's not about me now, is it? It's all about thee, lad – though God knows what'd happen if I weren't here to give you a shove. So pay some heed. I reckon it's time you stopped thinking about yourself and started thinking about that lass. I've said it before and I'll say it again. If you've any sense, you'll hang on to her."

Flushed with the old frustrated rage against him, I snapped back, "Don't you think that's what I want? Don't you think that's what I've always wanted?"

"Then do summat about it. Let's see what you're made of. Frame yourself. Get on out of this bloody hole."

I lay there gasping in the silence, thinking I was going mad, remembering how many times he'd flustered and humiliated me when I was a kid trying to learn to ride a bike, trying to learn to swim, trying to do better on the cricket pitch, while he shouted at me, breathing down my neck, knocking me off balance with his irascibility and scorn. But hadn't that boy grown into a man who had outstared terrifying acts of war and terror such as he had never known? I had watched men dying in their blood, and done my best to comfort them. I had watched cities burn. I had walked among the murdered dead of Equatoria and done everything I could to make it as difficult as possible for the world to look away. What more evidence could anyone want that I was a man among men? So how come he could goad out the child in me so easily? How come he could never admit for a moment that he was impressed by anything that I'd achieved?

"Leave me alone," I groaned at him. "Just leave me alone."

After a moment's silence he said, "I'm going nowhere."

"What the hell do you want of me?" I demanded. "Can't you see that I'm just about done for? Do you expect me to drag you with me every sodding inch of the way?"

"Are you listening to me, lad?" he retorted. "Didn't I just say that *I* wasn't going anywhere?" I heard a sudden pathos in his voice. "Do you think I don't know that I've had my time? It's gone, long gone, and I did what I could with it, and God knows it weren't all for the best. I can see that now. I can see how I made you and your mother suffer because I was trying so bloody hard to be a man. A man's man, I mean. One of the lords of the earth. But it's no good that way. Not any more. And I don't want to see thee making the same mistakes. So get on with you," he ordered, though an urgent, weary care now softened the rough impatience I knew so well. "Do summat different with your life. Do summat better if you can."

I'd never heard him talk this way before. Not even on his deathbed had he uttered so frank a note of failure and defeat. Instantly it took me back to the moment when he lay panting beneath me on the dusty cotton bales in the warehouse at Bamforth Brothers' mill. But it wasn't the superior strength of youth that had wrestled him down this time. His defeat was self-accepted, a weary admission that his life was over, and that he was consigning the future to me as a legacy of his own failure. It felt like an act of entrustment, one which recognized that I might fail too, as every generation did, but fail in different and perhaps better ways. And in that sense it was no defeat at all. He was going nowhere, because there was no need for it. This was the House of the Dead. He had nowhere else to go. He was one among the dead. He belonged here now.

Then it came to me. I'd been dragging his dead body through my dreams not because *he* was hanging on to *me*, but because *I* was hanging on to *him*. Thirty years had passed since he'd died and in all that time I'd never been able to let him go. So if he'd come back and was alive again and full of menace, as he'd been in my dream, it was because I'd kept him alive inside me. But alive in the wrong way. Alive as an unloved and domineering part of myself. Alive as something that ought to have been allowed to die a long time ago but still lived on as the corpse that I dragged with me through my dreams. And that was my problem, not his. After all, what was he in truth except what all the many grieving friends who had turned up at his funeral considered him to be: a decent, fallible, ordinary man, doing his best by his lights to hold himself together and get on with things? No, he was right – this wasn't about him at all. It was all about me.

And, when that came clear, I saw that, for all the things I'd done, all the wars I'd followed, all the passing celebrity I'd won for myself, I'd hardly begun to live my own life at all. And it wasn't Adam's life that I'd been living either. Despite what had happened between him and me, between mé and Hal, I wasn't Adam's proxy after all. The truth was that for years, as far as my stultified heart was concerned, I'd been trying to live out my father's sort of life when I believed I was living my own. That was why he was with me still. That was why he still haunted my dreams. And, yes, it was absurd that the realization should have come so late, to a man already a year older than my father had been at the time of his death. But I'd seen it at last, and I knew now what both of us needed. What we had both needed for a long time.

In a final act of complicity, knowing it was what his sad ghost most desired of me, I loosened my grip and, with an immense sadness of loss and completion, I opened my hands and let him go.

It was as if a door had been thrown open on a compression chamber. I felt a convulsive gust of release. Then came a sensation of the darkness round me swooping towards invisibly distant light, and I knew that he was gone. Inside me the feeling of emptiness returned, intensified now, as if nothing remained there that was indisputably mine. All bearings were lost inside that sudden vacuum. Like a nervous flicker of residual memory from another life, I experienced a few seconds of panic. Then the fear began to dissolve, for the emptiness felt charged with latent possibility. Boundaries which had earlier blurred into the darkness in alarming ways were now merging again, but with the curiously restful knowledge that there was no distinction between the molecules of which my body was composed and those of the rocks and the air inside this lightless crevice and of the world beyond. It was all one, and as familiar again to me now as it had been long before when I was a boy utterly immersed in the Pennine landscape of my youth.

That restored communion lasted for no more than a few tranquil seconds, before consciousness of the condition clicked in and I was outside it, observing myself and my situation once more. A sensation of weightlessness remained, like that of a seed head afloat on a freshening breeze. I could see nothing and hear nothing, but in that lenient silence a dark tide turned and feeling came rushing in.

I lay for a time with tears in my eyes, ruing all the years in which, instead of mourning my father, I'd buried him alive inside me only to forget that he was still there. But now he was gone. We were free of each other, and for the first time in as long as I could remember I felt a deep-reaching pang of love for him. He was my father, we were one flesh, and I was thinking that in the last challenge he'd given me the old bastard had never spoken a truer word. "It's about time you stopped thinking about yourself," he'd said, "and started thinking about that lass."

So that's what I did. I pulled myself together and levered my body up again. My fingers fumbled for the gap I'd found the moment before I banged my head. The slot between the roof and the top of the rock felt slim but just passable. I squeezed my shoulders into the gap, dragged my legs after me and pulled myself along.

I don't know how many more yards I crawled inside the earth, enclosed and supported by it. Exhausted, I kept muttering quietly, as if to someone or something other than myself. Meanwhile images flashed across my mind: my grandfather on my mother's side, hewing coal with his pick, deep underground in a South Yorkshire colliery; Maximilian Kolbe in the bunker with a donkey-headed figure praying beside him; the bodies of the many dead dumped in the streets of Equatoria; and the woman in the yellow turban wailing over the body of her child. Yet, whatever other images came at me, again and again I willed myself to see Marina beckoning me on, drawing me through the dark.

Eventually, with all sense of distance and time deleted, I looked up ahead and thought I saw the faintest glimmer of rosy light. It came like a shot of adrenalin to the heart. I closed my eyes, shook my head and looked again. Faint but unmoving, the glow was still there. It might have been a candle flame burning just a dozen yards away, or the residual light of an extinguished star. There was no way to tell. But illusory or not, it gave me a goal to strive for. It gave me hope.

I groped my way along the next stretch, listening to my laboured breath. The light neither vanished nor grew brighter. I was beginning to wonder whether it was no more than a mirage after all, when the incline turned steeper and I saw that the light was shining downwards into the passage from a hole in the roof. Not itself a source of light, the radiance was cast from elsewhere, just enough to show there was headroom here to stand and stretch my grazed and aching limbs.

A dozen wary steps across a random fall of stone and I was looking up an angled shaft wider than a chimney some twenty feet high. Shadows thrown by the light revealed ledges offering handgrips in the rock. I guessed that others had passed this way before me. Using the same grips and toeholds that a cave dweller might have found twenty thousand years earlier, I made the climb. At one point I was forced to perch with my feet astride the shaft as I fumbled for the next grip. Then my fingers found a purchase. I swung my foot back across the gap onto a ledge wide enough for me to push upwards. A second later my head pushed through the gap and my dark-adapted eyes were so dazzled by a brilliant glare that I might have dipped my head into the sun.

Light seared across my vision, obliterating more than it revealed. Only gradually dared I allow its radiance to filter through. When I did so, I saw how it was generated by the massed ranks of burning candles, hundreds of them, each raising a silent hosanna in what felt like a convocation of flame. A figure loomed over me blocking out some of the glare. Then a hand reached down to help me through the gap in the rock. Astounded, overwhelmed with gratitude to have come through, and filled with crazy exultation, I think I gasped out loud. When I looked up, an expressionless mask stared back at me.

Half climbing, half pulled, I emerged into the rounded chancel of a candlelit cave. The bulky figure whose hand I had taken stepped back from the edge, and I saw many other people waiting for me, silent, motionless, all of them caped in white. Through air redolent with beeswax and warmed by the heat of many candles, I might have been looking at a company of exiled angels or at the assembled spirits of the dead.

"Well done, old thing," said the figure beside me. "We were beginning to worry."

I stood blinking in the light, my mind adrift in a vague terrain between reality and dream. But I could smell the dry air of this cavern round me, my shins smarted where they'd grazed against rock, and somewhere I could hear the sound of falling water. I had to trust the evidence of my senses.

Turning my head towards the sound of water, I saw an arch of rock that sprang like a flying buttress across a green pool, and knew that I was back inside the same chamber where Adam and I had taken to the skiff. And here was Gabriella, still in her carmine gown beneath the white cape, stepping forward from the assembled crowd to greet me.

"So, Mr Crowther" – her smile contrived to mingle concern with a mild, ironical detachment – "like our friend Guerino you have made a journey to the underworld in search of your father. But did you find him there?"

"Yes," I heard my voice answer in the silence of the cave, "I believe I did."

"And did you speak with him?"

I nodded my head.

"And tell me," she pressed quietly, "did you have the good sense to say farewell to him and leave him in peace?"

"I think so. I believe that's what happened down there, yes."

"Then you are welcome back into the land of the living," she said at last. "I think you deserve our congratulation." Smiling, Gabriella put her hands together and began to clap.

Immediately Larry Stromberg, who stood a couple of paces behind her, did the same, and then every one assembled in the cave joined the applause, with a benevolent air of welcome and approbation.

Bewildered, embarrassed, I began to feel like the dazed centre of attention at a surprise birthday party. Looking around at these people who had been waiting for me here in the light while I was scrabbling on my hands and knees through the dark, I recognized some faces: Allegra, Meredith Page, Dorothy Ziegler, Orazio, Angelina.

"Forgive me," Gabriella said, as the applause came to an end, "that you were kept for so long a time alone, but you came among us in ways which were not foreseen." She opened her hands in an extravagant gesture of self-exculpation. "If only you had done as Adam asked, things would have been arranged with more consideration."

"Where is Adam?" I asked. "He was behind me in the cave, and then he vanished. I don't know what happened to him."

Gabriella turned and gestured to Allegra, who took the hands of two cowled figures standing beside her and led them towards me. When they pulled back their hoods, I was looking at Adam and Marina. Neither of them spoke, but Allegra said quietly, "This should have happened a long time ago. I hope you'll be kind to one another."

Gabriella opened her hands and said, "So you have your wish to meet with Adam and Marina after all. Now something much more difficult must happen. Come, Lorenzo. Come, Allegra. Let us leave these three to talk together."

As they walked away towards the arch that led out of the cave, Adam took Marina's hand and guided her to where, in a ring of flickering candles, a rock formation roughly shaped like a stooping figure seemed to peer down into the pool. Marina sat down on a slab of rock at its base. Still without speaking, Adam sat beside her and gestured for me to join them on a slab a few feet away.

Marina must have heard the sound of my arrival, but she gave no sign of it. I now knew that she would have been unable to meet my gaze even if she wished to do so, but I felt both rebuffed and held at bay by the resolute way she kept her head averted towards the sound of water falling into the pool. Though only a few feet away from me, she felt unreachably distant. When Adam too lowered his head as if in a meditative trance, the three of us sat in uneasy silence for a time with the rough stone figure looming above us.

Eventually Adam drew in his breath and said, "You must know that this is no easier for us than it is for you. But Marina and I feel we can't go back to see Hal until we have a fuller understanding of everything that happened all those years ago. About what happened between me and him for a start, and the part you played in it. And I know that I have to come to terms with my father just as you have with yours, but this is about more than that." He looked up at me sharply then. "And it's not just about the three of us, though God knows we need to look at all that again – at the way you hurt us both as badly as you did. But Marina and I need to talk about our mother too. We need to understand what happened to Grace – why she did what she did, I mean. And we think you know."

Whether he knew it or not, Adam could not have found a more unnerving way to begin what had to be accomplished between us. I looked across the short distance and the great gap of time and duplicity that divided me from these two people I had loved so much and lost so cruelly. How to cross that gap? Did they know what they were asking? My eyes shifted away, up at the figure that seemed to lean above them in a gesture of protection. But there was no protection here. Nowhere inside this cave could a Faraday Cage be found. And I had no real desire for one. I had emerged from that dark underground passage like a creature breaking a chrysalis. All I wanted now was honest air and light.

"It all goes back such a long way," I began uncertainly, "probably further than you think. Are you sure it's what you want? Are you sure you're ready for this?"

"Why else do you think we brought you here?" Adam answered with a firm voice.

"What about you, Marina?" I asked. "You haven't said anything yet."

She lifted her face towards me, grave, uncompromising. "If you're asking me whether I'm ready," she said, "I've been ready for thirty years."

And before she could add another word, I had decided that, for me too, after three long decades of self-imposed and self-defeating silence, nothing less than a confession of the truth of what had happened after the start of our trust game back in London all those years ago would do.

21
Loyalties

For several days after the trust game began, I looked for Marina everywhere, but she was nowhere to be found. I carried her absence with me like a constant ache. Three times I went to her flat unannounced. The door was locked, the lights unlit at night. I hung about the Bloomsbury streets hoping to bump into her. I went to the gallery where her work was exhibited and saw no sign of her. Then I rushed home, scanning the crowds, driven by the thought that she had been looking for me in my part of London while I sought her out in hers. Each disappointment intensified the almost pleasurable pain of knowing that my life was incomplete without her.

But events at work were catching up with me, and my mind was made up to break the rules of the game by telephoning her when I came home one evening and found a postcard lying on the doormat. On one side was Van Gogh's *Starry Night*, on the other just five words: *Are you missing me too?*

The telephone gave me only her voice on an answering machine, so I tried coaxing the tape: "I know this is against what we agreed, but yes, I'm missing you like mad and, what's worse, I have to be away for a few days. *Work.* Could be a week, though I hope it'll be less. Then we have to get together. Definite time, definite place. Okay? Let's do it or – believe me – I'll go crazy."

After that I phoned Hal, as arranged, to let him know my place was free for a few nights if he wanted it, and waited in vain for Marina to call me back.

I did get back to London early. Earlier even than I'd hoped. Early enough to hear noises in the spare room of the flat as I opened the door.

"Hi, Hal," I'm back," I called, surprised to find him there in the afternoon. I was sorting out some shopping in the kitchen when he came into the hallway, where he stood in bare feet, staring at me with a queasy smile.

"Been sleeping off a hangover?" I said. "I've got news that'll wake you up."

"Actually, Martin," he forestalled me, "I... I wasn't expecting you back quite yet. This is..." As I had often seen him do under question, he stretched his arms above his head, clasped his fingers there and brought them slowly down to where his hair floated in silver-grey fly-away wisps. "Well, it's a bit embarrassing, you see." Biting his lip, he tilted his head towards the door he'd closed behind him.

"Ah! You've got a... a friend in there?"

I took in his nod and the downward flicker of his eyes before their vigilant blue stare glanced up again, warding me away. I dipped my own eyes away from that gaze. and saw the pale bones of his ankles and the yellowish hammertoe on his left foot.

"Right. I see. Okay." Crouching down to the fridge, I put away the beers I'd bought, and heard him clear his throat. I frowned up at where he stood across from me, a big man blocking the narrow hall. "Well, I guess I'd better go out again so you can... sort yourselves out. Will half an hour be long enough?

"If you really wouldn't mind."

"No, of course not. Best thing."

"Yes," he agreed. "Best thing."

As the front door closed behind me, fury swept over me. How had I got myself into the ludicrous situation of being turned out of my own flat for someone else's convenience? It might have been less infuriating if he'd lightened the moment with a joke of some sort. That would have been more Hal's way – a cavalier, unembarrassed pleasure in his own foibles. But those clipped sentences, the stubborn intensity of his gaze... he'd wanted me out of there. He'd been silently willing me to leave.

It wasn't just curiosity, therefore: more an uneasy suspicion that made me duck into the coffee bar down the other side of the street, from where I could keep watch on my front door through the window.

I didn't have long to wait. The door opened. A woman came out and turned back round on the threshold before I could make out her features through the condensation. She hugged Hal's half-hidden figure at the door, not simply in affectionate farewell, but kissing him urgently, with passion, several times, before hurrying down the street in the opposite direction to the one I'd taken. By then I'd taken in the fact that she was black, which would have caused me no concern if I had not immediately recognized the cherry-red beret she wore.

I sat down at the counter hearing the blood in my ears.

When I got back to the flat, Hal was still there, waiting to apologize. With his bag already packed, he'd recovered his composure and was ready to strike the lighter note he'd failed to achieve earlier. He was surprised, therefore, by my baleful mood.

"So," he said, "what's your news then?"

"I've been given a new assignment," I answered without warmth. "Chief Africa correspondent."

"But that's marvellous," he exclaimed. "Congratulations. We must celebrate. Let me take you out to dinner."

"I don't think so."

"Look," he offered with a rueful smile, "about what just happened... I'm really sorry. We'll make sure it doesn't happen again, okay?"

I heard my voice demanding, "What the hell are you doing, Hal?"

Taken aback by my tone, he blinked. "But... I thought we had an arrangement." He looked away from my stare, then slowly back again. "Of course, if you're not happy with it... I won't do this again. Perhaps that would be best."

The way out was open. I merely had to step through.

"Yes," I said, "I think that would be best."

"Right, well… yes, I understand. Of course." He leant down to pick up his bag. "I'll be on my way then. Mustn't crowd you out of your own place."

At the door he stopped, put on his jaunty felt hat and turned, smiling at me – a wan, suddenly much graver smile. "I really am sorry about this afternoon, Martin. Wouldn't have had it happen for worlds. Are you quite sure I can't take you out – to make amends? We could talk about the new job."

"I'm tired, Hal," I said. "I'd rather not. It can wait."

"Well if you're sure…"

"Yes, I'm sure."

Still he hesitated. "We *are* still friends, aren't we? Wouldn't like my little weaknesses to have come between us…"

I nodded, and glanced away.

"That's a relief! Good man! Had me worried for a minute. Till next time, then."

He turned to the door, and was about to open it when the words burst out of me. "I know who it was. I know who you were with."

Slowly he turned back to face me. "Ah," he said, though it was little more than a sigh, barely a suppressed gasp.

To fill the intolerable silence I said, "I saw her leave."

"I see." He stood there, gripping his bag in one hand while he swept the other across his mouth and cheek. "Do you… do you want to talk about it?"

"Don't you think we should?"

Vaguely he nodded his head. "Do you think I might sit down?"

Leaving his bag in the hall, he followed me through into the sitting room. I asked if he wanted a drink, poured him the stiff whiskey he asked for, and then another for myself. He sat with his elbows on his knees and his hands supporting his head, staring at the rug on the floor.

"God knows what you must think of me," he said. "I can't expect you to understand."

"It was a hell of a shock, Hal."

"And you must be feeling ill-used." He nodded as if to confirm the thought. "But you see, the thing is… we had nowhere else to go."

He glanced up at me out of desolate space, still wearing his jaunty hat. I was thinking that London was full of hotels, that there had been no necessity to implicate me in this disastrous intrigue, and I was on the point of saying so when, to my amazement, I saw tears begin to slip in silence down his face.

I sat down across from him as he dragged a handkerchief from his trouser pocket and pressed it to his face. Then he took off his hat and ran his fingers through his dishevelled hair. "I'm sorry," he whispered. "I'm so sorry."

Clearing my throat, I said, "You know this can't go on, Hal."

"No, of course not," he said. "I can see that it puts you in an impossible position. I wouldn't dream of bringing her here again."

"It's not just here," I said. "You can't go on seeing her, Hal. Not like this. Not here, not anywhere."

I saw from the immediate weary dismay on his face that he must have tried to tell himself the same thing many times, but it took the uncompromising certainty of my voice to confirm the truth of it.

"Yes," he mumbled, "I suppose you're right." He picked up his hat by the brim and turned it between his hands. Then he looked up at me, his haggard eyes ardent with appeal. "I wonder if I can make you see?" he pleaded. "I know what you must be thinking, but this isn't the squalid thing it must appear, you know. We do love one another, Efwa and I. And we need one another too. We're both exiles, you see… Both exiled from warmth and understanding. You have no idea how hard it's been. I tried to make it work with Grace after I got back from Equatoria, but... well, the thing's just dead between us. It's been dead for years. My fault, I'm sure. I know it is. Don't get me wrong. I'm not blaming her. But I can't lie in a cold bed, under judgement, Martin. And I've been so damn lonely and demoralized since everything went wrong out there in Africa."

For a moment I thought he was about to break down completely. I saw the breath shuddering through him. But he put his knuckles to his teeth, biting back the distress, and managed to regain control. He unclasped his fist, wiped his mouth and began to speak again.

"I've done my best to keep up a front, but.... Well, the truth is I was just about at the end of my tether when Efwa came to talk to me at an exiles' meeting and..." He faltered there and glanced across at me in appeal. "You have to understand, neither of us was looking for anything more than a bit of care and concern... not at first..." Hal closed his eyes and raised his hand to fend off a response. "And of course, I feel rotten with guilt about Adam. Sometimes I wake up sweating in the middle of the night. And then I can't sleep.... But what can you do when lightning strikes? And the thing is, he's no good for Efwa. He thinks he loves her, but he just doesn't understand her needs. He doesn't know how to hold her and keep her. She's only his *dream* of Africa, whereas for me she *is* Africa, heart and soul... in her hopes and her fears, in her little weaknesses as well as in her strength. And the great thing is that she gives me hope. Hope that my life can still be worth something. She makes me feel alive again – though goodness only knows what she can see in a daft old fool like me! But I know I matter to her, Martin. I matter to her very much. We've become each other's life, you see. We're only any good when we're together. Yet there's nowhere for us simply to be..."

Again he turned those blue beseeching eyes my way. But asking for what? Understanding? A degree of sympathy? Consolation even? Or was he hoping that, out of love or loyalty, I might relent and assure him it was fine to carry on using my flat to make love to a woman who was his daughter-in-law and the wife of my best friend?

"But it's impossible, Hal," I protested. "Surely you must see that? Imagine what would happen if Adam found out. It doesn't bear thinking about."

"No, he mustn't," Hal said. "Of course he mustn't."

"Then how can there be any future in it? You know better than I do how unstable Adam can be. I'm not sure he could survive finding out about this." Watching him wince against the pain of that thought, I said, "I have to think about my loyalty to him too."

"Of course you do," he answered. "I know I've no right…" – he gave me a beggar's sidelong glance – "but this is between you and me, isn't it? You wouldn't ever tell him?"

"What did I just say? Never in a million years. But you've got to get your head straight. You should never have let this happen in the first place, and now it has to stop. You've got to end it, Hal. Right away, however painful that might be. There's no other way out."

His voice was little more than a whispered croak as he said, "But what about Efwa?"

"What about Adam? What about Grace?"

He sat there on the couch, staring at his knees, nodding his head.

"You don't even have to think about it, Hal. You know I'm right."

Loudly he drew in his breath and sat for a time with his eyes closed. "Do you think I might have another drink?" he said eventually, and glanced at his watch. "Then I'd better make for my train, otherwise I won't get back tonight."

Watching as I poured another whiskey into his glass, he said, "I imagine you must despise me now."

"Never," I declared. "I think you've been a damned fool, but which of us hasn't been – especially where women are concerned?"

He nodded, looking suddenly much older in the bleak light from the window, then turned to me again. "I think I'm going to need some support to get through this."

"I know."

He seemed to draw some comfort from the response. Two swift swigs at the whiskey began to restore his dignity. But I just wanted him out of the place now, and it came as a relief to hear him say, "I'd better be on my way." He put his hat back on and looked down where I sat frowning in my chair. "I know how hard this must be on you. But you have no idea how much your kindness and your confidence mean to me." Then he stretched out his arms towards me. "Would you give me a hug?"

Such a thing had never happened between us before. In the tough northern culture from which Hal and I came, men did not hug each other. But I got to my feet. He advanced towards me, gripped my shoulders in his big embrace and whispered fiercely, "You're a true son to me." His grip tightened for a moment, and the act felt like a dubbing – an honour unexpectedly conferred.

Not long afterwards, he left. From where I stood at the door, I watched him take a deep breath as he regained some composure from the wreckage of his inner life. Then he straightened himself and walked away, braving the indifferent street like a disgraced politician, head held high.

Less than half an hour later the telephone rang. I'd just stepped out of the shower and stood, wrapped in a towel, listening to an urgent voice on the answering machine saying, "Martin, will you pick this up please?"

It was Marina's voice. I rushed to lift the receiver and said her name.

"I wasn't going to do this," she began. "I was just going to take off and never see you or talk to you again. But I decided I couldn't do that. That it would be an act of cowardice. That I had to speak to you at least, and hear whatever hypocritical cant you came up with to justify yourself. I decided that I had to tell you exactly what I thought of you before writing you out of my life once and for all."

"Marina," I protested, astounded by her vehemence, "what is this? I don't understand. I've been looking for you everywhere. Where have you been?"

"Where have I been? I'll tell you where I've been. Like the deluded fool I am, I've been in Somerset, working on a painting for you. Then I came back today and went straight to your place, hoping that I might see you, that I might give it to you. So I was there, Martin. I saw."

"Wait a minute," I said. "This isn't right. I don't think you understand..."

"What's to understand?" she shouted down the line. "I saw it with my own eyes. I saw the two of you together. I saw her leave your flat. I saw the way you kissed her as she left. I mean, just what kind of rat are you these days? I know you've had lots of stupid affairs. You told me so yourself. But I can't believe you could sink so low as to include your best friend's wife among them."

"Marina," I said, "that wasn't me."

After a moment's silence she said, "Is that the best you can come up with?"

"I'm telling you the truth."

"The truth?" Her voice was harsh with sarcasm now. "Right. Okay. If it wasn't you, who was it?"

I stood in silence with the receiver at my ear, thinking quickly, in confusion.

"Come on then," she defied me. "Let's hear it."

"I can't tell you," I said.

"I see. You know who it is, but you can't tell me."

"Marina," I said, "you're going to have to trust me about this."

"Trust you?" The words were an incredulous scoff. "Well, to hell with you, Martin! I learnt a long time ago that I can't trust men in general, and now I know to my cost that I can't trust you in particular. I'm a painter, for God's sake! What I trust is my eyes, and I know what they've seen. And what they saw disgusted me. So get out of my life, do you hear? And stay out of it. Keep clear of me. Don't try to see me or talk to me ever again. As far as I'm concerned, you don't exist any more."

She slammed down the phone. The receiver buzzed in my ear. I stood in the silent room, shaking.

22
Coup

I rang back at once, but heard only Marina's voice on the answering machine. I spoke to it, believing her to be listening, but she didn't pick up the receiver. I tried again. Again my recorded pleas elicited no response. I must have rung six or seven times without getting through. After putting down the phone for the last time, I decided to go straight over to Bloomsbury to confront her with the truth about what she had seen.

My knock went unanswered, and though it was getting dark I saw no lights at her windows. I scribbled a note asking her to meet me, telling her how important it was that we talk things through, but even as I pushed the scrap of paper through her letterbox I knew that she must have gone away. She had left London with the explicit purpose of avoiding contact with me, and I guessed she would not be back for some time. Adam might know where she'd gone, but I quailed at the prospect of talking to him now.

Each day that week I rang her several times and got no reply. I wrote draft after draft of a letter trying to explain what had happened, but I couldn't bring myself to post even the one I detested least. I was too conscious of the impact it must have – on Marina first and then on the rest of the family as the shockwave of the truth passed on. Also, rightly or wrongly, I had given my word to Hal. *Never in a million years*, I'd said, contracting myself in perpetuity to protect him from the fall-out of his folly. Even though it left me in torment, there were moments when I thought that promise was for the best. At other times I would happily have consigned Hal to whichever fiery hole in hell a vengeful fate might choose for him. But because Marina was out of reach, and because every cell in my body resisted the prospect of confronting Adam, I was unable to act.

The plan to make me the new Africa correspondent was well advanced. The appointment would take me out of the country for months at a time, and I knew that I couldn't bear the thought of leaving before I had spoken to Marina. So, doing the only thing I could think of, I rang High Sugden in the hope that Grace might know where she was.

"Marina? Oh goodness only knows!" Grace's voice felt distracted and strained. "If she's not in Bloomsbury, I've no idea where she is. It could be that place she goes to in Somerset. Or somewhere abroad even. Italy perhaps."

"You wouldn't have addresses for her in those places by any chance?"

"Oh dear, Martin, you know what she's like. She's been almost a stranger to us for years now. She never tells me anything. I live half in fear of a policeman turning up at the door some day saying something terrible has happened to her."

"Marina knows how to look after herself."

"Yes, but..." Grace sighed down the line. "Anyway, why did you want to see her? Was it something important?"

"Well... It's just that I'll be abroad for quite some time, and I thought it would be good to see her again before I leave."

"I see. And will you be visiting your mother before you go?"

"I was planning to, yes."

"Then you might look in on us too. Hal's been gloomy since he came back from London last week. I can't do a thing with him. But you've always been able to cheer him up. Do come and see us, won't you?"

I heard the note of entreaty in her voice, but such a visit was the last thing I wanted. "I'm not sure, Grace." I said. "I'll try to come if I can."

When I drove up to Calderbridge that Friday, I found my mother sitting alone in the house among her potted plants, staring at the television, elfin-thin and pale, with shadows round her eyes as though grief had permanently bruised her there. Her appetite for food and life had vanished.

"It never feels like there's much point cooking just for one," she said, "and if I do throw something together I can't face it when it's done."

When I insisted on taking her out for a meal, she said that she hadn't the heart for it, and that it would be just a waste of money, but I refused to hear her protests. "What do you think Dad would say if he saw you like this?" I challenged her. "He'd not be happy to see you letting yourself go. He'd tell you to get out and enjoy yourself while you have the chance, wouldn't he? So come on. Go and put a nice frock on. We're going out, you and me. All right?"

I took her to a restaurant of which I'd heard good reports and told her to ignore the prices on the menu. When a gin-and-tonic had relaxed her a little, we talked about old times together, laughing over some of my impossible behaviour when I was a boy, and fondly remembering my dad. Eventually I said, "I've been thinking, mum. Maybe you should get a job. Not just house-cleaning once or twice a week. A proper job. One that will keep you occupied and interested and gives you the chance to be with people."

"What could I do?" she asked. "I'm too old to be a barmaid these days. The only thing I know is cleaning. Who'd want me for anything else?"

"You never know. We'll have a look in the paper when we get back, and see what's on offer. I bet we can fix you up with something." After a pause I added: "And while we're on the subject, there's something else I wanted to tell you: *I've* been lined up for a new job as well."

She listened in silence as I described the posting to Africa, nodding when I assured her that I would be given regular leave to come back home.

"It won't be like Vietnam, will it?" she asked eventually.

"Not at all." I made no mention of the war against Portuguese rule in Angola and the brutal conflict between Nigeria and the break-away state of Biafra. "In any case, I won't take the job unless I'm sure you're going to be all right back here."

"You know I'll not stand in your way," she said at once.

"The point is I need to know you're not just sitting at home on your own all day, grieving for Dad and worrying about me. You need a bit of new life. And you could do with some new friends. Now come on, let's enjoy this meal. We'll talk about it again in the morning."

The next day I opened the curtains on the view of Gledhill Beacon looming over the town under a dour sky. A solitary patch of sunlight brightened the rim of the quarry, which was gradually, year on year, reshaping the contours of the hill. Nothing stayed the same, it seemed – nothing except the knowledge that, however far I travelled across the world, this landscape would always speak to my soul in my native tongue.

Later that morning, I took my mother shopping in Calderbridge, and we bumped into Grace as she came away from the butcher's shop in the Market Hall.

"I see we've both got sons at home this weekend," she said to my mother. "How are you doing, my dear? You're looking brighter than the last time I saw you."

"It's been a treat having our Martin back. He's lifted my spirits no end."

"I'm so glad. I wish I could say the same for Adam. He turned up late last night. We weren't expecting him."

"Isn't Efwa with him?" I asked.

"No, she isn't," Grace said pensively. "I haven't had a chance to talk to him yet, so I'm not sure what's going on." Standing outside the butcher's stall in the smell of meat and sawdust, she fixed me with a meaningful stare. "It's a shame you and Adam weren't in touch. You could have travelled up together. Is there any chance you might come and visit us tomorrow? I'm sure Hal and Adam will be glad to see you."

"I don't know," I prevaricated. "I think I should spend all the time I can with my mum. Especially with this new posting coming up."

"Oh don't you worry about me," my mother volunteered. "I'm used to being on my own these days. You get on out to High Sugden, lad, and meet your friends."

"Tomorrow then," Grace said with a smile, before I could speak again, "round about tea time?"

The Sunday morning was spent doing a job my mother hadn't been able to face alone – sorting out my father's clothes and shoes. To the hollow sound of bells pealing across the town, I bagged up his charcoal-grey suit, his sports blazer and flannels, his cricket whites, a few shirts and ties and a reasonably new topcoat, all of which I would take to a charity shop when I got back to town. I had just finished putting the bags into the boot of my car when my mother came down from her bedroom holding a tin caddy.

"Will you deal with this for me?" she asked, averting her eyes from my puzzled frown. "While you're out on the tops. He loved it up there. I think it's best."

She handed over the caddy. The label stuck to its side said: *The Macerated Remains of Mr John Reginald Crowther, 48 Gladstone Terrace, Calderbridge.*

I looked back at my mother. Her eyes were brimming with tears.

I drove out to High Sugden knowing that I would make up the fourth corner in a quadrangle of deceit. For if Grace had betrayed Hal, and Hal had betrayed both his wife and his son, while Adam alone had kept faith, hadn't I, one way or another, betrayed them all? Not least myself? And however one interpreted that tangle of treacheries, it seemed impossible that so fraught an occasion could pass without disaster. For if the truth about Hal and Efwa was revealed, my own name might be cleared and a way opened back into Marina's confidence – but who knew what degree of anguish must be endured before that could happen? How long could it be before Grace's pain and rage drove her to throw in Hal's face the fact that she had long since cuckolded him with one of his best friends? And once that secret was out, what hope could there ever be of winning Marina back? These bleak questions jarred in my brain as I sat at the wheel of my car that Sunday afternoon, barely conscious of the road around me.

Halfway up the lane from Sugden Foot to High Sugden, I pulled over by a field gate in a dry-stone wall and picked up the caddy. Getting out of the car, I saw how an old stone stile beside the gate gave onto a sloping pasture of rough grass, where a flock of sheep grazed on the tussocks. At the top of the field a rugged slab of rock shaped like the head of a giant saurian jutted from the outcrop.

The wind barged at my shoulders as I crossed the grass with the caddy gripped in my hand. Panting, I made the last steep ascent around the lower ridges of the rock face, up a narrow cleft onto its flattened topmost surfaces and out onto the slab. I stood there for a time, gazing down on the sheep and the wooded lower valley. To the east lay a more distant prospect of derelict mill buildings and chimney stacks, and the glint of water where the river poured its torrent into Sugden Clough.

With almost suffocating sadness in that fresh, wild air, I unscrewed the lid of the caddy and looked inside. It was perhaps three quarters full of a buff-coloured granular powder, not the grey ashes I'd expected. This was all that now remained of the body which had once filled out the clothes packed into the boot of my car. A body from which, some thirty years earlier, the seed of my own existence had been sown.

I looked up to check that the wind pushing at my back was not about to change. With a sweep of my arm I sent the remains of John Reginald Crowther blowing out across the steep slope of that Pennine hill. The swarm of grains lifted with the wind, hung for a moment as though seeking the right direction, and quickly dispersed on the bright air.

Then I turned back to the car, heavy-hearted, and drove to meet whatever wretchedness might be waiting for me at High Sugden.

Three other cars already stood in the yard. I parked close to where the water clattered into the trough, and saw Grace walking towards the house down the path that led up onto the tops. A little way ahead of her loped a single English setter which raised its head when it spotted me getting out of the car. Halting briefly to sniff the breeze, it barked and came bounding down the track.

"You've lost one of the dogs," I called as Grace entered the yard.

"Hengist died a couple of months ago," she answered. "We had to have him put down, poor old chap!" She knelt to tousle the ears of Horsa, who stood beside me, panting, with his tongue lolling from his flews. "We miss him dreadfully, don't we, sweet boy?"

"I'm sorry to hear that. How's Adam today?"

"Desperately miserable, I think. He's been in bed most of the time since he arrived. And he won't talk to me: you know how tight-lipped he can be when he's in trouble. I'm sure things can't be going well with Efwa. You haven't heard anything, have you?"

"I haven't seen him for ages," I said.

"No? Well... I know how much your friendship has always mattered to him. Let's see if you can't open him up a little. Come on in. I'll put the kettle on."

As soon as we went through into the hall we heard the muffled sounds of raised voices coming from Hal's study up the stairs. Grace stood with her hand gripping the carved owl on the newel post, looking up the wide oak treads at the gallery beyond. "That doesn't sound good," she said. We both strained to make out the words but could distinguish only the tone. On both sides it sounded heated and bitter.

A bang came from the study, as of a fist crashing down on a desk. I felt Grace catch her breath beside me. Hal's voice shouted something that might have been, "Just get out. Get out." And then more clearly as the study door opened, "Just get out of my bloody study and leave me alone."

"All right I'm going," Adam shouted back. "God knows why I thought there was any point trying to talk to you in the first place! It's hopeless! And you know what sickens me most? It's the thought of how much I admired you once. When I think of the times I've tried to defend you against Marina! But she's right. You're just an egotistical bastard who cares about nothing but his own selfish interests. You've never been a father to me. You've never really listened to a word I've said. As for real feeling – I don't think you'd know a real feeling if it exploded in your face."

"Don't you dare talk to me like that," Hal shouted. "You know nothing about my feelings. Nothing."

"So what does that tell you? That you've never known how to show them, right?"

"I don't want to hear any more of this."

"Of course you don't – because you can't bear to face up to the fact of what a fucking disaster you are. A disaster as a father. A disaster as a husband. A disaster as a politician. A complete fucking failure of a human being."

"And what are you then?" Hal demanded. "A weakling who couldn't stand a bit of intellectual pressure at Cambridge. Someone who's thrown up every opportunity that's been put his way for want of courage and moral fibre. No wonder you come snivelling to me with some sob story about your wife. If you were any sort of man you'd have taken better care of her."

Then Grace's voice rang out up the stairs. "Stop it." she shouted. "Stop it at once. Both of you."

The air of the house hung about our heads, still as dust.

Grace stood white-faced at the foot of the stairs, her eyes tightly closed as though against intense neuralgic pain. But Adam had turned on his heel and walked along the gallery to the top of the stairs where he stopped and shouted "Bastard! Bastard!" at the study door, which was slammed shut against him.

He got halfway down the stairs, staring at us, amazed to find us standing in the hall as witnesses to his rage and humiliation. Then he stopped, sagged down on one of the bare oak treads and sat, still trembling with rage, holding his head between his hands.

"My darling," Grace gasped. "My poor, poor darling."

"Leave me alone," he snapped, fending her off with a flap of his arm. "Just leave me alone, will you?"

"You mustn't take any notice of him," Grace said. "Your father's been terribly depressed lately. He doesn't know what he's saying."

"He knows exactly what he's saying," Adam snapped back at her. "He knows exactly how to undermine what little confidence I have. The man's a monster. I don't know how you can bear to live with him. You should have left him years ago." When his mother failed to answer, he stared down at me, his face filled with hostility. "What the hell are you doing here?"

"Grace asked me to come and see you. Both of you. You and Hal, I mean."

"Oh yes? I suppose you're going to tell me you agree with him – that I was a fool to marry Efwa in the first place? That I've thrown my life away? Unlike you, of course, who's turned out to be just the sort of son that bastard always wanted? Well, as far as I'm concerned, you're welcome to one another. He's never been a father to me. I'd sooner die than be the kind of son he wants."

"Adam" – Grace reached out to him – "you mustn't think that way. It can only hurt you. What's been happening? What's happening between you and Efwa? You have to talk to me."

But Adam merely sat on the stairs with his head in his hands, staring down at his feet.

Grace glanced helplessly at me. I had no idea what to say or what to do. My strongest desire was to be out of that wretched house and running through the clean, wild air of the tops, running till my breath gave out or the blood burst in my ears. "Could you get us something to drink, Grace?" I said instead. Then I looked back at my friend. "Come away from there, Adam. Let's go through into the sitting room. Let's try and talk."

He glowered at me before rising and following me. I sat down in the buttoned leather chair by the window that faced south onto the garden, while he sank onto the couch across from me without saying a word. His lean features were dark with stubble. Not since that night in Cambridge years before had I seen him looking as desolate as this.

"Do you want to talk?" I asked.

"What's the point?" he scowled. "If I've learnt anything over this last week it's that words don't make a blind bit of difference. I tried talking to Efwa till I was blue in the face, and it got me nowhere. You've seen what happened when I tried to talk to Hal. What good do you think talking to you will do?"

"I don't know. Perhaps none. But silence can be worse, can't it?"

"I wanted to speak to Marina," he said. "I thought she might be able to help, but she's disappeared. I've no idea where she is. That's why I came up here. I couldn't stand another minute cooped up in that flat with Efwa not talking to me."

"She hasn't said anything to you then?"

"Not a word. But it's obvious she's having an affair. I've suspected it for weeks. She'd been unhappy for ages, and suddenly she brightened up and started taking trouble over her appearance again. Then it finally dawned on me. But when I tried to talk to her about it, she just got ratty and offended, so I was left with these rotten thoughts going round in my head.

Then something happened, about a week ago. She must have been dumped by her lover. She's been shut up in the bedroom most of the time since then, and won't talk to me. God knows who she's fallen for – probably one of the Equatorians from the exiles' group. One thing's for sure: she's not pining for me."

I looked away from his bitter scowl and saw Grace through the half-open door, standing in the hall with a tray of drinks, listening. Unaware of her presence, Adam said, "I had to get away last night. I couldn't bear it any more."

"But if you're right and the affair's over," I said, "can't you just give it some time? These things happen, Adam. Give her a chance to come round and start over again."

"You haven't seen her. You haven't seen the state she's in. I don't think there can be any going back." Adam's voice was breaking as he spoke. I thought he was about to weep. I looked away, hot with the knowledge that I only had to say, "It's Hal, Adam. It's your father who's seduced your wife," and the shock alone would have been enough to convert him from this abject wreck into a man ready to wreak murderous vengeance. That would have been it. No more deceit, no more equivocation, just the cruel fact of the case out there to be lived with, one way or another, once and for all, by each one of us – Adam, Efwa, Hal, Grace, Marina eventually, and me. But with a visible effort Adam pulled himself together. So I sat there in silence and watched Grace come in through the door with the tray of drinks trembling in her hands.

"I think we could all do with one of these," she said.

"That's always your answer, isn't it?" Adam snapped back at her.

"You have to stop this, Adam," Grace said with astounding severity. "I know you're hurting, but lashing out at those who love you won't do any good."

"And just who would that be?' The sarcasm was as caustic as his stare. "The only one of you who really cares about me is Marina. And you and Hal drove her into hiding years ago. God knows where she is now that I need her."

Rising to my feet, I said, "You're not being fair, Adam."

"Fair! You think there's anything fair about this world? And as for you – do you imagine I'm blind? Do you think I haven't watched you taking over my life?"

I was at a loss how best to answer the accusation when Hal's voice growled from the open door. "Face up to it, Adam," he said in a voice of calculated derision. "You've been given every chance in this life. No one's responsible for your failures but you."

"Leave us alone, Hal," Grace urged, "You'll only make things worse."

Hal stood motionless, glaring at his son. "Be quiet, woman. This is between me and him. He's not angry with you or Martin. It's me he hates, and he always has done. He hates me because he knows he'll never be half the man I am. Isn't that right, Adam?"

I heard Adam wince. When I turned to look at him his eyes were wide, his mouth open as if gasping for breath.

"You know something, you unspeakable fucking bastard?" he said at last. "I wouldn't be *twice* the man you are if it meant being in any way like you at all."

"Get out of my house," Hal said with cold, suppressed violence. "Get out and don't come back."

"Why would I ever want to come back here?" Ignoring Grace's pleas, Adam brushed past Hal and left the room. I heard the sound of his footsteps crossing the stone flags of the hall, and then that of the heavy studded door banging shut behind him.

From where she stood, staring at her husband in a fierce trance of disbelief, Grace hurried out after him.

Hal reached out a hand for the back of a chair and sat down, staring into the empty, soot-charred recess of the open hearth. Neither of us said a word. Through the window onto the yard I saw Grace leaning to speak to Adam, who sat with his hands gripping the steering wheel of his car. He shook his head several times. Holding on to the open door, Grace stared about her in dismay. There was a last brief exchange before Adam pulled the door shut and drove away. Grace stood with a hand at her mouth, watching him go,

"It's done," Hal muttered into the silence of the room. "Once and for all it's done."

"Oh God, Hal," I said, "I think you've just lost them all."

"I know," he said, "I know."

"I don't understand why you had to be so cruel."

His eyes studied me briefly, and then looked away. "Don't you?"

"No, I don't."

Almost wearily he said, "Then consider the possibility that it might have been for his sake." For a time Hal sat withdrawn in silence before shaking his head. "At least I didn't lie to him," he added at last. But he might have been speaking to himself.

I said, "You couldn't have hurt him much worse if you'd told him the truth."

"The truth?" Grace demanded from where neither of us had seen her standing at the half-open door to the hall. "What truth?" She advanced into the room, pushing back her wind-dishevelled hair. "What are you talking about?"

When neither Hal nor I answered, she arrived at her own conclusion. "You're talking about Efwa, aren't you? You know who she's been having the affair with." In the same moment her face blanched with another sickening realization. She turned her fierce, unforgiving eyes on me.

"You," she said. "It's you, isn't it?"

"No, Grace," I answered at once. "No."

She seemed instantly to accept the honesty of my unflinching gaze. Either that or some terrible intuition was already breaking across her mind.

"Then who?" she said in a voice charged with all the implacable power of a woman's desire for truth. "Who?"

*

In the years that followed I often wondered whether disaster might have been averted if I'd stayed on longer at High Sugden than I did that evening. But nothing I might have said could have proved stronger than the fate that had begun to gather about Hal's head from the moment he first succumbed to his infatuation for Efwa.

In any case, having once realized where the true guilt lay, Grace wanted me out of the house and gone. She assumed that I must have been complicit with Hal all along, and after that she had nothing more to say to me.

Nor do I know what she found to say to Hal. When I left High Sugden to drive back to London, they were sitting in a time-fused silence, waiting for whatever words emerged to shatter it for ever.

I drove back down England through heavy rain. The A1 unspooled through the darkness ahead of me. Every now and then I'd see a sign flash by and would be surprised to discover how far I'd travelled.

The traffic thickened as I entered London. It was well after midnight when I got home and found the envelope that had been pushed through my letterbox. The neat handwriting was unfamiliar to me, but when I unfolded the single page of the letter and began to read, I recognized the sender clearly enough.

Dear Martin,
I am writing this letter because yesterday I have come to your house and you are not there and soon I will be gone from UK. I don't know what to write because already I think you will think me as a woman who is not good at all. Maybe is so. I have done certain wrong things and I am feeling too too bad for Adam but God will decide. Now I have to go from my house here. Adam has raised his hand to me one time and even I think he would have beat me but he is a good man who

thinks it better that he hurts in himself. Maybe I am feeling better if he has beat me. But now he has gone for his father's house in High Sugden and I don't know what he will say.

I think now I have to go from UK before the truth can kill us. I have friend who will help me and I know that my family in Adouada has need of me now. After that I don't know. But I beg you please to tell Adam that I have fear for him . My heart is all hurt and I too sorry for the pain I have give. Now I have my trust in you even as Hal has trust in you. You are our good friend for all of us and we are all in God's hands .

From your friend Efwa

Throughout the next two days I tried to ring Adam, but got no answer. Then, on the evening of the second day, my own phone rang. It was Hal on the other end. He was so distraught that it took some time for me to piece together what he was trying to tell me.

Earlier that day, a group of children out playing on the moors had found a tidily folded pile of clothes on the edge of the dam beside the ruined mill near the head of Sugden Clough. On top of the pile, held down by a stone, lay a piece of paper with a brief hand-written note, of which they could make no sense.

While the girls were examining the clothes, one of the boys dived into the water. Several feet below the surface he found a white body suspended head down in the murk. The left wrist was tied to the iron axle bar of a cog wheel half-buried in mud.

Some two hours later the first policemen arrived on the scene. Knowing nothing of the laconic, despairing spirit which had once animated the poor drowned body, they too were perplexed by the note. It read quite simply, *Coup de Grace.*

23
Revenant

Thirty years after those events, the account I gave of them that night inside the water theatre at Fontanalba was not so coherent. I often hesitated. At some points I found it hard to speak at all. Briefly I considered omitting any mention of what had happened between me and Grace, but then I saw how my public loyalty to Hal would be inexplicable without the admission that it was the corollary of private guilt. Even so, I was doing my best to navigate my way past that difficult confession when I recalled the manner in which Grace had once remarked that sooner or later Marina would get the truth out of me. In that moment, Grace's reproachful figure pressed on my conscience. Nothing, it seemed, could be concealed for ever. And hadn't I promised there would be no equivocation this time? In any case, what point in telling the truth at this late stage unless that truth was complete?

The long silence after I had finished speaking felt intensified by the sound of falling water. Adam and Marina had come to the cave expecting to hear me confess my guilt, but what they heard was not what they anticipated, and I could feel them striving to adjust. Marina remained withdrawn and inscrutable, cloistered inside her darkness. Adam sat beside her with his hands tightly clasped in his lap, absolutely still. He had been weeping silently as I spoke, and for the first time I was struck by how much his haggard face had come to resemble his father's with the passing of the years.

"Did Hal ask you to tell us this?" he said at last.

"No – not in so many words."

"But he knew that you might?"

"I imagine so. I think he must have wanted me to tell you."

Adam voice was hoarse with grief. "I can't bear to think what my mother must have gone through."

Marina remained frozen inside her silence, her face averted as Adam made a visible effort to pull himself together. "There's been a tragic waste at the heart of all of this," he declared. "A waste of life. A waste of friendship. A waste of love. It looks as though one way or another we've made a mess of everything between us."

"Yes," I agreed, "I'm afraid we have."

"But maybe some of it is still redeemable."

"I'm hoping so," I said, perhaps too quickly. "I know that Hal hopes so too'

Adam shook his head. "I don't know about Hal. I can't even think about seeing him yet. Right now every nerve in my body is shrieking *To hell with him*." He turned incredulous eyes on me. "I mean, how do you forgive a father for stealing your wife, for God's sake? Or for driving your mother to kill herself?" Again he shook his head, as if to clear it of impossible thoughts. "What kind of saintliness would that take? Part of me is ready to murder him with my own hands for what he did." His expression had become a white scowl as he spoke. I could sense the old anger and bitterness rekindled inside him as if each word was a breath blown on still-smouldering coals. "Even at the time," he said, "when I didn't know the half of it, I hated the two of you more than I've ever hated anyone in my whole life."

"I know," I said. "I can still feel it." And I think that we must both have been remembering the moment in the Coroner's Court thirty years earlier, when having heard me endorse Hal's plausibly edited account of the events preceding Grace's death, Adam and Marina had stared across the crowded courtroom at me, both of their faces radiating hatred, and white with the cold, incredulous fury of those who know themselves betrayed.

Quietly Adam said, "But it turns out that you weren't just protecting Hal, were you?"

The question needed no answer, but it prompted me to say the difficult thing that I thought he needed to hear. "I don't believe that Hal was just protecting himself either."

"You mean me?" he frowned. "And you think that exculpates him?"

"I didn't say that. But he's my friend. He was my friend before all this began and he's been lacerating himself with grief and guilt ever since.

Worriedly aware that Marina had not yet uttered a word, I felt sure that she must be preparing some vehement condemnation of her father. Her face was turned away from me still. She sat motionless in her white cape, a marble statue of contemplation, revealing nothing of her feelings and leaving it to her brother to respond.

"You can't expect me to feel much in the way of sympathy for Hal right now," he said. "It's Efwa I'm thinking about."

"But wasn't she as much a victim of all this as the rest of us?" I said.

"Don't get me wrong. I'm not looking to blame her. Not after all this time. What would be the point of that? I'm just wondering what happened to her – after she returned to Equatoria, I mean." His eyes winced shut. "Chances are she's dead by now, like so many others, I suppose."

"Actually she's alive," I said quietly.

Adam's eyes widened again. "You saw her?"

"In Fontonfarom, yes. Somehow she survived the massacre there. She's been helping to run a makeshift orphanage in the old Middle School building. Of all the people I was looking for on my last trip, she was the only one I found." I hesitated for a moment before deciding to add, "I've got her on video, if you can bear to watch."

"You filmed her?" Adam exclaimed in disbelief. "What about helping her to get away? Wasn't there something you could have done for her? Didn't you think about that?"

"Of course I did. But she wouldn't come. And she *wanted* me to film her. She demanded it. She wanted the world to know what was happening in Equatoria. And there was no way she was about to abandon the children in her care. In any case," I looked up at Adam, "what would there be for her here?"

He opened his mouth to reply, but then turned wretchedly away. "Nothing," he acknowledged. "I failed her. I failed her years ago. I never saw her clearly. Not from the start in Equatoria, let alone in London." But now he was speaking more to himself than to me. "She badly wanted to have children," he said, "and I wasn't ready for that. I was too young. Or perhaps I was just too scared." He pushed a hand through his thinning hair. Then, like a man dazed by his own admission, he added, "The truth of the matter is that Hal probably understood Efwa better than I did."

"Who knows?" I said. "But sooner or later we have to forgive our fathers, don't we?"

Apart from the sound of the water falling into the pool, there was, for a time, only silence in the cave. All three of us were locked inside our own thoughts. Faced with Adam's anguish and Marina's continuing silence, I became convinced that I had made a terrible error of judgement in revealing the truth. Might it not have been wiser to get away from Fontanalba days ago after I'd done what I came to do? It would have been their choice whether or not they wanted to see their father again, and at least I would have left them with their illusions intact. And though such a course of action might have meant all kinds of loss to me, I had been living with loss for thirty years and was almost inured to it. But the truth was out now, and there was no going back. All three of us would have to live with the consequences, and for Adam, who was in so many ways the most vulnerable, they might prove disastrous.

But I had underestimated my friend and the degree to which the years had transformed and strengthened him. I heard him utter a small, dismissive laugh. Looking up, I saw him shaking his head at me with a perplexed and rueful smile. "What is it between you and me?" he said. "Ever since we first met, we've been confusing each other about who we are. When I came in here tonight I thought that you were the one who would be looking for forgiveness from me, and that it was my role to be magnanimous. But that's been turned upside down, hasn't it?"

"There's nothing I have to forgive you for," I said.

"Only half a lifetime of misjudgement!"

"Which only happened because I withheld the truth."

"And now I understand why," he said, "even though I think you were wrong to do it. Wrong for yourself certainly. Wrong for you and Marina too. And probably wrong for me as well. Haven't we all been living out a lie for all these years because of it? But it was a lie that came from care, and I can't blame you for it. In fact, I guess I should thank you for it."

"But then," I said, "I have to thank you too."

"You do? What for?"

"For my trip to the underworld, and for what happened down there."

Adam studied me with searching eyes. "We should talk more about that. But it sounds as though you kept your side of the deal."

Encouraged by his wry manner, I said, "So what about yours?"

He drew in his breath before answering, "I suppose I'll have to honour it. I can't see how else to put an end to all this – though it's going to take me some time to find the strength." He glanced down at his sister and stroked her hair with an affectionate hand. "But you and Marina need to talk to one another now. Alone, I mean, without me." His brow wrinkled in a frown as he looked back at me. "I don't know what else to say right now, except that I'm utterly saddened by everything that's come between us."

"Me too," I responded, and a moment later, to our mutual amazement, we found ourselves moving into an awkward embrace. Briefly it felt as though the long, conflicted scissors movement of our lives was resolving itself into a completed circle. Then he picked up a candle, walked away across the floor of the cave and disappeared into the darkness of the arch, leaving me alone with Marina.

Impassive as a statue of herself, Marina sat among candles beneath the figure in the rock. She had gathered the white folds of her cape about her, holding it closed just below her throat as if to protect herself against the cold. Yet it was not cold in the cave, and there were no winds to ruffle her hair or scatter the sleek fall of water into the pool. Her knuckles shone in the candlelight, her face was half turned away.

If Marina had been at all moved by what she had heard, her feelings did not show. I had told her everything, and she was giving nothing in return. Clearly my unpalatable truth was not what she had expected – how could it have been? – but her composure alarmed me. I was left doubting whether it would be possible to retrieve half a lifetime of loss and grief and guilt with a single conversation, but at least we had to begin.

"What about you, Marina?" I said. "I've no idea what you're feeling now."

She turned her sightless eyes my way. I wanted to meet them, but couldn't. "What do you want me to feel?" she sighed. "Gratitude that you've been honest with us at last? Regret that I didn't give you the chance to explain yourself all those years ago? Perhaps you want an apology for the way I misjudged you as badly as I did? I don't know what you can possibly want of me any more."

"I don't want any of that," I said. "What I want is to feel you here, present, feeling something – anything – I don't care what, so long as it's real. Anything but this cold distance. I can't believe in that. I was prepared for you to be furious at what had happened. Furious at me, furious at Hal. Furious at life and what it's done to us. I expected you to be outraged by the truth."

"It didn't even surprise me very much." She frowned and shook her head a little. "I always knew that Hal was lost to himself, forever confusing what he wanted with what was the right thing to do, always meaning well, and yet succeeding only in wrecking people's lives." She turned away again. "And why on earth should I be furious with you? You made your choice and took the consequences. But I'm not thinking about that now. I'm thinking about Grace." I caught my breath at that, but it was herself she was questioning. "I'm thinking about how I never really understood her – drinking the way she did, withdrawing inside herself rather than fighting him. I didn't allow myself to see that she was struggling simply to survive. And in the end, of course, she couldn't. He was too much for her. For all of us really." Marina was rocking a little as she spoke. "I've thought about her every day since then, and even after all these years part of me is still angry with her for doing what she did, for the harm it did, especially to Adam. Yet at the same time I can't forget the countless ways I hurt her and belittled her without even thinking about what I was doing or why I was doing it. Adam feels the same, I know. So it wasn't just Hal, was it? None of us were innocent in Grace's death – not even you, Martin."

I told her I knew this was true. I said that one of the hardest things for me was knowing that I was never worthy of Grace. Not on that fraught afternoon we spent together, when she was so miserable she hardly cared what she was doing, and not afterwards either. Certainly not towards the end. "She took the distance I kept from her as a judgement," I said, "though it was never meant that way. It was just the awkwardness with feelings of a young man out of his depth."

"And you don't think Grace understood that?"

"Perhaps she did. The truth is that I've always found it hard to think about Grace at all.

"But we have to, don't we?" Marina insisted. "Wasn't that what Adam was saying just now? That we have to face things –

especially the things that trouble us most. So we try to convince ourselves that we don't know them at all – until sooner or later something happens that we can't argue with. For me that was Grace's death. And it happened just at the point when I'd truly begun to understand something of her pain… to know how it feels," she added with an uncertain tremor in her voice, "to be betrayed by someone you love very much."

After an uneasy moment, I said, "I didn't betray you, Marina."

"You didn't trust me with the truth," she answered, "so it felt like betrayal."

"But you didn't trust me either."

"That's true. I couldn't trust you, because I asked you for the truth and you refused to answer me. What was I supposed to make of that? After that, everything was impossible."

"I couldn't tell you," I said, "because I loved you."

"Even though that meant wrecking both our lives?" I could feel both anger and sorrow behind the accusation. Something of the old, volatile heat had returned to her voice. "It didn't spare Adam much in the way of pain, and it certainly didn't save Grace. So tell me, Martin, would good *did* it do?"

I sat in silence, remembering and ruing the fateful trust game that Marina had asked us to play and how we had both been losers in the end.

"If I *had* told you back then," I said, "what do you imagine that would have done?"

"Who knows? If I'd known the truth, I might have confronted Hal before Adam did. I might have been able to strengthen Adam against him. I might even have found a way to help Grace. How can I know what might have happened? Probably it would all still have proved disastrous, but at least it would have been real."

Her blind gaze could not take in the anguish in my face. In that moment what I wanted more than anything else was to cross the space between us, to take hold of her – and somehow, through the immediacy of touch, scroll back the years and return to the night in London when she and I rediscovered one another and all things began to feel possible again. But time grants no such mercies, and the distance separating us stretched wider and was far less easily traversable than the one that Adam and I had crossed. Marina had turned her face away from me again. I could see only the sheen of her hair in the candlelight.

"So are you telling me that this is unredeemable after all?" I said.

"No," she answered dully, "not entirely. I dare say Adam and I will go back and try to do for Hal what we couldn't do for Grace – make it a little easier for him to face his death, I mean. Somehow we might even manage to forgive him. Like you said the other night, isn't forgiveness about as close as we can get to love, these days?"

"And what about us, Marina?"

"Us?"

"Yes, us. You and me."

"We both got things wrong," she said. "So of course we must forgive one another. It goes without question."

"But that's not enough. Not for me anyway."

When she averted her face, I said, "You know why I came to Italy."

"You came because Hal asked you to come. You were doing it for him – just as you withheld the truth for his sake all those years ago."

"Not true," I said. "Not true on either count. I think you know that. I think you know that I came here looking for you."

The sound of water falling into the pool, that susurration of white noise, filled the silence between us.

"I can't see your face," I said. "I don't know what you're thinking."

When she turned my way again, I saw only sadness without any sign of hope or expectation in her features. *This is how things stand,* they seemed to say. *We made them so. This is the price and consequence of who we are. We have no grounds for complaint.*

But I wasn't about to submit to her silence. "It's true that Hal's asked me to come," I conceded. "It's true that I was doing what I could to help him by coming here. But the real reason I came was for my own sake. I came here looking for you."

"Then perhaps you were doing the right thing for the wrong reason."

"Isn't that better than doing the wrong thing for the right reason? Or what I thought was the right reason? I've already wasted half my life that way. Don't ask me to throw away any more of it."

"I'm not asking you for anything."

"Why are you doing this?" I said. "Why are you withholding yourself this way?"

"Why did you withhold the truth from me?" she countered.

"I've told you already."

"And that kind of moral evasion is consistent with your idea of love? Do you really believe that anyone has the right to keep another person ignorant of something as vital to the whole fabric of their life as that?"

"No, not if they have something to gain from withholding the knowledge. But I didn't, Marina. I only had something to lose."

I watched her withdraw again into silence, putting a hand to the rock formation as if for support. But I had not made that journey through the dark only to lose her again as I had lost her all those years ago,

"I came because I want you back," I said.

Her chin tilted as she took in my words. Then she shrugged with a weary air of resignation. "It's too late. Everything's different now. That time's gone. We live in different worlds, you and me. You don't know who I am any more."

"I know who you are for me."

"You knew the woman I was thirty years ago. Everything in my life has changed since then. You know almost nothing about me now. You have no idea about my life, about what I do here, about what matters to me."

"You don't think that, after what I've just been through, I'm beginning to get some sense of it?" Some of the rapture of release I'd felt on first emerging from the tunnel had returned to my voice. "I don't pretend to understand everything that happened down there, but it feels as if it's altered everything. It feels as though something new can happen now. That's what I want. That's what I want with you. Everything is still possible. All you need to understand is that my feelings for you are as true now as they were that night in London. I loved you then, Marina, and I love you still."

"Why aren't you listening to me?" She tossed her head impatiently. "We're not the same people we were then. It must be obvious I'm not the person you once knew." Before I could argue she pressed on. "You don't have to take my word for it. You've seen the paintings I've done while I've been here. Do you think the woman you used to know could have painted them? Did you even recognize them as mine?"

With growing confidence I told her that I had indeed recognized her clearly in the huge mural on the walls of the painted room, that I'd seen her kneeling there, surrounded by all the dreadful things that life can do to us. I told her that her presence among those images had shown me just how much we must have in common still, because if I were able to paint my own self-portrait it would look a lot like that – a man on his knees in the middle of some heart-breaking atrocity or other.

Her lips had opened slightly. She uttered a half-suppressed gasp of astonishment.

"What is it? I asked.

"It's nothing."

"Tell me."

"It's just that for much of the time I was working on that painting I was thinking of you. Of your work. Of what you do."

"You see?" I said. "We do know each other after all."

"There's a difference," she insisted. "For you, the horror seems to be out there in the world. For me, it's in here." She put a hand to her chest. "Every detail of that painting is me, my self-portrait – not just the figure you focused on. I can still see it all. I only have to look inside."

"And you don't think that's true for me too?"

"I'm not just talking about remembering it," she said. "I'm talking about owning it, about admitting it as an undeniable part of who we are. Yes, I know that you've been enduring the most terrible things for years, observing them, reporting on them, capturing them on film. You must know far more about the atrocities out there than I ever will, but I'm not sure that you have anything other than a literal understanding of it all."

I shook my head at that, wondering what could be more literal and real than the devastations of war. But this wasn't what I wanted to talk about. "Does it matter?" I protested. "I think we both got lost in the sheer awfulness of things because of what happened all those years ago. But we can't answer for all of the misery in the world. And we don't have to let it blight our lives for ever. Not now. Not any more."

Candle flames swayed and flickered around us. She put the palms of her hands together and brought them to her lips as she rocked her body slowly back and forth. In little more than a whisper she said, "I don't even know what you look like now."

Moving closer, I reached over and took hold of her hands. She started a little as I lifted them to my face. Tentatively her fingers began to explore my temples under the receding hairline before moving with more confidence round the orbital bones of my eyes to the ridge and contours of my nose. They followed the creases etched from the curve of the nostrils to the taut line of my mouth and on into the groove above the lips. Stubble rasped as her palms closed over my chin and jaw. Her fingers made their way towards my ears and back to the temples. My skin trembled at a touch which felt as intimate and revelatory as a prolonged meeting of the eyes.

"You're older, craggier," she said at last. "But it's still you."

"Yes," I whispered, "it's still me."

Sensing that I was about to gather her in my embrace, she lifted her hands from my face and pulled away.

"Think about it, Martin – even if everything else made sense, the last thing you need is a blind woman in your life."

"Is that what's bothering you?"

When she didn't answer I said, "Listen to me, Marina. I've spent years since that time in London trying to forget you. I've tried and I've failed. It's the most dismal failure of my entire life. Why else do you think I haven't been able to hold another relationship together since then? Why do you think I got hooked on chasing catastrophes around the world? And yes, it agonizes me that you've lost your sight. But it doesn't change my feelings for you. It doesn't change anything. Not for me."

For a moment I felt I had won through. I sensed her teetering on the very brink of assent. Then she drew in her breath sharply and edged further away. "Let's not talk about this now," she said. "We're bound to get things wrong like this. I need time to think about everything that's happened tonight. And so do you. You need to come down. You need to rest. You need to get back inside your skin again." Supporting herself against the rock, she rose to her feet. Her free hand reached for me. "Give me some help to get out of here now," she said. "We'll talk again tomorrow."

Her voice left no room for protest or demurral, but her hand felt receptive to my touch. I took her arm to support her as we crossed the uneven floor of the cave, but once we came out into the entrance passage she freed herself, leading the way confidently through the familiar darkness. We stepped out through the door into the cold of the night air, where the cascades pouring down the façade of the water theatre shone like frost in the moonlight. Without pausing, Marina walked around the pool, making for the tunnel. Her silence felt inviolable and, as much as I wanted to seize this moment to make a further declaration, I sensed that it would be wrong to push her now. In any case, it was too late, because Larry, Orazio and Angelina were waiting for us in the night.

"Ah, there you are at last," Larry said. "You must both be exhausted. Martin, old soul, you'll be glad to hear that Angelina has some food for you. Then Orazio will show you to your bed." He turned to Marina. "As for you, my dear – Adam has filled me in a little about what you've been through. I think it's time that you too got some rest."

Many hours later I woke up to the sound of singing in the garden outside– a duet of female voices, softly accompanied by a lute. I remembered holding Marina the previous night, holding her just long enough to feel the truth of her response. I remembered eating something and then being shown to a bed, where I lay down convinced I would stay awake all night, only to plunge at once into unbroken sleep.

By the time the singing woke me, bright bars of daylight streamed through cracks in the shutters. I guessed that more than twelve hours must have passed. I crossed to the window, opened the shutter and looked down to where Allegra and Meredith were sitting on a marble bench, singing an Italian folk song in the green shade of a mimosa tree. Fra Pietro sat across from them, smiling with closed eyes as he fingered his lute. A blue haze of afternoon sunlight hung about them.

Though they must have heard the noise of the shutter opening, not one of them looked up. So I stood at the window unobserved, breathing the scented air, listening to the music, utterly present in the moment, and filled with the exhilarating conviction that, after long years of exile in the shadows, I had at last been returned to life.

24
Heartsease

When I came down from my room, the trio had vanished. No one else was about in the courtyard. I looked through the arch into the water theatre and saw that the cascade was not operating, so I passed on down the stairwell to the lower garden and the swimming pool, and found that area deserted too. I had no idea how many people were staying at the Villa. Maybe most of them had left? Or perhaps they were all assembled somewhere or had withdrawn for a siesta? In any case, I was impatient to see only one of them, and I was glad of this chance to come quietly awake before re-entering the world.

I dived into the pool and swam several lengths, delighting in the touch of water and the shimmer of light it cast among dark cypresses. When I hauled myself out, I saw Gabriella approaching from the direction of the stairs.

"So you are returned to us at last," she said.

"I must have been asleep for hours."

"Many, many hours. I think more than thirty."

I looked out in amazement as I dried my hair with a towel.

"It's true. I think also you must be very hungry."

"I'm famished."

"I will ask Angelina to prepare something for you. Later we shall all eat dinner together. You are welcome to be among us, if you wish."

"So everyone is still here then? All the people I saw?"

"Not all. Some have left. Some had left even before we came to greet you. And this will be the last night together for the others."

I recalled the feeling of emerging out of darkness into a bright otherworld, and the throng of people who applauded me in the cave. "This has all begun to feel a bit unreal," I said. "Like a dream or something."

"But are not dreams also real? Are they not sometimes more real than things we wrongly believe to be true?"

"Yes," I said, answering her smile, "I believe that sometimes they might be."

"Good! This is an improvement."

"If so," I said, "it may have something to do with the surprise you all jumped on me."

"Not *jumped*," she smiled, wagging a corrective finger at me, "*springed*."

"Not *springed*," I said, "*sprang*."

Gabriella flapped her hands in exasperation.

More seriously I said, "Marina and Adam must have passed on what I told them."

"Of course. And it seems that you are not so much a *meschino* as I thought. A little foolish sometimes perhaps, but not a wretch. This too is an improvement."

"I'm glad you think so. Is this why I'm now invited to meet your other friends?"

"Also because, as I have said, certain among them are already gone."

"The ones I might have recognized?"

"Perhaps."

"So are you going to tell me more about the mysterious Heartsease Foundation?"

"Dine with us tonight," she answered, "and find out for yourself. Also there is someone important that you must certainly meet."

I said I looked forward to it, and then finally got to put the question that had been on my mind throughout the conversation. "Have you seen Marina today?"

"Of course."

"How is she?"

"I think perhaps," Gabriella said, "I must leave her to answer for herself."

Angelina brought me a tray of food down to the pool. As she arranged a dish of gnocchi and some bread on the marble table, her Italian prattle felt as amiable as it was incomprehensible. I was relishing every mouthful of the food when Adam came to sit with me beside the pool.

He told me that he had been waiting for me to wake so that he could talk to me again. He had been thinking things over since leaving the cave. He wanted me to know that if I had told him the truth about Hal all those years ago, he might have been destroyed by it. Even as things were, he admitted, it had taken him years to pull himself together again after that disastrous time.

"But I want you to know that I understand just how much your silence cost you," he said, "and though there's nothing I can do to make up for that, at least I can keep my side of the deal and go back to see Hal."

"I'm glad to hear it," I said, trying to lighten things a little. "After all, a deal is a deal."

"Even though neither of us knew quite what we were letting ourselves in for."

We sat in silence for a while, each preoccupied with his own thoughts, until I glanced across at him and said, "Do you remember Jonas Cragg?"

"Of course," Adam laughed, "how could I forget old Jonas?"

"I think I believed in him rather more than you did."

"I was an incorrigible sceptic in those days," Adam said. "And the son of one too. It took an original like you to reopen my imagination."

"As you did mine, in a different way. You Brigshaws turned me over in every way imaginable. You did it between you back

417

then, and you seem to have done it again here. I certainly can't go back to the way things were. Not now."

"What about your job?"

"I think that's over," I said. "My career began in Equatoria, and that's where it should end. I've done what I can. I know that in the great scheme of things it doesn't amount to much. And I'm getting too old for it. There are other, younger people already doing it far better than me – some strong women among them."

"Perhaps you shouldn't be too hasty about that," Adam cautioned me. "You may feel differently once you're outside this enchanted place."

"I don't think so. I've no wish to crawl back inside my cage." When I looked back at him I saw him shaking his head. "What is it?" I asked.

"I wonder if we're about to make another switch," he said. "You and me, I mean. I've been thinking for a while that it's time I got out into the world again. I'm wondering whether it's time I went back to Africa."

"To Equatoria?"

He nodded uncertainly. "I think there may be things I have to offer there. Finding out what's needed first, then looking for appropriate ways in which the Foundation's resources might be able to help."

"Does this have anything to do with Efwa being there?"

"Not in the way you think. But what you told me about her has sharpened my thinking. I know that I let her down, Martin. I let her down in all sorts of ways. If there's anything I can do to help her now... Well, I believe I should do it. Don't you agree?"

I could see excitement in his eyes. I could feel it in his voice. But I was still unclear about his role in the Foundation, and I was puzzling over the strange rituals I'd seen in this place, that bizarre procession of fancy dress and masks a few evenings earlier. What could such elaborate fantasies have to do with

418

the pressing needs of a country that was suffering as Equatoria suffered? When I challenged him about it, Adam merely smiled. "What you saw," he said, "was part of our celebrations before some of our key speakers had to leave."

"You mean it was just a party, a social occasion?"

"Not just that. But what's so wrong with having a good time?"

"I still don't get it," I said. "You're going to have to say more."

Perhaps wary of my scepticism, Adam took some time to think before speaking. "As I told you the other night, we're about change," he said eventually. "The Foundation is concerned with the dynamics of change in general – social, political and cultural change, yes, but change in individuals too – which means it comes from the ground up, not top down. Above all we're about using the transforming power of the imagination."

I recalled the five-point mission statement on the first page of the folder in which Adam had filed his account of the meeting with Gabriella at the Springs of Clitumnus. I'd taken it for mere rhetoric at the time; now Adam seemed to be offering it as a serious and considered manifesto.

"That's still a bit on the vague side," I said. "I have a lot of questions."

"Then talk to some of the people here – particularly the students. They're the future. They're what Heartsease is about."

"And what about Larry's part in all of this?" I pressed. "All his stuff about the Mysteries of Isis and the Revenant of Fontanalba?"

"Ah," Adam glanced at his watch, "I can't explain that for you. If you really want to understand, you'll just have to experience it for yourself." He got to his feet. "Look, I have a meeting in a few minutes. Let's talk again later – at dinner perhaps."

As he turned to leave, I said, "Do you know where Marina is?"

"I haven't seen her all day," he said. "Try her studio. It's near the water theatre: turn left at the arch, it's at the end of the courtyard, looking out towards the orchard."

When I went back through into the courtyard I saw Allegra supervising two young men who were carrying clothes hampers through to the front of the house. "We have to return this lot to the costumiers today," she explained cheerfully. "How are you this morning?"

"I'm feeling fine. Surprisingly fine. I was just looking for your mother. I gather she has a studio somewhere here."

"It's over there." Allegra pointed to the end door of the building across the courtyard from the house. Then she raised her eyebrows at me and said, "Good luck!"

"You think I'll need it?"

"Don't we all?" she said, and turned back to her work.

By now it was late afternoon and the light was fading towards sunset. When I knocked at the door of Marina's studio it was opened, to my surprise, by Larry's friend, Giovanni, who was dressed in grubby overalls and wiping his hands with a towel. I told him I was looking for Marina. He nodded, turned and called her name.

"Who is it?" she answered.

"It's me," I said. "I've come calling on you. May I come in?"

A moment later I heard Marina say something in Italian, and Giovanni stepped to one side. The studio was lit by a large semicircular window above a workbench on the wall of the gable end. Wearing a blue smock and jeans, Marina sat perched on a stool there, doing something I couldn't see with her hands. The light from the window gleamed off her hair. She did not turn her head my way.

After a further brief exchange in Italian, Giovanni nodded to me again and went out, closing the door behind him. I took in the contents of the room: a sink with large brass taps, a number of buckets, a row of jars and bottles filled with coloured powders, a stack of plastic sacks piled beneath a banistered staircase, and in one corner an electric kiln with its door open and three shelves perched on stilts inside.

"You're a potter," I exclaimed.

"No," she answered. "Giovanni's a potter. He has his own studio in the village. He comes out here every now and then to help with the things I can't do."

Moving closer, I saw that she was turning a lump of clay in the palm of one hand, opening it, like the corolla of a flower, with the other. "I just like the feel of clay."

I cleared my throat. "The other night," I ventured, "you said we'd talk again."

Carefully she set down the unfinished pot on the workbench, got up from the stool and crossed to the sink, where she washed her hands clean of clay and dried them. I saw from the confidence of her movements that she knew the exact location of everything in the studio.

"Shall we stay in here," she said, "or would you rather be outside?"

"I like it here."

She returned to the stool and sat down again, facing me this time across the room. From outside the studio came a clatter of wings as a flight of doves rose and circled and shone against the evening sky. After a long pause I looked back at Marina and said, "So, where do we go from here?"

She ran the fingers of one hand through her hair. "Nowhere," she said. "We go nowhere. This whole thing's impossible."

"It's not impossible," I answered immediately. "Why should it be impossible?"

"Look at me." She lifted her defiant face as if to outstare me. "Do I have to spell it out for you? Just think about the kind of life you live. How could the two things possibly go together?"

421

"They don't have to. I've already told Adam – I'm giving up that life." She shook her head in dubious reproof. "And no, not because of you," I said. "Whatever happens between you and me, I'm giving it up because I'm through with it now. I want to be human again."

I heard the catch in her breath, saw her pass her hands through her hair again, and then bring them to rest at her cheeks, cupping her face.

"But I don't want to do it alone," I whispered, moving closer to her, "not now. I want to do what we should have done all those years ago. I want to make a life with you."

She lowered her hands, clasped them tightly together and then raised her head to face me. Even in that diminishing light, I could not believe I was invisible to her.

"Are you sure that's what you want?" she asked. "Are you really sure?"

"Yes," I answered, "I'm absolutely sure."

I saw the light of assent brighten her face. She lifted her hands, reaching for me through the dark. For the first time in too many years, we moved into a deep embrace. And then, for a time, we were both in tears. Perhaps both of us were thinking of that long-ago morning in Bloomsbury, when we agreed that the time and place of our next meeting would happen as a gift of chance. And because of that act of trust in life, and because of the failures of trust on both our parts which followed it, we had lost so much. Yet even so an assignation of love had been made that day, and it was time to keep it now.

"I love you, Marina," I whispered. Softly she answered me. Our embrace reached deeper still. Then she broke away from our kisses and led me across the studio to the stairs, and up into a simply furnished room, where our bodies eagerly found and recognized the lovers they had lost. As the dusk gathered around us, our acts of tenderness and passion redeemed the years of loss, fulfilling all the promises once made by a love that had got deferred through error, chance and circumstance, and yet remained strong enough to bless our life for years to come. We felt it now. We knew.

That evening, Marina and I were the last to enter the long chamber in the building opposite the water theatre which had been put into service as a dining hall. Allegra and Gabriella immediately approached us with a glint of purpose in their eyes.

"Well, it looks as though you two have begun to sort yourselves out," Allegra said, smiling at her mother, while Gabriella took me by the arm saying, "Come with me. I wish you to meet a very important person." She steered me across the room, past the table where Adam and Larry were sitting, towards a group of people who were chatting around an ornate fireplace. Among them stood a short man wearing an expensively cut woollen suit. His tanned, aquiline features wrinkled in a smile as he saw Gabriella.

"Ah there you are, *cara*," he said. "I've just been hearing about the work that Molly here is doing in Northern Ireland. I am most impressed. It seems that your adventure of the imagination grows stronger every year."

"With such good people how could it be otherwise?" Gabriella turned to me. "This is my husband Raffaele. His family have lived here at the villa since... oh I don't know when... Probably since Caligula came to make a bath *alle fonti del Clitunno*."

Raffaele gave me a shrug of amused despair. "My wife has an extravagant talent for exaggeration," he smiled. "Sometimes it confuses me also. But I think you must be Martin Crowther. Gabriella has been telling me of your work."

"Has she indeed?" I returned his smile. "I don't think she entirely approves of it."

"On the contrary. She expresses considerable admiration. But come, Angelina is ready for us, I think. Let us dine together with these young people" – he gestured to the three women and the black man in braided locks and a Manchester United football shirt with whom he had been talking – "perhaps they will teach us how to improve the world."

Gabriella made off across the room as we sat down. Looking around, I saw Larry holding forth to Adam at their table, while Meredith and Dorothy were laughing among a group of young people. In a distant corner, Marina and Allegra sat deep in conversation, and were soon joined by Gabriella. Meanwhile a line of people had formed at a bar where Angelina was ladling soup from a large tureen. Despite the chandeliered grandeur of the room, the occasion had a relaxed and informal feel. Raffaele touched me on the arm and opened his hands in an apologetic gesture. "Forgive me, I was forgetting. In this company one must serve oneself. Shall we?"

Given the chance, I would have preferred to be sitting beside Marina, but I glanced her way every now and then and was relieved to see her smiling. The people around me spoke engagingly about themselves, and I soon began to build a clearer picture of who they were and what they were doing in the world. I learnt that the Irish woman's brother had been gunned down five years earlier on the Shankill Road. Now she was running a drama group for people from both sides of the sectarian and political divide in Ulster, encouraging them to tell their stories and to find common ground in the wounds and losses inflicted by the violence of that turbulent province. The young black man came from South Africa, where he was a law student working as an intern with the Truth and Reconciliation Commission. One of the other women was Lebanese, a teacher from Beirut, who listened with critical interest as her friends discussed the problems they encountered in their work, and answered questions that Raffaele and I put to them.

When the meal was over, Raffaele pushed back his chair and turned to me. "I think I would like to smoke a cigar," he said, "for which pleasure I shall go into the garden. Will you keep me company?"

"It's a remarkable thing that Gabriella's doing here," I said, when we were outside.

"I do not always understand my wife," Raffaele smiled across at me. "Sometimes she even alarms me a little. But I confess I admire her very much." He eyed me with keener interest through a cloudy haze of smoke. "I understand you have been admitted to our beautiful water theatre. It is good to see it in operation again. Tell me, what did you make of that?"

"It was certainly an experience," I said. "And yes, more than a bit alarming too."

He seemed amused by the reply. "I think perhaps you are a braver man than I am," he said. "For myself I prefer to keep my wife's activities at a distance. I find it safer so. Of course I raise funds for her adventures. I introduce people to her work. And truly I believe in it myself. But the troubles of this world are so big…" He opened his hands in an expansive gesture. "We understand this, you and I, do we not? So I think you will agree that what Gabriella and the others are trying to do, imaginative though it may be, is too small in scale, and perhaps a little too fanciful to make much difference?"

I was about to press the subject further when he favoured me with a conspiratorial smile. "You and Marina," he said, "I understand there is hope you will be united at last?"

"More than hope," I said.

"Ah, then you are a very fortunate man. I congratulate you. I even envy you a little. Marina has not yet told you then?"

"I'm not sure I understand."

"She and I," he said with no sign of embarrassment, "we were lovers once. In the old days."

Despite my best efforts, the pang of jealousy searing through me in that moment must have reached my face. Immediately he added, "Please, do not be dismayed. It was a beautiful thing. I am sure she will tell you so. And there was no deceit. After all, Gabriella also has her lovers."

"Adam," I guessed out loud.

"For a time, yes." With a little shrug, Raffaele drew on his cigar again and looked up at the stars. "This night is also very beautiful," he said.

But my mind was elsewhere. I was thinking of Gail and of the other women with whom I'd made love during the course of the past thirty years, and how few of those encounters had been beautiful. As for Marina... What else could I have imagined? She was a passionate woman. Of course she too must have taken lovers, and if this attractive Italian count was among them, well... why not? I had never assumed that she would have kept herself chaste throughout those long years out of some self-denying loyalty to the memory of me. But neither, until this moment, had I thought too closely about it – and yes, the feeling hurt.

Raffaele stubbed his cigar on the stonework of the balustrade, took a breath on the night air, turned to me and said, "We are still friends, of course, you and I?"

"Of course... Why on earth not?"

"Good, good. That is how it should be. Perhaps it is time we rejoined the others?"

As we went back into the dining hall, he patted me on the arm and excused himself, saying that he must visit the kitchen to congratulate Angelina on the excellence of the meal. By that time all the tables had been cleared and people were now standing around in small groups, laughing and chatting together. Slipping past those who stood near the doorway, I made for the corner where Marina was still sitting with Allegra and Gabriella, who looked up at my approach.

"So," she smiled, "how did you find my husband?"

"He's certainly an interesting man." I reached out to touch Marina's shoulder.

Allegra was also smiling. "And quite a charmer, don't you think?"

"Yes, that too."

"Everyone finds him so," Gabriella said. "Even I adore him still! Now, tonight there is a final ceremony. It begins soon. We are hoping that you will like to take part."

I looked for Marina's response to this invitation. "Is that what you'd like?"

Before she could answer, Allegra delivered another arch smile. "Of course, if the two of you would rather be alone…"

Marina laid a silencing hand on her arm and lifted her face in my direction. "It would be a lovely thing to do together. There's something I'd really like you to see."

In the final chapter of *The Golden Ass*, Apuleius draws a veil over the rites by which his narrator is initiated into the mysteries. Having told us that he crossed the threshold of death, Lucius declares that he saw the sun shining at midnight and that he worshipped the gods of both the upper world and the underworld face to face. He then declines to say more about it, because there would be no point. If you haven't been there yourself, he says, you simply won't understand.

The rational sceptic I once was would have been infuriated by such claims to privileged esoteric knowledge. But in my more open-minded moments, it might have occurred to me that the same holds true about trying to explain to someone who has never made love just what the experience is like. Or telling the deaf about music for that matter, or someone born blind about light. In any case, after what happened later that night, I have a better understanding of the difficulties which Apuleius encountered. But I'll try to convey what happened to me.

Arrangements had already been made for the final gathering before the company was to disperse the next day. Some time after the conversation in the dining hall, Marina and I joined the long candlelit procession that passed out into the courtyard and through the archway leading to the water theatre. This time there were no elaborate costumes and no masks, just people in their everyday clothes, walking silently in pairs, each carrying a candle in a simple tin holder through the night. Marina and I were among those at the tail end, while Allegra and Giovanni walked together in front of us. Adam and Larry brought up the rear. Loudspeakers had been set up in a high window of the main house, from where the sound of Monteverdi's Vespers floated across the air.

Though a few leaks still dripped from the mythological figures at either side of the tunnel, this time no spurts jetted from their wineskins, mouths and shells. But we could hear the cascade of the water theatre in full flow, and when we came out on the far side, I looked up and saw the Revenant of Fontanalba gazing down where the silver cataracts poured among the figures and the beasts. In the radiance of a nearly full moon it was like watching the stone fabric dissolve into an insubstantial veil.

Ahead of us, each couple was parting company to walk on either side of the semicircular pool. Releasing Marina's hand, I followed Giovanni to the right, glancing across to where Allegra trailed a hand to guide her mother round the margin of the pool. But Marina was walking with her head held confidently high. Evidently she found all the guidance she needed in the sound of the cascade. When we met again at the centre of the façade, I took her hand once more, feeling its responsive warmth as we passed together through the door that stood open on the world below.

The music faded behind us as we entered the atrium of the cave. After we had passed through the inner door beyond, the sound of falling water faded too. Here the narrow passage forced us into single file. I walked slightly ahead of Marina still holding her hand. Candlelight flashed off chips of mica and burnished the colours in the stone. Again I was possessed by the sensation of entering a living organism, though with no apprehension this time of the massive tonnage of rock bearing down above our heads. In the company of so many other people it wouldn't have surprised me to hear laughter or chatter or nervous whispers somewhere, but the procession passed through the silence of the cave with the same hushed reverence with which we might have walked along the nave of a cathedral.

The comparison felt apposite. The last time I had come this way I had been so preoccupied with my own inner struggle between scepticism and trepidation that I had shut off much of my sense of wonder. Even so, some feeling for the power of the place had stirred me. Now I understood that this was truly sacred space. Sacred long before men found their way down inside its halls to worship there. Sacred of its own essential nature, prior to all stories and superstitions. Sacred because it was mysteriously *here*, a hollow place inside a hill beneath the moon. Sacred simply as a gesture of that primal energy through which a universe of matter, time and space was conjured into being, so that there was *something* – a magnificent, heart-shakingly beautiful something – rather than nothing at all.

Walking through the passages in the rock was like walking back into the same state of astonished expectancy in which I had wandered the hills and crags around Calderbridge as a boy. In that exalted state I had watched cloud shadows altering the contours of the landscape. I had listened to the clatter of beck water pouring among stones. I had marvelled at the way the winter light seemed to buckle in the wind. In those days I had begun to dream that I was a poet. My heart quickened to recall those times. Perhaps that dream might come again. Remembering how I had watched Marina dance on a sodden hillside in the smoky light of a thunderstorm, it occurred to me that, for all the frenzy and terror of the times I had endured reporting on the war zones of the world, I had never felt so completely alive as I did now, walking through this Umbrian hill with the woman I had loved for so long.

Some time before the rough track took its steepest incline downwards, I heard the sound of water falling into the pool. We took a turn, and I saw the candles ahead of me lighting the roof of the natural arch which led through into the vaulted chamber where Adam and I had pushed out in the skiff, and to which I had returned, having encountered my father in the dark hall of the dead. That was surely the right place in this limestone underworld for our company to gather. I was wondering what form the celebration would take when Marina halted beside me. "Can you see into the cave?" she whispered.

"Not yet, no. Just the entrance arch, but we're nearly there."

Marina turned her head towards Adam and Larry who were held up behind us and told them to come past. Puzzled by her hesitation, I leant back into the wall so that Larry could squeeze by me and follow Allegra and Giovanni, who had now moved on. By the light of his candle, I saw Adam lean forward, take his sister in his arms and lightly press his lips to her cheek before he too brushed past me and walked on down the slope.

"What is it?" I asked. "Don't you want to go down?"

"In a moment. I want to talk to you first. Tell me when the others have gone."

I looked down the slope, and saw the glow of Adam's candle pass beneath the arch some thirty yards away before it vanished into the dark.

"They've gone," I said. "Come here. Let me hold you." Keeping my candle away from her hair, I took her into the reach of my free arm. Evasively, she tilted her head away a little.

"Earlier," she said, "when you came back into the dining hall, there was something strange about your voice. It didn't feel as if quite all of you was inside it. What was the matter? Was it something that Raffaele said to you?"

"Yes," I admitted, "it was."

"He told you that he and I were lovers once?"

"Yes."

"And how did that make you feel?"

"I know this is foolish," I said, "but it made me jealous."

"I'm glad that you know. I was going to tell you myself, because I didn't want any secrets between us. And it's not foolish at all. I'm pleased that you're jealous."

"But it's completely irrational of me. After everything *I've* done. I mean."

"We only feel jealous about the things we prize," she said. "I like being prized by you. In fact, I love it."

I lowered my head to kiss her, but she lifted the tip of a finger to my lips and said, "Will you do something for me?"

"Anything," I said.

"Are you ready for another risk?"

"Are you daring me again?"

"No, not this time. I'm asking you."

"I'm yours," I answered. "You don't have to ask."

She said, "I want you to blow the candle out."

Only the still distant sound of water filled the silence of the cave.

"But how..." I began.

"I'll guide you there."

Without a word, I lifted the candle closer to her face, so that she could feel its warmth. Then I blew at its little crocus flame of light, and darkness as thick and black as any I had encountered in the halls of the dead shut down round us.

"Come with me," she whispered, taking a firm grip on my hand, "there's something I want you to see."

I let the candle drop and responded to her pull, feeling my way along the wall with my free hand. Marina drew me down the slope, walking not quickly, but with the confidence of someone who had made this dark journey many times before. Nowhere could I make out any glimmer of light. All I could hear was the tread of our feet on stone and the sound of water pouring into the pool. The slope steepened. She slowed down ahead of me. When the plunge of water into the pool sounded louder, I knew we must be coming out through the arch into the vaulted chamber, but not a candle flickered anywhere. Was she leading me by a different route than the others had taken? Now I heard the sound of her foot sliding cautiously across a rocky surface. She took a small step down, waited for me to do the same, and we progressed together haltingly down tier after shallow tier, until she pulled me around some obstacle she had encountered and I gasped out loud at the starry figure of light that appeared.

Some distance below me, a crowd of candles had been arranged so as to illuminate nothing but the formation of rock on which they stood. My hand tightened in Marina's grip, and I gazed for a long time, aware that this cave must be full of people, all quietly doing what I was doing – meditating in silent wonder on the power and beauty and strength of what was present to us all: a stack of rock shaped by random collisions of water and stone over thousands of years into the image of a female figure so grave and timeless that she must have been venerated as sacred by almost every generation preceding ours. Marina tightened her embrace about my waist. My hand moved to cover hers, and in the very moment when she whispered, "Have you seen yet?" a tremor of understanding passed through me in a stroke of midnight light. I knew now why the Revenant of Fontanalba was transfigured by his vision into a person who was no longer either man or woman because both male and female were now newly reconciled in him. And as surely as I felt Marina beside me – warm, alive and present to my senses, freely given to me as mine, yet still inalienably her own – I felt the light glittering from the figure in the rock softly illuminate a figure that had long been dark inside myself.

"Yes," I answered quietly, "I've seen."

Music sounded. Allegra had begun to sing. I turned my head to look in her direction. Her hair was now gleaming in the candlelight. Then I made out the people around her, coming to reclaim the candles they would need to light their exit from the cave. One by one they took their share in light. Soon the stone figure would have returned into the dark. I drew Marina closer to me. Gradually she came into focus as the first of the candles passed by, and it felt as though we too were being conjured out of darkness by the breaking of the light.

Already, somewhere across the earth, day was dawning, while elsewhere in the self-same moment midnight struck. And it was all one. The earth was turning even as we stood inside it. Beyond the prodigious variety of life in all its many forms, beyond all the divisions which, year in year out, devastate so many lives, it remained seamlessly itself, all one. I saw it and I felt it so, and because this was an experience, not just an idea, I knew that I was inseparably part of it. I knew too that I would not be able to hold on to this exalted state for ever, but everything would be changed by it, and never again would it be possible to live as though it wasn't so.

Still singing as she reached up to retrieve the last candle, Allegra would soon come across the rocks to join us. But for now the whole cave resonated around us to the rejoicing sound of her song. And it was like listening to darkness singing. It was like listening to light.

Author's Note

The characters of this novel are all fictional, as are the places that feature here. There is a real village called Fontanalba, located not in Umbria but in the Haute Savoie, and I have borrowed its ancient legend of a revenant for purposes of my own. The Umbria to which I have shifted that legend is as imaginary as are, say, the Italian settings of Elizabethan plays, and the Equatoria of this novel will not be found in any atlas. Though none of its politicians are intended as portraits of actual people, living or dead, some of its troubled history was suggested by that of Ghana's First Republic. Calderbridge bears a distinct resemblance to Halifax, my hometown in Yorkshire, and the inscription over the door of the fictional house, High Sugden, was actually carved above the entrance to High Sunderland Hall, which may have been the inspiration for Emily Brontë's Thrushcross Grange. I remember seeing that house in ruins when I was a boy.

A novel gets written in solitude, but many people contribute to its composition. Not for the first time I owe much to my friend Richard Lannoy, who introduced me to the legend of Fontanalba when he was researching the mythopoeic landscape of Le Val des Merveilles. The account which Fra Pietro gives of the life and death of St Maximilian Kolbe was drawn from Diana Dewar's fine biographical study, *Saint of Auschwitz*. And like all novelists, I also stand in debt to Apuleius of Madaura, the ancient African godfather of the novel form.

This book might never have been conceived at all if Kate Noble had not made the generous loan of her cottage in Umbria many years ago. Many other friends have helped and encouraged me since then, and in particular I need to thank John and Antoinette Moat, Jules Cashford, James Simpson, Sacha Abercorn, Adam Thorpe, Patrick Harpur, Sebastian Barker (who published part of the 'Clitumnus' chapter in *The London Magazine*), Alexis Lykiard, Andrew Miller, John Latham, Diane Skafte, Professor Liliana Sikorska and the members of my writing workshops in Bath, London and at Cardiff University, as well as friends made in Ty Newydd, Totleigh Barton, Lumb Bank and Clun.

I owe a huge debt of thanks to my resolute agent, Sarah Ballard, who made a number of insightful notes on the manuscript at a crucial stage. Sadly my former agent, Pat Kavanagh, did not live to see the completed version of a book to which she gave characteristically kind encouragement, but I wish to acknowledge my heartfelt gratitude for more than twenty years of her counsel, help and friendship. I am also immensely grateful for the faith placed in this novel by Alessandro Gallenzi and Elisabetta Minervini, my publishers at Alma Books. The book has greatly benefited both from their corrective help on matters Italian, and from the consummate exercise of editorial skill. Once again, however, my principal debt is to the indispensable contribution made to the work by the patient and always truthful readings of my wife, Phoebe Clare.